the reckoning

JAMES JAUNCEY has written for adults, young adults and children. He lives on the edge of the Scottish Highlands and when he is not writing he plays the piano in the Funky String Band. He is also on the board of the Edinburgh International Book Festival, the world's biggest literary festival.

The Witness, James Jauncey's previous book, was recommended by the Richard & Judy Book Club, was a *Scotland on Sunday* number-one children's bestseller and was shortlisted for the Royal Mail Scottish Children's Book Awards 2008 and the Highland Children's Book Awards 2008.

Praise for The Reckoning:

'*The Reckoning* combines page-turning excitement with serious political and ethical issues' *Herald*

'This is both a tense thriller and a moving boy-into-man story' *Daily Telegraph*

'It had me turning pages at three in the morning, quite unable to turn out the light and settle down until I knew what would happen next. And next, and next . . .' *Arran Voice*

'*The Reckoning* is tense and exciting, it's only too credible, it asks difficult questions, has a charismatic central character and an atmospheric setting, and doesn't shy away from death. What more could you ask?' *Bookbag*

JAMES JAUNCEY

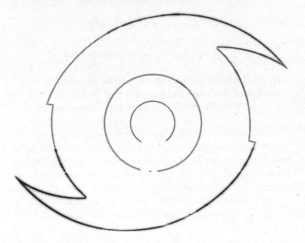

the reckoning

YOUNG PICADOR

First published 2008 by Young Picador

This edition published 2009 by Young Picador
an imprint of Pan Macmillan Limited
20 New Wharf Road, London N1 9RR
Basingstoke and Oxford
Associated companies throughout the world
www.panmacmillan.com

ISBN 978-0-330-45402-5

Copyright © James Jauncey 2008

1 3 5 7 9 8 6 4 2

A CIP catalogue record for this book is available from
the British Library.

Typeset by Nigel Hazle
Printed and bound in the UK by CPI Mackays, Chatham ME5 8TD

For Anna and Jake
with love

'I have no color prejudices nor caste prejudices nor creed prejudices. All I care to know is that a man is a human being, and that is enough for me; he can't be any worse.'

Mark Twain

Whale Island

ONE

It was like two worlds. Overhead, the sun beat down from a clear blue sky. A hundred yards ahead, the dunes had already disappeared.

Fin stopped and waited, feeling his bare arms turn to gooseflesh. Even at the height of summer the sea mist brought with it a chill. A deadening of sound and vision. A sense of reality suspended.

He could feel ribs of sand pressing into the arches of his feet. The warm water lapping round his ankles. The air was still, but the mist needed no wind for movement. Dragon's breath, boiling up out of the sea. That was how Fin had always thought of it. The sigh of ancient, leathery lungs in some vast dark cavern, fifty fathoms below.

Now the mist brushed up against him, rolled around him, as if deciding whether to smother him or sweep him away.

There was a strident call, somewhere between a long honk and a grunt. The ferry, making her way out to the islands, the sound of the siren distorted by the fog.

The islands. We were one of them till they built the bridge, he thought. He had liked to think of himself as an islander when he was a kid. A Whale Islander. Different. That's how he'd felt as he'd watched the occasional visitors step down on to the jetty. Proud and independent, piratical even. But now all he could think of was starting university and getting away on to the mainland. And just ahead of

3

him, invisible in the mist, the bridge hung like a thread of hope across the narrows. He could hear a muted rumble as a vehicle crossed it.

The morning's inactivity on the beach had left him feeling sluggish. He wished he had brought a fleece. Still, the twenty-minute walk back to the village would warm him up. He stepped from the water on to firm wet sand and set off homewards. Not even the thickest sea mist – and this one seemed to be thickening by the minute – could disorientate him on this stretch of shore. He had walked it hundreds – no, more like thousands – of times in his eighteen years. He knew every sweep and promontory, every dune, almost every rock pool, between here and home.

Any minute now he would come to the first pier of the bridge, rising up through the fog like a great steel-and-concrete giant's leg. He could hear another vehicle approaching now. Closer. Slowing and stopping. Directly ahead of him. The sound of a door opening. Someone getting out. A voice.

Fin walked forward. The pier materialised beside him, towering into the murk. He looked up but could see nothing.

He paused as a second door opened. There were footsteps, no more than thirty feet above his head, on the far side of the bridge. The vehicle had been heading towards the mainland. Now there was a scuffling sound, raised voices, then a cry. Scarcely human, more like the shriek of a seabird. Followed by a fleeting glimpse of movement in the mist. And then a dull, wet thud.

Fin stood where he was, rooted to the sand. There was a long moment of silence. Then a short burst of frenzied splashing. Then silence again.

He began to run.

He was almost on her before he saw her. The splashing started again as one leg drummed the shallows where she lay half in, half out of the water. Fin could see the sleek black curve of rock on which she had landed, a porpoise arcing out of the sand. A couple of feet in either direction and she would have missed it, for what difference that might have made. The way she lay, sprawled across the rock on her back, she looked like something discarded. But her eyes were open and they widened as she focused on Fin. She was in her early twenties, he guessed. She had high cheekbones, dark hair falling across a chalk-pale face. She was slim in jeans and sweatshirt, now soaked. But for the colour of her skin she could have been Maia, he thought, his heart thundering in his chest as he knelt down beside her in the water.

The fog swirled around them now, so thick he could see no more than a couple of yards beyond her.

She opened her mouth but no sound came out.

He leaned forward, put his head close to her face.

Her whisper was almost inaudible. 'Help . . . me . . .'

'I'll help you,' he said.

She groaned and her eyes clouded in pain.

'I'm . . . frigh . . . tened . . .'

She looked up at him.

He didn't have his phone on him. What the hell should he do? Leave her to get help? Stay with her and hope someone came along? Shout out at the top of his lungs?

'Please . . . hold . . . m—'

Her body shuddered and little flecks of foam appeared at her lips.

'Your hand?'

Her eyes flickered.

Fin reached down and took it. Despite the chill damp

air, her hand was warm and the skin felt very smooth. The fingernails were bitten low.

'It's OK,' he said, feeling hopeless. 'You'll be all right. There'll be help along soon.'

She had begun to pant. More foam bubbled at her mouth, pinkish now.

He longed to run away. But he also wanted to comfort her, take her in his arms if need be. He was terrified of hurting her. Her head lolled back over the rock, though she had moved it to look at him, so her neck couldn't be broken.

'I'm going to get you more comfortable,' he said.

He let go of her hand and it fell at her side. He shuffled round in the water to kneel behind her on the edge of the rock. Then lifted her head and took it on his lap. He laid one palm against the side of her face and felt the tiniest pressure from her cheek. With the other hand he stroked her head. Through the seawater tang came the scent of shampoo.

'Is that all right?' he asked.

She gave a little grunt.

'You're OK,' he said again. 'I'm here. With you. There'll be help soon.'

She was panting again, faster now and shallower.

'It's all right.' He could feel his voice rising in his throat.

Her eyes were starting to lose focus. She was slipping away from him.

'Stay with me,' he whispered. 'Please. Please. Don't go.'

He was rubbing her cheek now with one hand and stroking her hair with the other.

'It's OK, it's OK . . .' He was repeating it like a mantra, over and over again. 'Stay with me, *stay* with me . . .'

And then suddenly she was gone.

For a moment the mist eddied above his head and thinned. A wafer of sunlight fell on her face, and Fin caught a swift movement aloft, the flash of a gull's wing against the blue.

Then the mist closed around them once more. The shocked young man kneeling in the water with the stranger's head cradled in his lap.

TWO

Separated from the mainland by a narrow channel, Whale Island was five miles long and a little over a mile and a half wide. In former days it had been known for the whaling station from which it took its name, two small fishing communities, a herd of wild goats and a shrine to St Brigid, who was reputed miraculously to have saved the crew of a stricken ship run aground in the island's Goat Bay during a storm. Now, since the building of the bridge, some visitors still made a kind of pilgrimage to the shrine, but most simply came for the sheltered beaches and the picturesque fishing village of Easthaven.

Today the mist had spared Easthaven, a sunlit mosaic of glinting water and upturned boats, white cottages, stacks of orange lobster pots and lengths of blue synthetic rope.

In the back seat of the police car, Fin registered none of it.

The car was drawing to a halt at the harbour. One of the policemen was saying something to him.

'Sorry . . . ?'

'I said, you all right, son?'

He nodded.

'Don't want us to come in with you?'

'No, thanks.'

'Did all you could, you know.'

'I guess so.'

'Get your mum to put the kettle on. Make you a cuppa. We'll be back later to take a statement.'

Fin climbed out of the car and stood in the sunshine, every moment of the last hour vivid in his mind. The short minutes leading up to the girl's death. Then, almost immediately afterwards, the footsteps approaching. The appearance out of the mist of a short, balding, bespectacled man in a suit splashing through the shallow water in his shiny shoes. The moment of surprise as he took in the sight of Fin and the girl. Then shaking his head, saying in clipped tones, 'I tried to stop her.' And shocked and dazed though Fin was, his feeling that something was not right . . .

He stepped out of the sunlight and into the alley that ran between the cottages. He was glad the police hadn't insisted on seeing him to his door. If his father was in, he'd assume the worst before Fin had even opened his mouth. He always did. That was Danny Carpenter's way. Or had been since the accident which had crippled him, half Fin's lifetime ago. And right now a bawling match with his father was the last thing he needed. Thank God it was his mother's Saturday off.

He paused at the front door, frozen at the thought of the normality that lay the other side. He had just held someone's head on his lap as they died. And through there his mother would be tidying or emptying the washing machine or making a cup of coffee . . .

He took a deep breath, then opened the door. And realised at once that today nothing was normal.

Sounds came from the sitting room. Kath Carpenter and someone else, another woman. Their voices low, intense. Although he couldn't hear what they were saying, the sense of drama was palpable, even through the closed door.

Fin stood in the crowded kitchen wondering what to do.

He didn't want to intrude, but he wasn't sure how much longer he could contain what had happened.

The living-room door opened and his mother came out.

'Hey, sweetheart! Heard you coming in. Back already?'

Fin tried a smile and failed.

She frowned. Over her shoulder he could see the television through the living-room door. She was not a daytime television-watcher, not even at weekends. But now it was on, though the sound was off. It was showing scenes of devastation in some crowded city street. Rubble. Wrecked cars. Shattered market stalls. Dark stains on the ground.

'You all right?'

He shrugged. 'I guess.'

She lowered her voice and smiled. 'Can it keep, whatever it is? See . . . I've got Sally here. Just back from the city.' She gestured at the television. 'She got caught up in . . . that. She's in a bit of a state, poor love. She was passing the West Indian market when it went off. The market was packed. And, trust Sally, she went in to help . . .' His mother's voice faltered. 'She saw some dreadful things.'

Fin tried another smile. 'Yeah. It'll keep. I'm going upstairs.'

Kath put her hand on his arm. 'Have a good natter later, eh?'

'Sure.'

He climbed the narrow stairs and stopped on the little landing at the top. On the shelf below the skylight was an old brass barometer. The weather had been good for the last week, the needle holding resolutely to the extreme right. Now it was swinging back towards the centre.

Number Thirteen, Easthaven, like most of its neighbours, had six rooms. Three bedrooms upstairs, two small, one slightly larger. Kitchen, living room and bathroom downstairs. Despite the historic character of the village, and the building restrictions that went with it, one or two incomers had found ingenious ways to create more space in the low, cramped cottages. But most of the islanders simply made do with things as they'd been arranged two hundred years ago, when the cottages had first been built. There were only thirty of them, clustered in a vague semicircle around the harbour. There were no street names, just Easthaven. Fin had always liked that. Number Thirteen, Easthaven. It felt as if his cottage was something important to the village, a solid part of what made it into a place. And solid they were, these cottages, with their gable ends to the sea so that the winds and rain and spray battered the windowless end walls, not the vulnerable front doors and windows. Fin liked that too. That someone had thought about it. Worked out how to minimise the ill effects of being so close to the water. Though it meant that there was little space or light between the cottages, as they hunkered down in short rows under the lea of the hill that rose to landward.

Now Fin opened the door to his left and went in. Maia's room. It was a few months since he'd last been in here. It looked as if she'd just tidied it. Books, music and movies neatly arranged on the shelf, bedcover drawn up and her old threadbare teddy sitting watchfully on the hump of the pillows. Knick-knacks crowding the little dressing table. Bead necklaces hanging round the frame of the mirror. *Blue Planet* poster behind the bed. But it smelt empty, musty, as if it was too long since the window had been opened. Fin felt the ache of longing start, the lump rise in his throat. Could Maia have died? Frightened, alone like the girl on the beach? It was nearly a year now since they'd last heard anything from her. Eighteen months since that

11

awful Christmas Day when she'd left home – forever, she'd said. Though over the following months there had been texts, the occasional phone call, and one weekend when Kath and Fin had taken the overnight bus to visit her at university. But finally, at the end of last summer, a jubilant postcard: *Got a job!* Then silence.

Anger, confusion and a deep ache of loss. These were what Fin felt whenever he thought of Maia, his adored older sister. Her twenty-second birthday just last month and nowhere to send her a card. For so long his guardian and protector. The one who cleaved her way through life's choppy waters, leaving Fin to paddle along comfortably behind. He could understand why she'd left home. Danny had worn her down, their clashes becoming more and more intense as she started at university and all her passion found its focus in her studies, her concern for the environment. Not that Danny, a former fisherman, could argue much with that. But her education, her way with words, made him feel clumsy and inadequate. Fin could see that. And, no matter how often Kath intervened, he took every opportunity to undermine her. To snipe at her student way of life, her friends, her clothes, her taste in music, her airy-fairy politics, as he called them. Until finally, that day, seated round the table for Christmas dinner, Danny had gone too far. And Maia, beyond tears, her face tight with rage, had gone upstairs, packed a suitcase and walked out of the house, leaving a half-finished plate of turkey on the table. The worst thing of all was that it was Fin who had started it. Rising to some snide remark from Danny about the dreadlocks he had started to grow, when he should have known to keep his mouth shut. Especially on Christmas Day. Then Maia had stepped in to say that actually they had been her idea, that he'd look like her idol,

Bob Marley. And so the argument had escalated until the two of them were screaming at one another and eventually even Kath had given up trying to get them to see sense and had sat there in her paper hat, head in hands, staring at her best tablecloth.

Still, despite his feelings of guilt, Fin could see that since Danny's accident, the chemistry between his father and sister had soured beyond repair, and anyway neither of them was able or willing to compromise. Maia had been only six months away from the end of her studies, so perhaps the gesture of leaving had been more symbolic than anything. But why had she then cut them *all* out of her life? What had happened? Was it the job? A relationship? An opportunity overseas? Did she have any idea how hurtful the unanswered texts had been? The unreturned phone messages . . . ? Now, of course, Fin had given up, assumed she'd got rid of the old phone. But until today, a few minutes ago, he had never allowed himself to think the very worst.

He threw himself down on the bed and buried his face in the pillow, hoping that maybe some scent of her, some reassuring trace remained. He was relieved when the tears came, though he wasn't sure whether they were for the dead girl, or his sister, or both.

Later he got up again. This was no good. It wouldn't bring Maia back. He plumped the pillows and smoothed the cover down. He knew his mother paid occasional visits to the room when the house was empty. A couple of times he'd caught a whiff of her perfume around the door. He also knew that his father wanted to reclaim the room so they could tidy away some of the junk that cluttered the small house.

'She's not coming back, woman. You know that as well as I do. And even if she did, I wouldn't have her . . .'

Sometimes Fin wondered why his mother hadn't left long ago. Got herself a flat in Cliffton, on the mainland, where she'd been brought up. But she had a stubborn streak, Kath Carpenter. Like mother, like daughter. And he knew there was a part of her that still, despite herself, believed Danny's disability, his self-pity and bitterness, were challenges she would eventually overcome. So for the time being, Maia's room waited ready for her return.

Well, his mother could visit it as much as she liked, thought Fin, closing the door. But that was the last time he would go in there till Maia came back. He crossed the landing and went into his own room. Lay down on his own bed and breathed deeply. This was his haven. No matter what went on, he could usually put himself back together in here. This was the place where he thought about things, imagined them, created them. Where, sometimes, things happened that made him feel he was marching to the beat of the universe.

He closed his eyes. At once the young woman's face filled his mind. Her imploring look as she asked him to hold her hand. He opened his eyes again quickly. Focused on the narrow workbench which spanned the whole wall beneath the window.

There was his laptop, speakers perched on the window-sill behind it. And there, taking up most of the rest of the bench space, was the Carpenter Patent Beer Dispenser. His own invention. It had been there for over a year now and he hadn't yet had the heart to dismantle it. From the centre of the bench rose a metal arm, slightly shorter than his own, with an elbow joint halfway up and a claw for a hand. Pulleys ran like sinews from the shoulder to the claw. In front of it sat a pad on which were set a can and a glass, held in place by an adjustable frame. When the laptop was

14

on, all he had to do, from anywhere in the room, was say, 'Beer, please!' and the arm would bend, the claw would lift the ring pull and the frame would release the can as the arm lifted it free, tilted it and poured the contents into the glass. In theory. In practice it had succeeded once out of a dozen attempts, an expensive way of ruining his bedroom carpet. Still, it had been a near-triumph at the time. He'd scrounged some bits and pieces from Mr Newton, the design teacher, made the arm and claw and holding frame in the school metal workshop and got hold of a copy of some voice-activation software from a kid whose father worked for an engineering firm. Once he'd fine-tuned the prototype, his plan had been to try something much more ambitious, the Carpenter Patent *Ice Cold and In Your Hand* Beer Dispenser, although that would have involved buying a mini-fridge and taking up the carpet to fix a set of rails to the floor between the bench and the bedside, and he wasn't sure what his mother would have thought about that. Though he knew what his father would think, and not hesitate to say: 'Contraptions. Don't see the point of 'em. You should be outside getting your sleeves rolled up, rather than sitting in your room all day. Christ, boy, I was at sea when I was your age, doing man's work. I *was* a man at seventeen, but your generation . . . you're bloody soft.' Maybe you're right, Fin would have been tempted to say, but look where being a man got you. Though in fact he would have bitten his tongue yet again and watched as his father limped out of the room, with that twisted, dragging movement of his left leg that sometimes made Fin want to scream.

As a small boy, Fin had always had the idea that one day he would build the best toy in the world. It would be the most fun, exciting, fast, scary, fantastic, lovely thing anyone had ever made. It would be better than the best computer game, the best movie, the best story, the best construction kit, the best wildlife film and the best fairground ride. It would be all the things he looked forward to or longed for, rolled into one. And as time went on, when his parents were arguing, if he got into bed and put his pillow over his head and thought about the best toy in the world, it seemed to blot out all the badness. But his attempts to build it had always ended in dismal failure, because he had no idea what it was. The closest he'd got was a model of an autogyro, a kind of simple two-man helicopter. Making something that actually flew would have been a major breakthrough. But although the rotors spun furiously as it sped along the bench, they lacked the power to lift it off. And little by little it had dawned on him that perhaps this fabulous toy could only ever exist in his imagination.

Then, during his last year at school, an even more intriguing thought had struck him. Maybe the toy *was* his imagination, pure and simple. The place where he was entirely free to think, do, or be anything he chose. And if that was the case, perhaps the virtual world might be more interesting than the physical, tangible, three-dimensional world of Useful Things, whose design was where he'd so far imagined his future might lie. So he'd abandoned the Carpenter Patent Beer Dispensing devices and begun drawing and sketching. Then he'd downloaded some free software on to his laptop and started experimenting with simple animations of everyday objects. Halfway through the autumn term the head of design and technology had passed him on to the Art department. And now, on the strength of a short animation he'd made over the Christmas holidays, he had an unconditional place on the animation course at Northwestern University and a project to complete for the beginning of term. Storyboards for a thirty-second animation on the theme *Life Is a Bowl of Cherries*. Although at this moment it seemed like a distant planet . . .

Downstairs he heard his mother and Sally saying good-bye. The front door opening and closing. Then his mother's footsteps on the stairs.

THREE

The policemen returned late in the afternoon. Kath made them a cup of tea and they sat, all four, round the small table in the kitchen.

They were polite and friendly, Kath thought, and considerate of what Fin had been through. One asked questions, the other scribbled in a notebook. A well-rehearsed routine.

She could tell that Fin was shaken. When she first went into his room she thought he might have been crying. His eyes looked puffy and some of the brightness seemed to have gone out of his face. As she listened to him, sitting on the end of his bed, she found it hard to believe that this was her son, telling her how he'd looked after a dying girl, alone in the fog on the seashore. And when he finished, and shrugged, and said, 'Well, that's it, there's nothing more to say,' she couldn't help feeling that something else had happened out there in the mist. That he had crossed a line. And her heart gave a tug as she realised that this was the beginning of losing him.

But now, as he talked with the policemen, answering their questions in a level voice, sure of what he had seen and heard, repeating his answers when they asked him to, Kath felt nothing but pride. He seemed to have filled out over the summer. The shoulders were broader, the planes and angles of the face more pronounced, the skin a rich glowing brown. And, once she'd got used to them, the dreadlocks, deep chestnut and shot with streaks of honey from the salt and sun, did lend a certain rakishness to his look, she had to admit. There was no doubt he was handsome. How would Maia look now . . . ? Kath dug her nails into her palms and forced herself to concentrate on what was happening here in the kitchen.

'And you're certain you heard two voices?'

'Certain.'

'Could you tell who they were?'

'No. But I guess it was the man in the suit and the girl.'

'Talking to one another?'

'Not really. At first just one saying something. I think it was the girl. Then nothing for a while.'

'And then?'

'Then the other person getting out of the car. Then a bit of an argument, a scuffle maybe. But very short.'

'What next?'

'The cry.'

'Straightaway?'

'Yes.'

The writer nodded and closed his notebook as his colleague downed the last of his tea, then said, 'Thank you, young man. You've been very helpful. And thanks for the tea, love.'

Kath smiled. 'So, what now?'

'Well, it looks like suicide. In which case there'll be an inquest. We might need to call your son as a witness. We'll let you know.'

'Do we . . . Do you know her name?' Fin asked.

'Yes. It's Charlotte Svensson. She worked on Seal Island, at the Institute, as a researcher. The gentleman you met, who was driving her, was Mr Hunter. He's the head of security there. We've also spoken with the director,

Dr Whitelands. It seems she'd been suffering from depression for some time. They were sending her off on sick leave to the mainland. Mr Hunter was taking her to Cliffton to get the train. When they got on to the bridge, she said she was feeling sick and asked Mr Hunter to stop the car. She went to the parapet while he waited in the car. Next thing he knew she was climbing it. He says he shouted at her to stop, and she shouted back that it was too late. He made a grab for her but she jumped. He couldn't do anything about it.'

'I guess not.' Fin looked down at his empty teacup.

'How old was she?' Kath asked as the policemen made their way to the door.

'Twenty-two,' replied the questioner.

The same age as Maia. She showed them out and closed the door behind them.

'So she was from here . . . on the islands,' said Fin, still staring into the bottom of his cup. 'I thought she'd be a tourist . . . That kind of makes it worse, doesn't it?'

Kath shook her head. 'It's horrible whoever she was . . .' She reached across and took Fin's hand. 'Look, this is really hard for you, love, I know. What d'you think would help? A bit of distraction? Go into Cliffton and see a movie, maybe? Just stay in, watch some TV? Go and see Poacher?'

Fin thought for a moment. 'Reckon I'll go over to Poach's.'

Kath smiled. Difficult though it was to admit, there were times when friends made for better medicine than parents. 'Good idea,' she said.

Then the smiled faded and her heart sank as the familiar step echoed up the alley. The slow, laboured sound of one foot being placed firmly on the ground, then the pause and shuffle as the other was dragged behind it.

Kath got up and went to the door. 'I'll explain it all,' she said over her shoulder to Fin. 'You go and get ready.'

But before Fin could rise from the table the door was flung open. Danny Carpenter stood in the doorway, red-faced and bleary-eyed. He swayed, then planted his stick firmly in front of him and said loudly, 'So, what the police doing here in my house, eh?' His gaze fixed on Fin. 'What you been up to? You been in trouble? Because if you have, I swear to God, you'll feel the end of . . .'

He swayed again.

Kath put out an arm to steady him, but he brushed it away.

'Get off me, woman.'

She ignored him. 'He hasn't been in trouble, Danny. Quite the opposite . . .'

'All right, all right.' Danny took several unsteady steps into the room, grasped one of the chairs vacated by the policemen and slumped into it. 'So he can tell me himself. Can't you, Finlay?'

Fin edged back in his chair as the beer fumes hit him.

'Look', said Kath, 'he's just had a very difficult experience, and he's been helping . . .'

'It's all right, Mum,' said Fin. 'I can tell him.'

'Go on, then,' said Danny. Make me believe you, his look said.

'I was under the bridge when someone committed suicide. At least . . . that's what the police said.'

His doubt failed to register with Danny. 'What you mean, committed suicide?'

'Fell,' said Fin. He seemed reluctant to say 'jumped', thought Kath. 'In front of me. Landed on a rock and broke her back. That's what I think it was, anyway. And I . . . I was with her. While she died.'

Now he was biting his lip. Kath wanted to go and put her arms round him. But she knew that would only incite Danny further. Fin managed to retain his composure and meet his father's suspicious gaze.

'And what were you doing . . . under the bridge?'

'Danny. For God's sake, let him—'

Danny waved a dismissive hand and glared at Fin across the table.

'I was on my way back from the beach.'

'Not at work then . . .'

'No, Dad. It's my Saturday off.' He was doing his best to sound reasonable. Kath could only guess how he must be feeling.

Danny snorted. 'Your Saturday off. Oh yes. From Kettle's Cafe. Serving tea to tourists. What kind of a job's that? Girl's work, that's what—'

'Look, Dad, we've been through all this before.' Fin started to get up from the table.

'Sit down!' Danny bellowed. 'I haven't finished.'

Fin looked at him, hesitated, then sat down.

'See, you wouldn't get a proper job looking like that, anyway. That hair of yours . . . like a bloody rat's nest. So . . . my point is,' he blinked slowly, 'when you going to get it cut?'

Kath stepped forward. 'All right, Danny. That's enough.'

Danny half turned and scowled. 'You stay out of this, Kath.'

But now Fin was on his feet. Kath could see the vein pulsing at his throat.

'I'm going out now, Dad.' Fin moved round the table and made his way to the door.

Danny gaped at him dully. Then his face clouded with

rage and he fumbled for his stick, which was hanging on the back of the chair beside him. Kath ignored him and followed Fin into the alley.

'We'll go to the movies another day, yeah?'

Kath did her best to smile, but her heart went out to him as she watched him walk away down the alley.

Then she braced herself and went inside again.

FOUR

Across the road, at the end of the alley, Easthaven's harbour was enclosed by two concrete walls that ran out from the land like the crooked claws of some giant crab.

In the years since his father's accident, Fin had lost count of the number of times he had walked out along the seaward wall, climbed the rusty rungs and sat down on the top, staring out to sea. Now it was a clear, still evening with no trace of the shrouding mist. On the northerly horizon the ferry was making her way back from the islands. And to the east there was the bridge, spanning the few hundred yards between the island and the low green hills of the mainland. His means of escape . . . but something else now too.

Charlotte Svensson. Who was she, lying there broken on that porpoise rock, alone and terrified and in agony? In the intensity of the moment she had been a life that was about to go out. That was all. And everything. Now . . . she was dead, but she had crashed into Fin's life, and he felt unfamiliar tremors around him, as if he was in the aftermath of some seismic shock. Where was she from? What had she been doing at the Institute? And the most insistent question of all, had she really jumped?

'Hey, Fin!'

He turned around. A tall fair-haired figure was beckoning to him from outside the Ship Inn, the pub that stood on the corner where the road curved round into the harbour.

Had it not been low and white-painted like the cottages, it would have seemed incongruous here in Easthaven, the only hint of commerce on the harbour front of this otherwise sleepy village. But the Ship Inn had been here at least as long as most of the other buildings and, apart from the addition of benches and sun umbrellas in the summer, its outward appearance had changed hardly at all in two centuries.

Fin stood up, climbed back down the rungs and set off towards his friend.

Poacher leaned against the wall beneath the ancient harbour lamp by the door to the public bar. Over six feet tall, with pale blue eyes and a tangle of tawny curls, he was dressed in a sweatshirt, denim cut-offs and sandals. He looked like a beach bum. He *was* a beach bum. Or would have been had his dragon mother not press-ganged him into working in the pub every holiday, where he'd been taking orders, preparing and serving food, and washing dishes ever since they'd bought the place three years ago. Though, in truth, it was no great hardship for Poacher, since one of his two passions was cooking. He was never happier than when he had his sleeves rolled up, oil sizzling in a pan, a sharp knife to hand and something to chop. Fin loved the way his friend's large, clumsy-looking hands could slice and dice with such precision.

Poacher's other passion was the sea. Until this summer he'd spent every moment he wasn't at school, or helping in the pub, in the water with a surfboard. Then he had discovered sea-kayaking. And now the banana, as he called it, the strange-looking yellow fibreglass craft that sat on the grass outside the Archers' family home, was the only thing he could talk about apart from food. And even then he'd named it after something edible.

'You look crap.' Poacher had never seen the point of conversational niceties.

Fin shrugged. 'Yeah, well . . .'

'D'you want to come over to mine?'

'OK.'

Poacher fetched his bike from behind the wheelie bins.

'How was work?' Fin asked.

Poacher rolled his eyes. 'Mental. Coachload of geriatrics all wanting sausages and chips.'

They walked away from the harbour towards the new part of Easthaven. New in that it had only been there for fifty years. A collection of bungalows and modern two-storey houses that sprawled up the hill behind the harbour. The Archers had the end-of-row bungalow on the imaginatively named Seaview Terrace. Like Poacher himself, everything about it was large, from the bedrooms to the garage to the fishing gnome that peered patiently into the pond in one corner of the garden. Fin was amazed that no one had stolen it yet.

They began to climb the hill, Poacher wheeling the bike. 'So why you looking so crap, then? Your old man been at you again?'

'Yeah . . . partly . . .'

'What about, this time?'

Fin put up a hand, grasped a handful of hair.

Poacher nodded. 'The dreaded dreads, huh? So nothing new?'

'True . . . but . . . there's something else.'

'OK. Wait, don't tell me . . . one of your contraptions came back to life and broke down your bedroom wall? No? Well . . .'

'Look, Poach . . . this was serious. Weird. Seriously weird. I don't know . . . let's get to yours first. Then I'll tell you.'

'Hmmm . . .' Poacher raised his eyebrows. 'The plot thickens.'

Fin envied the Archers their space, after the low ceilings, small windows and thin partition walls of Number Thirteen.

Now the house was empty. Poacher's younger sister, Dee, was spending the evening with friends. His mother, the Camp Commandant as he and his father had christened her, was exercising her iron will at the pub. And his father . . . Apart from the odd appearance behind the bar, no one ever seemed to know where Stan Archer, a thin, harmless-looking man, was or what he did. Least of all his son.

Poacher rummaged in a fridge the size of a telephone kiosk. 'Wanna beer?'

'No, thanks. A Coke would be fine.'

Poacher draped himself over a kitchen chair. A sprawl of tanned limbs. He cracked open his can and raised one eyebrow.

'So . . . ?'

Fin leaned forward, elbows resting on the kitchen table.

'So . . .' He found it hard to meet Poacher's eye. 'I . . . er . . . I saw someone die today.'

Poacher's jaw dropped. He put down the can on the table.

'No shit! How? I mean . . . what happened?'

Fin told him.

Few things reduced Poacher to silence. But when Fin finished, he simply sat there in amazement.

Fin's mouth felt dry, his limbs stiff. He took a sip of Coke. Stretched back in his chair. 'The worst thing was that all the time I was with her, all I could think about was Maia.' He shook his head and rocked forward again. 'Jeez, Poach, what a day. First this, then I get home to find that Sally's there with Mum, basically in pieces because she got caught up in that bombing on the mainland yesterday – in that street market—'

'Oh yeah,' Poacher interrupted. 'I saw it on TV at work. Quite a few people killed. Horrible. And they're saying maybe it was a racist attack. It was some kind of ethnic market. Virtually all the dead were black.'

Like you. The words came into Fin's mind with such a jolt that he lost his train of thought.

'So then . . .' He struggled to recover himself. 'So then . . . like to crown it all, the police come round to take a statement from me and they tell me that the guy from the Institute who was driving her said she jumped . . .'

Poacher looked up. 'Yeah?'

'Well, I don't think she did. I think . . . she was pushed. In fact, I'd put money on it.'

'You *what* . . . ?'

'I don't think she jumped.'

'My God.' Poacher's eyes widened. 'Why – I mean, what makes you think that?' He picked up his neglected beer and took a swig.

Fin paused. How *did* he know? In the same way he'd known the moment she died.

'I . . . I don't think I can really explain. A hunch, I guess you'd call it. But it's a really strong hunch, Poach. The Institute guy told the police he was trying to stop her jumping, trying to restrain her. That's what they said. So maybe the fog was distorting sounds. Maybe I wasn't hearing things clearly. But it was all going on right above my head. And the second person who got out of the car –

28

him, I guess – didn't run to the parapet. He walked quite slowly.'

Poacher frowned. 'Maybe he didn't want to do anything that would frighten her?'

'Possibly. But if she really wanted to jump, why did she cry out like that?'

He needed so much for Poacher to believe, for someone to believe, so that he wasn't alone with this feeling that the truth was going to be lost here. But Poacher looked unconvinced.

' OK . . . first of all, why would the Institute head of security want to bump off one of his own people? And then, even if he did, the bridge is a pretty random place to do it. I mean . . . it might not have been foggy, for a start. Then what would he have done?'

Fin drummed his fingers on the tabletop. 'I don't know. I don't know the answers to any of it. You might be right.'

Poacher nodded. 'Maybe the fog *was* distorting the sounds, like you said. Maybe there was more going on than you actually heard . . .'

'But she didn't want to die, Poach. It was in her eyes. And anyway, she said so. She was terrified. Surely if you're trying to commit suicide, you're not going to be frightened of dying.'

'I dunno . . . people change their minds. I saw a documentary about a guy who jumped off the Golden Gate Bridge in San Francisco. One of the only ones ever to survive. And he said that the minute he jumped he knew he'd done the wrong thing and all he wanted to do was stay alive for his wife and kids . . .'

'Maybe.' Fin shrugged wearily. 'But there was something else too. When he, Hunter, came down to where we were, there was something . . . not right about him. He seemed

really cold – I mean not particularly upset or anything . . .'
Fin got up and began to pace. 'I can't believe we're having
this conversation, Poach. It's just so . . . so bloody weird.
This morning none of this had happened. Life was normal.
And now . . . here I am, and you don't really believe me.
And all I know is that *I* don't believe – don't ask me why
– I just don't believe she jumped.'

Poacher nodded thoughtfully. 'Weird. It certainly is
that. Fin's weirdest day.' He brightened. 'Good name for a
movie. Fin's weirdest day.'

'Lousy name,' said Fin. 'No one would go to it.'

'I would.'

'Yeah, but you're my friend.'

Poacher smiled. 'That's me. Peter Oliver Archer. Friend
to the stars – of Easthaven.' He got up and walked over
to put a large hand on Fin's shoulder. 'Look, I'm taking
the banana out tomorrow. Got a friend coming over from
Cliffton, the Duck. He's cool. Anyway, we're heading down
to the whaling station at Salvation Cove. Maybe go over to
the sea caves on Seal Island. Why don't you come with us?
He's got a two-man fish. He's picking me up at nine. It'll be
good. Take your mind off things.'

'Thanks. I'll think about it.' Now Fin felt drained.
'Reckon I'll make a move, Poach.'

'OK. Text me before nine if you want to come.'

'Will do,' said Fin.

He went outside into the summer dusk and walked
slowly down the hill. On the far horizon, the Gannet Rock
lighthouse blinked its warning into the emptiness of the
vast quiet ocean.

FIVE

A mile out of Easthaven there was a fork in the road. To the right, it ran north towards the island's second village, Goat Bay. To the left, it headed south to the causeway that crossed a mile of tidal flats and linked Whale Island with its smaller neighbour, Seal Island. *Green Energies Research Institute – 3 miles*, read a sign which was dominated by the silhouette of a wind turbine.

'It's the Institute Open Day in a couple of weeks,' said Poacher as the van slowed at the fork, then swung left. 'We're doing the beer tent. Fancy coming?'

'If the beer's free,' said the Duck, who was driving. A small wiry character, clad all in black, he was a couple of years older than the other two. There was a quiet energy about him that Fin found intriguing.

'You wish,' said Poacher.

Fin had never given the Institute a lot of thought, much less its annual Open Day. Though he saw the signs every year, the invitation delivered to each household. He had been eleven years old when Green Energies had bought Seal Island from the family of the late Lord Highgate, the wealthy and eccentric former owner. Fin had been aware at the time that there had been controversy about the sale, though he hadn't understood why. Now he knew that it was the bridge that had been the issue. It had been part of the package – bribe, his father had called it – that the authorities had offered Green Energies to bring their

31

Institute to this far-flung and not very prosperous corner of the country. They would pay three-quarters of the cost of construction. And while no one had any problems with the Institute itself – wind-energy research was something few people argued with on the island, it seemed – the idea of the bridge had had all the force of an axe, splitting the island neatly in two: those who thought that it would help bring in money not only from the Institute staff and its visitors, but also from tourists who would now be able to come here more easily; and those who wanted the place to remain as it had always been, an island, and not become overrun with coach parties and yobs on motorbikes and ice-cream wrappers. Needless to say, the bridge had proved another wedge between Fin's parents. Kath welcomed the change, the potential prosperity. Danny fought the idea with every ounce of strength in his twisted, angry body. Fin merely watched in fascination as construction began and the two halves of the bridge inched out from opposite shores, until one day there was no longer any daylight between them.

Poacher and the Duck chatted as the van trundled southwards. They had an easy camaraderie that made Fin feel like a silent observer. Today it suited him. There was too much going on in his mind. He gazed ahead to where, in the far distance, he could just see the tip of one turbine blade pass over the shoulder of Seal Island's single hill, then another, then another, like the spokes of a runaway wheel careering along the horizon but going nowhere.

Charlotte Svensson. He turned the name over in his mind. What kind of life had she had there at the Institute? Was she very clever? A scientist? Had she liked being shut up on Seal Island? Or was that not how the people who worked there felt? Because it certainly seemed to outsiders as if the place had been turned into a kind of fortress since Green Energies had taken over. First there was the causeway, although that had always been there, a kind of reverse drawbridge which disappeared under water for an hour and a half twice a day when the tide came in. Then there was the high wire fence around the perimeter of the island. Well, they were doing top-secret research there, so fair enough, Fin supposed.

He was jolted from his thoughts as the van turned off the road and on to the rough track that dipped down towards a small rocky bay.

'I guess that's where they boiled them up,' said the Duck, pointing to the tall red brick chimney that towered above the narrow strip of shingle beach. 'Boiled the whale blubber to make oil for lamps and soap. And they called this place Salvation Cove.' He gave a soft laugh. 'Whose salvation would that have been, then?'

'Old Albert was in the pub the other night, talking about it,' said Poacher. 'Albert Smith – he runs the whaling museum. Says they're going to start running whale-watching trips from here.'

'A load better than harpooning them,' said the Duck.

They parked the van a little distance from the chimney. Unstrapped the kayaks from the roof and unloaded the paraphernalia on to the grass. Wetsuits, paddles, helmets and provisions.

Fin stood and watched, trying to keep out of the way as they sorted through the equipment. He could sense their excitement, but he felt disconnected and anxious and in two minds as to whether he should have come at all. Though he guessed Poacher must have mentioned something to the Duck about what had happened the previous day. They were both doing all they could to make him feel welcome and put him at his ease.

The Duck. How had he come by a name like that? There was nothing obvious. No waddle. No weird nasal laugh. No upward flick of hair at the nape of his neck. All Poacher had told him was that he lived for travel and was currently working as a handyman for a rich couple in Cliffton to earn money for his next trip. There was something gypsy-like about him, now Fin came to think about it. And a clear, knowing look in the deep-set brown eyes.

Now he passed Fin a wetsuit and told him to get ready.

'Going to be my passenger today. OK with you, Fin?'

'Sure,' Fin said. 'Thanks. Though you'll have to keep me straight.'

'No problem.' The Duck was choosing between two pairs of paddles.

'You OK?' asked Poacher as Fin struggled into a wet-suit. It felt cold and clammy against his skin.

Fin nodded.

'Just do what he says. You'll be fine.'

There was no trace of yesterday's mist. Within a few minutes Fin could feel the heat of the sun warming up the skin of the suit. A dazzle of sunlight on the water made him squint. When they were ready they carried the kayaks down to the water. The Duck held theirs steady as Fin pulled on his helmet, then squeezed into the narrow moulded seat and hooked the skirt of the spray-deck into place around him. Then the Duck showed him how to balance the kayak with the paddle as he took his place in front.

'Ready?'

Poacher leading, they paddled slowly out of the little bay. Then turned towards Seal Island and the caves.

SIX

For the first few strokes it seemed to Fin that the slim craft was so delicately balanced that the slightest wrong movement would capsize it. But as he relaxed and tried to follow the Duck's rhythmic, muscular roll, paddle dipping and rising on alternate sides, he began to realise that, slim as it was, the kayak sat much more steadily in the water than he had thought it would.

They pulled away from the shore, and the clear green water gradually darkened as the seabed fell away. Fin felt that familiar tightening in the pit of his stomach. It was ironic, he often thought, that the son of a trawlerman should be frightened of deep water. Yet it had scared him since the first time he'd been out mackerel fishing with his dad in better days – before the accident. Then, a few hundred yards beyond the harbour walls, he'd watched as they hauled out the writhing silver-blue beauties, one after the other, and the line had seemed to go on forever, and his imagination had suddenly filled with the thought of all the fathoms of dark water that lay beneath the boat, and the monsters that might be lurking there. Too young to see the disappointment in his father's eyes, he'd begun to cry and said he wanted to go home. And even now he still found those deep ocean trenches that went down into the blackness for miles and miles, populated by creatures that had no eyes and were armour-plated to withstand the pressure of the water above, an infinitely more terrifying thought than the furthest reaches of space.

Now they were paddling out of Salvation Cove and across the mouth of the channel that separated Seal Island from its larger neighbour. The tide was high and there was no sign of the causeway. Straight ahead, across a few hundred yards of calm open water, was the headland at the north-western tip of Seal Island. In its cliffs lay the caves.

Poacher was alongside them now.

'Which one shall we do?' he asked.

'Cathedral?' suggested the Duck.

'Yes.' Poacher gave a little flourish with his paddle. 'Fin's first time. We should do the Cathedral.'

'Do you need permission from the Institute?' Fin asked him.

'To go to the caves?' Poacher laughed and shrugged. 'Probably. But hey . . .'

'I shouldn't think they even know about them,' said the Duck.

Poacher set off ahead.

After a few minutes the cliffs began to gain height. The kayaks drew closer and a tall shoulder of rock materialised, jutting out into the water. Poacher made his way to the seaward side, then turned into the angle where it joined the cliffs, and disappeared.

Fin and the Duck paddled on.

'Here we go', said the Duck.

The entrance was wide but low, little higher than a normal door. The kayak slid through and for a moment all went dark. Fin could hear a murmuring echo, the gentle wash and slap of water. The kayak rocked slightly as the Duck stopped paddling and said quietly, 'So, what d'you think?'

As Fin's eyes adjusted from the brilliance of the sunlight, all he could do was gasp.

'Cool, eh?' said the Duck, turning round and grinning.
Fin nodded.

Thirty or forty feet above his head towered a vaulting ceiling of solid rock. Either side the water lapped at the feet of the columns and pillars and buttress shapes that rose up the walls of the cavern. At the far end, at least a hundred feet from the mouth, there was a sloping strip of shingle in the centre of which, like an altar, sat a large rectangular slab of fallen rock, perfectly lit by the shaft of sunlight that fell from an unseen opening high in the roof of the cave.

They paddled forward. The water was milky green around them, but growing gradually clearer as it became shallower, until in the last few feet before the bows rode the shingle, it was like glass and Fin could see every stone and frond of seaweed, every sea anemone and sponge and small fish that darted about the seabed.

Poacher was already hauling his kayak out of the water.

Fin climbed out and gazed around him in amazement. He had never been in a cathedral, but it took very little to imagine this vast space echoing with voices and some robed priest where Poacher now stood by the altar slab, looking out over the glassy floor. How were caves formed? By the constant surging of the sea, he supposed, scouring away at the soft limestone walls, churning around the boulders that he could see now through the clear water. When there was a storm it must be like being inside a washing machine in here.

Poacher had produced a bag of sandwiches and cans of soft drink. Now he was sitting down with his back to the stone. Fin walked over and sat down beside him.

The Duck was rummaging in his kayak. He stood up brandishing what looked to Fin like a short length of plumbing pipe. Then Fin noticed the finger holes.

Poacher grimaced. 'Put it away.'

The Duck shook his head. 'You know the deal. Pay our respects to Neptune.' He turned to Fin. 'It's not the Institute's permission we need, it's his. This is his place, see. We don't belong here except with his say-so.'

Poacher caught Fin's eye and winked.

The Duck walked to the far corner of the shingle, then turned to face them. He put the whistle to his lips and began to play.

The low breathy notes rang out and seemed to fill the whole cavern with a mist of sound, so eerily, hauntingly beautiful that the hairs stood up along Fin's arms.

Standing apart, at the very edge of the pool of sunlight, his face half in shadow and absorbed in his playing, the Duck looked, in the wetsuit, like some kind of gypsy warrior.

He played on, the melody rising and falling like the wash of the sea. Fin closed his eyes and let the waves of sound sweep through him, lifting him up as if he was floating to the roof of the cave.

Something made him open them again. Out in the centre of the cave there was a movement beneath the water. Then it was gone. He blinked. It was at the darkest part of the pool, between where the light from outside reached and the shallow sunlit water at their feet.

There it was again.

The Duck played on.

It was large and dark, but of indeterminate shape. It was moving slowly, almost cautiously towards them. It stopped, hung still in the water. More of a stain than something solid.

The Duck played a scale. It was as if he was running up a circular staircase, the notes chasing one another higher and higher till Fin had to look away from the water and glance up to where he could almost see them in the sunlight at the roof of the cave.

At the peak of the crescendo the Duck stopped. As the sound died there was a gasp from Poacher. The shape spun in the water and was gone.

Poacher and Fin looked at one another open-mouthed as the Duck walked back towards them, a faint smile playing around his mouth.

'What was that?' said Poacher. He sounded nervous.

The Duck shrugged.

'C'mon, you saw it.'

'Yeah. I saw it.'

'So what the hell was it?' Poacher tried to smile.

'Your guess is as good as mine.' He put the whistle back in the kayak. Walked over and picked up a can of Coke. 'Pay your respects to Neptune and anything can happen.' He cracked the can open and drank. 'Better that than ignoring him.' He sat down on the shingle and took a sandwich.

Poacher passed the sandwiches to Fin and took one himself.

A magical thing had just taken place, Fin thought. The shaft of sunlight. The breathy notes of the whistle. The dark Shape in the water. The other-worldly figure of the Duck . . .

'Jesus!'

Poacher was sitting forward, staring at the water.

Out in the middle of the cave, the dark shape had returned. There was a swirl below the surface and a soft splash. A sleek dark head appeared. Two round inquisitive eyes. Dripping whiskers.

'A seal. Goddammit!' Poacher burst out laughing.

The sleek head dipped below the water again.

The Duck nodded and smiled.

'A seal,' Poacher repeated. He settled back against the stone.

Yes, thought Fin. But what brought the seal in here?

'What were you playing?' he asked the Duck. 'That tune.'

'No tune. I was just making it up. Like always.' He paused thoughtfully. 'But I don't usually get a result like that.'

'You don't usually play like that,' said Poacher.

'Yeah.' The Duck smiled. 'That was kinda weird, I admit. I was thinking about this story while I was playing. Heard it the other day from an old guy.'

'What story?' asked Fin.

The Duck glanced at them both in turn. 'You want to hear a story?'

'Go on then,' said Poacher. Fin nodded.

'OK,' said the Duck.

SEVEN

'An old man and woman lived in a cottage by the sea,' the Duck began. 'They had seven sons and were very poor. As they grew up, one by one the sons went off to sea and became fishermen and moved away to find themselves wives and start families, until eventually there was only one left. He was their pride and joy. A strong handsome lad who honoured his mother and father and worked hard the whole day long to put food on the table and fire in the hearth. He vowed he would stay with his parents and take care of them till the end of their days.

'One night there was a great storm. The wind beat around the cottage and the waves crashed into the shore. The mother and father and son were sitting round the fire, trying to stay warm, and there came a knock on the door. "Who could that be," asked the old woman, "at this hour and on a night such as this?" "Answer the door, son," said the old man. "No one should be out on such a night." So the young man got up from the fire and opened the door and in came a tall stranger in a dark hooded cloak. The cloak was soaked through and strands of seaweed trailed from it. It looked as if the stranger had come from the sea itself. "Come in," said the old woman. "Come in and sit by the fire." Without saying a word or taking off the cloak, the stranger sat down on a stool. And in the flicker of the firelight they could see that the visitor was a tall woman with a pale face and eyes that were cold and dark as the ocean. But still she said not a word.

'"You are welcome to the warmth our fire can give," said the old woman, "but alas, we are very poor, and since the storms came our son has not been able to go out fishing, so we have no food to offer you." Still not saying a word, the stranger felt inside the cloak and brought out a satchel from which she took seven fine silver fish, which she laid on the hearth. The old woman thanked the stranger from the bottom of her heart and at once set to cooking. The smell that filled the little cottage was mouth-watering. When the fish were done, she set the rickety table with four wooden platters. But the stranger shook her head. "Do you not wish to eat?" asked the old man. "My wife cooks the best fish for miles around." But the stranger merely indicated that she wished to sleep. "We have no room here," said the old woman. "But if you wish, my husband can show you the little stable where we keep our goat. You will be comfortable there in the straw." The woman nodded and the old man took her outside and showed her where she could sleep, warm in the straw beside the nanny goat.

'The old man went back indoors and, after eating the delicious fish, went to bed. But because of the noise of the storm he was unable to sleep. In the middle of the night a shutter started to bang. He got up to close it and saw a light coming from the goat's stable. He pulled on his coat and went outside, and through the one grimy window of the stable he saw the strangest sight. Still hooded and wrapped in her cloak, the woman was floating in the air above the straw and the sleeping goat. Around her, also in the air, seven candles floated in a circle. Although he could hear nothing because of the storm, the stranger seemed to be singing to herself as, one by one, she snuffed out the candles. Feeling puzzled and more than a little ill at ease, the old man went back to bed. Next morning, when he woke up, the storm had died away and the stranger had gone. It was a beautiful morning and, not wishing to upset his wife, the old man said nothing of what he had seen during the night. For the first time in several days, the son was able to go out fishing again.

'For a few weeks all was well. The weather stayed calm, the young man caught plenty of fish and life continued as normal. Then, one day, the dreadful news came that the eldest son had been lost at sea, washed from his boat by a large wave. Time passed. The couple's grief had only just started to abate when the news came that the second son also had been lost at sea, plucked from his fishing boat by a wave. Months passed and then came the terrible news that the same fate had befallen the third son. And now the old man set to thinking back on what he had seen through the window of the stable that night: the sinister black-clad woman floating above the straw and one by one snuffing out the seven candles. Now at last he plucked up courage to tell his wife. "Oh, you old fool," she cried. "If only you had told me at the time. She must have been the sea-witch, Neptune's daughter. When I was a young girl my mother taught me a charm that would have protected us from her wickedness. But now it is too late and she will surely take every one of our beautiful sons in return for those fine silver fish she gave us. Oh woe is us!" And she began to cry. "No, it is not too late," said the old man. "We must get word to the other three that they must not go to sea again. They must give up their boats and find work on the land. And our youngest son shall go and warn them." At this, the old woman looked less forlorn.

'So that very day the youngest son set off to warn his three surviving brothers. The weeks passed and no word came, until at last, one evening, up the path to the cottage trudged the youngest son. He looked weary and sad, and the old woman let out a cry to see him, for even though he had said not a word she knew at once what news he bore. When he had eaten and drunk he told them the story of how he had travelled around the country to find his three brothers, and each time he was greeted with the same dreadful news – that the very day before he arrived the brother had been washed from his boat and lost at sea. At this the old woman sprang to her feet and cried out that their youngest son, the beloved only survivor, should never set foot on a boat, or he too would surely suffer the fate of his older brothers. And so he returned to his work with a neighbouring farmer. Every day he set off and from dawn to dusk he bent his back to the plough or the scythe and every evening he trudged home wearily along the path that followed the cliffs to his cottage. And sometimes he would pause on the clifftops at sunset and gazed sadly at the sea, and think of his poor lost brothers.

'Then, one evening, he was returning as usual and a great storm blew up and as he came to the cliffs he saw a ship had been driven on to the rocks, and the crew were struggling to get ashore. I can't watch these good sailors drown, he said to himself, so he ran to the cottage and fetched a rope and threw the rope to the sailors, and one by one they made their way safely to the shore. But as the very last man was almost out of the water, the young man saw a huge wave coming in from the ocean. He had never seen such a wave in all his life and for a moment he was frozen as it towered up higher than the walls of a castle and crashed down over the ship, smashing it to smithereens, then rolled on towards the beach. Now the young man let go of the rope and turned towards the land and ran for all his life, but he was too late. The wave was still as high as a house and coming in faster than a galloping horse, and he had gone only a few paces when it broke upon him and swept him out to sea and he was never seen again. The very next morning the old man and woman packed up and left their cottage, never to return.'

The Duck nodded to himself.

Then he stood up and walked over to the kayak.

Unwilling to break the spell, Fin and Poacher followed in silence.

EIGHT

Maia looked up from the screen and realised with a start that it was dark outside. Her eyes hurt. Her shoulders too. She pushed back in the swivel chair and stretched. Then moved forward again and read the last paragraph one more time, corrected a spelling mistake and pressed Save. She logged off and shut down the computer. She retrieved her bag and left the building, nodding good-night to the security guard as she went.

Outside, the footpath lighting punctuated the darkness like a trail of glow-worms. It was too late to eat. She'd make herself toast and a cup of tea. The newsletter was coming along well since Terry had asked her to take charge of it. Although he still fed her the raw material – the thoughts, comments, news – she gave it shape and structure. She gave it power, she liked to think. She was his editor.

The thought filled her with warmth. She had never met anyone like him in her life. In fact, she was quite certain that there was no one else like him in the world. So kind and thoughtful and caring. Yet firm, full of purpose and direction. And so inspiring. In her wilder moments Maia thought she would happily die for him. And tonight he had singled her out for his special attention, his special care. She felt a momentary weakness at the knees. Quickened her step.

He never said anything but she always knew. It was just a look, the trace of a smile, a slight raising of one eyebrow, unnoticeable to anyone else. And it could come any-where. At any time. As they passed in the corridor. When he stopped by her desk to give her something. Across the crowded staff cafe. Once every couple of weeks. And at those moments, regardless of what she was doing, her at-tention was drawn to him, as if for a split second he was beaming all his personal magnetism her way.

The first time she had been stunned and flattered. She'd walked around all the following day with the feeling that she was hugging herself to contain this marvellous, pre-cious, extraordinary secret. Then there had followed an agonising two weeks of waiting, hoping, doubting, looking to every gesture, every nuance of voice or glance. Until it happened again. Then, a few months after she'd got used to it, there had been a dreadful few weeks when he'd seemed to ignore her. Later he'd explained that he felt she hadn't been doing her best work over the previous few weeks, and that if they were all to succeed, he needed every one of them to be giving their all, all the time. And she'd realised at once that he'd been right.

But now she had settled into a good working rhythm, and part of the pleasure of it was not knowing when the next moment with Terry would be.

She shouldn't have worked quite so late, she thought. She needed to relax before she went to join him.

Close though she'd become to her room-mate, at this moment she was glad Lottie was away. She'd have the place to herself for the next half-hour. She went round putting on lights. Kettle on and two slices of bread in the toaster. She ran a bath. Selected a chill-out track on the iPod.

She took the tea and toast through to the bathroom and put them down on the stool. Then undressed and got into the bath. She lay there, luxuriating in the warm water, feeling it easing away the tension in her shoulders, the back of her neck.

She smiled to herself. Life could hardly be better. She was doing work she felt passionate about. She had made several good friends, especially Lottie. And then there was Terry. Last time she'd been shopping she'd bought a dress with a big floral print that she knew would look good against her skin.

She drank the tea and ate the toast, dropping crumbs into the bathwater, then got out and went back to the bedroom. There on the chest of drawers was the photograph of her and Lottie where they'd first met, at the Groeneberg Industries' induction programme. Three weeks at Schloss Adler, a fairy-tale castle in Austria, surrounded by mountains and forests and lakes. Forty of them, from all over the world. Forty young idealists, burning to make their mark on the future. She could still remember her cheeks glowing with pride as Walter Groeneberg himself, who had flown in especially from Great Falls, Montana, had told them on the first day that they were the hope of the planet. Some of the finest young minds on six continents, he'd said, gathered here to learn how together, in the coming years, they could push back the frontiers of sustainable energy. 'Together we can create a clean planet,' he'd declaimed. *A clean planet*. How those words resonated in Maia's mind now. Not a day went by when she didn't come across the mantra in what she read, or wrote, or what her colleagues said, or what she herself thought. As if, during the daily consciousness-raising meditations at Schloss Adler, the idea of a clean planet had somehow entered their bloodstreams to give them a superior sense of purpose, an understanding of the importance of their mission, that raised them above the level of normal people. And Terry's supreme gift was his ability to win people's hearts and keep them true to that vision.

This was to be her family from here on. That was the other message she'd heard at every turn during those three extraordinary weeks in Austria. Now, in her heart and soul, she knew it for the truth.

She slipped the dress over her head and put on some of her favourite eyeshadow. Some lipgloss. A dash of perfume.

She looked in the mirror. Yes. Tonight she would make Terry happy.

NINE

The smashed window of the Scout hut gaped. Albert Smith stood looking at the glass that littered the ground below it with an expression of weary resignation. He shook his head.

'At least they didn't take anything,' said Sally Light-foot.

At this moment she was secretly glad of Albert's misfortune. It helped take her mind off the events of a couple of days ago, which continued to assail her in great vivid surges of noise and smell and images of such horror she could never have imagined. There was no telling when they were coming, and they rocked her sideways, left her gasping and dizzy. Flashbacks, they were called. She supposed that if she couldn't get them under control, she might have to go and see someone. But that would be a last resort. She hadn't lived alone for twenty years to go rushing for help as soon as something bad happened. And anyway, she believed in the healing power of the sea. If you lived close to it, as she did, it worked away at you day and night with its rhythm, its ebb and flow. Yes, the sea was her friend and she would never leave it, never move away from Whale Island. Even though it was the sea that had taken the man she loved.

'Come on then. Let's get to work.'

Kath and Fin had volunteered to come up and give a hand. Yobs from the mainland, it had been. As usual. No islander would have done this. And just when the developers were coming to talk about the possibility of incorporating the museum into the new whale-watching centre they were planning to build at Salvation Cove. Poor old Albert. She glanced at him fondly. The museum was his pride and joy. A few months after Irene, his wife, had died of cancer – nearly ten years ago now – a load of paraphernalia had turned up in someone's farm shed, stuff that had been stripped out of the whaling station when it had been abandoned. Albert had volunteered to sift through it, just for something to do, and there he'd discovered a fascination for history. He'd persuaded the parish council to let him have the disused Scout hut as a museum. These days he spent at least half his time up there, pottering about, cataloguing, labelling, arranging.

The yobs had taken nothing, as far as Sally could see. But they'd wrecked a lot. Display cases smashed. Photograph frames broken. More glass everywhere. The whaling life had made tough demands on instruments and tools, so they were well enough made to survive having been kicked around the floor. But it was a godalmighty mess nonetheless, and she could see that Albert was fighting back tears.

Kath had brought up a dustpan and brush, newspaper and bin bags. She and Fin were carefully sweeping up the glass, wrapping and bagging it. Sally looked at them kneeling on the floor, dark heads bent together, and felt a rush of affection. Kath Carpenter was like the daughter she never had. She could remember when Danny had first come home with her, the day he'd taken her into the Ship Inn, and everyone had spent the evening surreptitiously glancing at this exotic, dark-skinned beauty, unlike anyone that had ever lived on Whale Island before. And Sally had known, right then, even though there were twenty years between them, that they'd become friends. And they had. She was a brave woman, Kath, if a bit too stubborn for her own good sometimes. She put up with a lot from Danny. A lot more than she needed to, thought Sally, though she guessed Kath had her reasons. Anyway, she hoped that once Fin was gone Kath would rethink the whole situation. Maybe leave him, much as Sally dreaded the thought if it meant her friend leaving the island too. Meanwhile, Kath still had Fin for another couple of months, lovely lad that he was. He was brave too, come to think of it. The way he put up with Danny, and had stayed the course, unlike Maia – and that was a tragedy that made all their lives harder. But Fin's temperament was different from his sister's, more thoughtful, dreamy even, whereas Maia was fiery, impulsive, volatile. And then that business on the beach with the girl and the bridge – just a couple of days ago. God, she'd been so wrapped up in her own drama, she'd hardly given it a thought. That would have been tough for Fin, tough for anyone.

She began collecting up scattered photographs. What *was* going on at the moment? The bombing. The young girl's death. Now this . . .

'At least they'll still be able to see what we've got here.'

Albert placed a brass sextant in the last remaining space on the surface of the central table and stood back with a sigh.

All the debris had been cleared up. Fin had used Albert's tools to fix a piece of plywood over the broken window. The entire contents of the museum were now arranged either on the tabletop, in the display cabinets that had survived, in rows along the floor or propped against the skirting board. The one thing that hadn't been touched was the whale's jawbone. A huge curved section of yellowing bone nearly three metres long, it still hung on two chains from the ceiling.

But Fin's eye was drawn to the vicious-looking harpoon that stood in one corner along with a selection of long-handled flensing knives.

'Will they really want to show this stuff in a place where people are going to pay to watch whales?' he asked.

Albert smiled for the first time since they'd arrived. He was small and slightly hunched, with a fringe of white hair around a bald dome.

'That's precisely the point,' he said. 'It'll remind people of what terrible things we used to do to the wretched creatures, so when they see them the experience will be all the more powerful.'

'I'm glad they don't do it any longer,' Kath said.

'Well, they do,' Albert replied. 'Just not here. Other countries still go whaling. Here we've stopped doing it to the poor old whales. We just blow each other up instead.' He caught Sally's eye. 'Sorry, love, that was thoughtless of me . . .'

'It's OK,' said Sally. 'Are we finished, d'you reckon?'

Albert glanced around and nodded.

'Come on then.' Sally smiled. 'Let's go down to the Ship. I'll buy us all a drink.'

They turned to leave and Fin's eye was caught by a photograph resting on the edge of the table. It was faded black and white, and although it was dated 1952, it looked like something from another age altogether. A man in oilskins and a sou'wester operated the winch that was hauling a large whale alongside the ship on whose pitching deck he stood. For a moment Fin imagined him as Danny. He wondered what it was like to look down for one instant of terror and see a cable snag, then wrap itself around your leg, before you were jerked off your feet and screaming to your mates to cut the motor, your shoulder blades being wrenched from their sockets as you clung to anything that would stop you being dragged overboard, and all the while the cracking, searing agony in your thigh . . .

'You coming, love?' said Kath.

He went outside.

TEN

Ten o'clock on a Monday night in July, and the Ship Inn was doing a roaring trade. It was still light enough for people to sit outside at the wooden benches and tables overlooking the harbour. The day's heat hung in the air.

Sally led the way inside, into the small, low-ceilinged bar. It was festooned with ship's brasses and old photographs. At one end, the dartboard was surrounded by a red-and-white lifebelt. A ship's clock hung above the bar and on the bar itself was a jar almost full of coins, with a label asking people to give generously to the Cliffton lifeboat appeal.

Shirley Archer, Poacher's mother, was behind the bar. She looked up and waved as they came in, a large woman with cropped blonde hair and a tight black T-shirt declaring: *I got my sea legs at the Ship Inn*. The bar was packed with locals and visitors. There was hardly room to move, let alone anywhere to sit. But as they pushed their way towards the counter, a party got up from one of the tables in the window and Kath made for it.

While Sally waited her turn at the bar, Kath, Fin and Albert settled themselves at the table.

'Thanks for helping out,' said Albert. 'It was good of you both, especially you, Fin, after . . . well, what happened at the bridge.'

'It's OK,' said Fin. 'It was no trouble.' It was strange. Although he wanted to forget all about the other day, he also wanted to keep talking about it, in case he might stumble across something he'd overlooked, something that would convince him that she really had jumped. Then he could let it all go.

'She was from the Institute, I heard?' Albert went on.

'Yes.'

'D'you ever think about all those people down on Seal Island?' Albert mused. 'That we never see hide nor hair of them?'

'Can't say I do really,' Kath replied.

'I mean, it's not like the old days,' he continued, 'Lord Highgate's day. When the estate folk were forever up at Easthaven for one reason or another.'

Sally arrived with the drinks. She set them down on the table.

'Cheers.' Albert took a sip of his beer and wiped froth from his upper lip. 'We were just reminiscing . . .'

'*You* were just reminiscing,' said Kath.

They all laughed.

'*I* was just reminiscing about Seal Island in old Highgate's day. How we always used to see them. But we never see anyone from the Institute.'

'Except the buses,' said Sally.

'Ah yes, the security training programme.' Albert nodded.

'I've always wondered what security guards have to do with wind energy,' said Kath.

'Some of the big wind farms they're building are in pretty hair-raising places. Probably cheaper – and safer – to have their own in-house muscle.'

'Pity they don't come and spend their money here,' said Sally.

'I'll drink to that,' said Albert, raising his glass. He

turned to look at Kath. 'Did you hear Gus Steerman has been back?'

Kath halted with her drink halfway to her lips.

Sally glanced at Albert and frowned.

'No, I didn't,' Kath said. 'When?'

'Last week. Looking up old friends, I heard.'

'Well, he didn't call on us,' said Kath. She shook her head.

Why has Albert brought this up? Fin wondered. He could see his mother's discomfort and it made him angry. He'd always thought of Albert as a kind of genial elderly uncle. But mentioning Gus for no apparent reason – that seemed tactless. Gus Steerman. A name that was banned at Number Thirteen, Easthaven, for the simple reason that Danny felt betrayed by him. The owner and skipper of the *North Star*, Gus had been Danny's boss for nearly twenty years. And Danny had served him faithfully, come hell or high water, as his first mate. But after the accident Gus had simply ditched him, or so Danny said. 'The bastard never even came to see me in hospital,' he was prone to tell anyone who would listen. 'Cut me out, just like that. Good as chucked me on the scrapheap. Not so much as a fiver did I get from him.' And there had been something odd about it, everyone had to admit. Because Gus was generally liked and respected on the island, yet he seemed to have broken the unwritten rule that old shipmates looked after one another. Most of all skippers and crewmen. And to make things worse, he'd sold the boat for a decent sum shortly after and left for the mainland.

'Better not tell Dad that,' Fin said now.

Kath nodded.

Albert looked at her. 'I didn't say it to stir things up for you, love. Just to let you know, in case, well . . . as Fin says, we wouldn't want Danny getting all in a lather, would we . . . ?'

Kath blushed and reached over to pat Albert's hand.

'Thanks, Albert. Glad you told me.'

Fin put down his pint. He needed to get outside. It was hot and noisy and crowded in here and he wanted space to think. He stood up, made his excuses and pushed his way out through the crush of drinkers.

The sun had set now, but although the sky was drained of colour there was still a midsummer lightness. The outside tables were crowded and one group had taken their drinks over to the harbour wall. Their voices and laughter rang across the still evening water.

They were sitting a little along from Fin's thinking spot. He toyed with the idea of going left beyond the harbour, past the cottages and out to the rocks. But it seemed like too much effort. He turned right to walk inland, up the hill, then saw movement on the harbour wall. They were climbing down, clutching bottles and glasses, and starting to make their way, some of them a little unsteadily, back round the harbour towards the pub.

Fin walked towards them. They were young, in their twenties, four men in shorts and T-shirts, two women in sundresses. They were giggling and swaying, and one of the women leaned heavily on her partner.

The harbour wall made it too narrow for them to walk abreast. Fin stepped aside as the first three passed him, the two women and one man. As the remaining men drew level, the one nearest lurched towards him, deliberately, it seemed to Fin, shouldering him aside and at the same time letting drop the nearly empty pint glass, which smashed on the concrete.

Surprised and shocked at the unexpected physical contact, Fin moved back. But the young man stepped forward and thrust his face close to Fin's. He was clean-cut with short-cropped hair and a body-builder's physique.

'That was clumsy, wasn't it?' He paused and grinned. 'Monkey man . . .'

For a split second Fin wondered whether he'd heard properly. Then his heart began to pound. This was something he had only ever read about, something he had never imagined happening to him . . . He stood, staring stupidly at the young man, his feelings in turmoil.

'So . . .' said the young man, 'gonna pick it up then?'

The two other men were standing level, looking on. The other three had stopped and turned around.

'Oi, Sean,' called out one of the girls.

Fin said nothing. He broke eye contact and stepped to one side. But Sean moved with him, blocking his path.

'I said . . . gonna pick it up?' He paused again. 'Monkey man.'

'Leave off it, Sean,' called the girl.

'Just let me past, please,' said Fin. His mouth was dry, blood drummed at his temples.

Sean looked at him for a long time. 'Yeah, OK.' He stepped aside. 'Back to your monkey tree then.'

Summoning every ounce of self-control, Fin took a couple of steady paces forward. Then his spine prickled at the presence of someone behind him and a voice, so close that he could feel the breath on the back of his neck, said softly, 'Fucking nigger.'

Fin felt his moorings snap. A red wave of fury crashed through him, all the tension of the last few days exploding, as he spun round, swinging his fist as he went. It glanced across Sean's nose and caught him on the cheekbone. Fin heard his knuckles crack. Sean gave a startled grunt and

59

backed away, tripped and fell to the ground, narrowly missing the litter of broken glass. Fin fell on him and they rolled over together, as Fin grabbed a handful of hair and tried to batter Sean's head on the concrete, Sean yelling, 'Get him off me, get him off me!' and Fin biting down on something soft and fleshy and tasting blood. Sean roaring now like an angry animal. Hands grabbing Fin's arms and legs, a fist pummelling at his head, a foot in his ribs that drove the breath from him, then writhing and rolling and trying to throw them off, then a stomach-churning moment of nothing, weightlessness, before the crashing shock of cold water and the plunging down below the surface.

By the time Fin had hauled himself up the rungs in the harbour wall, a crowd had gathered. Shirley Archer had emerged from the pub to take charge, standing arms akimbo, glaring at Sean and his companions, daring anyone to challenge her authority.

Fin stood, sodden and dripping. Feeling, in front of the crowd, like some figure from a pantomime.

Kath was pushing her way through the bodies. She reached the front and looked at him in horror, but to his relief came no closer.

'I'm OK.'

'That's good then,' said Shirley Archer in her no-nonsense tones. 'So now you can tell me what was going on.'

Fin looked at Sean, who was being held by his companions. Whether for comfort or restraint, Fin didn't know and didn't care. He had one closed eye and a bloody wound that looked like a bite mark on one forearm. He met Fin's eye and his face twisted.

'He called me something . . .' Fin began. Then faltered. He felt angry and dazed and ashamed. He didn't think he could bring himself to repeat it in front of this crowd. He looked away from Shirley, who stood waiting. His knuckles hurt. His head and ribs hurt. And he had begun to shiver.

Help came from an unexpected quarter. One of the two girls, the one who had told Sean to leave off it, now spoke up.

'He did,' she said. 'He was right out of order. Can't take his drink, can you, Sean? Says things he shouldn't. Racist things.' She looked across at Fin and held out a conciliatory hand. 'Really sorry, mate.' She turned to Sean. 'If you ask me, you got what was coming.'

Sean glared at her but she looked away in contempt.

'Right,' said Shirley Archer, 'now we know. You, Sean – if that's your name – we don't stand for racists here. So you can piss off back to wherever you came from. And I don't ever want to see you in my pub or this harbour again. Do I make myself clear?'

Sean scowled and grunted. He and his companions trooped off in the direction of the car park, the girl who had spoken up gesticulating as they went.

Shirley turned to Fin.

'And you, young man – I don't care what people say to you. I don't like brawling in front of my pub. Bad for business. And you're bloody lucky the tide wasn't out. So get home and get dried off.' She paused. 'And next time you need to dust up a racist thug, you ask me first.' She winked, then turned and strode back inside. The crowd dispersed, Sally and Albert with them. Kath and Poacher stayed behind.

Poacher put an arm around Fin's shoulders.

'You OK, man?'

Fin nodded.

'Who was he?'

61

Fin shrugged. 'Some guy. Pissed.'

'What did he say?'

Fin shook his head.

'Wish I'd been here.' Poacher gave his shoulder an affectionate squeeze. 'Anyway, better get back to work.' He pulled a face. 'Catch you afterwards?'

'Maybe,' said Fin.

He glanced at his mother, still waiting for him at a discreet distance.

He thought she looked close to tears.

ELEVEN

Throughout his teenage years Fin's bedroom had gradually acquired an almost complete wallpapering of posters. Music ones. Movie and TV stars. Sports heroes. And, of course, girls. Some of the posters faded and torn. Some shiny and new. A chronicle of his changing fantasies and dreams. Then, on his very last day of school, he had come home and, in a grand gesture, torn them all down. All except one.

Now he pulled the duvet closer around him. Despite the warm night, he felt cold inside. His knuckles were bruised and his ribs hurt. He'd allowed Kath to clean up the cut to his chin and put some ointment on his hand, then make him a cup of tea, which he'd taken up to his room. But he hadn't felt like talking.

He eased himself back on the bed and looked up at his one remaining poster – of a handsome young black man in boxer's shorts and gloves. Bare-chested, head bent forward, left fist leading, looking straight at the camera. *Float like a butterfly, sting like a bee*, ran the caption. Why had he kept it? He didn't really know. Perhaps because Muhammad Ali was so much greater than any of the rest. A true legend, an all-time hero, not only as a sportsman but also as an activist, a statesman, an inspiration to others. Perhaps simply because he looked so good, with his perfect physique. Or because Fin liked the words of the caption and the images they conjured. Perhaps, even, because it was common knowledge that Ali now suffered from Parkinson's Disease – which seemed to make him more real in a way, more human. In any event, something had stayed Fin's hand when he had reached the poster of the world heavyweight champion, though it had never occurred to him until now that it might have been simply because Ali was a black man.

Fin had been lucky, he supposed. In eighteen years he had never given his colour more than a passing thought. Strictly speaking, he and his mother and Maia were half-castes, though most people they knew referred to them as black. It was only when people were uncomfortable, or trying to be polite, that they called them 'coloured' or 'mixed race'. In any case, their colour had never been an issue on Whale Island. And Cliffton Secondary, thanks to a firm head teacher, could claim to be as free of racism as any school in the country. So Fin had grown up considering himself just like all the other kids he mixed with, white, black or anything in between.

Yet now, in just a few days, the issue of race had twice crashed in on his consciousness. The bombing in the market first of all. *Like you.* Ever since that moment with Poacher, he seemed to recall the glimpsed scenes from the television in a clearer, harsher light. And now, this Sean. He felt shocked and angry and even ashamed, as if he had been cheapened by the racist abuse, by his own violent reaction. He had never hit anyone before in his life. Not in real anger. But neither had he ever heard such hatred directed at him as there had been in Sean's voice.

Had Muhammad Ali ever been called a fucking nigger? It would've been a brave man to do so, thought Fin, looking at the perfect torso, the fists, the unflinching eye. Though the likelihood was that he had been. He'd won his first world title in 1964, only a year after Martin Luther

King's famous 'I have a dream' speech, urging people of every colour across the United States to stand together against inequality. Yes, Fin thought, Ali would have known what it was like.

He turned over and winced at the sharp pain in his ribs.

Sometimes he wished he knew more about his ancestry. A one-night stand between Kath's mother, a hotel chambermaid in Cliffton, and a Brazilian deckhand named Lincoln, off a Panamanian-registered freighter. That was all anyone, including his nan, knew. Not a home town. Not a photograph. Not even any idea of whether Lincoln was his first or second name. Only that he was 'ever such a handsome devil' as his nan would say, with a twinkle in her eye and a mischievous elbow in the ribs of Fin's step-grandad, Tommy, a retired plumber with whom she had discovered a new lease of life in her seventies . . .

There was a crash as the outside door was flung open. Then a roar.

'Finlay!'

Fin's heart sank.

He got out of bed, pulled on his jeans and went downstairs.

Danny was waiting at the foot of the stairs, leaning on his stick, in the tiny hallway between the kitchen and sitting room. Behind him, on the back of the front door, hung his red trawlerman's survival suit. It had been there since he'd last taken it off, nine years ago, and he refused to let it be put away. He kept it there to torture himself, Fin sometimes thought, and made a point of hanging his own coat over it whenever he could.

Sometimes Danny would go down to the fishermen's mission in the evening. Sometimes he'd go in the afternoon.

Sometimes he'd get there in the morning and stay there all day, till he was chucked out or one of his mates brought him home. Fin could tell at a glance how long he'd been there. Today it had been an all-day session.

'Been brawling, have you?' His words were thick.

Fin nodded. There was no point arguing.

'Right outside the pub . . .'

The sitting-room door opened.

'He was attacked,' Kath said. 'Verbally—'

'You. Shurrup. Or I'll give you verbal.'

Kath glared.

'Someone called me a fucking nigger,' said Fin. 'So I hit him.'

'Fucking nigger, eh?' Danny eyed him blearily. 'Well, it's what you are, isn't it?'

Kath's hand moved so fast that Danny didn't see it coming. It caught him on the side of the face and made him stagger backwards, flailing with his stick to keep his balance.

'Don't you *ever* speak to my son like that again.' Her voice was like ice.

Danny's eyes were watering. Already a red weal was appearing on his face. He looked around, blinking as if unsure what to do next, then mumbled, 'Gonnabed.'

Elbowing Fin out of the way, he hauled himself upstairs and slammed the bedroom door behind him.

For the second time that evening Fin stood stunned to silence, unable to believe what he had just heard. Then the fury started to bristle in his veins again. He swung round, fists clenched, and started up the stairs. But Kath caught hold of him.

'No, love.' Her voice quiet now. 'It won't do any good for any of us.'

Fin turned on the stairs.

For a long moment they looked at one another.

'Please . . . ?'

Fin breathed deeply. Forcing the rage to recede. Then nodded and stepped down.

'I'll make us some tea,' Kath said.

Fin went into the sitting room and flung himself down on the settee. What was happening to him all of a sudden? Was he going mad? Was the world going mad? Why should anyone care about the colour of his skin? First Sean. Then his own father, for God's sake.

Kath came through with tea and a plate of biscuits on a tray. She took a seat beside him. Passed him a cup. Then sat with her own for a while, thinking.

'There's something I should tell you, sweetheart,' she said at length. 'About what happened just then. See . . . well, you know how much your dad changed after the accident. And one of the things was he started making . . . remarks, about how dark you are. How much darker than me and your sister.'

It was true. Kath and Maia were both a kind of café au lait that, were it not for the tight curls and slight flaring of the nostrils, might have placed them anywhere from the Mediterranean southwards. But in Fin's case, some quirk of the gene pool had endowed him with a much richer pigmentation. At his darkest, like now when he had spent a lot of time in the sun, his skin was a deep toffee colour.

'So anyway . . . the long and the short of it is that he started saying you couldn't be his.' She had begun to twist her wedding ring around her finger. 'Now he's no racist, your dad. That's one thing he isn't, whatever he said just now. He married me after all.' She smiled. 'But he *is* jealous –' she put a hand on Fin's arm – 'and if you're

67

thinking what I think you're thinking, sweetheart, the answer is he's wrong. You're mine and his and no one else's. That's God's honest truth. But the trouble is, he won't believe me. He's got it into his head that I had an affair. And nothing will budge him.' She paused. 'I hate to be telling you this, love. But it's the only way for you to understand.'

Fin shrugged angrily. Nothing anyone could say right now would make him feel better about Danny.

'What about a DNA test?'

She shook her head. 'He won't hear of it. I've tried that one and he just flies off the handle.'

'We could do it anyway. Then show him—'

There was a crash from upstairs. The ceiling shook.

'Oh God!' Kath pulled a face. 'He's fallen out of bed. You'll have to give me a hand.'

'Leave him there,' said Fin.

Kath shook her head.

'Come on.'

Fin followed her upstairs to where Danny lay sprawled on the bedroom floor, shirt half unbuttoned, trousers round his ankles. Snoring heavily. He had not so much fallen out of bed as failed to get into it. Fin looked down at the naked thigh with a mixture of revulsion and pity. He had never seen it before. Danny had taken good care that no one did, apart from Kath. The scarred flesh was loose and puckered where the muscle had wasted and the whole upper section of the limb was twisted and misshapen. It didn't look entirely human, Fin thought, more like something that might have been brought up in the *North Star*'s nets. The idea of having to walk on it made Fin wince.

'Come on. You get him under the arms,' said Kath. 'I'll take the other end. One . . . two . . . three – heave!'

It took them several attempts to get him into bed. Danny

continued to snore throughout. By the end they were both giggling like children. They pulled the covers over him and went downstairs.

'God, what an evening,' said Kath, dabbing at her eyes. 'I could use a drink.' She glanced at her watch. 'Eleven thirty. Will you be OK for work tomorrow?'

'Sure. What d'you want?' Fin went into the kitchen.

'Bacardi and Coke. If there's any Bacardi.'

Fin found the bottle and poured the last of it into a glass with Coke from the fridge. He took it back into the living room with a beer for himself.

'Cheers,' said Kath.

'Cheers.'

They clinked glasses. Then sat in silence for a little while.

'Maybe he doesn't want me to be his son anyway,' said Fin. Surprised at the lump that rose in his throat as he said it.

Kath put her hand on his. 'I don't think he knows what he wants any longer,' she said. 'He's not the man I married . . .'

'So . . . why don't you just – leave him?'

A squall of conflicting emotions crossed Kath's face.

'I've thought about it, love. Believe me, I've thought about it. Never harder than right now.'

'What's stopping you?'

She stared into her drink.

'I suppose . . . first of all, I grew up without a father and I didn't want that for you two. Not at any cost. So in the first years after the accident, when you were younger, I reckoned that . . . well, any father was better than none.'

'And now?'

She shook her head.

'What else?'

'Well, for one, I don't think he'd survive without me. He can't really look after himself properly any longer, what with the booze and painkillers. And for another, because we need his disability allowance. I don't earn enough at the shop to keep us all.'

'I'll be gone in two months.'

Now she pulled a face. 'I know you will.'

'Then there'll be one less mouth to feed.'

She nodded. 'I've said to myself for a long time that I'd think about it properly when you leave. If nothing changed . . .'

'And has it?'

She laughed grimly. 'What would you say? After to-night . . . ?'

'So?'

'So . . .' She looked down again, colour creeping into her cheeks. 'There is one other thing . . . You might find it hard to believe. But I do still love him. There are moments when I get glimpses of the old Danny, the one who swept me off my feet. And then I think, that's something worth fighting for.' Now she looked up at him. 'I know that must sound crazy to you – after what he's put you and Maia through. And maybe it is. Some people might call me self-ish. But when the time comes and you meet someone you really love, Fin, perhaps you'll understand. It's a hard thing to give up.'

Even when they say their son's a fucking nigger? thought Fin. Even when they drive their own daughter away? But he kept the thought to himself. Instead he asked,

'Mum, has anything like this ever happened to you . . . ? I mean, this evening . . . that guy . . . ?'

She turned on the settee and tucked her feet under her

so she could face him. 'You've been so sheltered, you know, love. Here on the island. And at school . . . Wasn't like that when I was a kid. Growing up with your nan, on benefits, in a two-room flat down at Cliffton docks. Darkie. Wog. Coon. Sambo. Oh, I had my share of name-calling. And worse. Even when we first came here. Though it was more subtle here, of course. Because of your dad, because of the Carpenters. But for the first year or so, it was there. Glances. Gestures. Whispers. Even body language. Things people assumed about me. Things people didn't assume about me.'

'What changed it?'

'Sally, bless her. She spotted what was going on. One night we were in the pub together and someone made some stupid remark. She just got to her feet in front of everyone and said they should be ashamed of themselves if they couldn't welcome someone whose only difference was the colour of their skin. And that was it. There's never been anything since. Not that I've been aware of.'

She drained her glass.

'I know I was really lucky with Sally. But the honest truth is – and I hate to say it – there's racism everywhere. Whatever people say. It's just that as you get older you get better at dealing with it. Knowing where not to go. Who to avoid eye contact with. And most of all, how not to rise to it, how not to feel hurt. But sometimes you come across a Sean. An ignorant animal who probably doesn't even know why he feels so much hatred. So maybe, Fin, love, what happened this evening was a good thing. Kind of a preparation. Because there might not be much racism here on the island, but once you leave here, once you get out into the world, I think you need to be ready for it.'

She leaned over and kissed him on the cheek. Then got

to her feet. 'Come on, it's late. We've both got to work tomorrow.'

'I'll stay down a bit longer,' said Fin.

She looked at him. 'You all right?'

'I'm fine. Just not ready for bed yet.'

Kath left the room.

For a long time Fin stared into the empty fireplace.

TWELVE

Maia sat on the bed, still in her dress, staring at the photo of her and Lottie in Austria. She had no sense of how long she'd been there, but dawn light was starting to seep into the room. She couldn't help glancing at the empty bedroom across the little passage.

He'd waited until she was getting dressed again to tell her. He had wanted to prepare her, allow her to feel relaxed and calm, before breaking the news, he'd said in his quiet, considerate way.

But nothing could have prepared her for this. Lottie was dead. It felt like a blow to the stomach, and she sat down on the chair with his clothes on it. How could she be dead? Last time Maia had seen her had been on Saturday morning at breakfast. She'd seemed a little distracted perhaps, but only because she was getting ready to go off on her six-weekly leave. She was getting a lift to the station later on in the morning. And now . . . that was it. She'd never borrow Maia's make-up again. Never argue about which movie to watch. Never forget to clean the bath. Suicide. The thought kept slipping away from her. She couldn't grasp it properly. Why, why, why? Lottie had had everything to live for. She was attractive and clever. She spoke several languages and understood the science much better than Maia did. She was passionate about their work at the Institute . . .

Maia probably didn't know, Terry had explained, but Lottie had a history of depression. She kept it under control with medication, and they had her under constant observation, but lately she'd begun to show signs and they'd arranged for her to go to a specialist clinic for a few days. And it had happened on the way.

So the iron pills, the anaemia – that hadn't been true. They'd been antidepressants. Maia cast her mind back. Perhaps she *had* seemed a little on edge over the last couple of weeks. Not quite the normal lively, cheerful Lottie. But that was a far cry from suicidal depression . . .

'You'll need time to take this in. We all will.' Terry had lowered his eyes. 'You could stay here. The room next door. The bed's made up.'

But she was dressed now. She shook her head. She wanted to be back in her own room, however empty it might feel.

And only when she got back – How long ago? Two hours? Three? – had she noticed that someone had been in and tidied up Lottie's possessions. The usual clutter of clothes and cosmetics, CDs, books and papers was now neatly arranged in piles around the cottage, ready to be packed away and removed.

Birds were starting to sing outside. The room was beginning to fill with thin, watery light. She felt very alone. For the first time in months she thought of her mother and brother, the cramped little house at Number Thirteen, Easthaven, her bedroom and the *Blue Planet* poster that had started it all. There was a huge emptiness inside her. She put her head in her hands and began to cry.

THIRTEEN

Over the next two weeks it seemed to grow a little hotter every day. The days were cloudless and the nights were still. Even on the ocean side of the island, there was hardly a breath of wind to stir the grasses on the dunes. By the end of the second week, the whole place seemed to shimmer and dance with heat.

The cafe was just round the corner from the Ship, on the road leading inland through the new part of the village. Dot Kettle, the owner and Fin's boss, complained endlessly about not being on the harbour front like the pub. But as far as Fin could see, it made no difference where it was, since Kettle's Cafe was the only choice visitors had.

He had taken the job because he wanted the money and knew it would be good to have something to get him out of the house over the summer months. But he had taken it also because after the pub, where Poacher, naturally enough, had first call, the cafe was the second-best place on the island for girls. Not that he and Poacher were in competition. Fin's taste was for dark-haired soulful types, with heads full of questions and eyes brimming with tender secrets. Poacher, on the other hand, liked cheerful blondes with hourglass figures, who wore denim and guzzled Chardonnay. His current girlfriend, Claire, was true to type. A trainee beautician whose family had a holiday cottage at Goat Bay, he'd met her at Easter, and now she was due back in a couple of weeks' time. Poacher was besotted. If she didn't text him at least twice a day, he fell into a black gloom. Fin observed this and congratulated himself on not being caught in the same trap. If he was going to be with someone, he wanted them to be there so they could see each other, talk to each other face-to-face, touch each other, not just speak or text over the airwaves. And that, he had decided, could wait till he was at university. For the moment the cafe suited him well. It permitted him the thrill of the chase and, if he was lucky, the odd conquest. But since most of the customers were visitors, there was no real danger of anything too serious developing.

Now, however, the flattening heat had dulled his appetite for the chase. And in any case, something else was happening. He was becoming incapable of looking at any woman in her early twenties without being reminded of Charlotte Svensson. Not even the stupefying routine of tables, freezer, till, dishwasher, tables could drive her from his mind. And the more he thought about her, the more he wanted to know about her. He had been present at her death, a moment of extraordinary intimacy, the last person she'd seen on earth. And now he felt bound to her. He couldn't let her fade from his memory, a complete stranger, pale and terrified in the mist. He needed to know who she was, where she had come from, what she did. Otherwise their encounter would have had no meaning. And anyway, the more he thought about her, the more clear in his mind he was that she hadn't jumped.

This weekend was the Institute Open Day.

He would see what he could find out there.

Saturday dawned hot and sultry. On the landing, the needle of the barometer had swung left and come to rest on Stormy.

After breakfast Fin had walked down to the harbour where the Institute was running a combined minibus-and-boat service, as necessary, every half-hour, all day. Now, crossing the causeway at low tide in the minibus, they were in a strange limbo where clouds and water and tidal flats were indistinguishable. Fin wanted to call out to the driver to stop so they could get out and stand there in this no-man's-land like creatures of uncertain element.

At the far end of the causeway, the normally closed security gates were open wide. A few yards the other side of the gates was another sign like the one at the road junction, though this one said: *Welcome to Seal Island. Home of the Green Energies Research Institute. Renewable energy for a clean planet.* Ahead and slightly to the right rose Seal Island's solitary high point, the prosaically named Lookout Hill. Beyond, concealed from both Whale Island and the mainland, were the house and grounds of Little Knossos, as the estate was formally called, and the turbine park.

Now the minibus skirted the hill, passed through a large wood and emerged in an open area of grass and parking space. The house, a mansion-like building, was visible beyond, through trees. As they stopped, sounds of amplified music rang towards them. A path led through the trees and out on to a large expanse of neat lawns and borders, dotted with a number of marquees and a stage where a crowd had gathered to watch the band.

Fin made straight for the beer tent. In the heavy air, the smell of alcohol was almost overwhelming. Eleven o'clock in the morning and the place was already packed with sweating bodies and shining faces. He fought his way towards the bar, where Poacher's head bobbed back and forth beyond the crowd. He caught Fin's eye and nodded towards the far end of the bar. Fin found himself a space and waited as Poacher handed over four plastic tumblers of beer, took the money and, ignoring the waiting customers, moved along to where Fin stood. His black *I found my sea legs at the Ship Inn* T-shirt was soaked with sweat.

'You going to be here all day?' Poacher asked.

Fin shrugged. 'D'you get a break?'

'Yes.' Poacher glanced over his shoulder. 'But not till about two. It's pretty manic in here right now.'

'I can see.'

At that moment Shirley Archer emerged from a side tent carrying a couple of teetering stacks of plastic glasses. She saw Poacher and Fin and her eyes narrowed. She set down the glasses and called the length of the bar,

'Oi! No time for that. There's customers waiting to be served.'

Poacher rolled his eyes.

'See you at two, then?'

Fin nodded and went outside.

There was a low rumble of thunder.

He scanned the lawn. There were various village-fete-like activities being manned by Institute staff. Some small tents housed Green Energies displays of one kind or another. And there, opposite the doors of the main house, was the one he was looking for. *Information*, read the sign at its entrance.

His heart began to beat faster as he walked over and went in. Framed by the silhouette of a turbine that covered the whole rear wall of the tent, a middle-aged woman sat at a table covered with leaflets.

'Hello.' She smiled. 'How can I help you?'

'Would it be possible to speak to Mr Hunter?'

'May I ask what about?'

'It's . . . um . . . a personal matter.'

'I'm afraid he's rather busy today.'

'Does he take a break?'

'Perhaps. But I don't know when, I'm sorry.'

'I'm going to be here all day.'

'Is it urgent?'

'Yes, I guess it is.'

'Well . . . I – I suppose I could try him. Who shall I say wants to see him?'

'Finlay Carpenter.'

'Finlay Carpenter. And . . . will he know what it's about, Finlay?'

'I expect so. It's about Charlotte Svensson . . . I'm the one who found her – under the bridge . . .'

'Oh.' Her expression changed. 'Oh, I'm so very sorry. That must have been terrible for you. Yes, you would certainly need to speak with Mr Hunter. Let me call him.'

She picked up a mobile and dialled.

'Eugene? It's Rosie, at the information tent. I have Finlay Carpenter here, wanting to see you . . . Finlay Carpenter . . . yes . . . about Charlotte . . . yes . . . OK . . . no . . . not possible today, I understand . . . OK . . . OK . . . during the week? . . . all right . . . yes, I'll tell him. Thanks.'

She put the phone down.

'He'd be happy to talk to you, Finlay. But he apologises, he can't manage today. Our busiest day of the year, you understand. But he says to please call and make an appointment for next week.' She handed him a card. 'Just dial the main reception. They'll put you through to his office.' She smiled. 'I'm sure he'll tell you what you want to know. Now enjoy the rest of the day here.'

'Thanks. I will.'

He left the tent.

So Hunter wouldn't see him. Not today anyway. Though

surely he could have spared five minutes if he'd really wanted to. Where did that leave Fin? He'd taken a deliberate chance, mentioning Charlotte to the woman, to see how she'd react. And she'd seemed sympathetic enough, not defensive, not as if she was covering up anything. Though she had given him an odd look when he'd told her his name, as if she recognised it . . . But Hunter was the one. Fin needed to be able to see the man's face as he spoke about Charlotte and answered his questions. That was how he'd really know. It would have to be next week.

FOURTEEN

At the far end of the lawn a knot of people was standing by a sign: *See the turbines. Tours every hour on the hour.* He looked at his watch. There was one in ten minutes' time. He might as well go and learn something about what they did here. He walked over and joined the waiting visitors.

In due course the minibus appeared and a dozen passengers got out. Some walked away, heads bent in conversation. Some sauntered off, blank-faced and bored, as if nothing could interest them on a sullen day like this.

'OK, folks,' the driver called. 'Climb aboard.'

Fin was last in. The only seats left were the three that formed the bench at the back. An elderly man had taken the one on the driver's side of the vehicle. Fin took the near-side seat, leaving the centre one empty. The man glanced at him as he sat down. Fin smiled. The man looked away. He was familiar, for some reason. The shop – that was it. He'd seen him in there buying groceries. He was tall, bespectacled, with a full head of grey hair, wearing walking trousers, lightweight walking boots and a faded polo shirt. He would have been pleasant-looking, were it not for the fact that his face was closed and expressionless.

On his lap was a small satchel. Now he took a notebook from it and began to scribble with a pencil. He held the notebook in such a way that Fin could not have read what he was writing if he'd wanted to. The gesture was almost childlike, as if he was writing secrets in a diary.

The minibus moved off, leaving the house and lawns behind.

'Welcome to the Little Knossos estate,' said the driver, speaking into a microphone. 'The house was built in 1908 by the first Lord Highgate, who had bought Seal Island a year previously. Lord Highgate was the proprietor of a London newspaper, the *Chronicle*. The newspaper rose to the peak of its success in 1900, when Lord Highgate agreed to help fund the excavation of the palace of Knossos in Crete by the English archaeologist Arthur Evans. In return the *Chronicle* received exclusive rights to report on the discovery of these fabulous treasures of antiquity. That is how Lord Highgate earned his money and his title, and the estate came by its name.'

The driver spoke in a lifeless monotone, as if he'd re-cited his patter once too often. Beside Fin, the elderly man ignored the driver and continued to scribble in his note-book.

'. . . the walled garden to your left. Today we grow our own organic vegetables. And to your right, the stable block, where we house visitors and conduct training.' The driver pointed to a foursquare stone building with a bell tower and an arch through which Fin could see a large courtyard. 'And there –' he indicated a steel-and-darkened-glass building that rose in stark contrast beyond it – 'that's the no-go area, the research laboratories. We call it the Pentagon, though it's only got four sides.'

The elderly man snorted in what sounded to Fin like irritation.

But the driver had more. 'There, just behind Hangman's Rock –' he pointed to a low hill visible above treetops to the left – 'is the entrance to the old labyrinth. There used to be tin mines here on Seal Island, though they were worked

82

out and abandoned by the late-nineteenth century. When Lord Highgate bought the island, he opened the main mine up to recreate the labyrinth of King Minos of Crete. He was obsessed with Crete – and with good reason, you might say, since he made his fortune from it. Anyway, he recreated the labyrinth in the tunnels and shafts of the old mine – to entertain his guests. By all accounts he made it pretty frightening. But whether they had a Minotaur in it, no one knows . . .'

The elderly man put down his notebook and looked at Fin.

'Do you know the story of the Minotaur?'

Surprised by the directness of the question, Fin hesitated. Then nodded. As a boy he had often been to Seal Island. Before they'd sold up, the liberal-minded Highgate family had encouraged Whale Islanders to use the place when they were not there, to enjoy the estate and its well-maintained grounds. The first time Danny had taken Fin to see the labyrinth, he'd explained how it was based on a terrifying underground maze that had existed in olden times, at the centre of which had lived a monster, half-man, half-bull. As they'd peered into the mouth of the dark tunnel that ran down into the earth, and from which had seemed to come a faint rumbling and whispering, Fin had clasped his father's hand in terror and asked if they could go somewhere else. And his father had gathered him up in a reassuring hug and said, 'It's just a story, son, just a story.' Those had been the good days, before the accident.

'You know of Theseus and his quest to slay the monster? To overcome the terrors of the labyrinth and become a man?'

This was very odd, thought Fin.

'Yes, I do,' he said aloud.

The man nodded in what might have been approval.

'So few young people know anything of the ancient world, these days,' he said. Then returned to his notebook.

Now the minibus had halted in front of high wire gates that opened in a fence. To the left was the shore, to the right the shoulder of Lookout Hill. The driver leaned out of the window and swiped a card through a reader mounted on a stand at the roadside. The gates swung open.

'Welcome to the Green Energies turbine park,' he said. 'No photographs from here on, please, folks.'

The gates closed behind them as the minibus pulled away, followed the line of the shore for a few hundred yards, then crested a small grassy rise. And there, concealed in the natural bowl formed by the shoulders and concave slope of Lookout Hill, stood a dozen turbines, slender columns reaching into the leaden sky like steeples, blades motionless in the still, unbreathing air.

'The Twelve Apostles, we call them,' said the driver.

The first thing Fin noticed was that they were all of different heights. The blades were of different thicknesses and proportions to their columns, and they all seemed to be pitched differently. Beyond, only partly visible over the shoulder of Lookout Hill, in what must have been a second hollow, stood a thirteenth turbine. Much taller than the others, this had one blade frozen in the twelve o'clock position. It had to be the one whose tip could be seen from Whale Island. So if the others were the twelve apostles, who or what did that make this one? he wondered.

His neighbour had now put down his notebook and was staring intently out of the window.

The road ran straight ahead for about half a mile. Every

84

hundred yards or so, a service track ran off and looped around a turbine. The minibus now moved slowly along the road.

'So . . .' said the driver, 'twelve prototype turbines of different designs. All facing into the south-westerly prevailing wind. All visible only from out at sea. And all with an uninterrupted flow of wind.' He seemed to have come to life now. 'Nearly thirty years of advanced technology and precision engineering – that's what's gone into these marvels. As you probably know, Green Energies is one of the world leaders in renewables, and when work is completed on the GE Super Turbine –' he pointed over the shoulder of the hill towards the thirteenth – 'we're confident that it will revolutionise world energy supply, reducing reliance on fossil fuels to next to nothing.'

'So what's the secret then?' asked a middle-aged woman sitting directly behind the driver.

The driver laughed. 'We're not telling. But currently there's an efficiency ceiling with wind turbines of thirty-five per cent. No one has yet managed to crack it. In other words, there's no wind turbine in the world capable of generating for much more than one-third of the time.'

The road ended in a turning circle.

'Can we get out?' someone asked. 'See the Super Turbine?'

'Afraid not,' replied the driver with a grin. 'More than my life's worth.' He swung the minibus round the circle and began, at little more than walking pace, to head back the way they'd come.

Fin's neighbour seemed to have lost interest and was staring out to sea.

'You were saying . . .' prompted the middle-aged woman. 'Thirty-five per cent capacity.'

'Yes,' the driver replied, 'that's the current limit. Because wind speed isn't constant, and also because above certain wind speeds turbines have to be shut down to avoid damage. An ideal site for most current turbine models is somewhere that has a near constant flow of non-turbulent wind throughout the year and doesn't experience too many sudden bursts or powerful squalls.'

'What about topographic acceleration?' asked a studious-looking young man. Showing off, thought Fin.

'You mean siting turbines in high places where the wind accelerates as it's forced over a hill or ridge? Well, we didn't do that because we weren't allowed to here. But that has its own benefits because it means our test site is as challenging as it possibly could be.'

They had reached the gates again. They swung outwards as they approached. There was another, louder rumble of thunder.

'So,' the driver went on, 'as I was saying, the GE Super Turbine is going to revolutionise world energy supplies – by breaking through the thirty-five per cent capacity ceiling, and then some! We're aiming for nearly eighty per cent. And that'll raise the wind-energy stakes to a whole new level worldwide. In most places where there's any wind at all, it'll reduce the need for fossil fuels to a fraction of the energy requirement.'

'And how's it going to reach that eighty per cent?' asked the woman.

'Revolutionary science,' said the driver with pride. 'I'm not giving away any secrets if I say a combination of gearing, blade construction and pitch, and our own patented yaw-drive system – the mechanism that keeps the rotor facing into the wind as the wind direction changes. So those beauties'll keep turning and keep stable in anything short of a hurricane. Believe me, the GE Super Turbine is going to be the nearest thing to perpetual motion there's ever been.'

Fin's neighbour, who had been slumped in his seat staring out of the window, turned to Fin with a look of fierce indignation.

'That,' he said, 'is a travesty of the truth. Wind power is *not* perpetual motion.'

He looked away again. Snapped shut his notebook and placed it back inside the satchel.

The minibus pulled up outside the main house once more. As the engine died there was a flash of lightning and a deafening crack of thunder, nearly overhead, it seemed. Followed almost immediately by the impact of fat raindrops on the roof of the vehicle.

The first few passengers out made a dash across the lawn to the tents. But by the time Fin reached the door, the rain was coming down in solid sheets. A few yards away, round the side of the main house, was what might once have been a tradesmen's entrance with a small porch. Fin sprinted for it and a moment later was joined by his neighbour from the bus who looked out of breath and dishevelled. He fumbled in his satchel for a small silver box and a bottle of water, took a pill from the box and swallowed it.

For some time the two of them stood in the shelter of the porch, listening to the rain crashing down around them. There were several more flashes of lightning and ground-shaking thunderclaps before at last the thunder moved on, growing fainter, and the rain began to ease a little.

'Zeus hurled thunderbolts from the top of Mount Olympus when he was angry,' said the man. He took another sip of water, then put the satchel and bottle down on the ground at his feet.

Fin nodded. He felt that this strange, disquieting person was trying to connect with him, but didn't seem to know how. And Fin wasn't sure whether he wanted him to. But the rain was still coming down. He would get soaked if he moved.

'If he were here today, of course, we would be living in a perpetual thunderstorm. So much stupidity. So much injustice. The ancients were *truly* civilised. We just think we are. But we're not.'

Fin wasn't sure whether he was expected to reply.

'The ancients are hardly taught any longer,' said the man. 'But they should be.' He peered out. 'There is everything to learn from the past.'

He bent down for his satchel and walked out into the rain.

Fin watched him go.

What could he learn from his own past? he wondered. That there had been a single moment in his life, in the life of the Carpenter family, when everything had changed? A single moment when something maybe as small as a speck of dust or a grain of sand had caused a section of winch cable to snag and, in the years that followed, a lively, happy family to be almost torn apart? And if so, had it happened at random, or was there a reason for it, some greater purpose, which only God, or fate or the universe knew about?

Fin shrugged. These were questions, not answers . . .

The rain had almost stopped.

He began to move away from the porch and his foot caught something which went skittering across the gravel. He looked down. The man's pillbox. He picked it up and put it in his pocket.

FIFTEEN

Fin had looked in all the obvious places. The man was nowhere to be seen. Now he made his way back to the beer tent. The thunderstorm had done little to clear the air, and Poacher was blinking sweat from his eyes as he served pints of lager to the crowd of customers at the bar. He saw Fin and glanced down to check the time on his mobile phone. Then moved along the bar to where Shirley Archer was serving another group of customers. He spoke to her and she nodded. He smiled at Fin and gave the thumbs-up.

'I'm starving,' he said once they were outside. He pushed a sticky hank of hair out of his eyes.

Beyond the beer tent was a smaller tent, a green-and-white striped gazebo, proclaiming itself to be the Green Energies salad bar – *All Our Own, Organically Grown!* Poacher glanced at it, grimaced and strode out for the car park, from which wafted the smell of hamburgers.

They ordered at the caravan, then found a bench and sat.

'So, how you doing?' Poacher asked, taking a bite of burger.

'I'm OK,' Fin replied.

'Any more about the girl?'

'Trying to forget about it.'

Poacher nodded approvingly.

'And the bastard at the harbour?'

Fin shrugged. 'Him too. Trying to forget about that too.'

'Wish I'd been there to help you sort him out.' Poacher chewed in silence, then looked up. 'Hey! Y'know what? Claire's not coming here after all. Some family issue. I'm going to hers instead. The Camp Commandant has given me time off.'

'That's good,' said Fin.

'You bet it's good,' said Poacher. 'She's just moved into a flat with her friend. It's close to the curry quarter, where all the Indian shops and restaurants are. Cool part of town.'

'When you going?'

'Tomorrow night. For a week. Can't wait.'

'How'd you persuade her – your mum?'

Poacher grinned. 'Told her Claire's got me a week's work experience as a porter in Chesterfields, one of the posh downtown hotels.'

Mrs Archer had a distinct vision of her son's future. She saw him in a sharp dark suit at the reception desk of a five-star hotel, smiling and saying, 'Yes, madam. No, sir. May I arrange for your luggage to be taken to your room?' And Mrs Archer believed that for the next three years her son would be studying hospitality at Northwestern College. Poacher had other plans. His taste for greasy hamburgers notwithstanding, he saw himself among the flames and pots and pans during the week, then out on the ocean at weekends. The plot, he'd confessed to Fin, was to enrol for hospitality studies, then switch to the chef course without telling his mother. Fin suspected this was a recipe for disaster and had told him so. There was, after all, a reason for her nickname, he had pointed out. But Poacher was adamant that he could get away with it.

'And has she?' Fin asked. 'Has Claire fixed you up?'

Poacher grinned again. 'Said she could get me a day in the kitchens at her friendly local Balti house.'

Fin smiled. 'Well, I'm not saying anything.'

The rain had stopped now and the band were beginning their afternoon set. Fin and Poacher wandered back towards the stage.

They stood listening for a while. Then Poacher shook his head.

'This music's shite.'

'What time've you got to be back?'

'Three.' He looked at his mobile. 'Forty minutes.'

'Let's go and check out the labyrinth. I haven't been there since I was a kid. It's not far.'

They walked through the grounds towards the sea, forking left where the way to the right led to the turbine park. Now the road became a track, following the shore. The sky was darkening again, the air growing heavier. Even the waves seemed dead, rolling listlessly on to the beach.

'Poach –' said Fin, 'do you think we're different – you and me?'

Poacher looked confused. 'How d'you mean?'

'I mean because of our colour. You white. Me black. Does it – matter to you?'

Poacher stopped and looked at him. 'You've got a better tan than I'll ever have. That's for sure. But I wouldn't care if you were purple. You're my best mate, Fin. That's what I care about.'

'Honest?'

'Honest. Look – what's up? You been stressing about that creep? At the harbour.'

'No. Well, yes, I guess . . . Him. And the bombing. And a conversation I had with my mum. I mean – maybe I've just been very . . . blinkered all my life . . .'

Poacher looked thoughtful. 'Well, yeah, maybe you have, living here . . . Just because I don't think you're different, doesn't mean that other people won't. Whoever bombed that market, for instance . . .' He nodded. 'Yeah, you'd be different to them, all right.'

Without warning, the rain came again. Fierce and stinging.

Fin and Poacher sprinted for the pines that stood back from the shore. But there was little shelter there so they ran on till the wood grew dense enough to keep the worst of the downpour at bay.

They stopped, breathless and soaked, beneath a spreading tree which was close to the edge of a large clearing in which stood a cottage. Although it was only three o'clock in the afternoon, the lights were on.

'Must be staff accommodation,' said Fin. 'I think there are cottages all over the estate.'

The rain continued to come down.

After a little while Poacher began to fidget and glance at his mobile.

'I'm going to have to make a run for it soon,' he said. 'Or I'll be mince.'

A few minutes later the front door of the cottage opened and someone stood in the doorway, looking out at the rain. After a moment he turned and stepped back inside. But not before Fin had seen his face. It was his attacker, Sean.

He grabbed for Poacher's arm. 'That's him. The guy . . .'

But Poacher wasn't listening.

'Gotta go. Catch you later.'

He turned and sprinted off through the trees.

Fin stood where he was, heart pounding. So he worked here at the Institute. Sean. A racist thug. As well as Charlotte Svensson. What kind of a place *was* this?

Now Sean was there at the front door again, pulling up the hood of a jacket against the rain. Fin shrank behind the tree and peered round. There was someone else too. Sean stepped out into the rain and ran for the trees on the far side of the clearing. His companion, a girl, bent to lock the cottage door. Even before she straightened up so that he could see her face, Fin knew from her posture, her movement, who it was.

She followed Sean, racing across the clearing to shelter.

Leaving Fin clutching at the tree for support, his heart pounding like a trip hammer.

It was Maia.

SIXTEEN

Albert Smith locked the Scout hut and began walking the mile back to Easthaven under storm clouds shot with crimson by the setting sun. This evening he felt younger than his years. The development people had spent all afternoon with him, looking through the collection of whaling memorabilia and listening to him talking about the island's whaling history. He was confident that he'd managed to convince them it would be worth having a small museum as part of the new whale-watching centre. It had been a good afternoon. And now Sally Lightfoot was going to cook supper for him.

He looked down the hill at the harbour and houses, already half in shadow, and on towards the point, to where her small white cottage stood, still in sunlight, a little apart from the others. Sally hadn't been herself since the bombing. It had shaken her much more than she was letting on. She was strong, Sally, but she had an unusual sensitivity too. Albert considered himself rational, a man who liked to find explanations for things. But Sally's premonition – there was no other word for it – last summer, about the yacht running aground, had baffled him. Particularly since he'd been the one to whom she'd recounted the strange waking dream a full three days before it had played itself out in real life in the still waters of Goat Bay. It had left him intrigued, but also a little shaken. And he'd found himself looking at her in a new light.

The road dipped down the hill, the first of the new houses only a short distance ahead. A van was pulled up on the pavement and someone was ferrying loads of possessions out of the house. It had belonged to the old widow who'd died a couple of months ago. Aggie Wright. He hadn't known her well. A quiet soul, last of one of the old island families. And that was always a sad thing, one more link with the past broken.

It took him a moment to recognise the tall fair-haired man who was now carrying out two heavy boxes. It was Gus Steerman, former owner of the *North Star*. Danny Carpenter's old skipper. Of course. Gus was Aggie's nephew, so probably her closest living relative. That's what he'd been doing back here over the last few weeks. Selling the house. Sorting out Aggie's stuff.

He looked up as Albert approached. Put the boxes in the van and stepped forward with a ready smile.

Albert had always liked Gus, despite the difficulties with the Carpenters. The man struck him as warm and capable. The sort of person you could trust to make the right decisions about things, if a little intimidating sometimes. He was a big man, six foot four, with a reputation for toughness and straight talking. All of which, Albert had always thought, made Danny Carpenter's tale about Gus leaving him in the lurch rather implausible.

'How are you, Albert?' His handshake was firm. 'Been up at the museum today?'

'Yes, I have. Good to see you.' Albert nodded at the house. 'Sorry about Aggie.'

Gus shrugged. 'Eighty-seven. She did well enough.'

'And how long since you left now?'

'Nine years. Nearly ten.'

'You're looking well.'

Gus smiled. 'Can't complain. Business does well. Got a timeshare in Florida. We spend part of the winter there.'

'Better than the fishing then . . .'

'You could say so.' He paused, looking almost wistfully down the hill to the harbour. 'Though you never completely get it out of your bloodstream. I didn't want to quit, you know. But, well . . . the quotas, not to mention the Spaniards and Russians, freebooting bastards. It was all going down the pan. And there were, well . . . other things.'

Albert nodded. 'And . . .' he racked his memory, '. . . Linda?'

Gus shook his head. 'We split up. Pretty soon after leaving the island. Things weren't going too well by then.'

'Sorry to hear that,' said Albert.

'Just the way it goes. Anyway, I've remarried. Lovely lass from the south. Jackie.' He looked at the house. 'Well, better get on. Still got a load of stuff to shift before it gets dark.'

'Yes, I'd better get on too,' said Albert. 'Good to see you again, Gus. And I'm glad things are going well for you.'

'You too, Albert. Take care of yourself.' He went back up the path to the front door.

Albert walked slowly down the hill. He was glad of the encounter. It confirmed his belief that Gus was a good man. He seemed to have mellowed in the years since he'd left. Though Albert was surprised to hear about Linda. The island was not an easy place to keep secrets. Yet he didn't remember ever hearing any gossip about the Steermans. They must have kept it well under wraps.

He quickened his step at the thought of Sally's airy front room with its big picture window looking out on the bay. The bottle of wine in the fridge. The fish browning in the pan.

SEVENTEEN

Fin chose the cliff path to Coldheart Farm. He needed to be by the sea. To smell the salt on the air and feel his stomach churn as the ground plummeted away to the saw-tooth rocks and sucking pools below. Anything to remind him he was alive, to keep him from feeling that he was losing all contact with reality.

After Maia had sprinted away across the clearing he had stood there for a long time, unable to move. Unable to absorb what he had seen. His sister, evidently at home at the Institute. Why was she there? Why hadn't she been in touch? Why was Sean there? What did she, a black girl, have to do with him, a racist thug? It wasn't just that the questions were baffling, they were hurtful, a slap in the face. And then there was Charlotte Svensson. Maia might have known her. What did that mean for Maia's safety if he was really right about Charlotte's death?

Eventually anger had taken over and he had walked furiously away from the cottage. If she was here, so close by, without their knowledge, after all the heartache of the last year, then to hell with her. He certainly wasn't going to be the one to make contact.

He'd got straight on the next minibus back to East-haven.

Back at home he had been relieved to find he had the place to himself. Danny was at the mission, watching sport on the widescreen TV as he did every Saturday afternoon. Kath had gone to Cliffton for the afternoon with a friend and was then going to the quiz night at the Ship. Fin wandered around the house, unable to settle, his mind spinning. He felt hurt, angry, worried, confused. He tried Poacher but his phone was off. He was probably clearing up at the beer tent. In the end he had made himself something to eat, turned on the television and tried watching a movie. *The Godfather*. He'd never seen it before, but he was too distracted to concentrate. He watched for an hour, then went to bed and suffered disquieting dreams about severed horses' heads and underground tunnels.

This morning his thoughts had begun to spin before he was even fully awake. He had lain in bed wondering what to do. Simply go and see her after all? Tell his mother? There wouldn't be any point involving his father. He'd just go berserk. But then what if Maia *wouldn't* see them? That would finish Kath, he knew. No, for his mother's sake he would have to try to find out more about Maia's circumstances before he said anything. And if there was anything funny going on at the Institute, that might not be so straightforward. It was going to be hard though – keeping it all from his mother.

Only as he was getting dressed had he felt in his trouser pocket and found the silver pillbox.

He had been sitting at the kitchen table with a cup of tea, turning the little box in his fingers, when Kath came in, still in her dressing gown.

'You look tired, love.' She bent and kissed him. 'You OK?'

'I'm fine.'

She glanced down. 'What's that? A pillbox?'

'Yes. Someone dropped it. Yesterday. At the Institute

opening. An old guy. I've seen him in the shop, I think. Quite tall, a bit strange, eccentric.'

'Odd way of talking?'

Fin nodded. 'Like, not conversation. He just tells you things.'

'Ah, that sounds like Mr Turner. Up at Coldheart Farm.'

'OK,' said Fin. Everyone knew there was a recluse at the farm on the headland. He'd been there for about five years, though no one knew much about him.

'Only see him once a fortnight,' Kath went on. 'When he comes into the shop to buy his provisions.'

Fin opened the pillbox. There were half a dozen pills, of several different shapes and colours. Inside the lid were the silver hallmarks and the letters N and T, which had been scored by hand. He showed it to Kath.

'Mr Turner. Wait a minute – Neil . . . no, Nigel . . . no, Norman. That's it.' She reached out to flick the kettle on. 'I'll give it to him next time he comes in.'

'Maybe I'll take it up to him myself. Could do with the walk. And he probably needs the pills.'

'Well, if you're certain. But . . .' she looked at her son, 'he is a bit of a recluse. Bit weird, some people say . . .'

'You mean be careful? *Mum!* I'm nearly nineteen, you know.'

'Course you are, love.' She smiled. 'I'm sure he'll be grateful.'

She made herself a cup of coffee and took it back upstairs.

Fin had remained at the kitchen table, turning the pillbox in his fingers. The silver felt warm to his touch.

Now the village was a mile behind and the path had

levelled out, following the edge of a huge field of ripening wheat that covered the headland.

Fin had never been to Coldheart Farm, though the chimneys were just visible from the road to Goat Bay. Surrounded by the emptiness of the crop fields and the ocean beyond, it had always seemed to Fin that it must be a bleak and isolated place. An image the name did nothing to dismiss.

Two brightly coloured slivers were slicing through the calm waters a couple of hundred yards offshore. Poacher and the Duck. Heading up the coast today. Probably aiming for one of the coves on the way to the lighthouse at the northern tip of the island. After he'd seen Mr Turner, he might go on and try to meet up with them. He'd thought that a walk would help clear his head. But all it had done so far was make him realise how complicated the situation was. He longed to see his sister, but he felt angry with her and at the same time anxious not to do anything that might blow it with her. He needed to talk this all through with someone.

Poacher. Solid and practical where he, Fin, was more dreamy. Poacher would help him keep his feet on the ground. And the Duck, perhaps. He would give good advice. Fin had thought about him from time to time since their day at the caves. Scruffy-looking. A biker, you might think at first glance. Someone who'd left school at fourteen and read survival magazines. And yet there was something deep and calm and clear in his eyes. And that whistle playing. The thought of it put the hairs up on the back of Fin's neck. The story did too. The monstrous black wave rearing up out of the ocean to reclaim what rightfully belonged to it.

He was almost at the farm now. There was a track leading through the field a little way ahead. Fin turned up it and walked between walls of waist-high wheat, the dusty, grainy smell filling the sultry air. Then the track passed straight into the farmyard, where a small, elderly car was parked in an outhouse. Fin walked up to the back door and knocked.

There was no reply, so he knocked again.

Eventually footsteps approached and the door opened.

Norman Turner looked out at Fin and said nothing.

Fin was prepared. He held out the pillbox and said, 'You dropped this yesterday. At the Institute. I thought you might need it.'

The man nodded and held out his hand. 'My mother gave me this,' he said.

They stood there. Was this going to be it? Was it up to Fin to make the next move? To turn and walk away?

'Well . . . I'm glad you've got it back,' he said eventually.

Norman Turner nodded. 'Did you walk from East-haven?'

'Yes.'

'Come in. You'd like a drink.'

'Er . . . I don't want to trouble you.'

His eyes came to life. 'I'm not mad, you know.'

Fin didn't know what to say.

The older man turned and went inside, leaving Fin to follow him.

EIGHTEEN

Fin stood by the table in the centre of the large farm kitchen, while Norman Turner let the water run cold at the sink and filled two glasses.

The kitchen was a surprise. Fin would have imagined bachelor chaos, unwashed dishes, food not put away, half-read newspapers. But it was tidy to the point almost of sterility, like an operating theatre. Which was not to say modern. The fittings looked ancient and in need of a coat of paint. Fin could see not a single appliance, not even a toaster or electric kettle.

Norman Turner handed him a glass of water and stood watching in silence, his own glass untouched, as Fin drank.

Fin felt the awkwardness burning across his chest. He longed to be away from here. He looked round the room for something, anything that might provide a talking point. His eye fell on a picture hanging on the far wall. The only picture, the only decoration of any kind, in the whole room.

It was a lifesized portrait, head and shoulders, of an old man with a towering forehead, bald skull, flowing white locks and beard, and a look in the stern, creased eyes that seemed to combine enquiry and wisdom. The face was familiar, thought Fin. But before he could think who it might be, his attention was distracted by the small table directly below the portrait, and the strange object that stood on it.

It was a wooden wheel, about the size of a dinner plate, supported on a triangular stand that allowed it to turn. Attached to the rim of the wheel was a succession of what looked like small hammers. Each hammer was hinged, so that those around the top half of the wheel lay flat against the rim, while those on the bottom half hung down.

'My shrine to perpetual motion,' said Norman Turner, drinking from his glass. 'Leonardo da Vinci. The greatest mind the world has ever known. And the overbalanced wheel.'

Memories of science lessons surfaced. 'I didn't think . . .' Fin began. Then stopped, recalling the moment in the minibus the previous day when the driver had mentioned perpetual motion. The older man had reacted almost as if it had been a personal insult.

But Turner finished his sentence for him. 'That perpetual motion was possible?'

Without a further word he set down his glass, walked to the door, opened it and left the room. Fin stood in the kitchen. Had he been too late, the offence already given? Should he take this opportunity to leave? His host unsettled him, he felt uncomfortable here. But at the same time Fin found him intriguing. Maybe it was knowledge – the sense that this strange man knew things; perhaps it was simply whatever mistrust of the Institute they seemed to share, each for his own reasons . . .

Fin followed him out of the kitchen and down a short passage which led into a large panelled hallway with a stone fireplace and a heavy mahogany staircase.

'Here,' came a voice from the room that opened off the hallway to the right.

Fin entered a space that was all he had imagined the kitchen might be, and more. This was the bachelor's midden. Though in truth it was more of a professor's laboratory or an alchemist's den. A large blackboard stood in the fireplace, covered with mathematical formulae and equations. Books and papers were strewn across the surface of a baby grand piano that had been pushed into one corner. Here was the half-eaten meal, a puddle of congealed gravy, the plate balanced on a bookshelf. A mug of undrunk, mould-encrusted coffee on the mantelpiece. The room itself had the same dark panelling as the hallway, but light flooded in from a south-facing bay window.

Dominating the room were two large wooden workbenches which stood side-by-side against the wall facing the fireplace. On one was a much larger version of the overbalanced wheel from the kitchen. This wheel was at least a metre in diameter, and the hammers were perhaps a third of that length. Standing in its frame it reached more than halfway to the ceiling. On the other bench stood a triangular contraption a little over a metre high. The right angle gave it a flat base, one vertical side and one slope of forty-five degrees. Inside the triangular frame, curving down from the apex to the foot of the slope, was a kind of chute ending in a little ramp which extended beyond the foot of the triangle. On the ramp sat a metal ball, slightly smaller than a golf ball. At the apex of the triangle stood a square metal box that was plugged into an electrical socket. Just below it, but at the very top of the slope, there was a hole through which, Fin imagined, the ball must drop on to the chute and return to the ramp. The box, he guessed, must be some kind of powerful electromagnet. In the space remaining between the workbenches and the door, a rack of joiner's tools had been fixed to the panelling. Saws and chisels, hammers, augers, planes, screwdrivers of all shapes and sizes.

A change had come over Norman Turner. Now there was light in his eye, a different timbre to his voice, as he gestured around the room, then pointed to the workbenches. 'The overbalanced wheel. And the Taisnerius device. Two medieval conundrums.' He nodded to himself. 'But not for very much longer. They are opening their secrets to me.'

Fin couldn't think of anything to say. Not that his host would wish to hear, anyway. More memories were returning. Fragments of Newton's Laws of Thermodynamics which, among other things, he was almost sure, demonstrated the impossibility of perpetual motion. He stepped closer to the workbenches and looked at the contraptions. The ideas seemed fairly obvious. Once the overbalanced wheel was set in motion, the force of each successive hammer flying forward as it reached the apex of the circle would pull the wheel around until the next hammer reached the apex, flew forward, pulling the wheel round some more, and so on ad infinitum. With the other device, he imagined that the magnet, if that was what it was, must drag the ball up the triangle's slope for it then to drop through the hole just before it reached the top and roll back down the curving chute to the foot of the slope, ready to be dragged up again in an apparently endless cycle of ascent and descent. Those were the theories. Although in practice – unless what Fin had been taught at school was plain wrong – they would never work. The wheel would succumb to friction sooner or later. Probably sooner. And the triangular device was relying on a rechargeable magnet to pull the ball up the slope.

'So this,' Fin said, choosing his words with care, 'is your alternative to what they're doing at the Institute, right? Make these work. Then harness them. And you solve all the world's energy problems. An infinite supply of free energy.'

Now, for the first time, Norman Turner smiled. It was only a half-smile, as if it had escaped him before he could bring it under control. But it transformed his face.

'No one has been here before,' he said. He looked Fin in the eye. 'I trust you. What is your name?'

'Fin. Finlay. Carpenter.'

'Norman Turner.' He held out his hand. A formal gesture.

Fin shook it. 'I know.'

'How?' He looked surprised, even faintly alarmed.

'My mother. She works at the shop. I think you buy your groceries there.'

'Ah.'

Fin's eye was drawn back to the contraptions. 'Riddles, you said these were. So at the moment these are – like, unfinished experiments, right? I mean, Leonardo didn't actually build a perpetual-motion machine. Not one that worked. Did he?'

Norman Turner shook his head.

'So, I mean – how close are you to . . . ?' He pointed at the wheel.

'A matter of weeks.' The older man indicated the blackboard. 'Are you a scientist?'

Fin shook his head. 'I did science at school. And I like making things. Or I used to. Now I'm more interested in making . . . virtual things, I suppose. Animation. That's what I'm going to study at university.'

Turner ignored Fin's reply. He continued to point at the blackboard.

'This is the formula for a zero-friction coefficient. Or will be, when it is complete. The Institute talk about their own revolutionary technology.' He paused. 'All I can say is that they have a surprise in store. The Turner device – that is what it will be called – will entirely eliminate inertia and drag. It will do what its name suggests. It will turn. Forever. And it will do so without the assistance of the wind.'

There was pride and defiance in his voice.

'So isn't all this –' Fin gestured at the room – 'isn't it secret?'

Norman Turner looked at him. 'I said I trust you.'

'Thank you,' said Fin. 'But wouldn't people want to get their hands on your – your knowledge? I mean, people would kill for this, wouldn't they?'

'You mean this is not like the Institute?' he replied. 'No electric gates, no security doors. You are right. But the land is open on all four sides of the house. I can see anyone who approaches. I have sensors on the cattle grid at the main road. On the farm buildings.'

'So you knew I was coming? Even up the track from the cliffs?'

His host nodded.

Now it was definitely time to leave, thought Fin, his palms suddenly clammy. But still there was one more question he wanted to ask.

'D'you know much about the Institute? I mean, what kind of people work there? You seemed to . . .'

Norman Turner stared out of the window at the large wheat field in front of the house.

'When I came here, five years ago, I had not the slightest idea of its existence. Ironically.' He gave a short, dry laugh. Like the smile, it seemed to escape from him. 'But now I know about it, yes. A great deal about it. The Internet is both a curse and a blessing. In this case, a blessing. The Institute is part of the Groeneberg Group, founded in Great Falls, Montana, in the early 1980s, by the visionary – their description – technologist Walter Groeneberg.

He was the only child of a farming family from Skyline, Montana. Both parents were Baptist preachers. Groeneberg was a gifted child who was accepted to study at the Massachusetts Institute of Technology at an unusually young age. He graduated with distinction, but not without controversy, after having founded a right-wing group called the Homelands Society—'

An alarm began to trill in some other part of the house.

'Ah. My constitutional.' He walked out of the room and turned it off. When he didn't return, Fin followed and found him in the kitchen. He was putting on a pair of walking shoes.

'My heart, you see,' he said. 'At midday I walk for half an hour. Every day. Without fail.'

His tone left Fin in no doubt that the audience was at an end.

'The Institute –' Fin said, hoping Norman Turner might at least finish his sentence.

Turner looked at him. 'You are a resourceful young man, I can tell. I used to be a teacher, you know. And there is nothing I can find on the Internet that you cannot.'

He turned towards the back door, then paused as if he'd forgotten something.

'Thank you for your visit, Finlay. May I call you that? It was . . . kind –' he seemed to struggle with the word – 'of you to return my pillbox. Our conversation has been pleasant. I have very few. If you cared to visit again, I would be glad to see you.'

As Fin followed him he noticed a small framed photograph sitting on the windowsill. It was of a young girl, maybe thirteen years old, with long dark hair and brown eyes, wearing a white school shirt and striped tie.

'Is that your daughter?' Fin asked.

Norman Turner stopped.

'My niece,' he said.

He opened the back door.

In the sunlight it seemed to Fin that Turner's eyes watered.

NINETEEN

Where the track met the cliffs Fin paused and gazed up the coast. No specks moved on the still, heat-dazed waters. He had been with Norman Turner much longer than he'd anticipated. Poacher and the Duck would be at Lighthouse Point by now. He turned right and began to walk back towards Easthaven.

The air was heavy and his head swam with the strangeness of the encounter. The frustration too of being on the brink, it felt, of some kind of revelation about the Institute, or at least its founder.

What sort of life did Norman Turner lead there, alone in Coldheart Farm, with his contraptions and his pristine kitchen? His conviction that he could compete with Green Energies? Could he really be on to something? The figures on the blackboard had been meaningless to Fin. All he had to rely on was his own, admittedly limited, scientific knowledge. Now a picture was materialising. Overweight, perspiring Mr Goldsmith, an eccentric if ever there was one, pirouetting in front of the blackboard in imitation of an asteroid spinning on its endless journey, as he explained that, in theory, a body travelling through space would move forward at the same velocity forever. Newton's First Law of Motion. But the reality, Mr Goldsmith went on, is that even space is full of outside agents, of which the asteroid itself was one, down to the most microscopic particles of dust, all of which eventually act upon the moving body to slow it down. In other words, space is not a complete void, much less our own atmosphere-heavy, air-polluted earth. So unless it's in a sealed vacuum, nothing will move forward unaided forever. And Norman Turner hadn't even begun to demonstrate how he would harness his contraptions to produce energy, which was where Newton's Second Law of Thermodynamics came into play. No system operating in a cycle can be absolutely efficient. In other words, as Mr Goldsmith had so vividly explained, not only can you not make a machine that will run forever, you can't make one that will produce energy without consuming itself as it runs.

So according to known science, Norman Turner's machines simply wouldn't work. For five hundred years the impossible dream of perpetual motion had drawn the gifted, the power-hungry, the obsessed, the plain deluded, like moths to a flame. Norman Turner was probably just one more of them. And eventually he too would have to submit to Isaac Newton's laws, and just run out of steam, or consume himself. These thoughts startled Fin. He wasn't used to looking at the world like this, making these strange connections between ideas. It was as if the body of Charlotte Svensson had crashed through his youthful fog and triggered something that made him alert to a whole new set of realities, a more intense version of the world he'd known until now. A version in which it was obvious that Norman Turner's delusion, his obsession with his unworkable contraptions, wasn't the whole story. There was something there that reminded Fin of his father. Veiled and complex as such things could be, he guessed that it was hurt and anger. Not of the same quality as Danny's. Of course not. But hurt and anger nevertheless.

He gazed north again, imagining Poacher and the Duck

with their kayaks drawn up in a shingly cove, relaxed and cheerful from the exertion of the journey. A scene of carefree companionship. He envied it. Envied the Duck his quiet, wry self-assurance, envied Poacher his simple, sunny outlook on life. Found himself longing yet again for the day, in slightly over two months' time, when he would take the bus over the bridge to Cliffton and the next stage of his life would begin.

A few paces away, a gull had found some current in the lifeless air, an updraught from the cliff. It planed alongside him, keeping pace with him as he walked. He turned to look at it and as he did so it swivelled its head to stare back at him with one unblinking orange-rimmed eye. For a moment it held his gaze. Then, in a single liquid movement, it swooped away out of sight below the rim of the cliff.

TWENTY

Terence Whitelands ran his finger down the long bow of Maia's naked back. She gave a soft sigh and settled into the bed. Her skin was warm and smooth and the colour – somewhere between milky coffee and caramel – aroused him more than anything else he knew. The arousal sharpened by that familiar gnaw of guilt that always accompanied it. This was wrong. A betrayal. Almost an act of treason, whispered the voices of his ancestors. But they were hypocrites, he knew. And this was also necessary. His finger lingered in the hollow at the base of her spine. Quite apart from the pleasure she gave him, she was smart and hard-working and he had every confidence that she would serve her purpose well. Beyond that, he did not care to think at this particular moment. He had made a truly discerning choice when it came to Maia. Even his initial misgivings about her return to the place of her upbringing had proved groundless. The induction programme had done its work and she'd shown not the slightest interest in making contact with her family. And she seemed to be recovering well from the shock of her room-mate's unfortunate death. Another necessity. Although, of course, she would never know it.

Yes, Maia Carpenter was one of his successes. Although her brother . . . now there was an unexpected fly in the ointment. Terence had quizzed Eugene thoroughly over events at the bridge. He had had to agree that it was a one-in-a-billion chance that the Svensson girl should have landed at the feet of a relative of one of the staff, let alone her room-mate's brother. And neither of them could have anticipated the further irony that the cretinous Sean should have picked on the same young man for his drunken antics at Easthaven. And now the youth, Finlay he was called, had turned up at the Open Day, asking questions about Charlotte. Eugene was going to have to keep a close eye on him. Take him in hand if necessary.

Sean. Terence sighed. An ex-para whose short, inglorious military career had ended in dismissal for stealing ammunition, Sean Rafferty was nothing more than a bully-boy in perpetual need of a gang. A bully-boy, what was more, who couldn't hold his drink. But he was an exceptional leader of the labyrinth programme. Terence had seen recruits who would not have looked out of place in a bare-knuckle ring emerge from the labyrinth on their knees, ashen-faced, whimpering. Well, Green Energies needed tough security operatives, and the Project needed the toughest, most committed of them all. And Sean was the man to deliver them. Currently the Seal Island Institute was supplying more recruits to the Project than any other Green Energies training centre in the world. Which would do Terence's career no harm at all.

So Sean was still here, gated for the next month, and chastened by the dressing-down Terence had given him. Which was just as well, since there was another batch of recruits arriving in a couple of days' time. And there were the finishing touches to put to Operation Korma . . .

Maia was drifting into sleep. He'd let her stay, for once, he thought. She had earned it. He smiled to himself, got out of bed, pulled on his bathrobe and went over to the window. Summer dawn was breaking. Mist carpeted the

114

lawns. The air was still, and all around Little Knossos order prevailed. If only his father could see him now, how proud this would make him. Dr Terence Whitelands PhD, Director of the Green Energies Seal Island Research Institute and Security Consultancy, Regional Leader of the Project. The small boy in Bloemfontein, South Africa, who had gazed so admiringly at his father's police inspector's uniform forty years ago could no more have flown to the moon than imagined a future such as this. And how strange, he thought, at the age of forty-five, that he should still feel the absence of his father's approval like an ache.

But it was not Bloemfontein and the vast skies of Africa that were summoned now by thoughts of his father. Rather, the grim, grey clouds of England, and the two of them on their knees together on the cold floorboards of the rented flat, muttering the guttural Afrikaans prayers in that language that had always seemed to Terence to fill his mouth with stones and thorns and the dung of oxen. At home in the morning, before Pappie went off to work in the shabby grey security guard's shirt and trousers, for which he had swapped the smart blue uniform of the South African Police. In the evening when he came home again. Terence taking the full force of his father's hand or, worse still, his leather belt, when he faltered or stammered or forgot the words, or sometimes simply fell asleep there where they knelt. And the terror of the weekend walks, when Pappie tested him on his Bible knowledge, and would wait until they got home to administer more punishment if he had not learned well enough. A stern father and an unforgiving God his childhood companions . . . Terence could smile now. He regretted none of it, even though he had long ago relinquished the God. It was what had made him into the man he was now, a man tempered by hardship, who knew himself well. A man capable of making difficult decisions and remaining true to his purpose in life.

He turned back from the window and looked at Maia. She had pulled up the sheet and now only her head was visible with its nimbus of dark curls against the surrounding whiteness. Though he could plainly see the generous contours of her body through the thin covering. She was deep in sleep now, peaceful and beautiful.

Thinking of difficult decisions . . . this one would be hard if things didn't turn out as he wanted them to. Oh yes. But still he would do what had to be done.

He slipped off the bathrobe and pulled on running shorts and a singlet. He would run the coastline this morning. Five and a half miles around Seal Island. He needed to sharpen his focus. He bent down to pick up his trainers. Paused. Stood up again. He would run barefoot today.

TWENTY-ONE

Despite his earlier vow, Fin went upstairs and without hesitation turned left into Maia's room. Even the act of opening the door was enough to bring life to the otherwise still, silent room. Dust motes danced and swam in the afternoon sunlight streaming through the window and on to her bed. The thin curtain swayed and a startled spider scuttled along the windowsill.

He went straight to the window and opened it as wide as he could. He looked through the CDs, chose one of her favourites and put it on the old player that sat on top of her chest of drawers. Then he took off his shoes, moved the teddy bear off the pillows, and lay down, hands crossed behind his head.

Memories returned. The fair at Cliffton, when he was maybe eight years old. The lights and music and toffee apples. The rough and dangerous-looking men and women who ran the stalls. The stomach-churning rides and then, inevitably, the throwing-up. And Maia with her arm around him on the ferry on the way home. So grown up, so sure, so . . . safe. And the time they cycled over to Salvation Cove and walked round the headland with a tent to camp alone on the sandy beach beyond. In the summer dawn they'd swum naked, the cool water like liquid velvet on their skins. Then a pair of early-morning hikers had appeared and they'd crouched, giggling, behind rocks till the coast was clear again. And always the sense that she knew how things worked. She would make sure they were all right. She would look out for him. Even when she started to get serious about the woes of the world. Ticked him off for eating junk food and putting money in the pockets of the planet-polluters, sweatshop-supporters, child-enslavers. For not looking out for the Fairtrade label. Most of all, ranted at him for leaving his bedroom light on, for not recycling his soft-drink cans, for being plain dumb and unaware as he admired some tourist's sleek, gas-hungry sportscar. Yet always the tenderness, which maybe only Fin and his mother in the whole world knew about. But it was there, however much he annoyed her, however tormented she became by the injustices that she saw around her. There in a particular way their eyes might meet, sending a peal of silent laughter bubbling up through him. Or in her head on his shoulder as they watched television together. Even after the accident, when the rows with Danny had started and she had begun to push Fin away when he tried to console her, even then, he had still known that nothing could ever touch that place where they truly loved one another. And on the day she had finally walked out, her rage so intense that even Danny was silenced by it, he had known that that place was still safe. That the waves crashing in on it from the outside world could never break it.

But that had been eighteen months ago and it was hard to keep believing when all there was was silence. Yet now he knew that she was not only alive, but nearby. Working for an organisation that for three hundred and sixty-four days of the year hid itself away behind tall fences, security gates and half a mile of tidal flats. An organisation whose employees, it seemed, were liable to throw themselves from high bridges and beat up young black men for no apparent reason.

How could he possibly understand this? He sat up and glanced around the room, as if there might be clues waiting for him in her possessions, or in the way the sunlight fell across the foot of the bed, or in the arrangement of the furniture, or even in the music – Bob Marley's 'No Woman, No Cry', its lazily wistful pulse redolent of Jamaican heat.

Unless she was being held there against her will, she must have chosen not to make contact. That was the thought that kept returning, the thought that admitted a cold draught to this warm, sunny, sleepy room filled with the sounds of the Caribbean. Perhaps now she would somehow sense that her place in the house had been brought back to life again. Perhaps she would feel some kind of tugging at her heart-strings. She was only a few miles away, after all.

The walk out to Coldheart Farm and back was beginning to catch up with Fin. His limbs and eyelids were growing heavy . . .

'She's not coming back, you know.'

Danny stood in the doorway, leaning on his stick.

Fin blinked and sat up, struggling for consciousness.

'I said, she's not coming back.' He paused, breathing heavily from the exertion of climbing the stairs. 'And even if she did, I wouldn't have her. So you can turn that bloody music off. Get back to your own room.' He coughed. 'If it was up to me, I'd have had all this stuff out in the street a long time ago. But your mother says keep it. Your mother says she'll be back. Your mother says she'll be wanting in again one day. Your mother's gone soft in the head.'

Fin sat on the bed looking at his father. Now he felt no anger, no need to argue or hit back. He knew that Danny was wrong. She might not be coming back here. Not yet, anyway. But she was back on Seal Island. The knowledge gave him strength.

'What you looking at me like that for?' Danny's eyes narrowed. He shifted his weight on the stick.

Fin got up from the bed and walked to the CD player, switched it off.

'Whatever you say, Dad.' He turned to close the window.

He heard his father shuffle and tap across the landing, the bedroom door being pulled hard shut.

He tidied the bed and stood for a moment in the empty room, glancing around as if in one final sweep for clues.

'What the hell's going on, Maia?' he muttered to himself as he left the room and closed the door.

He went downstairs. The kitchen clock said four thirty. He was going to meet Poacher at six and take the bus over to Cliffton with him. See him off on the train to Claire's, then catch the last bus home again.

An hour and a half to kill. He really ought to start putting some thought into the holiday project – Life Is a Bowl of Cherries. He went into his own room, turned on the laptop, gazed at the screen for a minute, then connected to the Internet and typed in 'Green Energies'.

TWENTY-TWO

Poacher stank of aftershave. His jeans were ironed and he was wearing a crisp new polo shirt, pale blue.

'The Camp Commandant bought it for me. Said I needed to look smart. For Chesterfield's.' He grinned. 'Aka the Punjab Palace.'

He slung his bag in the luggage locker and they boarded the bus, found seats near the back. Poacher could hardly sit still. He drummed his fingers on his knees and beamed.

'Train gets in at ten thirty. She's meeting me at the station. We're going straight out to see some of her friends. Have a few drinks. Then back to her place.' He paused. 'For a night of lu-u-urve.'

The message alarm sounded on his phone. He studied the screen, then tapped in a reply.

'That's her. Just checking I'm on my way.' He turned to Fin, eyes momentarily dreamy. 'Could be the big one, y'know, Fin. I've never felt like this before about anyone.'

'Sure.' Fin was glad for his friend, if slightly envious. What would he give right now for a little excitement, a little romance, instead of all the crap that seemed to greet him at every turn.

The bus moved off. In a couple of minutes they'd be on the bridge. The first time Fin had been across it since the day of the fog.

'And I wasn't joking about the Punjab Palace. She knows the owner's son. He was at college with her. She's got me a

121

couple of shifts in the kitchen there. I'll be checking out all those sauces and spices. It's going to be brilliant, Fin . . .'

They were on the bridge now. Another hundred yards. The sun was going down behind Beacon Hill. Long shadows of the suspension cables slanting across the road. Just about . . . now. He looked at the parapet. Imagined her poised, like a bird ready for flight.

No. It wasn't right.

And then they were past the place, gathering speed as the mainland approached and the road opened out ahead.

'Hey! Where did you go?'

'Sorry.' Fin looked back to Poacher.

'I was just saying about working at the curry house – and I lost you.'

'Yeah . . . see . . . it's the first time I've been over the bridge since – well, you know . . .'

Poacher nodded and gave him a sympathetic look. But Fin knew what he was thinking: You're not still on about that, are you? So how was he going to respond to Fin's next question? Fin didn't want to dampen his friend's excitement about his trip, but he'd decided, while staring in mounting frustration at the computer screen, that he had to talk to Poacher about what had happened at the Institute. If only to find out whether he'd noticed anything that Fin hadn't.

'Yesterday morning. At that cottage. When we were in the trees. Did you see anything?'

Poacher looked at him. 'The rain pissing down.'

'No. I mean, inside. Inside the house.'

'Like what?'

'People. Think . . .'

Poacher frowned. 'A guy came to the door just as I was leaving.'

Fin nodded. 'Anything else?'

Again Poacher frowned. Then shook his head.

'No girl?'

'No. Why?'

'Because there was one with him. And Poach, it was Maia.'

Poacher's eyes widened. 'Maia? You sure?'

'You'd know your own sister, wouldn't you?'

Poacher nodded. 'Yeah, I guess I would.' He let out a long breath. 'Maia! Whoa! But – I mean, what the hell's she doing there?'

Fin shrugged. 'There's something else, too. The guy. The one you saw. He's the racist creep from the harbour.'

'*What?*'

The couple in the row in front turned around.

'Yes. Sean. So something pretty weird is going on, Poach. What with Charlotte Svensson and now Maia *and* Sean. I don't have a good feeling about the Institute. But I don't think I can just march in there and talk to her. Even if they'd let me in – which I doubt. Look, either she's made the choice not to be in touch with me and Mum – don't ask me why – in which case I think she'd just tell me to piss off. Or something else is going on. And I guess that's what I'm really worried about, Poach . . . that maybe something's happened to her.'

'Have you told your mum?'

Fin shook his head. 'I don't want to. Not till I know a bit more. I think it would kill her, knowing Maia's here but not being able to see her. I dunno – it's all getting really complicated . . .'

Poacher squeezed his arm.

'Know what I think? You don't have to do anything right now. You can wait a few more days. I'll be back next weekend. Then we can decide what to do. I'll help you, Fin.

I will, really. Maybe I can get into the Institute and talk to her. The Camp Commandant knows them all pretty well. She'll fix it for me.' He smiled. 'We'll sort this out together, Fin. You and me.'

Fin nodded. A lump rising in his throat.

'Thanks, Poach.'

TWENTY-THREE

Sally stood at her cottage door and watched Albert make his way slowly, a little unsteadily even, along the path back to the harbour. He was a dear man. And a good friend. She always looked forward to their evenings together.

Ten thirty and it still wasn't completely dark. A pale dusk luminescence lingered faintly in the northern sky. She stood for a while listening to the gentle lap of the waves on the rocks at the foot of her little patch of garden. She breathed deeply, taking in lungfuls of sharp sea air.

Then she turned back inside, put on some soft music and began to tidy the kitchen. She was touched by Albert's continuing concern that she was all right after the bombing. That she was coping with the after-effects. He was too tactful to ask outright if she needed counselling, but she knew that was what he was suggesting. And proud though she was, because it was Albert, she didn't mind.

For the last twenty years Sally had believed that anyone who could survive the experience of hearing that rap on the door on a filthy January night, and knowing, even before she'd placed her hand on the door-handle, what she was going to learn from whoever it was who waited grave-faced on the doorstep – anyone who could live through that, and the grim days and weeks that followed, could live through anything.

But now she wasn't so sure. The carnage – there was no other word for it – that she'd seen in that busy street, the spreading slicks of blood, the body parts, detached from their owners as if by an explosion in a doll factory, the screams of the injured, the panic-stricken shouting of friends and relatives, but most of all the sheer indiscriminate savagery of the blast, ripping through market stalls, shopfronts, human flesh and bone, making no distinction between male and female, young and old, black and white – though it was mostly black – she was haunted by it all. She couldn't deny it. During the day she couldn't get it out of her head, while at night she had strange, troubling dreams of which she could remember nothing the next morning, but which left her with a sense of panic and foreboding.

She poured the dregs of the wine into a glass and took it through to the sitting room, with its picture window looking out on Easthaven bay. A couple of lights twinkled in the harbour. Then the faintly shimmering expanse of the narrows. And beyond, a dark shadow on the horizon, the mainland.

What kind of people would do that? she wondered. Set off a bomb in a crowded market full of innocent people going about their normal business. Knowing that it would kill many and horribly maim many more. What kind of hatred must the perpetrators have felt towards those people they'd never met? And since, in Sally's experience, people tended to hate only what they feared, in what way did they fear them? What on earth would anyone have to fear from a market full of ordinary people? But of course it wasn't the people themselves they feared. It was what they stood for. In this case, not being white – if the group that had claimed responsibility for the bombing was to be believed.

She drained the glass and took it back through to the kitchen. Then she walked around the cottage putting lights out.

126

A little later, lying awake in the darkness, she remembered the one thing she hadn't mentioned to Albert. She'd had another of those strange waking dreams. A couple of days ago. Sitting exactly where she'd just been sitting half an hour ago, on the settee in the living room, looking out through the picture window at the narrows. She could recall every detail and now it made her shiver under the bedclothes. Though it had been a still, hot day, a violent storm had seemed to blow up. Rain lashing into the island. High winds whipping the narrows into an angry churn of sea. The mainland invisible beyond. And then, out in the middle of it all, the sea had seemed to undulate, to swell upwards like the sinuous back of some animal uncurling itself from sleep, until the dense black water had gathered itself into a great curling wave that towered up and rolled forward with increasing speed through the narrows towards the bridge.

Sally sat up and put on the light. She was breathing fast. She drank water from her bedside glass. Surely it couldn't have been real. Another weird after-effect of the bombing, it had to be. And yet . . . it had had the same vivid quality, the same intensity as the vision of the yacht before. That had scared her enough. This scared her a lot more.

She picked up her book and settled back on the pillows. But it was almost dawn before she finally fell asleep, light still on, book in hand.

TWENTY-FOUR

On Wednesday evenings the salon stayed open until ten o'clock. It was always busy. And noisy. The midweek manicure and facials crowd treated it as an alternative to the after-work session in the pub. By closing time the counters were strewn with almost as many empty glasses and wine bottles as cosmetics.

Claire's feet hurt. She had the beginnings of a headache, but she was happy. This was how life should be. The job was better than she could have hoped for. Hard work, yes. But fun and exciting. It made her feel that she was where things were happening, among glamorous, sophisticated people who moved on a bigger stage. She could imagine herself becoming one of them, in time. And then there was Peter – she didn't like to call him Poacher; that was for his mates. Peter. It sounded more . . . serious. She could love someone called Peter. She did love someone called Peter. If she'd had any doubts before, the last three days had chased them away like clouds on a spring day. From the glossy blonde crown of her head to the tip of her pearl-pink toe-nails she loved him absolutely. She loved the clean line of his jaw and the roguish blue eyes. She loved the broadness of his shoulders and cute bum. She loved the way he made her laugh, the way he could be so big and so gentle at the same time. And almost best of all, she loved the fact that all her friends fancied him too. But he was hers and – her heart cartwheeled – she was his.

She hummed as she walked down towards the Curry Quarter. Ten fifteen. He was off at ten thirty. Today Mr Singh had given him the early-evening shift. 'He'll make a jolly good chef one of these fine days, that young chap of yours,' he'd declared in his singsong voice, as she'd waited for Peter to change out of his kitchen clothes at the end of the lunchtime shift the previous day. 'He's a good worker. He picks things up quickly. He's welcome here any time.' Raj, Mr Singh's son, had leaned over the bar as they left and given her a big wink. 'Yeah, babe. Good geezer, that Pete.' She smiled to herself. Maybe they could do something together. She could give people beauty treatments. Peter could cook for them. A spa hotel. That's what they should do. Find some nice place out in the country and start a small exclusive hotel. One day. Not yet though. There were too many good times still to have in the city, and—

The explosion sounded close and far away at the same time. The sharp, loud bang and echoing after-boom that made the air quiver around her and brought everything to an instant standstill. People frozen with shocked hands to their mouths or ears. Eyes turned towards the cloud of smoke, sickly orange in the sodium street-light glow, that drifted up into the night sky.

And then the spell broke. Movement returned. People started to run. The sudden clamour of anxious voices. Car horns. Distant sirens. And Claire's own breathing as she joined the stampeding crowd. The rattle of her high heels on the pavement. Her heart thundering in her chest. Running as fast as she had ever run in her life. Towards the curry quarter.

Poacher opened his eyes to a world visible only through a strangely flickering fog. A moment ago he had been dropping the final batch of peeled potatoes into the huge, twenty-litre pot of boiling water that stood on one of the banks of gas hobs lining one wall of the kitchen. Now, for reasons he couldn't entirely grasp, he seemed to be lying on his back at the foot of the cooker, still clutching the potato peeler in one hand, but unable to move on account of the section of heavy metal shelving that lay across the upper half of his body, pinning him to the floor. His head swam and his ears rang. Nearby he could dimly hear what sounded like someone groaning. Out of the corner of one eye, spreading across the floor, he could see a dark puddle, which might or might not be tandoori sauce. He couldn't really feel anything. He didn't know whether he was injured. In fact, he was strangely calm lying here. A gas explosion. That's what it must have been. Soon rescuers would arrive and lift this thing off him and get him out. And Claire would be there, anxiously waiting for him. He pictured her soft sexy smile as he walked out of the rubble towards her, grey with dust, his clothes ripped, like the hero in some disaster movie. His senses were returning. He sniffed the air. There was no gas smell. So they must've turned it off by now. Well, that was all right. But the groaning was getting worse. 'Hey, Imtiaz,' he called out. 'You all right?' There was no reply. 'It's OK. They'll be here any minute. To get us out.' But the groaning continued. He couldn't do anything about that.

He tried turning to see where the light was coming from. It was difficult because the top of his head was jammed right up against the foot of the cooker. And the shelving across his chest meant that he couldn't wriggle back to give himself any more room to turn. But in the end, ignoring the sharp pain of something metal and unyielding that gouged into his scalp, he managed to move his neck enough to look up.

The light was coming from outside because there was no longer any roof. It was street lighting, veiled by the thick cloud of dust that hung in the air. He could see jagged shapes. Timbers, masonry, wiring, plumbing. The kitchen was a single-storey extension at the back of the building. His heart tripped. Had there been a second storey, he would not be looking up now. But this was too painful, this thing digging into his scalp. He began to let his head go and, as he did so, his gaze was snagged by something directly above him. The flame-blackened bottom of the twenty-litre pot, brimful of potatoes and boiling water. It had been edged off its ring by the blast. Now it balanced on the very edge of the range, four feet above his head. Ready to topple.

Very gingerly, heart thumping, Poacher lowered his head to the floor. His ears still rang, though now he could dimly hear sirens and other sounds of activity. Including what he thought might be voices, close at hand. The noise of rubble being shifted.

Staying as still as he could, he called out, 'In here. In the kitchen. Help. We need help.'

Then, hardly daring to breathe, he closed his eyes and thought as hard as he could about Claire.

Claire had lost a shoe. Her lungs were bursting. Blood pounding at her temples. She rounded the corner and stopped, gasping, to take in the chaotic scene that greeted her. Already blue police lights flashed at both ends of the street. Ambulances were arriving, policeman stringing up no-entry tape, trying to control the milling crowd of on-lookers, rescuers and survivors, who were now starting to be led from devastated buildings in varying states of shock and bloodstained disarray.

The blast had destroyed about a hundred yards of street

frontage. Claire stood fighting back tears as she tried to figure out whether the Punjab Palace was among the buildings that had been hit. But it was impossible to tell. There was not enough left of any of them to know which was which. And since they were all restaurants anyway, the debris in the street, dismembered tables and chairs, here a buckled brass tray, there a smashed statue, offered no clues.

She kicked off her remaining shoe. Began to walk slowly forward, ducking under the police tape. She felt light-headed, as if her feet were no longer in proper contact with the ground. She could see now that the Punjab Palace was the second-to-last in the row of devastated restaurants. But it didn't matter because Peter was going to be alive. And she was going to walk calmly over there and dig him out with her bare hands if she had to.

She picked her way through the chaos, stepping over lumps of masonry, ignoring the glass that cut her bare feet, ignoring the mangled, bloodied objects that tried to draw her gaze into the rubble where they lay, ignoring the tears that now poured down her cheeks. One thought only in her mind, one prayer. Be alive, Peter. Please, please. Be alive.

She was twenty yards from the Punjab Palace when the second bomb went off.

Coldheart Farm

TWENTY-FIVE

No one spoke much on the way back from the Cliffton crematorium. Shirley Archer had hired a minibus for the immediate family and a handful of close friends from the island, including Fin and Kath. A couple of car-loads of relatives from further afield followed behind, along with various others of Poacher's friends from the mainland. The Duck, in leathers and helmet, brought up the rear of the solemn little cavalcade on a motorbike.

As Fin had watched the coffin glide forward and the curtains close silently behind it he had wondered, with a feeling of detachment bordering on unreality, about what was inside the polished wooden box with its brass handles and its covering of lilies. What was left of his friend? Had the explosion blown him into pieces? Had he been crushed or sliced up by flying glass? Or had the blast simply hurled him into something solid? He would never know, of course, nor wanted to really. All he could think was that whatever was in the box, it no longer had much to do with his friend. If Poacher was anywhere now, the smile, the laugh, the roguish looks, the essence of him, he certainly wasn't in that casket that was shortly to be incinerated at one thousand degrees Celsius, its contents reduced to bonemeal. No, Poacher was gone, a small bright burst of raw energy speeding off out into the universe. And what if there was reincarnation? What would he come back as? Fin knew what he would have liked to come back as, and the thought made him smile, despite the solemnity of the occasion. Poacher would have wanted to come back as a celebrity chef with a beautiful blonde girlfriend and his own five-star hotel in some surfers' paradise. Though Fin suspected that that wasn't quite how reincarnation worked. More likely his friend would come back as a monk with some lesson to learn. Or maybe a kitchen cockroach.

Only as they crossed the bridge and the island rose up into the sunlight before them did it strike home to Fin that Poacher was truly gone. They were going back to the Ship Inn for cake and tea, or something a little stronger than that for those who wanted, or needed, it. And Poacher wouldn't be there. Would never be there again. Now Fin felt a kind of numbness creeping over him. It seemed as if everywhere he turned these days there was a new shock awaiting him, intent on closing him down like some failing computer.

Shirley Archer had organised a couple of the staff to make sandwiches and prepare the tea. Now she was ushering people into the bar, making sure they had a cup and plate and enough room to stand or sit. Fin watched her and thought, This is how she's coping with it. Keeping busy. Letting herself run on autopilot. Stan Archer stood red-eyed at the door, shaking people's hands as they came in and looking as if he might crumple at any moment. Dee, Poacher's sister, just looked bewildered as she handed round sandwiches, scarcely able even to acknowledge the kindly remarks and looks of sympathy she received. After a little while she left the room and Fin heard feet going upstairs to the sitting room they kept in use over the bar. He wondered whether he should go after her, but he couldn't face it, and he guessed she wanted to be on her own anyway.

He looked around the crowded room. It seemed odd to

136

hear such muted conversation in what was normally such a raucous place. And the faces. Some solemnly composed, some softened in sympathy, some resolutely cheerful. All wearing the masks they felt appropriate to the occasion. But what were any of them really thinking or feeling? Fin hadn't a clue.

There was an arm at his elbow.

'You all right, man?'

He turned to see the Duck. His stomach plunged. No one had asked him how he felt today. Everyone's attention was focused, naturally enough, on the Archers.

Fin tried to smile, failed. 'I . . . I don't know.'

'Crowded in here. Come outside, eh?'

The hand was steering him towards the door.

They left the bar and walked out along the harbour. It was high tide. Three small boats rocked at their moorings.

'This is going to be tough,' said the Duck.

Fin nodded.

'We're going to miss him, aren't we?'

'Yes.'

'Poor old Poach.' The Duck shook his head. 'Bastards. Whoever did it.'

'I can't believe it. That he's not here.'

'We had a great last trip together. Up to Lighthouse Point.'

'I saw you.'

'And now he's gone.'

They walked on in silence.

'Bastards,' said the Duck again. 'Ignorant, murdering, bigoted bastards.' He shook his head. 'Let's hope they get theirs when the time comes.'

Today, scrubbed and clean-shaven, the Duck looked younger. Fin was surprised by the savagery in his voice.

137

'Where . . . d'you think he's gone?' Fin felt embarrassed by his own question.

But the Duck nodded. He stretched out his arms and described a wide circle, taking in earth, sea and sky.

'Here. There. Everywhere.'

They walked another few yards, then scrambled up on to the sea wall and turned, legs dangling over the seaward side, to stare out at the ocean in silence.

'How did you know?' Fin asked eventually.

'Know what?'

'That this is where I always come . . .'

The Duck shrugged. 'Seemed like a good place.'

They were silent again. Fin felt no need to say anything. His mind was quietening for what seemed like the first time in weeks. He could feel the tension leaving him.

The Duck fished in his pocket and produced a box of matches and what looked like a half-smoked roll-up. He lit it, inhaled deeply and held his breath for several seconds, then exhaled a long stream of aromatic smoke. He held out the stub to Fin.

Fin shook his head.

The Duck took another deep drag. Then tossed the butt into the water.

'Listen to it,' he said softly.

'To what?'

He gestured in front of him.

Fin glanced down at the waves lapping at the concrete a couple of yards below his feet. The water a prism of blue, green, dark amber.

'Not the waves. The ocean.'

Fin looked up and let his focus come to rest on a point halfway between his feet and the horizon. At that distance no movement was visible. And yet . . . if he concentrated

138

. . . was it possible that he sensed something? Not so much a sound as a pulse. Long and slow and deep. Something that came from some deep, ancient place below the waves, perhaps even below the bed of the sea. Or was it simply the blood coursing through his veins? It was soothing, whatever it was.

The Duck smiled wistfully. 'We're all part of that. You. Me. Poacher . . . wherever he is. That's why we should try not to worry about him too much, y'know . . .'

Fin raised his eyes to the horizon.

'Maybe. But it's the ones who're left behind that it's so tough for. His mum and dad. Dee – I don't think she knows what hit her. And Claire. She's not even here. She couldn't face it. It must be terrible for her. I mean . . . she was there, right there – when the second bomb went off . . .'

The Duck reached out and touched his arm.

'You can't feel for everyone, man. You can't carry all their stuff as well as your own. You need to look after yourself first. Then you can take care of everyone else. If you still want to.'

He paused, catching Fin's uncertain look.

'He phoned me, y'know. When he got to Claire's. Said you're dealing with some heavy shit – though he didn't say what.' He looked at Fin. 'He really cared about you, man.'

Fin swallowed. 'I know.'

'Look, now's not the time. But I'm here. When you feel like it, just let me know. If there's anything I can do to help, I will.' He looked away for a moment, then back. 'This is really hard for all of us. We'll get through it together.'

He patted his pockets and pulled a face. Then fished inside his jacket and took out a dog-eared notebook and a pencil stub. He scribbled in the notebook, tore off a corner of a page and handed it to Fin. 'Here's my number.' Then swung himself down off the sea wall.

'We can't bring him back, you know. So we have to try to move on. Which doesn't mean forget him.' He half-smiled. 'We won't be able to anyway.'

He lifted his hand in salute and ambled off in the direction of the car park.

Fin watched him go, then returned his gaze to the ocean, to that mid-point between harbour and horizon. He concentrated, reaching with all his senses for the pulse. But there was nothing there. Just the sound of his own breathing and the lap of waves below his feet. After a while he climbed down from the wall. He made his way back to the Ship and went inside.

TWENTY-SIX

That night the heat was stifling. Fin slept fitfully. He woke and threw off the sheet. Got up to open the window as wide as he could. Then fell back into bed and dreamed of the Institute, where Poacher was serving beer in a big white tent beneath the turbines. But the spinning blades kept slicing at the arm with which he was trying to operate the beer tap, and the customers were getting impatient as the plastic tumblers filled up with blood. Meanwhile, at a table in one corner, Maia, Sean and Charlotte Svensson were chatting among themselves, looking up from time to time to laugh at Poacher and his predicament.

Fin woke again, this time in a pool of sweat. He lay on his back for a long while, staring up at the ceiling. Poacher had been dead for over a week. It still seemed impossible. For the first few days he had been like a sleepwalker. Numb. Moving through life barely conscious of what was going on around him. But now, along with the pain of Poacher's absence, Maia was starting to push her way back into his thoughts. Perhaps that was what the Duck had meant by moving on. Maia was the one who was still alive. His sister. She was the one he needed to do something about. Poacher would have agreed with that. He had been going to help Fin reach her after all.

Fin turned on his side and watched light creep into the eastern sky as he ran through what he had so far found out about the Green Energies Group. The corporate website had told him little of interest. Headquartered in Great Falls, Montana. One of the world's largest investors in sustainable energy. Involved in wind-farm development in more than thirty countries. Known principally for the quality of research undertaken at six centres throughout the US, Europe and Asia, of which Schloss Adler in northern Austria was the main one. Research and development currently focused on the GE Super Turbine. But no details of the research centres. No information about who worked at them. Not even a photograph of any of the places. Unsurprising, he guessed, given the revolutionary technology, the commercially sensitive nature of the business.

But over the next few days he had persisted, working his way through the hundreds of pages of references thrown up by an Internet search for 'Green Energies'. And eventually, after following links to articles, technical reports, blogs, discussion forums, chatrooms and message boards, he had been rewarded. On a site posted by a group of Danish eco-activists, buried among the now familiar rantings about disfigurement of the landscape, danger to wildlife and, of course, corporate greed, he spotted something that caught his attention at once. Green Energies, claimed the writers, were reputed to run a controversial induction scheme for new employees, who were selected on the basis of intensive psychometric testing and then inducted in a two-week programme which allegedly combined elements of Eastern mysticism and neurolinguistic adaptation techniques borrowed from the CIA and other intelligence agencies. The writers didn't spell it out, but the inference was clear: Green Energies systematically indoctrinated their new employees. No theories were advanced as to why this might be the case but, the writers continued, Green Energies were notoriously secretive, and although there had been various allegations of illegal practices, nothing had ever come to court, for the company was also known to retain infamously aggressive lawyers. The piece concluded with a startling assertion: Green Energies claimed one of the lowest rates of personnel turnover of any organisation in the world, almost as low as the armed forces.

For twenty-four hours Fin had been torn between the certainty that Maia had been brainwashed and the probability that the writers were yet another group of lunatic conspiracy theorists. And then the bombing had driven all such thoughts from his mind.

But now they were back again. Another item on the growing inventory of unsettling possibilities associated with the Institute. And with them the conviction that he had to see Maia as soon as he could. How, though? He began to regret the conversation he'd had with the woman on Open Day about Charlotte Svensson. Everything had become so much more complicated since then. If he now rang up and started asking about Maia, they might well become suspicious. And that was without introducing Sean into the equation. No. He would have to find a way of getting on to Seal Island undetected . . .

Norman Turner. The thought came with the first sleepy squawk of a seagull. His antipathy towards the Institute was obvious. Perhaps he would be able to help. And anyway, there was the tantalising thought of what he had been about to say, that day . . .

Fin sighed and turned over. He closed his eyes. He would go back to Coldheart Farm this evening, as soon as he finished work.

In a subdued way, people were being unusually nice to him since Poacher's death. Fin noticed it in the cafe, starting with Dot Kettle herself. She had smiled at him twice this morning, her face taking on an expression usually reserved for her infant granddaughter and one or two of her longest-standing customers. Sally Lightfoot dropped in at lunchtime for a bottle of mineral water, and later on in the afternoon Albert Smith came by and sat for ten minutes with a cup of tea. Neither made any particular effort to engage Fin in conversation, but he knew that the reason they were there was to see if he was all right. He didn't mind. In fact he was comforted. He was also glad of the steady stream of customers throughout the day, the heat driving them in for ice creams and cold drinks. Like Shirley Archer, he was better busy.

Six o'clock came quickly. He helped Dot to lock up, then walked up the lane to Number Thirteen, wondering exactly how he was going to frame his request to Norman Turner. He went in and stopped in surprise to see Kath and Danny sitting together at the small kitchen table, a pot of tea between them. A sight he hadn't seen for as long as he could remember.

'Hey, darlin'. Like a cup?' Kath smiled and patted the empty chair beside her.

Fin's surprise must have registered plainly. Danny looked up and also smiled.

''S'all right, son. Your mum and I were just having a natter. Nothing serious. But . . .' he cleared his throat, 'I want you to know that I'm right sorry about your pal. A terrible thing.' He shook his head. 'And . . .' now he shifted in his chair, 'your mum says I'm to say I'm sorry . . . that I've not been around the last couple of days . . .'

Try the last nine years, thought Fin. But he nodded all the same, startled by the apparent sincerity in his father's voice.

'We lost a young lad, y'know. On the first boat I was on. Before I joined *North Star*. Well . . . young – I was young too. The same age. Not that we were close, not like you and your – Poker. But we were shipmates all the same. Hundred miles south of Iceland. A force 10. Sleet like bullets. He forgot to put on his harness. Wouldn't have lasted two minutes in that water.' He shook his head. 'It's a bad, bad thing – when a young life gets taken away like that. Things have to go on, of course. But you never really get over it, never get used to it . . .'

Fin still stood in the doorway. Kath caught his eye.

'Thing is,' Danny went on, 'it's tough any way you look at it. And I sometimes wonder whether it wouldn't have been better if I'd gone over the side too, rather than ending up like this.' He looked at Fin. 'At least your pal knew nothing about it . . .'

'Yes, well . . .' Kath pushed her chair back abruptly and got up. 'Fin needs something to eat.' She glanced at the kitchen clock. 'And you've got your darts night, haven't you?'

Danny seemed lost in thought.

'You'll be wanting to get down to the mission,' said Kath pointedly.

Danny looked up and nodded. Reached for his stick and heaved himself upright.

'See you later then.' He shuffled to the door, back bent like a man twice his age.

Kath went to the oven. 'Can you wait twenty minutes? I've got you a nice steak pie.'

Fin could sense the anger in her movements.

'Sure, Mum.'

'God!' She banged her hand down on the work surface. 'Will he ever get over it?'

'I don't know . . . But – well, at least he was trying.'

This was unlike him, Fin thought, to be defending his father. But it was true. Danny had been trying, to start with anyway. And considering what he'd said after the incident with Sean, it seemed to Fin like a definite step in the right direction.

Kath turned round with a weary gesture.

'You're right, love. He was. But still he's like a broken bloody record.'

Fin sat down. Watched his mother put the pie in the oven.

'So what's changed? I mean, apart from what obviously *hasn't* changed. But, like, him trying all of a sudden . . .' He gestured at the table, the teapot and cups. 'You and him.'

Kath closed the oven door. Turned to stand facing him, arms folded.

'I gave him an ultimatum. Told him if he didn't shape up, I'd be off.'

'You didn't . . .'

She nodded.

'Hey Mum, that's amazing!'

'Yes.' She gave a tight smile. 'After what happened the other week . . . and our conversation . . . I just thought, well, finally – enough is enough.'

'And he's taken it to heart . . .'

'Hmmm.' She turned away. 'We'll see.' She began to take plates from the cupboard. Passed them to Fin to lay the table. 'Oh, by the way, that guy from the Institute. The one who was driving . . .'

'Hunter?'

'Yes, Hunter. He was here this afternoon. Wanting to see you. Said you'd tried to contact him at the Open Day. Said you wanted to talk to him about the girl.'

'Charlotte, Mum. Charlotte Svensson.' She couldn't just go on being 'the girl'. She had a name. And it was it important that people used it, even if she *was* dead.

'Sorry, love. Charlotte. Anyway, I told him you'd had rather a lot on your plate since then. Which was probably why he hadn't heard from you.'

'And . . . ?'

'He seemed quite happy. Said you had his phone number if you still wanted to see him.'

'Fine. Thanks.'

'So . . . what did you want to talk to him about?'

Fin shrugged. 'Try and find out a bit more about her. Like . . . oh, I don't know . . . it's hard to explain, but – I don't think I can really let go of her while she's still a stranger. Does that make any sense?'

Now she smiled. 'Yes. And I'm glad you told me.' She reached across and took his hand. 'Because to be honest, love, I've been worried about you. What with everything that's been happening. And now . . . Poacher . . . It seems like the last straw. But you're OK? Really OK? I mean . . . you'd tell me if there was anything else bothering you . . . ?'

Fin disengaged his hand from hers. Of course he wouldn't. He was nearly nineteen. He'd tell her *some* things but not *anything*. And she knew it as well as he did. But right now they needed to go through the motions, for both their sakes. He smiled. 'Yes, Mum. I'm OK. Well, I am and I'm not – you know what I mean. But sitting around won't bring Poacher back. I just want to get on now. Do my job at Kettles. Try and enjoy the rest of the summer. Get ready for uni.'

Kath stood up and planted a kiss on top of his head. 'Good. That's all I needed to hear.'

TWENTY-SEVEN

So she had finally done it, thought Fin. He felt proud of her. Even though he knew she should have done it years before. In time to stop Danny making Maia's and his teenage years a misery. In time to stop him driving Maia away. But now she'd done it. And Fin was pleased for her, because even if it didn't work, even if she'd left it too late, he could see how important it was to her to have taken a stand at last. And not just for her, for him too . . .

He made his way along the cliff path towards Coldheart Farm. The day's heat hung in the air and there was a suggestion of thunder now, a smudge of cloud on the western horizon.

Maybe something good would come out of the incident with Sean after all, he thought.

He walked up the track through the wheat field, crossed the yard and rang the doorbell.

There was a movement in the kitchen. The face of Norman Turner at the window. It withdrew and a few moments later the door opened.

'Finlay.'

'I – I . . . hope you don't mind . . . I wanted to talk – well, ask you something. About the Institute.'

Norman Turner closed his eyes. 'The Institute. Ah yes. We discussed it when you were last here . . .' He opened his eyes and paused expectantly.

'Um . . . could I – maybe . . . can I come in?'

He nodded.

'Yes, please come in. I was having my supper.'

'Oh . . . I don't want to disturb you. I mean . . . I can come back another time.'

'Come in.'

He turned and Fin followed him into the kitchen.

The room was as tidy and empty as last time. On the table was a glass of water, a plate containing the remaining mouthful of what looked like baked beans on toast, and a thick book open at a page of mathematical tables. For a moment Fin felt almost overwhelmed by the loneliness of it. His eye fell on the photograph of the schoolgirl and lingered there, as if to confirm that there was at least some vestige of humanity in Norman Turner's strange universe.

Turner sat down in his place and forked the final piece of toast into his mouth.

Fin hesitated for a moment. Then took a seat across the table and waited as Norman Turner wiped his mouth, took a drink from his glass of water, then closed his eyes again.

'Your question, Finlay. What was it?'

'When I was here – last time . . . just before you went for your walk . . . you started to say something about the founder of Green Energies. Some group he started . . . ? I looked online like you said, but I couldn't find anything – not about that, anyway.'

'Ah.' He looked at Fin. Nodded. 'You do have to be persistent. With an appetite for digging for bones. Which their lawyers are very good at burying.'

Fin had a sudden image of Norman Turner standing with a spade in front of a pulsating mountain of electronic data. Digging obsessively, all through the night . . .

The older man went on. 'Walter Groeneberg. The Home-lands Society. Yes. He was nearly expelled from MIT—'

'MIT?'

'The Massachusetts Institute of Technology. Where he was studying. The Homelands Society was a survivalist club. A group of students who went out into the woods at weekends and during vacations and lived off the land. Built camps. Killed their food. Preparing, they said, for the day when society collapsed. But there was an incident. One autumn semester they invited a young freshman to join them. Took him into the woods. Then hunted him. The experience left the freshman severely traumatised, or so he alleged. But the incident never went further than the university's governing body. Groeneberg personally conducted their defence and argued that this was no more than a longstanding ritual within the society, a kind of initiation rite. They were admonished and ordered to close down the society, but there the story ended. I don't know that it even made the press. Even then Groeneberg had a nose for sharp attorneys.'

'Seems so.' Fin nodded. 'I found a site that claimed Green Energies put their new recruits through some kind of weird programme when they join. Something to do with neuro-something and some Eastern stuff. The suggestion was that the techniques are dodgy, illegal maybe – and that some people might have tried to take them to court about it, but that their lawyers were too smart.'

'Ah.' Norman Turner nodded. 'The induction programme. Yes. You did well to find that.'

'You know about it?'

'Since we're in . . . competition –' a smile brushed his lips – 'I've made it my business to find out whatever I can about them. It's all in the public domain, of course. But some of it only just. Where did you come across this site?'

150

'It was some Danish eco-warrier-type outfit. I spent hours on the Internet and that was the only mention of it that I found.'

'And do you believe it?'

'I . . . I don't know.'

Now Norman Turner looked at Fin. 'What makes you so interested in the Institute, Finlay?'

Fin hesitated. Could he really take this strange man that he hardly knew into his confidence? It was why he had come here, of course. But with the moment at hand he felt uncertain.

Norman Turner waited.

'Well . . . it's – to do with my sister. And another girl I didn't really know. Though not in that order.'

Sitting at the kitchen table, Fin told him everything. From the moment Charlotte Svensson had fallen through the mist to the moment he had seen Maia at the cottage door.

Norman Turner listened without expression. When Fin had finished, he sat for several moments tapping his fingers against his glass.

Then he said, 'And do you think I can help you?'

'I don't know.' He looked at the older man. 'I . . . I hope so. It's why I came here.'

'Have you told anyone else?'

Fin shook his head.

'Not even your parents?'

'No.'

'And you have good reason for that?'

'I think so.'

'Why don't you just take your suspicions to the police?'

'Because I don't think they'd listen to me. Or at least, not take me seriously. They've already swallowed the

151

Institute's story about Charlotte Svensson. And anyway, that's all I've got – suspicions. I don't have any proof of anything – except that Sean's a racist. And I guess the only way I can really find out more about any of this is by seeing Maia – if she'll see me. But I don't think I can just walk on to Seal Island and ask for her at reception. And I thought . . . well – maybe that's where you could help me . . . I mean . . .' he hesitated, 'what do *you* think . . . about the induction programme – about the Institute? Do you think there could be something . . . dodgy going on there?'.

Norman Turner looked at him.

'Dodgy . . . Well, Finlay, it's true I've unearthed some un-savoury facts about Green Energies. Yes. But had I looked as closely at practically any large corporation in the world, I've no doubt I would have found equally disturbing things. That's simply the world of big business. Where power and profit are sometimes put before human considera-tions. Even when the product is something like sustainable energy.' He leaned forward. 'One day, Finlay, you'll come to realise that nothing on this earth is either all good or all bad. I'm sure Joseph Stalin loved his mother. I'm sure Mahatma Gandhi lost his temper. The word is "duality". And that's what makes the world an interesting, if con-fusing – sometimes even dangerous, place.' He drummed his fingers on the table top. 'As for the induction programme – I can see how you might imagine that it could be some form of brainwashing. And you may be right, as you may be about the other girl's death. I don't know. But I agree that it's important you try to see your sister. In fact, I believe it's the only thing you can do.'

'And . . . do you think I'm right not to try to do it – like, officially? I mean, not ask anyone's permission? Not call? Just turn up there?'

152

'Given what you've told me, Finlay, yes, I think you are right.'

' OK . . .' He hesitated. 'So – do you have any idea how I could get on to the island?'

Norman Turner turned to glance at the portrait and wheel, as if seeking inspiration. 'Well . . . I suppose I could take you. I could make an appointment to see someone there – whoever their public-liaison person might be. I have a professional interest in what they do, after all. They would let me in. A harmless eccentric . . .' He gave a wry smile. 'And if you're in the back of my car, you could simply get out once we're on the island and away from the security cameras. Then you can make your way to her quarters and wait for her.'

'What if she lives with someone?' Now that they were discussing the practicalities, Fin felt suddenly unsure of himself. 'With Sean?'

'You'll have to use your wits.'

'But what if she's not there? If I have to wait. I mean . . . you won't be able to just – hang around . . . till I'm finished . . . will you?'

Norman Turner nodded. 'No. I'll leave something behind. Like I did before.' Again the wry smile. 'But deliberately this time. So I have a pretext for returning if need be. We'll make a rendezvous.'

'And . . . if she doesn't want to see me?'

His host lifted a hand. 'Listen, Finlay. You can continue to raise objections till the crack of doom. But this seems to me like your best chance.' There was authority in his voice now. 'Maybe I could put it another way. You're old enough to understand it when I say that perhaps you feel a responsibility, a duty even, to these two people – to your sister and the other girl, Charlotte Svensson. Do you? Or can you simply walk away from this because it's starting to seem too difficult?' He turned to look at the shrine again. 'In *his* day they still burned people for thinking some of the things he thought. But he believed in the importance of scientific truth. And you, Finlay, the reason you're here is because you believe, I think, in human truth. In stripping away the lies and deceptions that you fear may surround both their circumstances.'

'Yes.' Fin nodded. 'Yes, I do.'

'Good,' said Norman Turner. 'Then I'll make an appointment with the Institute and let you know. Do you have a mobile phone? Give me your number.'

He stood up and fetched a notepad from a drawer. When he had taken down Fin's number he looked at him and said, 'What made you think I would help you?'

Fin was not sure how to answer. 'Because . . . because – I reckoned you knew things about the Institute. And you seemed, well . . .'

'Unconventional?'

Fin nodded.

'Someone who might not kowtow to authority?'

'Yes.'

'You said you had reasons for not speaking of this with your parents. But what about friends? Do you not have a friend you could have discussed it with?'

'Well . . .' Fin hesitated. 'Yes – one friend. We'd started talking about it. My best friend. But then – he was killed. In the bombing. A fortnight ago.'

'Oh. I am so very sorry.' For the first time since he had met him, Fin saw emotion enter Norman Turner's face. 'Are you all right?' he went on. 'That must be a hard loss to bear.'

Fin nodded.

'Especially on top of everything else.' His eyes creased with sympathy. 'A hard, hard loss.'

Fin swallowed. 'Yes.'

'I know what it's like to lose someone,' Norman Turner said after a while.

'Do you?'

'Yes. Not that they died. Not like your friend. But I doubt I'll ever see them again.'

He paused as if waiting for Fin's permission to continue.

'Who was that?' Fin asked.

Norman Turner pointed to the photograph of his niece. 'My brother's daughter. Amy.' He nodded to himself. 'My brother died of cancer when she was a few years old. We were not close, my brother and I. But they lived nearby and I was fond of Amy. She was like the daughter I never had. I used to see her at weekends. Her mother never particularly liked me. But she saw that there was a bond between us and it suited her to have someone who would take Amy off her hands sometimes, once her husband was gone. I'd never married, you see. And I like to think I became a kind of father to Amy. Am I boring you, Finlay?'

'No.'

The moment of emotion had passed. His voice had become matter-of-fact, as if this story belonged to someone else.

'I taught history in a secondary school,' he continued. 'Ancient history was my chosen subject, the Greeks and Romans. But there's little interest in the classical world these days, so I settled for so-called modern history. It was a big school, fifteen hundred pupils. A decent enough place, though there were rough elements there. And I was always something of a target. The oddball bachelor. Psycho Turner.

155

Or Normal Norman, when they were being ironic. Oh, I knew. Every teacher does.' He took a sip of water. 'Then Amy moved up from her primary school. My school was her local secondary, you see. And almost at once she began to be bullied. Because of me. Now, I could bear it on my own account. It was nothing I hadn't experienced before. I'd been sent away to boarding school when I was young, and I was bullied mercilessly there. But I couldn't stand to see my niece having to suffer such cruelty. And one day, Finlay, I did the thing no teacher should ever do. One day when I was tired, had too much marking to do, an unruly class – I no longer remember why – I lost control. Laid hands on one of the bullies in anger. And he reported me. Of course I was suspended. Well, the disciplinary proceedings dragged on. Meanwhile, encouraged, no doubt, by the local community, the young man and his gang began to ostracise me. Ignorant, small-minded people in my neighbourhood started harassing me. Before long I was being spat at in the street, having my car tyres slashed and excrement put through my letter box. I became depressed. I tried to kill myself and ended up in hospital.'

Had he ever told this to anyone else? Fin wondered.

'I spent several months in hospital,' he went on. 'I was surprised that Amy never came to see me during that time. When I came out I learned why. Her mother, who by then had begun another relationship, had taken her out of the school and they'd moved away to live with her new part-ner, leaving no forwarding address.

'In the end I resigned before the disciplinary hearing took place. My neighbours continued to harass me so I also sold my house and moved. I lived in my car for six months. I remember hardly anything of it except driving around the country, living off coffee and biscuits, until I found this

156

place where I knew I could settle quietly. Where I wouldn't be bothered by people. Where I could get on with my research. My parents had left enough money for me not to have to work if I lived frugally.'

He paused, then glanced again at the portrait and wheel. 'Without him, Finlay, I don't think I would have survived. He was my companion during those months. Leonardo. Him and his genius. He gave me a reason to keep going. His courage to venture where no one had gone before. To challenge the conventions of his day. To ignore what other people said or thought about his ideas. And that was when I decided to continue his work on perpetual motion. I'd been fascinated by the idea since I first came across it when I was . . . not much older than you.'

Norman Turner sat back in his chair and looked at Fin. 'Why is he telling me all this? you are asking. Well – because, like you, I also mistrust the Institute. Because you seem to be a decent young man, and I'd like to help you. And because this is a small place, this island. People will find out that you've been up here. They'll say things about me, as people always do about those they see as different. And I would prefer that you knew the truth.'

Despite the dry delivery, Fin sensed that within the older man a door had begun to open.

'Thank you,' he said. 'But can I ask you something?'
'Yes.'
'Have you tried to contact her since? I mean . . . how old would she be now?'
'Nearly nineteen.'
'The same age as me.'
Norman Turner smiled.
'So have you tried the Internet? The social networking sites? You might easily find her that way . . .'

Turner gave another sigh. 'She was thirteen at the time. Highly suggestive, I'm sure – as pubescent girls are. And her mother would have turned her against me. I'm almost certain of it. Otherwise she would surely have contacted me. You see, Finlay, I've come to understand that I prefer to live with the memory of her daughterly love and innocence. I don't want to run the risk of finding out it is no longer there.'

He stood up and took his glass to the sink to refill it.

'So there it is – that's why I understand your loss.'

Fin nodded, uncertain what to say. 'I – er – think I should be going now . . .'

He stood up and put out his hand. Not sure whether Norman Turner would take it. 'Thank you very much for helping me.'

'I look forward to seeing you for our little . . . date with the Institute,' said Turner with the trace of a smile.

He took Fin's hand. His handshake was firm and warm.

TWENTY-EIGHT

Maia believed that she could handle most things. But she had to admit that she was struggling to come to terms with Lottie's death. The sense of loss swept through her at unexpected moments. When she was at her desk, or standing in the queue at the staff cafe. And, of course, whenever she walked back into the cottage, her eye drawn to the empty bedroom across the little passage from hers. Sometimes it left her feeling weak-kneed and tearful. At others, listless and disconnected.

Now she flipped through the favourites on her iPod, looking for the track she wanted. But when it came on she didn't feel in the mood for it. She got up and went to the window and stood staring out at the trees, reduced to dark shapes in the falling dusk.

To make things worse, Terry too seemed to have been more affected by Lottie's death than he was admitting. He was so distracted. So busy with God knows what. It felt like weeks since she had last been with him, weeks of waiting for that particular look, but being constantly disappointed. It stretched time into a long, dull ache. Seeking diversion in the evenings, she'd had people round to the cottage for pizza a couple of times, and once Sean had asked her over to his flat in the stable block after work. They'd commiserated about Lottie, shared a bottle of wine and watched a movie. But she didn't really like him. He seemed coldly single-minded. And while she knew he was good at what he did, she suspected that he had a cruel streak which made her want to keep him at arm's length. Anyway, he was always going on about her skin, which seemed to fascinate him, and she guessed that he'd only invited her in the hope that he might get her into bed. Which was not going to happen. Fit though he was, Maia had never found him in the least attractive. The muscle bulges that came from regular working-out did nothing for her. And now the yellowing black eye – the result of sorting out a small problem in the labyrinth, he had explained smugly – made him look repulsive.

She turned away from the window and made for the kitchen, then changed her mind and crossed the corridor to Lottie's room. She went in and without putting the lights on sat down on Lottie's bed. Terry had said that they'd find someone else for her to share with. But they hadn't yet. She sat still, listening to her own breathing. Trying to imagine Lottie's last few days. Lying here in bed at night, maybe not sleeping, wrestling with her depression. Wondering how she was going to do it . . . For all the ups and downs of her own life, Maia could hardly imagine the agony someone would have to be in to think of killing themselves, let alone the practicalities of it. Pills? Cutting her wrists? Drowning? Suffocation? Jumping?

No. She thumped her hand into the pillow. This wasn't right. Lottie hadn't been ill. She was certain of it. A little distracted perhaps, she'd noticed that, but not depressed. They lived together, after all. Maia would have known. But Lottie had been full of energy, working as hard as she always did, making plans for her next leave. That wasn't the behaviour of someone who was planning to do away with herself, thought Maia. Though how she was supposed to square that with what Terry had told her, she didn't know . . .

Lottie had been as good a friend as Maia had ever had. Which was saying something, since Maia didn't readily open up to people. Danny had cured her of that; as he'd changed, she'd gradually withdrawn inside the thickest shell she could pull around herself, afraid to let him see the least glimmer of her inner thoughts and feelings, in case he hauled them out of her and trampled on them.

Even once she'd left home, she had kept her guard up. At university, she knew people had thought her cold. But she couldn't let anyone in close. It had been a kind of abuse, she now realised, Danny's constant sniping and undermining. But because she'd been a teenager, she'd responded in the worst way possible, sulking or lashing out, when what she should have done was simply ignore him, leaving him to stew in his own sad, twisted life.

So she'd immersed herself in her studies, choosing the library over the student pubs and coffee shops, and after three years she'd been rewarded with a first-class degree, which had given her the confidence to start applying for serious jobs. Within two months of graduating she'd been taken on by Green Energies. She would never forget the feeling of getting on the plane to Vienna. It was as if she were literally taking flight, leaving behind her old earth-bound existence for a new life on some higher level. She'd never felt so good before, never believed that it was possible to feel so good.

And of all the extraordinary things that happened during the three weeks at Schloss Adler, meeting Lottie had been the best. The common experience, the daily meditations, some basic chemistry . . . she still wasn't sure what had brought them together, but they'd connected at once, as if they'd known one another all their lives. Maia remembered it so well, talking through the night in their shared room, two strong young women, their idealism ablaze in this fairytale castle in the forests of central Europe.

So she'd been shocked and thrilled at the end of the three weeks to learn that they'd both been posted to the research institute on Seal Island. Shocked that she was going home, thrilled that her new best friend was going with her. Though in the event, she'd found that she felt almost no connection with the place at all, despite its link to her past, nor any desire to make contact with her family. Now Green Energies was where she and Lottie belonged. They were, as they had chanted morning, noon and evening, 'one family for a clean planet'.

Lottie, the better scientist, had been put straight into the research programme as a junior laboratory assistant. Maia had been placed in the communications team. And while at first she had been a little envious of Lottie, and her role in the crucible of this new technology, Maia had soon found that the task of communicating their message of a clean planet seemed every bit as worthwhile, and sometimes a lot more exciting. Their friendship had intensified in this new environment and even when Terry had singled Maia out for his special attention, it had seemed not to come between them.

But now . . . Lottie was gone, Terry was unavailable, and Maia felt adrift and miserable. She had a headache coming on. She got up and left Lottie's room, closing the door behind her. Went back into her own room and looked in her drawers for painkillers. She couldn't find any. Maybe they were in her bag. It was a deep patchwork affair with wooden handles, and full of junk. She should clear it out, she thought. She upended it on her bed and poked through the contents. There was the foil strip of pills, and there . . . something unfamiliar. A memory stick, but not hers. She looked at it, then remembered. It was Lottie's. Of course. She'd picked it off the floor of the sitting room where Lottie must've dropped it, a couple of days before she left. Maia had been on the way out at the time and had popped it into her bag, meaning to give it back. Then Lottie had gone and she'd forgotten all about it in the drama that followed.

Now she held it in a cupped hand and looked at it with a sense of guilty curiosity. There might be private things on it. But Lottie was dead. Private things might offer some insight into why she was dead. And if it was nothing but work, then it wouldn't matter anyway, would it?

Leaving the contents of the bag strewn across the bed, she went into the living room and sat down at the table in the window. She turned on her laptop and connected the memory stick. She waited for the contents to come up on the screen. There were six files, all named with meaningless strings of characters of the kind familiar to anyone involved in the more technical aspects of the research programme. She tried to open the first file and was asked for a password. Passwords, she had always thought, were like birthmarks – just one of the many intimate details that you couldn't avoid getting to know when you lived with someone. She typed in Lottie's and let out a breath as the screen cleared and the file was revealed. A dozen pages of unintelligible formulae, short paragraphs of technical description – something to do with blade pitch – and diagrams. She moved on to the next file. More of the same. And the next. What was she looking for? She didn't know. A clue, she supposed. Anything to support this uncomfortable feeling that Lottie hadn't, wouldn't, couldn't have killed herself. She got up and went into the kitchen, poured herself a glass of wine and took a packet of cheese biscuits from the cupboard. Then she returned to the desk.

The next file she opened was the same as the previous three. But as soon she opened the fifth her pulse quickened. It was all text, blocks of different typefaces suggesting that they had been cut and pasted from different sources. Maia skimmed the file. Newspaper reports, mainly from South Africa, it seemed. Maybe this was some personal project Lottie had been doing for Terry. The thought gave her a small pang of jealousy. She took a sip of wine, then leaned forward with her elbows on the desk and began reading from the beginning.

The first piece was a short news report, a couple of paragraphs, dated 1973, about the dismissal from the Bloemfontein Police Department of an Inspector Christian Blankard on grounds of gross professional misconduct. It was followed by an equally short editorial comment, from the same newspaper, dated the following day, noting that unusual as such dismissals were, they were nevertheless essential to the maintenance of probity within the Bloemfontein Police Department. 'We must never allow one rotten apple to spoil the whole barrel,' concluded the editorial piously. It struck Maia as odd that in neither piece of writing was the nature of the misconduct explained. Though perhaps, given the climate of the day, with conflict over apartheid at its height, it was a simple matter of security not to divulge such details.

She scrolled down to the next page and caught her breath. Now there was a black-and-white photograph that had not yet loaded on to the page when she had first skimmed through the document. Solemn in front of the camera, in what Maia took to be his South African police inspector's uniform, was a man who looked uncannily like Terry. 'Former Police Inspector Christian Blankard: multiple violent rapes', read the caption. To the left of the photograph was a heading which read: 'Blankard victims testify to Truth Commission'. For a moment she was unable to concentrate on the text that followed, so striking was the likeness between the inspector and Terence Whitelands. Her eye kept returning to the image until she could only conclude that this person had to be a very close relative of Terry's, most likely his father. The same dark hair and parting. The same clean jawline and slightly swarthy complexion. Most of all, the same eyes. Dark, intense, unfathomable. Were it not for the name . . . She shook her head. Despite the name . . . It had to be.

She began to read. The article was dated 1995, twenty-two years after the first. It was more a feature than a news report. It dealt with one of the many scandals to come to light after the end of apartheid and the white domination of South Africa. The testimony of the victims to the Truth and Reconciliation Commission was part of the process that enabled the country slowly to start healing its wounds. In this case, the scandal was twofold: firstly, that over a period of ten years a serving white police officer had violently raped seventeen women, all black or coloured, who had been brought in for questioning about a variety of offences ranging from shoplifting to terrorism; secondly, that although, thanks to the bravery and persistence of one of his victims, a young lawyer, he had finally been disciplined and dismissed from the police force, he had never faced criminal charges, and now, at the time of writing, was thought no longer to be resident in South Africa, although his whereabouts were unknown. The article paid close attention to the story of the young lawyer whom the inspector had raped, not once but twice, the first time on the evening she was brought into the station for questioning about her association with a client suspected of activities against the state; the second time, two days later, when she was released and he followed her in his car then dragged her into the bush on the edge of the township to rape her and beat her so severely that he left her for dead. But she survived. And once she had recovered her health she set about bringing him to justice, slowly and at great personal risk from the police death squads who were determined to silence her. She took cover in the heart of the township, moving every couple of days for more than two years so she could not be tracked down, constantly on her guard against informers, while she began to identify his other victims and persuade them to give her their evidence until eventually she had compiled a dossier that the authorities could not ignore.

Maia sat back and toyed with the glass of wine, but didn't drink. Her heart was racing with indignation and admiration for the young woman. She was brave and principled, as Maia hoped she would be were she ever to face such evil. But the man. Blankard. What a pig. *Surely* he couldn't be anything to do with Terry. She scrolled back to the photograph. Felt the sinking in the pit of her stomach. Yes, he could. The resemblance was so strong. Terry's father. A racially motivated rapist. Her mind began to spin. And if he was, did Terry know about it? He would only have been a child when the crimes were committed, after all.

She read on.

The next item was from a London newspaper, dated a couple of years after the South African feature. But where the feature had left Maia with a feeling of sick outrage and anxiety, this report filled her with horror. Terence Whitfield, aged thirty-five, a renewable-energy consultant, was convicted of assaulting Miss Chantelle Kingston, aged twenty-seven, in her flat. This time the photo, unsmiling before the police camera, was unmistakably Terry himself. Had Miss Kingston's flatmate not returned at the critical moment, the report said, Miss Kingston had no doubt that the assault would have been much more serious and, judging from the defendant's demeanour, could well have led to rape. As it was, said the judge, handing down sentence, this was a wholly unwarranted, racially aggravated assault of a particularly unpleasant nature and he had no hesitation in sending Whitfield to prison.

Oh God. Terry too . . . Now Maia's heart was thundering. He had beaten up a woman. A black woman like her. Who had Chantelle Kingston been? A girlfriend? A casual pick-up? A prostitute even? Did it matter? Had Maia ever seen any hint of violence in his dealings with her? No. Something controlled, a kind of fierce, contained energy beneath the concern and gentleness. But no violence. Nevertheless, the thought of it made her feel ill . . .

She stood up. She was trembling. The small room felt confined. She needed to get outside so she could think clearly.

It was a sultry evening, the air heavy from the day's heat, scents of pine lingering. She walked away from the cottage, through the trees, towards the beach. Her mind spun. Could she picture Terry lifting his hand against her? No. It seemed impossible. But then, until it had happened, she could never have imagined the verbal abuse she would receive from Danny in the years following the accident.

She had reached the shore now. She kicked off her shoes and walked on to the beach. She sat down and stared out to sea. It was still and shining dully, like pewter. She picked up a handful of warm sand and let it run through her fingers.

Whitfield. Whitelands? Why the name change? Out of

shame? Or to conceal the criminal record? The two names were not so very different anyway. Both meant the same thing really. She thought back to the South African police inspector. Blankard. What did that mean in Afrikaans? she wondered. *Blank* . . . it could mean white. And why had Lottie been researching it all? To warn her, Maia? Was that it? Maia's palms were suddenly clammy. Was that . . . could that be why Lottie was no longer here?

She shook her head. No. Surely not. Her imagination was starting to run away with her.

Perhaps Lottie *had* been jealous of her and Terry after all. Especially if she had been depressed. And this was to have been some kind of ruse to spoil things.

She stood up again.

Well, whatever he might or might not have done, she would swear on the holy bible that Terry was the gentlest, most considerate man she had ever met. He had given her more in the last few months than her father had in her whole life, even counting the years before the accident. And as for being a racist . . . ha! It was the colour of her skin, he told her repeatedly, that was one of the things he most admired, that most excited him about her.

She felt a sudden twinge of guilt. Everyone had a right to secrets, didn't they? Everyone had things in their past they'd rather forget. And now she'd betrayed Terry's trust by prying into matters that were none of her business. Anyway, they were all family here at the Institute, weren't they, and families supported one another through thick and thin – at least if they were halfway decent they did. She owed it to Terry – and to Green Energies – to put it all out of her mind. Lottie's death, Terry's past misdemeanours, even his father's unsavoury activities – if he really was Terry's father; she mustn't allow them to cloud her judgement, to get in the way of the two things that were most important to her in the whole world. Her work here at Seal Island. And Terry himself.

She brushed the sand from her skirt and headed back towards the cottage.

TWENTY-NINE

The mist had rolled in as they reached the causeway, and now, somewhere near the middle of it, it was almost impossible to tell what was water and what was sky. Fin was sitting in the back seat, a knot gathering in his stomach as he waited for the moment when the security gates would materialise out of the murk.

Was this the stupidest thing he had ever done? Putting his trust in this strange, eccentric man with his mad project and sad past? How reliable was he? How likely to forget what they were there for and wander off on some tangent that might leave Fin stuck on Seal Island with nothing but a long swim home? All Fin had was the belief that, for all his oddness, Norman Turner wanted to help. And right now he was the best chance Fin had of making some kind of contact with Maia. The only chance.

'Time to get down.' Norman Turner spoke over his shoulder.

Fin dropped to the floor behind the front seats and pulled the travelling rug down to cover himself as well as he could. He wondered whether this was strictly necessary, but the older man had been insistent. 'We must leave nothing to chance, Finlay,' he had said, retrieving the rug from a cupboard in the back passage of the farmhouse. He'd seemed in unusually high spirits as Fin had walked in earlier that morning, after Turner's insistence that he come to the farm rather than be picked up in the village. 'The fewer

170

people see us together, the better.' And he had been humming to himself ever since they had left.

The car rolled to a halt. Fin smelt the brine on the air as Norman Turner rolled down the window and waited in silence. A tinny voice squawked something at him, and he replied with his name and the name of the person he was meeting at the Institute. The windows went up and after another pause the car rolled forward.

'We're through.'

Fin remained on the floor as they had agreed. His heart was now beating fast. The car travelled a few hundred yards then slowed to a halt again.

'Are you ready?'

'Yes.'

'Then I'll phone you as I leave.' There was an avuncular note in Norman Turner's voice. 'If there's no reply, or you're not ready, I'll phone again as soon as I've arranged to come back and pick up my pillbox.'

Fin threw off the travelling rug, reached for his small backpack and opened the car door.

'Good luck,' said Turner without looking round.

Fin climbed out and closed the door as quietly as he could. It sounded loud in the silence. The car pulled away and a few moments later was swallowed up by the mist. He stood by the roadside, feeling its chill touch on his skin. What would his mother think if she knew what he was doing? What did she think anyway? He'd told her that he needed to get out of the house for twenty-four hours. To be on his own, to start putting himself back together again after Poacher. He was going to go down to Salvation Cove for the day. Take his tent in case he decided to spend the night there, he'd added for good measure. 'OK, love,' she'd said. 'If you're sure that's what you want to do.'

He slipped his arms through the straps of the backpack and stepped away from the road. He could see no more than a few yards ahead, but if he strained his ears he could hear the muted breaking of waves on the shore. He had already decided that it would be safest to follow the shore-line, away from where he imagined the security cameras would be. The mist would make it easier for him, though he would have to watch where he was going.

He headed for the sound of the waves, picking his way carefully across the rough ground. Shapes began to gather themselves out of the gloom. Tumbledown walls, grassy ridges where foundations had once risen. Sad piles of stones. The ruined village. Had it ever had a name? He pictured hardy fisherfolk and their low, smoke-blackened cottages, the men away in their boats, the women mending nets, trudging off to Easthaven with wicker creels on their backs, barefoot children at their skirts. How did places die? Was it famine, or disease, or just that it became too hard to make a living here? He tried to imagine the exodus. Men and women bowed and aged before their years, snivelling hollow-eyed children, trudging out of the village without a backwards glance. Heading to the mainland for work or charity or cheap rooms in some stinking, overcrowded back lane, if they were lucky. Leaving behind nothing but empty cottages and a scattering of fresh graves. And now, just half a mile from here, the island had been brought to life again, not by the sea, but by the wind. A different kind of harvest, one that would never fail so long as the oceans continued to warm up and cool down. Maia knew about this place. But what about other people at the Institute? he wondered. Did they ever visit it and stop to think?

He moved on, the space between his shoulder blades prickling.

For as long as Fin could remember, Danny had had a collection of Ordnance Survey maps. They covered the coastline for a hundred miles in either direction of Whale Island. He remembered his family teasing his father about them – before the accident, of course – and asking why he needed so many maps of the land when he spent all his time at sea, and Maia, quick as a flash, saying, 'In case he gets shipwrecked, of course,' and them all laughing. Then Danny looking thoughtful and shrugging, and saying that he just liked them, no point asking him why, he just did, and there didn't have to be a reason for everything. Now Fin was grateful to him. They had often studied the map of the islands together, and the lie of the land ahead was clear in Fin's mind. Seal Island was roughly the shape of a very lumpy letter T. Little Knossos sat in the left armpit, with the turbine park, sheltered from the north by Lookout Hill, on the lower edge of the left arm. The ruins, marked on the map simply as 'settlement', stood on the right arm. A short way down the stem of the T the land rose into the headland that bulged out around the foot of the small hill crowned by Hangman's Rock, before dropping down again to the entrance to the labyrinth and, beyond that, the long curving strip of beach that fringed the wood where Maia's cottage was.

His heart quickened as the ground began to rise through the mist ahead of him. He was close now. But he had not gone far when he heard the muted sound of voices. He stopped. There was a series of barked commands, and the irregular thud of feet. He stood still, wondering what to do. Then noticed that the thud of feet seemed to fade in an odd way, as if they were not so much receding as being swallowed up by something. Perhaps they were going down into the labyrinth. Whatever was happening, he didn't want to get caught up in it.

He waited till the sounds died away. Then moved off again. The mist was as thick as ever. Something loomed in front of him. A tree. And another. The beginning of the wood. He threaded his way between the trees till a lessening of the gloom indicated a clearing ahead. He paused at the edge. There was the cottage, solid in the mist. All was still. In the deadening silence, Fin's heartbeat thundered in his ears.

For a long time he stood and stared at the cottage. Then he walked out from the trees and up to the front door. He knocked. There was no reply. He knocked again. Still no reply. He scanned the eaves of the cottage for cameras, but could see none. He walked quickly around the building, glancing through windows, but no one was there. For a moment his confidence faltered. Was it really her that he had seen here? He was tempted to go round again, looking inside properly for signs of Maia's presence, possessions he might recognise . . .

He turned and walked back into the wood, far enough not to be visible from the clearing should the mist lift. He found a large tree, took off the backpack and checked the time on his phone. Midday. Maybe she would come back for lunch.

He sat down with his back against the trunk to wait.

THIRTY

Albert Smith went round the Scout hut opening the windows as wide as he could. Walking up the hill from Easthaven, he had watched the mist drift in to cover the southern part of the island. But here the sky was an unbroken blue. Sunlight streamed through the windows and open door and fell on the untidy piles of whaling memorabilia that lined the table and floor.

He hadn't felt much like coming up here since the place had been vandalised. But yesterday morning there had been a letter from the whale-watching people to say that as long as the old slipway didn't need too much work, the project would go ahead and would definitely include a small museum. They would be back in touch once the survey results were through.

This morning he had left the house with a spring in his step. He would start sorting things out properly and redo the inventory while he was at it. First though, he needed to let the old place breathe. And while it did, he would have a cup of tea.

He took the one wooden chair outside, along with the canvas satchel containing his Thermos. He sat down in the sunshine, undid the flask and poured himself a cup. Easthaven lay below him, a cluster of whitewash and stone around the harbour. The sea sparkled beyond, then disappeared under the thick quilt of fog.

He and Sally had had a drink together in the Ship last

night. Well, it was important to support the Archers, to help them to see that life went on. And Shirley Archer was a strong woman, no doubt about that. A survivor. She'd make sure the family was all right. Though on reflection he wasn't sure that going to the Ship had been such a good idea for Sally . . . That poor boy's death had really shaken her. Just when it seemed she was starting to get over her own experience. And last night she had seemed . . . not exactly agitated – Sally always managed to appear calm, no matter what was going on – but opaque, like the fog. She admitted to him that she was sleeping badly, and she told him about another of those peculiar waking dreams. An enormous wave. Well . . . setting aside the very strange incident of the yacht running aground, you didn't have to be Sigmund Freud to figure out that a dream, even a daytime reverie, about a giant destructive wave was likely to have something to do with her recent experiences.

He sighed and sipped his tea. What Sally needed right now was a bit of calm – like the sea out there this morning. Sunlit. Deep blue. Unruffled. He'd have to keep an eye on her. Though it wasn't only Sally who was suffering. These events, these single moments of destructive force, set off waves – the idea seemed not to want to leave him alone this morning – that overtook so many people in their outward surge. There was the poor young lad, Peter – Albert prayed it had been quick and painless. The next to be caught up were his family. Then that pretty young lass he had been going out with – along with Fin Carpenter, his best friend. Then their families. And friends and relatives of the Archers, like Albert himself. Then *their* friends and relatives. How many households had the actions of those bombers touched? And Albert was thinking only of Peter Archer. Seven other people had died in the attack, and more than a hundred had been injured. No one had yet claimed responsibility, but the police said it bore the hallmarks of the previous attack, the one Sally had been caught up in, and they were treating it as a concerted, racially motivated campaign. They were urging the public, especially in ethnic communities, to be at their most vigilant.

He finished his tea, shook out the dregs on to the ground, and stood up. His eye was drawn to the last white cottage on the left, beyond the harbour, a little apart from the others. One of the pleasures he and Sally took in each other's company was a good gossip. Nothing malicious, of course. But a look at island life under the microscope, or through the telescope, depending on how you chose to see it. Who was doing what? Where were the undercurrents? It was, he supposed, a way of feeling connected to all those people whose lives eddied around them. Anyway, something she'd said last night had intrigued him. He had mentioned his encounter with Gus Steerman, adding that he'd been surprised to learn that Gus and Linda had been having problems at the time they'd left the island.

A fleeting look of sympathy had crossed Sally's face. 'You were nursing Irene at the time. Of course you wouldn't have heard the rumours.'

'What were they? The rumours . . .'

'That Linda Steerman was having an affair.'

'While Gus was at sea, I suppose.'

Sally shook her head. 'No. That was the odd thing. It seemed she was as good as gold while he was away. According to whoever was putting the rumour about . . . and you never know, do you, where it starts? Someone sees something. Someone else says something. And in no time the story has a life all of its own. Anyway, she was the model wife while he was away, apparently. It was only when he was on shore that she misbehaved.'

Albert raised an eyebrow. 'Seems an odd way of going about it.'

Sally had shrugged and smiled again. 'In my experience, Albert, dear, so much in life is not how one expects it to be.'

She was right, he thought now, carrying the chair back inside. He liked things to be logical and orderly – which was doubtless why he had taken on the job of looking after the museum. But reality was often so much closer to the random, ill-assorted piles that littered the inside of the hut and now challenged him to sort them out.

Well, all right, he thought. I'm up to the challenge.

He took off his jacket and set to work.

THIRTY-ONE

A strange wind blew through the Institute whenever the labyrinth programme was running. It carried with it a fine grit of suppressed expectation that invaded the workings of the normal daily routine and left everyone restless, on edge.

Maia had seen the coach arrive the previous evening, seen the faces at the windows taking in their new surroundings, some eager, some obviously apprehensive. And now, a few hundred yards from the desk where she sat, they were being tested to the very limits of their physical and mental endurance. 'Green Energies Security Consultants foil turbine terrorists', 'Green Energies Security Consultants win new conflict-zone contracts', 'World first for Green Energies Security Consultants at new icecap energy farm' – she'd written the press releases herself. The more the world came to rely on sustainable energy, the more vulnerable the installations became to threats. And these guys were the toughest around. But even among the tough guys, as Sean had said, there were sheep and goats. And at this very moment, hundreds of feet below ground, they were being sorted into their respective species.

Maia had never been into the labyrinth. It was out of bounds to everyone except Sean and his team. She imagined it was a network of tunnels where, perhaps, the men were confronted by some modern version of the minotaur, some terrifying psychological and physical challenge that they had to overcome. Sean had told her a little about the programme, the training and evaluation objectives, the ten-point axis that featured psychological stability, stress management, emotional response, upper-body strength, lower-body strength, cardiovascular fitness and other things she couldn't remember. But what actually went on in there he wouldn't tell her, and she was left to guess. She'd seen the faces of the participants when they came out, and her rational mind told her she was better off not knowing, though another, less civilised, part of her longed to find out.

She always felt distracted on these days, this morning doubly so. Try as she might, she couldn't ignore the thought of Terry and that woman he'd assaulted. She sat at her screen and struggled to engage with the relentless out-pouring of information from the Green Energies Seal Island Research Institute to the world beyond. A slow, steady tide of reports, press releases, scientific papers, research studies, web pages, all promoting the excellence – no, the pre-eminence – of Green Energies' work, without ever, of course, revealing the technological secrets at its heart. It was rather like Sean's description of the labyrinth programme, she thought, a picture painted only with the broadest of brushstrokes. But it seemed to work. With eighteen months still to go until the unveiling of the Super Turbine, Green Energies' stock had never been higher on the world's equity markets.

Not that wind power was universally popular, of course. And part of the job involved countering, pre-empting or if possible spoiling the arguments of the various opposing camps, such as the environmentalists, who worked themselves into a froth over the habitat of horned snails and other zoological or botanical curiosities. But they never had any money, and as long as governments could be dissuaded from getting behind them, they weren't much of a problem. Middle-class Nimbys, however, the category Maia most despised, were often surprisingly well organised and persistent in their efforts to resist anything they considered unsightly or noisy being planted in their backyards. And then there was the old adversary, relentless, monolithic, still lumbering on – the nuclear lobby. Well, as far as Maia was concerned, it didn't matter how clean the energy itself might be, because burying spent plutonium with its half-life of five hundred millennia was tantamount to giving the planet a vast dose of lethal poison.

Maia had long ago convinced herself that clean, renewable energy was so critical to the future survival of the planet that nothing – snails, pristine landscapes or terawatts of nuclear energy – should be allowed to get in its way. This was what she reminded herself when she found her attention wandering or her enthusiasm for the job on hand waning. But right now, with this febrile, unsettling atmosphere around her, as well as her gnawing thoughts about Terry, she could barely concentrate.

She looked at her watch. Twelve thirty. Half an hour till lunch. She returned her attention to the screen and the press release about the new strategic alliance formed by the Institute with the Windlab Symposium of Ashgabat, Turkmenistan. She tried to imagine the dry winds that must blow ceaselessly across the steppes of central Asia. Wondered what it would be like to live a thousand miles from the sea.

The longer Fin sat under the tree, the more his thoughts seemed to tie themselves in knots and the more his tongue felt like cotton wool. What if he had to wait here all day? What if she didn't live here after all? He opened his backpack and fished for one of the bars of chocolate he'd brought. The sweetness made him feel more grounded. He looked at the cottage to see if, by any chance, she might have slipped in unnoticed while he was lost in his thoughts. But he could sense its emptiness mocking him across the clearing. He scanned the trees beyond for signs of movement, then felt his pulse quicken as he was rewarded with the glimpse of a figure approaching down the path through the wood. A figure with the rapid, almost angry steps of someone who was flustered. The figure stepped out into the clearing and Fin's heart turned a somersault.

It was Maia.

He didn't want her to see him till he was ready. He slipped behind the tree, peered round the trunk. But Maia looked neither left nor right. She strode straight down the path to the front door, opened it with the key she already held in her hand and went inside without closing it.

For a moment Fin simply stood and stared after her, his heart pounding. Whatever else might have changed in the last eighteen months, the way she dressed hadn't. Still the same sandals, short denim skirt and cotton top. Dark curls pulled back off her face with tortoiseshell combs. The bag was new though. A large patchwork affair with wooden hoops for handles. All this he absorbed in an instant, as his mind started to race again and a cold sweat broke out under his arms. This was not someone who had sauntered home for lunch. This was someone who had had to come back unexpectedly, perhaps because she'd forgotten something, and resented it. Which meant that she wouldn't be staying long. If he was going to make his move at all, it had to be now. He reached for the backpack and stood up, then walked out of the trees, across the clearing and up to the front door.

THIRTY-TWO

He could hear her moving around in one of the rooms off the short passage that led in from the open front door. He stood on the threshold for several moments, trying to take control of his emotions, then knocked at the open front door.

A pause. Then, 'Coming.'

Moments later she appeared in the passage. She took a couple of steps towards the front door. Then stopped. Her eyes widening.

'*Fin . . . ?*'

'Hello, Maia.'

'Wh . . . how . . . I mean, what are you doing here?'

Her face seemed to collapse, almost as if she'd been hit. Then recover itself as pleasure, guilt, confusion flashed across it in quick succession.

'I came to see you.' He was still standing in the doorway. He longed to step forward and hug her. But she remained motionless.

'Oh my God, Fin! Why . . . how? Like – *how* did you know I was here?'

'I saw you. At the Open Day.'

She seemed lost for words.

'It was just luck,' he said, trying to keep his voice level. 'I came for a walk down on the beach with Poacher. The rain came on. We went into the wood. To take cover. And I just happened to see you here, at the door.' He paused. A lump rose in his throat. This was all wrong. He wanted to be saying the important things that clamoured in his mind, like: How could you come here and not let us know? What have we done to you? Do you realise you're breaking Mum's heart? And do you have any idea how much I miss you?

But instead, before he could stop himself, he blurted out, 'Poacher's dead, Maia.' And burst into tears.

She put a hand to her mouth.

'Oh no, Fin . . . what happened?' Her face creasing in sympathy.

'He was killed in that bombing. A fortnight ago.' He fumbled in his pocket for a tissue. 'Staying with his new girlfriend.'

'Oh God, Fin – I'm so sorry.'

The hug came at last. Though even in his wretchedness, Fin was aware of a stiffness about her. Her body somehow at odds with her emotions.

'No, *I'm* sorry.' After a little while he pulled away. 'Coming here to crack up on you wasn't part of the plan.' He forced a smile.

She nodded. Traces of shock and confusion still evident in her face.

'So what *was* the plan?' Now she looked awkward. Clasped her hands together. 'I'm not coming home, you know. I *can't*. Not till that bastard's six feet under.' She paused, caught her breath. 'That . . . that's not what you've come to tell me – is it?'

Fin shook his head.

'Pity.' She said it to herself. Then gave him an apologetic look. 'So. Why did you come?' She tried again.

Fin swallowed. 'Because you're my sister, Maia. Because we haven't heard from you for so long and because . . . I love you.' He'd never said that before. He felt the blood rush to his face. 'And I thought maybe you'd . . . gone. For good. But you're here on Seal Island.' He made a conciliatory gesture. 'And I guess I just want to know why.'

Now again he could see the conflict in her face. And with Maia, where there was uncertainty, anger was never far away.

'But if you really don't want me here, I'll go. Right now. Leave you alone.' He took a step away from her.

Maia chewed her lip. Looked down at the ground, then at the trees beyond. Colour flooded her cheeks.

'Yes. I think it would be better, Fin.'

Although he had rehearsed this moment in his mind, along with all the other possible endings to their conversation, he had never believed it would happen this way. Now that it had, he felt like the skipper of a boat that has struck rocks. Was this the end then? The last time he would see his sister? Ever?

'OK. I'll . . . I'll go. But there's one thing I want to say . . .'

'Go on.'

'There's something not right here, Maia. At the Institute. And I'm worried. Really worried. That guy who was here in the cottage, the day I saw you. I know him. Sean. We got into a fight. He called me a fucking nigger. He's a racist, Maia. And what are you doing with a racist like that? I mean . . . what does he call *you*?'

Now the anger blazed up in Maia's eyes. 'OK, that's enough. It's time you went.' She turned to go inside.

'But that's not all,' Fin called after her. 'There was a girl who worked here. Charlotte Svensson.'

Maia stopped. Turned round.

'What about her?'

'She fell off the bridge.'

'I know.'

'I was there. When she died.'

Maia's mouth dropped open.

'I was walking home from Cable Sands. She almost landed on me.' He looked Maia in the eye. 'But I don't think she fell . . .'

For the second time Maia's face seemed to collapse. All the anger and defiance left her in an instant.

'You'd better come in,' she said.

Ever since Fin could remember, Maia had been a pacer. Unable to keep still when she was agitated, or excited, or simply gripped by a thought. Her ceaseless movement had been almost as much a feature of his childhood as the ebb and flow of the tides around Whale Island. And now, as he sat on the settee and recounted what had happened beneath the bridge, Maia paced up and down the narrow corridor between the furniture and the wall of the little sitting room, arms crossed at her chest, head lowered in concentration. When he came to relate how Eugene Hunter had finally appeared, she stopped him several times and asked him to describe in more detail what the head of security had said, how he had sounded, his behaviour.

When he had finished she said nothing, but kept pacing, hugging her thoughts to herself as if afraid they might somehow escape.

'You knew her?' said Fin at last, unable to stand the silence any longer.

She seemed to ignore him. Continued pacing. Then stopped. She pointed through the opposite wall of the living room.

'There. She slept there. She was my room-mate.' Her eyes brimmed with tears.

'Oh Maia. You too . . .'

She nodded wretchedly.

For a moment Fin thought she was going to give in to the tears. But she sniffed and recovered herself.

'Lottie Svensson, my best friend.' She paused. 'My one-time best friend.'

'I'm sorry, Maia. Really, really sorry.'

Brittle though she could be, Fin longed to put his arms around his older sister and comfort her. Feel the comfort of her too, if he was honest. He looked at her wrestling to keep her emotions under control, and wondered about Green Energies and their induction programme. Could she have been – altered – in some way? Could he see a change in her? Outwardly, not much. Her hair was cut a little differently. She might, he thought, be wearing different make-up. And inwardly? Everything he had seen so far suggested she was still the same angry, passionate, restless, headstrong, confused sister he had always known – and adored. So more than anything, he still wanted to know why? Why his sister hadn't been in touch with him when she was just five miles away. Even though she hated Danny, even though she might hold Kath partly responsible for Danny's continuing reign of misery, Fin knew of no reason for her to blame him. And there was no getting away from it. The real turning point had not been her leaving home. It had been the job. But now, ironically, it seemed they were being drawn back together by the Institute, by the dead girl who'd crashed out of the mist at his feet. Nothing in life could have prepared him for a moment as strange as this. It seemed to Fin it was the only safe route he had with Maia, for now anyway. He took it gratefully.

'So what . . . what do *you* know about Lottie, Maia?' he said gently. 'About how she died?'

Maia sat down. Not beside him on the settee, but on the wooden chair at the table at the window, where there was a laptop and papers. Beyond, mist still swirled through the clearing, framing her face with drab grey.

'We were told,' she said slowly, 'that she committed suicide. Not how, at first. But later we heard that she had asked Eugene to stop on the bridge, that she was feeling ill and thought she might be sick. Then she made a run for it. Climbed the parapet . . .'

Fin was startled to notice that she was doing what Kath did. Twisting the silver ring she wore on the fourth finger of her right hand as she spoke. Round and round. A sedentary alternative to the pacing.

'But she wasn't depressed. She had no reason to do it. I know. I *know*, Fin. I was her room-mate, for Chrissake. She had everything going for her here. They said she was on antidepressants. But I'm sure she wasn't – that they were just vitamin pills. But they tidied up all her stuff before I could check. Then they took it away. Left nothing.' Her voice had begun to crack. 'There's nothing left of her.' She gestured despairingly around the room. 'No trace left of Lottie . . .'

Her shoulders heaved, and this time she could not hold back the tears. Fin made to get up from the settee, but she held up a hand. He waited while she left the room and returned with tissues. She sat down on the wooden chair again, crossed one leg over the other and turned her shoulder towards him. Don't come any closer, the gesture said.

'Do you know what happened?' he asked. 'I mean, why she might . . . not have committed suicide?'

Maia paused. Then shook her head.

'There was nothing going on here? She wasn't in trouble?'

This time her shake of the head was more emphatic.

After a long moment's silence Fin said, 'You don't think she jumped. Neither do I.' He looked at her, willing her to return his stare. Which she eventually did. 'So what should we do about it?'

Now she sounded defensive. 'I don't want to *do* anything. I just want to know. For her sake.'

Fin looked at her in disbelief.

'But . . . but if she didn't jump, that means she was pushed. In other words, she was murdered, Maia – I mean, you can't just *know* about something like that. You have to *do* something. *We* have to do something.'

'Like what?'

'Like go to the police.'

'I – I don't think that would be a good idea. Look, this is Institute business. Anyway, the police have already put in their report.'

'But . . . I don't understand. We've got new evidence to give to them . . .'

She gave him the contemptuous look that had always made him feel like a five-year-old on his first day at school.

'No we don't, Fin. What evidence? We have two people speculating, that's all. We don't have a shred of evidence between us. Voices in the mist – that's all you've got, Fin. And a feeling – that's what I've got. A feeling that my best friend wasn't suicidal. A feeling that what they told me were antidepressants were plain ordinary vitamin supplements. Voices and feelings, Fin. The police would just tell us to piss off.'

He had forgotten this trick of Maia's. Her ability to deflate him, leave him feeling winded. Now he struggled to recover himself.

'So . . . you're saying that although we both suspect Lottie was murdered, we should do nothing about it?'

'Yes.' She sounded defiant.

Fin paused. He felt angry now. 'You know what that makes me think?'

She shook her head.

'That you're covering something up. Protecting . . . I don't know what.'

'No! That's—'

'Then why can't we go to the police?'

'Because I don't know that I'm right. You don't know that you're right. And there's important stuff going on here. No one would thank me for calling the police back in again, taking up everyone's time.' Her voice was losing its edge. Becoming softer, younger. 'So yes, in a way, I am protecting them, I suppose.' She smiled at him, the full seductress's beam, lips parted, white teeth gleaming, dark eyes flashing. 'But not in the way you think.'

She was good-looking, his sister; there was no denying it. But Fin wasn't going to fall for this trick either.

'Does this place really make you so happy that you'll do that for it?' he asked. 'The work. The people. Not seeing us . . . me – just down the road?! Have I done something to deserve that?'

Her expression changed. She shook her head. 'Of course not. It's not you, Fin. It's just him. I can't come back while he's still there. And, well . . .' her voice began to lose conviction, 'since I can't see you, I thought it was easier not to have any contact. Less upsetting for you and Mum. D'you understand that?'

He returned her look. 'Not really. You could have rung. Sent a postcard. At least met us somewhere. Maia – we didn't know what had happened to you. You might have been dead, for all we knew. Like Lottie.'

He regretted it as soon as he said it.

Her eyes blazed. 'Yes. Well. It's time you went. I've got to get back to work.'

'All right,' Fin said, his heart pounding. 'I'll go. But at least tell me if I'm going to see you again. Will you come and meet us? Me and Mum.'

She had turned her back on him now, and was gathering up papers from the table.

'I don't know,' she said. 'Maybe. Maybe not. But I'll tell you one thing: you'd better not show up here again like this. It could get me into real trouble.' She turned round. 'By the way – how did you get in?'

'I – I got a lift in. With someone who had a meeting.'

She raised an eyebrow. 'Can you get back out the same way?'

'Yes.'

'Good. Well . . . you'd better get going.' She reached for her bag and placed a sheaf of papers in it.

Fin stood up. 'OK. But Maia – if you could see us, it would mean everything to Mum. She's given him an ultimatum, you know. Told him she'll go if he doesn't shape up.'

'Hmm.' Maia sounded sceptical.

'Well . . . will you ring me? At least.'

'I'll . . . try.'

'OK. Bye then.' He stepped towards her. She didn't resist when he hugged her. But this time he was even more aware of the stiffness.

He walked out of the cottage and across the clearing.

Only when he reached the shelter of the trees did he realise that beneath all the other undercurrents – the

191

obvious confusion and ambivalence about Lottie's death, the strangely divided loyalty to the Institute, the frankly unconvincing excuse for her silence – the emotion his sister had been transmitting most for the last half-hour had been fear.

Maia was afraid.

THIRTY-THREE

Once, when Fin had been seven and Maia ten, they'd taken buckets and nets and gone round the point beyond the harbour. There was a pool there, someone had told Fin, that held the biggest shrimps on Whale Island. Monsters. The size of sausages. It had been a summer's day, hot and cloudless. They'd made their way round the point, out of sight of Easthaven, bursting with the sense of adventure, the promise of great bounty. They hadn't told Kath or Danny where they were going. All the way there they'd imagined their homecoming, buckets brimming with giant shrimps, Kath and Danny beaming with pride as they sat down to the shrimp supper of all time.

It had taken them a long while, almost all morning, but eventually they'd found what they thought was the pool. It was right at the end of a long finger of rock that ran out from the shore. They had to splash through shallow, sandy pools to get on to it, then scramble along the spine, with its knobbly, slippery coating of limpets and seaweed, sidestepping the deep water-filled crevasses that split it along its length. When they came to the pool they were only a few feet from the sea, washing around the tip of the rocks, chest deep, limpid green and cool-looking.

And there had been shrimps there. Not quite the size of sausages, but plentiful all the same. Prancing and scuttling, skulking under stones and fronds of weed. Translucent in the clear water like ghosts. They abandoned their nets and set about catching them in cupped hands, standing knee deep in the water and waiting till the little crustaceans swam into place, then snapping shut their palms and lifting them quickly out of the water, squealing at the tickle of tiny legs and feelers before dropping them into the buckets.

The day wore on. The sun beat down and the buckets filled. They began to grow weary. They shouldered the nets and made their way back along the spine of rock, treading like cats to avoid spilling their ghostly treasure. To be halted by a ten-foot expanse of surging tide where the shallow, sandy pools had been that morning. And Maia had rounded on him.

'This was your idea. What do you suggest we do now?'

Fin fought to hold back the tears of helpless terror that were starting to well.

Maia walked to the very edge of the rock and looked down. The water was clouded with sand churned up by the movement of the tide. There was no way of telling how deep it was.

She turned back to Fin. 'Well,' she said furiously, 'we obviously can't stay here. So we're going to have to swim for it. The sooner the better, before this gets any deeper. And I really, really hope you make it, Fin, because I really, really don't want to have to tell Mum and Dad that you've drowned. This is all your fault, you and your monster shrimps. You . . . you idiot!'

And unfair though it was, her rage had galvanised him to flop down into the surging water after her, buckets and nets abandoned, and grip her hand as they half-hopped, half-swam across the chin-deep channel, gasping and spluttering mouthfuls of salty water as the current tried to tug them round the point and out into the bay beyond. But they'd made it. And they walked home shrimpless,

194

in sodden shorts and T-shirts, to be met with a roasting from Danny for going off without saying where. And only then had Maia burst into tears. Fin had watched her sob into Kath's bosom, and Kath had comforted her, stroking her hair and saying, 'There, there, sweetheart, you're safe now. It's OK. It's OK.' And Fin had realised then that his big sister had been truly afraid. But later, as he lay warm and safe in his own bed in the moments before drifting off to sleep, it was the anger in her face that he remembered. And he knew, even then, that it was what had saved them.

The mist was as thick as ever. It brushed at him as he retraced his steps through the wood, keeping the sound of the sea on his right this time. But now the mist was chilling and clammy, whereas before it had been merely dense. He stopped and took out his phone. Two o'clock. He felt as if he had been there for ages. But it was only a little over an hour. He dialled Norman Turner's number and was relieved when he answered. He was still on the island, eating a sandwich in the Institute car park. But the earlier excitement seemed to have left him, Fin noticed. When he asked how Fin had got on, his voice sounded flat.

As Fin moved on through the trees a breath of wind stirred. Ahead, the mist began to thin and the outline of Hangman's Rock hill gained definition. He swung left to skirt the landward side of the hill, and saw a figure. It was no more than twenty yards away and it had its back to him, bent forward, hands on knees, in a posture of exhaustion. A moment later another figure appeared beside the first and sank soundlessly to the ground. The faint breath of wind had now become a breeze. Holes were appearing in the mist, ragged patches of blue sky, veiled glimpses of glinting water. And more figures were becoming visible. Fin glanced around for cover. If the mist cleared he would be in plain view of them, whichever way he went.

A few paces to his left a drainage ditch ran towards the shore. He dropped to the ground and crawled towards it. It was thigh deep, with a trickle of brackish water in its bed and a fringe of coarse, spiky grass. He rolled into it, feeling his trainers sinking into mud which released a strong sulphurous odour. He wriggled out of the backpack and, crouching, peered through the fringe of grasses.

The mist had now almost evaporated. Sunlight bathed the figures who had joined the first two. Nearly a dozen now. Like marathon runners at the end of a race, they looked spent, lying or sitting or standing in various postures of physical collapse. But unlike marathon runners, there was no smiling winner among them. No. This was a group of men who seemed shocked by what they had experienced, faces slack with relief at whatever ordeal they had completed.

They were all dressed the same. Black baseball caps, black T-shirts, black combat trousers tucked into black army boots. They ranged in age from the early twenties to middle age. Despite their exhaustion, they all seemed lean and muscular, men who kept themselves in good physical shape.

There was some kind of commotion beyond Fin's line of sight. Heads turned in the direction of the entrance to the labyrinth. Moments later another similarly clad figure stumbled into view, with the inert form of a companion draped over his shoulder. He staggered towards the group, tipped his companion head first on to the ground and collapsed himself. He lay there, knees in the air, chest heaving.

At that moment there was a shouted command and the figures started to clamber to their feet. Fin's heart began to race as Sean strode into view, also dressed in black, but minus the cap and carrying a clipboard. He was joined a few moments later by two other men, who appeared to be his assistants. At another command the men fell into two ragged lines. All except the figure who had been carried from the labyrinth. He now lay motionless on the ground where he had landed. Sean walked over to him. Stood for a moment looking down. Then said something to which there was no response. He shook his head and gave the man a vicious kick in the ribs. The man squirmed and grunted in pain, then heaved himself to his feet and shuffled into place in the waiting line. A final command from Sean, and the men moved off at a weary trot, back along the track towards the Institute, the two assistants bringing up the rear. Sean hung back for a short while. He appeared to be scanning the ground for something. Whatever it was, he didn't find it. He shrugged and set off after the men at walking pace. Within a couple of minutes they had all rounded a bend in the track and disappeared from view.

Fin waited a little longer to be sure no one else was going to appear from the labyrinth, then climbed out of the ditch. His trainers were coated with foul-smelling orange slime. He wiped them on a clump of grass. Then, curiosity overcoming him, he walked round the foot of the hillock, past where the men had gathered. Just as he remembered, the grassy gulley deepened as it approached the entrance to the labyrinth. But now a tarmacked track ran along its bed. And at the end, where once there had been a dark gaping maw, there was now a pair of heavy steel doors.

He stood for a few moments looking at the doors, remembering the fear he'd felt standing here as a child, his imagination bristling with the horrors that might lie in wait in the depths of those old mine workings.

Then he turned away. As he retraced his steps around the side of the mound he spotted a black baseball cap lying half concealed behind a tussock of grass. He bent down to pick it up. Above the peak it had the words: *Green Energies Security Consultants*. Fastened to the peak itself were two small, round pin-on badges. One said simply: *Sean – The Boss*. The other had no words, but an emblem. It was like a comb with a row of curved white teeth, all of the same size except the left-hand one, which was twice as long as the rest and had a dripping red tip. He held it his hands, turning it over, wondering what it stood for.

Then he unshouldered the pack and put the cap inside it.

He set off along the shore towards the rendezvous with Norman Turner.

THIRTY-FOUR

An hour later Fin was back at Number Thirteen. He could see the flicker of the television through the sitting-room window. It wouldn't be Kath – she was at work. Which meant only one thing. He opened the front door as quietly as he could, but he had not reached the foot of the stairs when Danny's voice called out.

'That you, son?'

'Yes,' Fin replied.

The television went silent. He could hear his father's shuffling movement. He waited.

'You're back early.'

At least it wasn't an accusation.

Danny appeared in the kitchen.

'Thought you'd gone camping.'

'Yes. Changed my mind.'

Danny was standing with one hand on the back of a kitchen chair. Fin could smell beer on his breath. But he seemed steady enough on his feet. And he didn't have that red-eyed, bleary look that Fin dreaded.

'Not in the mood?'

'Something like that.'

Danny nodded. 'Not thinking too much about the Archer lad, eh?'

'No.'

'That's the stuff, son. So . . . fancy a cuppa?'

'You mean, do I want to make you a cup of tea?'

Danny grinned. 'Good lad.'

'Sit down,' said Fin. He switched the kettle on. 'Just going upstairs to dump my stuff.'

Danny was trying, there was no doubt about it. Even though it infuriated Fin that he still couldn't call Poacher by his name . . . Even though at this moment a cup of tea with his dad was the last thing Fin felt like. How would he react if he knew where his son had really spent the morning? What would he say to the news that Maia was so near, on Seal Island? Fin wasn't about to find out. That was one thing he was clear about. Perhaps the only thing.

'Kettle's boiling.' Danny's voice carried upstairs.

Fin dropped the backpack on the bed and went down to the kitchen.

'So what you been up to this morning?' Fin asked, even though he knew what the answer was going to be.

Danny didn't say anything till Fin had placed the two mugs of tea on the table and sat down opposite him.

'Went for a walk.'

Fin gaped in disbelief.

Danny grinned again and nodded. 'Walked along the beach. Took me a while. But I made it to the far end and back.'

'Hey!' said Fin.

'Decided it was time to get off my arse. Get some fresh air. Make sure the good one doesn't pack up on me.' He patted the uninjured leg. Then pulled a dismissive face. 'Getting bored with the Mission. Same old faces, day in, day out. Give them a break for a while. Might even take up studying something.'

'Studying . . . really?'

'Computer, maybe. Learn how to use that Internet. Do an evening class in Cliffton. Get the bus.' He gave Fin a sidelong glance. 'I know what you're thinking: your mum's been getting at me.' He shook his head. 'Well, OK, she has. But I been doing some thinking of my own too, see. Since your pal died. Made me figure you're only here once. Don't want to be a miserable bastard for the rest of my life.'

I'll drink to that, said Fin to himself. 'Poacher would be pleased to know that, Dad,' he said out loud. He took a sip of tea and raised a silent toast to his mother and her ultimatum.

'Dad, d'you know anything about the Institute?' he asked on a whim. 'I don't mean what they do – more what . . . kind of organisation they are?'

'How do you mean?' Danny looked at him sharply.

'I mean . . . well, there they are, down on Seal Island. There must be fifty or sixty people working there – that's what I reckoned when I went to the Open Day. And we never see them. They might as well not be there. Have you ever met any of them? Or have any of your friends down the Mission?'

'Why you interested in the Institute all of a sudden?' His eyes narrowed. 'Not about to go all green, are you? Like your sister.'

Already Fin was regretting the question. 'No. Just wondering. Because Charlotte, that girl, the one who . . . fell. She worked there . . .'

Danny nodded and grunted.

'Anyway . . . I was just thinking about it this morning.'

'Well, since you're asking . . .' The familiar sourness crept back into Danny's voice. 'Yes, I did. They advertised for a driver when they first started up. Nothing long distance. I could have done it easily – in an automatic. Here to Cliffton station, here to the airport. Picking up visitors. Taking them back again. That kind of thing. But they gave it to someone from the mainland. Even though I was the only islander to apply. Something about not being able to get insurance for someone in my condition.' He looked at Fin. There was no pride in his face now. 'No good for anyone or anything – story of my bleedin' life. Anyway. Bastards. That's what I think of the Institute.' He pushed away the mug. Reached for his stick and levered himself out of the chair. 'I'm going back next door.'

He shuffled out of the room, leaving Fin looking after him. No 'Thanks for the tea'. No 'Nice to get a chat, son'. How little it took to plunge him back into his anger and self-pity and hatred for the world.

Fin got up and washed the mugs, then left the house. He walked down to the harbour and out to his place on the wall. He hadn't been back since he and the Duck had sat here on the day of Poacher's funeral. He climbed up and turned to face out to sea. There was no trace of the earlier mist in any direction. He peeled off his shirt and sat for some time, feeling the heat of the sun soaking into his body.

He had seen Maia, spoken to her, touched her. And now his feelings were in turmoil, his mind a cacophony of questions. *Why* had she not got in touch with him? What was she frightened of? Was she really at the Institute of her own free will . . . ? He had started to talk to Norman Turner in the car on the way back to Easthaven, but the older man's mood had changed. The boyish sense of adventure had gone. And although he'd listened attentively when Fin spoke, and offered what advice he could, he'd seemed preoccupied, almost withdrawn. When Fin had asked him if anything was the matter, he had smiled and thanked Fin politely for his concern and said that he just felt a little tired, he was not used to so much excitement.

And for a moment, disappointed though he was, Fin had felt concerned for the older man with his odd ways, almost fond of him.

He glanced down to where a patrol of small silver fish slid through the clear green water below his feet, maintaining perfect formation as if joined by tiny invisible wires. Fin would have given anything to be one of them right now. Preferably the one at the back, swimming happily along without a care. Following everyone else and not having to give a moment's thought as to where to go or what to do next. Instead of which he felt like one of the sacrificial Athenians, lost in the labyrinth, alone and terrified, with no lamp to light the way forward.

What did he know that was certain, that he could lay out on his mental workbench like the components of one of his contraptions? Not much really. One girl had died in suspicious circumstances. Another, feared missing, had been found. And the organisation they both worked for employed a vicious thug. What would Leonardo da Vinci have made of it? What leaps of the imagination would he have summoned to assemble the components into some perfectly running, smoothly functioning machine? Or would there have been too many weak links, too much speculation and thin air? Yet it was the hunches, the blind leaps of faith, of the imagination, that had brought some of the greatest minds to their discoveries. And Fin's instinct told him that something was wrong on Scal Island. Very wrong.

Should he tell his mum? Go back to the police? Confront Hunter? Right now he didn't know and couldn't think. God, he wished Poacher was still here. He would give anything just to hear his voice, see his big cheerful face, talk through everything that had happened with his best friend, someone he trusted . . .

He could feel his back beginning to burn. He turned over and stretched out on top of the wall, put his rolled-up shirt behind his head and shut his eyes. Through his closed lids the sunlight was making black spots in his vision. He had been frowning with concentration, he realised. He let the muscles of his face relax, and the spots dissolved into dancing pinpricks of light, myriads of them, like the synapses firing away overtime in his brain.

THIRTY-FIVE

It was mid-afternoon when Maia's phone rang and Terry asked her to meet him in his office. There was an unfamiliar note to his voice that made her feel instantly anxious.

Her unease increased when she entered the office and saw Eugene Hunter. They were both sitting at the low table in the corner opposite Terry's desk. Through the glass wall she could see past the trees to the sea, now in full sunlight after the morning's mist. Terry gave her a brief smile and nodded to the remaining seat. Eugene's face betrayed nothing. There was not a person on Seal Island – apart, perhaps, from Terry and maybe Sean, and Maia wasn't even certain about them – who wasn't a little afraid of Eugene Hunter. Stockily built, with wire-framed spectacles and the trace of a Zimbabwean accent, he looked in his dark suit like a bank manager. But his raison d'être was to ensure that nothing compromised the security of the Institute. He trusted no one, and for that reason most people at the Institute, including Maia, reciprocated his distrust. The office joke went that in place of a brain he had the tiny brass workings of a Swiss watch, while his heart had simply been removed at birth.

Terry waited till Maia had settled into her seat, then picked up a remote control and pointed it at a screen set into the opposite wall. The screen came to life with grainy images from a security camera. They revealed a figure standing in the approach to the labyrinth, then turning and walking away, jerkily, frame by frame.

Maia's stomach plunged.

It was Fin.

'You recognise him, OK?' asked Eugene.

Maia wondered if they could hear her heart pounding. She was going to have to tell them the truth. Or a version of it at least. Oh God, how could Fin have been so stupid? She'd been in an agony of confusion as she watched him walk away from the cottage. Torn between the hurt she knew she was causing him, her own uncertainty about Lottie's death, the news about Sean, and a strangely powerful yet contradictory feeling of loyalty to the Institute, to Terry. Which, little by little, over the next couple of hours, had seemed to reassert itself until she was burning with indignation at the way Fin had dared to march into her life, presuming that she wanted to see him. He had no right. And even if he *had* been there when Lottie had died, it was nothing more than coincidence. Life was full of coincidences; they didn't come with any entitlements.

'Yes. It's my brother,' she replied.

'Do you know what he was doing here?'

'Yes. He came to see me. This morning.'

'How did he know you were here, Maia?' asked Terry.

'He said he saw me at the Open Day. By chance.'

'And you believe him?' asked Eugene.

'Yes, I do.'

'So why did he come to see you today?'

'He said he wanted to talk to me.'

'What about?'

'He said he missed me. He was upset that I hadn't been in touch.'

'And why hadn't you? Easthaven's just a few miles away.'

'That's my old life.' Maia shrugged, then gestured at the building around her. 'This is where I belong now.'

Eugene and Terry exchanged glances.

'Maia,' said Terry, with a look she couldn't penetrate, 'did he mention that he was there when Lottie died?'

Now her heartbeat doubled.

'Yes,' she said. 'Yes, he did.' She hesitated. 'So . . . you knew . . . ?'

'We knew,' replied Eugene.

'Why . . . ? Why didn't you tell me?'

'Because we thought it would make the whole thing more difficult for you,' said Terry.

'But it was a very odd coincidence, all the same, wasn't it?' Eugene now.

'Yes, it was.' Where was this conversation going? she wondered.

'What did he say about it?' It was Eugene again.

'Just that he'd been there when she . . . er . . . fell. And I told him she was my room-mate. That was a . . . a big shock to him. And he said – he said he felt very sorry for her.' She looked down. 'And for me too,' she added.

Terry nodded. In sympathy, Maia thought.

'How did you leave it with him?' Eugene again.

'I had to tell him to go. He wanted to stay. He was . . . still upset with me . . .'

'And will you get in touch with him?'

She hesitated. 'No.' Then looked from one to the other. 'Have I . . . ? Have I done something wrong?'

To her surprise it was Eugene who shook his head. 'Look, Maia, if I wanted to make trouble for you, I could say that you should have reported what happened at once,

207

OK? Though in the circumstances I can see why you didn't. But we have to take all intrusions very seriously, you understand? Which is why we have to ask you these questions. I can see you've been honest with us, OK. And I'm sure if he comes back, you'd let me know right away, eh?'

It was not a question.

'Yes. Of course,' she replied.

'So then, one last thing, do you know how he got in?'

Maia thought. 'He said something about a lift. With someone who had a meeting here. But I – I didn't ask him any more about it. I just wanted him to go. I'm sorry . . .'

Eugene and Terry exchanged glances again.

'He's . . . He's not still here, is he?' Maia asked. 'I mean – you didn't find him?'

'No,' Eugene replied. 'We only got these through half an hour ago.' He pointed at the screen. 'Some mix-up in the control room.' Then he nodded. 'So. Thank you, Maia. That's been very helpful, OK. You can go now.'

Maia felt a flood of relief. And in the moment of getting up from her chair, she caught Terry's eye and he gave her the look. The slightest curl of the lips, an instant of fire in the dark eyes, imperceptible to Eugene. She made it out of the door and down the stairs before slumping on to the settee in the reception area, her heart beating wildly as she fumbled through her bag, pretending to look for something.

Much later, as she dressed in the shadowy room, the sleeping form plainly visible in the summer night, she realised that all the day's tensions, all her anxieties about Lottie, about Fin and his visit, had simply fallen away over the last three hours. Eclipsed by the presence of this extraordinary man, his understanding and vision, his care and concern, his magnetism. Whatever he had done in the past, she didn't care. She could forgive him anything. Looking at him now, lying there, breathing softly and peacefully, she felt almost ashamed that she could have doubted his tenderness. She gave a sigh of deep contentment as she opened the door and slipped from the room. Her world was back in order again.

Terence Whitelands watched the shadows swallow her. Heard the door click shut. And also sighed. Such a beauty. So young, so . . . fiery. Like a lioness. Was that in her blood, her genes? Was that what awakened the impulses he had to fight so hard to contain, and in so doing found himself taken to new and unimagined heights of pleasure?

There were several other non-whites working here on Seal Island. But Maia was the only one who, all being well, would return to Schloss Adler for the assimilation programme. Though she didn't know it yet, Maia was living proof that with the right grooming, a quarter-blood could be brought into the fold and moulded to the thought patterns, the behaviour, the ideology of her genetic superiors. It had been a stroke of genius by the Committee to recognise that the presence of token non-whites in the organisation would serve to deflect unwanted attention, a kind of necessary window dressing, while the pick of the crop were observed and prepared for the assimilation programme. An even more inspired step to acknowledge that in the final analysis there would simply not be enough Aryans to control the planet, and a compliant, thoroughly assimilated subordinate class of quarter-bloods would be essential to effective administration. Would it be possible to 'turn' three-eighths, or even half-bloods? The Committee had decided not. Where more than two of the great-grandparents were of the lesser races, the genetic stock was simply too inferior, the blood too polluted. 'That kaffir blood is like spent plutonium, yah,' he remembered his father saying. 'Poisons everything and sticks around for a helluva long time.' Christian Blankard's litany, as he had driven his ten-year-old son up and down the country at weekends, visiting the 'townships', as he called them. Brixton in London, St Paul's in Bristol, Handsworth in Birmingham . . . Pointing out at each stop how this was the cancer at the heart of a once-great nation. How, soon, England would be like Africa, and then all would be lost. He had made no secret of the bitterness he felt at having left the Dark Continent just in time, only to discover that the country he had always most admired was heading the same way. All they could do, he had told his son repeatedly, was be vigilant and pray.

But now . . .

Terence stretched, yawned and permitted himself a glimpse of the new world order. A glorious reckoning, a majestic vision of racial purity. The planet washed clean of the brown scum that had risen through the cracks and crevices of even the most apparently unassailable strongholds of whiteness and now lay like a film of old, rank grease across the face of civilisation. There would be ghettos, of course, where labour was required. But they would be fortresses, designed not to keep invaders out but the inhabitants in. And what the lesser races believed to be their trump card, their bargaining counter in the struggle for supremacy, the black oil, which by no coincidence was to be found in those very same inhospitable corners of the earth as their black populations, would be neutralised by none other than the Super Turbine. In a single stroke, the ages of fossil fuel and so-called multiculturalism would be swept into the landfill of history. Black skins and black energy a mere footnote.

That had been the true genius of Walter Groeneberg's vision, that the superior race should be dependent on their inferiors for nothing except labour.

And the Project was now well under way. A bombing here, the assassination of a prominent black figure there. Negritude, for the purposes of the Project, was a broad church. Arabs, Africans, Asians, Orientals, Native Americans, Aboriginals – any non-Aryan, in fact – all were legitimate targets. Operations would remain anonymous. There would be no hysterical jihadis ranting in the media about the true path to purity. Oh no. No fanatical towel-heads with nitroglycerin corsets. The strategy was to sow fear and confusion, little by little, with no warnings, in ever widening circles, until at last they began to turn on themselves like rats in a trap. By which time Green Energies would wield so much power through the universal adoption of the Super Turbine that the leaders of all civilised nations would pay good heed to whatever utterances issued forth from Great Falls, Montana.

And Terence himself? He was a realist, a pragmatist. Not so self-important as to believe that his name would be carved in stone alongside those of the founders of the new world order. No. He saw himself more as a favoured commander, perhaps even a general, who already had two resounding successes to his credit, Operation Gumbo and Operation Korma, and a third, Operation Couscous, on the way. Terence's father had idolised Jan Smuts, the Afrikaans general who had proved such a thorn in the flesh of the British during the Boer War, with his brilliant use of guerrilla tactics. Strike and withdraw, strike and withdraw – that was how Terence pictured himself; planning his campaign, knowing his ground, meticulously choosing his next target, leaving nothing to chance. While the pick of Sean's trainees were like the Boer riflemen. Hardened sharpshooters, invisible to their enemies, who excelled in stealth and destruction. Oh yes . . . his father would have been so proud of him.

He breathed in, savouring the traces of Maia's scent on the sheets. Wondered sleepily if she suspected anything. The Committee had run a risk in deciding to send her somewhere this close to home. But she had responded so well to the induction programme that they had grasped the opportunity to test its efficacy still further by exposing her to her childhood environment. And to her, or rather the programme's, credit, Maia seemed so far to be resisting. What they hadn't allowed for was the quite extraordinary misfortune that of all the people at whose feet Charlotte Svensson could have landed, it would be Maia's brother. A nosy little bastard, as it transpired . . . It would be hard to give Maia up, Terence was well aware of that. Though if there was a real danger of her jeopardising the Project, she would have to be got rid of without hesitation. For the moment though, it all seemed manageable enough. Another couple of evenings here with him, soon, for Maia. And a visit by Eugene to the Carpenter family. That ought to keep things straight.

He turned over and closed his eyes, regretting that he hadn't told her to stay.

THIRTY-SIX

The little pool of light at the end of the narrow passageway between the low fishermen's cottages was, to Fin, a kind of beacon. All his life it had spilt from the kitchen after dark, drawing him home, signifying safety, no matter how foul the weather, how murky the night. But this evening, in the summer dusk, he approached it with an anxious heartbeat echoing his footfall in the alley.

He had dozed off on the harbour wall and woken an hour later with a thundering headache. For the next three hours he had walked. Out to Cable Sands and on along the cliffs beyond. The headache had left him, and in its place had grown the conviction that he had to tell his mother about Maia. By the time he reached the bridge for the second time, huge and shadowy, almost mythical in the fading light, he had begun to wonder how he could possibly have kept it from her for so long.

This time he had paused under the bridge. The tide was in, and the exact spot was now underwater. But he stood for several silent moments on the shingle, among the razor shells and bladderwrack, and gazed at where he thought the rock was. What kind of fate ordained a person such a violent death? He knew some would say that there was a grand puppet master out there, pulling the strings, reeling people in when their time was up. But Fin rebelled against that idea. What did it say about the choices people made in their lives? The effort and worry they put into trying to do things right? That they were all futile? That whether or not he told Kath about Maia, nothing would really change? No. He shook his head fiercely. If the decisions Fin made had no effect on anything, then he might just as well lie down right there and wait for the tide to come in . . .

Now he opened the door to Number Thirteen and went in. Though the kitchen light was on, he could tell at once that the house was empty. He felt relieved but also frustrated. He still had to have the conversation, and part of him wanted to get it over as soon as possible.

There was a note on the kitchen table. 'Nan's poorly. Going over to see her – spending the night. Back tomorrow lunchtime. Sausages for your supper in the fridge. Mum xxx PS Mr Hunter from the Institute was round again. Said he wanted to see you.'

So Kath was in Cliffton. Which meant that, with no one to cook his supper, Danny would be at the Mission, for all he'd said about it earlier. And Hunter had been here again. That brought a knot to Fin's stomach. Why had he come? What did he want? Could someone have seen him on Seal Island this morning? Had Maia said something? Surely not . . . But there was something else too. His mother would normally have rung him on his mobile to let him know where she was going. Why not today? He felt in his jeans pocket. No phone. Perhaps he'd put it in his rucksack that morning. He went upstairs to his room and checked. No. Could he have lost it on Seal Island? Unlikely. He'd used it once, to call Norman Turner, then put it back in his pocket. He would have to call Coldheart Farm on the house phone. See if he'd left it in the car. But hang on . . . he couldn't. The older man's phone numbers were both on his mobile. Oh well. He would just have to go up there in the morning.

He went back into the kitchen and turned on the grill.

Unwrapped the sausages. What was he going to do this evening? Normally he would have called Poacher and gone over to hang out at his place, if he wasn't working behind the bar. Normally . . .

'Dammit, Poach!' he said aloud. Blinked back tears as he put the sausages under the grill.

No one who knew Poacher could possibly have wanted to kill him. Though that, of course, was the problem. The people who killed him hadn't known him. He was just an anonymous enemy, perhaps not even a human being in their minds. Fin remembered his history teacher explaining how the long-distance weaponry of the twentieth century had forever changed the way people thought about war. For the first time, you could kill without being close enough to see your enemies' faces. It had allowed people to kill on a much larger scale without compunction, she'd said. Fin hadn't understood at the time. He did now. And the greatest irony of all was that Poacher hadn't even been their intended target. Just what the army called 'collateral damage', the bland phrase they used to describe the act of casually killing innocent bystanders. If he were to meet one of the killers, would he know? he wondered. Would he sense Poacher's blood on their hands . . . ?

His thoughts were interrupted by a smell of burning from the grill.

It wasn't until half an hour later, sitting at the kitchen table, his meal finished, that he thought of the Duck and his offer of help on the day of the funeral. Was he someone with whom Fin could talk all this through? He hesitated. 'Hey, man, don't beat yourself up, we're all part of the one universe,' or words to that effect, had been all very well at the time, but was that what he needed now? A flute-playing, story-telling stoner? And yet the Duck who had

215

paddled the kayak across the water to the caves had been strong, focused, decisive . . .

Fin went back up to his room and rummaged through the pile of pocket-emptyings on top of his chest of drawers. Found the scrap of paper on which the Duck had scribbled his number, thankful now that he hadn't transferred it to his mobile. Then went back downstairs again to the house phone and dialled.

The sky had grown hazy towards evening, and now it was a dark, overcast night. The heat like a blanket. He made his way down the alley and turned right at the end. The Duck had suggested meeting at the Ship, but Fin had said he would prefer somewhere quiet, where they could talk and not bump into people he knew. They'd settled on the beach car park just along from the Mission.

Fin paused at the harbour, glancing around as he always did to see if there was anyone about. But the darkness was thick tonight and he could hardly make out the harbour wall. There was only the slap of the water and the creak of mooring cables to tell him that the tide was in. He walked past the Ship, and as he turned the corner he had a sudden sensation of being watched.

He walked on, resisting the urge to quicken his pace. There were bungalows and cottages on the right now, and a rocky strip of shore on his left, the sea moving like some restless sleeping animal at his side. Thanks to street lamps and some light from the cottages, the way was only partly in shadow. But the presence of light did nothing to relieve the prickling between his shoulder blades. He stopped under a lamp and crouched as if to do up his trainer, glancing back the way he had come as he did so. The road was empty. He walked on, more quickly than he intended, and was relieved when he drew level with the Mission, its light spilling in broad swathes across the road. He glanced at the windows, pictured his father at the bar, proudly telling his mates about his walk along the beach . . .

He heard the bike before he saw it, the throaty rumble, then the single headlight swinging down the hill. He hurried on towards the car park.

The Duck was removing his helmet as Fin arrived. They walked some distance out on to the darkened beach and sat down on the sand.

'Thanks for coming,' said Fin.

'No sweat.' The Duck shrugged. 'So . . . what's up?'

To the wash of unseen waves, Fin told him everything.

The Duck listened in silence.

At the end he let out a long breath. 'Whoa, Fin. You been in the wars, man.'

'Seems so.'

'OK.' He nodded to himself. 'So . . . what do you think's going on?'

Fin lifted a handful of sand and let it run through his fingers. 'I think . . . number one, Maia's been kind of brainwashed – I don't know how else to describe it, or to explain how she could be here and not have made contact with us. But why, I don't know. I mean . . . it makes it sound like some kind of cult, doesn't it? But a sustainable-energy cult – wind power . . . ?' He shook his head. 'Number two, Lottie did something, or discovered something, maybe some commercially sensitive secret, that meant she was a threat to the Institute, so Hunter pushed her off the bridge. Or perhaps she and Hunter were, like, an item and something went wrong – though, having seen them both, I can't really imagine it. Anyway, whatever happened, Maia knows something about it and now she's scared the same thing

217

might happen to her. But she won't admit it, and she's really defensive about the Institute . . .'

'OK.' The Duck drummed his fingers on his knee. 'And what about Sean? Where does he fit in?'

'I don't know.' Fin shook his head. 'Maybe not at all. Maybe it's just coincidence. They probably need a bullying creep like that to train their security heavies. Maybe it's as simple as that. Though if Maia knew what he was really like, I don't think she'd put up with him for thirty seconds. Unless . . . Unless that's the brainwashing again.' Fin shrugged, then suddenly remembered something. 'I found his cap this morning – after I'd seen him outside the labyrinth with the trainees. He'd dropped it earlier, I guess. Had a badge with a weird little emblem on it.'

'Like what?'

Fin sketched the curving teeth in the sand between them. 'See that?'

The Duck squinted.

'The big one at the left-hand end had a red tip. Dripping, like blood, maybe.'

'Hmm. OK.'

'So . . . what do *you* make of it all?'

The Duck leaned forward, chin on knees, and stared into the darkness.

'I think,' he said after a long silence, 'that there's a time for trying to sort things out on your own and there's a time for putting your hand up and saying, 'Too much.' Look, man, you're dealing with a heavy load here. Quite apart from Maia and the Institute, there's Poacher not being around. That's a big enough deal on its own.' He reached across and touched Fin's arm. 'Remember what I said at the funeral – about taking care of yourself? Well, now's the time.'

218

'Meaning?'

'Meaning – first off, tell your folks. She's your sister, but she's their daughter too.'

Fin nodded. 'I'd kind of come to that decision.'

'Good. And second, go to the police. You have to, man.'

'But I . . . I don't think they'll listen to me.'

'You gotta take that chance, Fin.' There was urgency in the Duck's voice now. 'Look at it this way – if anything bad happened to Maia and you hadn't done everything you could to prevent it, you'd never forgive yourself.'

'True . . .'

'I'll come with you, if you want. Happy to. Honest. Look, talk to your folks. See what they say.' He started to get up. 'I've got to get back to Cliffton now. But listen, I was going up the coast tomorrow with the kayak for a few days. I could come here first. Just to be around, lend a hand if you need it . . .'

'Well . . . OK, thanks. But can I call you tomorrow? Once I know what's happening.'

'Sure. Call any time. I'll keep the mobile on. And why don't you give me your number too – just in case.'

Fin recited the number from memory. 'But I left it up at Coldheart Farm, so I won't have it till tomorrow,' he added. 'Anyway, thanks. Really. Thanks for everything.'

The Duck pulled on his helmet. 'Like I said, no sweat, man. I told you we'd get through this together. It's just a different "this".'

In the car park Fin stood and watched as the tail light climbed the hill and the noise dwindled. Then he turned for home.

He was almost back at the Ship when a car came round the corner, headlights on full beam, engine racing. Half blinded, he saw it slew towards him, on the wrong side of the road, and for an instant he believed he was going to die. Then, at the last moment, his reflexes took over and the next thing he knew he was in the herbaceous border the other side of the low garden wall of the bungalow on his left. Out of sight, the car raced away down the road.

For a long time he lay shocked and winded, breathing in the smell of plants and moist earth, not quite sure what had just happened to him. But eventually he clambered to his feet and brushed himself down, then checked himself for damage. There seemed to be none, though his legs were weak and his heart beat double time. Curtains twitched along the road. He was glad that this cottage was empty, its occupants away. He walked unsteadily to the garden gate and let himself out.

At the harbour he paused in the light that pooled from the bar window of the Ship. He was trembling now. The bar looked warm and safe, full of people. Shirley Archer was behind the counter, joking with customers. But he would just invite a quizzing by going in, and he didn't trust himself not to say more than he intended.

He stared across the harbour into the darkness, his breathing calming at last. What had actually happened? A car had come round the corner from the harbour, going too fast, and had veered across the road towards him. A drunk leaving the Ship. Some people did drive when they'd been drinking here. They knew the nearest policeman was in Cliffton. That was what he wanted to believe. But it didn't explain the sensation of being watched, nor the nagging thought that the car had been driven at him deliberately. Whether to kill him or merely frighten him, he didn't know. But if this *was* a warning, then surely it was about something more than just visiting Maia . . .

He could hear people coming to the pub door, saying their goodbyes. He walked away into the shadows.

Back in the house he stood for a moment listening to his father's snores. Then he went into his room. He took off his shoes and lay down on the bed. He turned off the light and stared into the darkness for a long time, until the beating of his heart slowed and he fell asleep at last.

THIRTY-SEVEN

Danny surprised Fin by joining him in the kitchen for breakfast. Normally on a Saturday he didn't appear till mid-morning. Now he forked up a rasher of bacon and announced that he was going to get the bus over to Cliffton and join Kath. 'See that your nan's OK,' he said. 'Do a bit of shopping maybe. Get the tea-time bus home.'

From the moment he'd woken up, Fin's mind had spun with what had happened the previous evening. His hands had trembled as he'd washed, got dressed, cooked the bacon. Now he gave a distracted nod.

Danny pulled a face. 'Didn't you hear me?'

'Sorry.'

'I'm. Getting. The bus. To Cliffton.'

Danny hadn't been to Cliffton for as long as Fin could remember. It seemed to Fin that he always found reasons not to go. As if he was ashamed of his disability, afraid he might be mocked by strangers.

'Hey! That's great, Dad,' Fin said. 'Will you be OK?'

'Course I will, son. Right as rain. And your mum could do with a hand.'

There were moments when this new Danny stretched Fin's credulity.

'Well, have a good time then,' he said, as enthusiastically as he could.

Half an hour later Fin left the house and walked down the alley to the harbour. There he hesitated for a nervous moment, glancing in all directions before turning left towards the cliffs.

The sky hadn't cleared overnight. The air was trapped between low cloud and a sullen ocean. It made him feel thick in the head. Yet as soon as he let his concentration wander, the image of the car filled his mind, headlights blazing, coming straight at him. He forced himself to focus on the path in front of him, following the cliffs until Coldheart Farm loomed from the haze. For all its isolation, for all the strangeness of its occupant, it seemed a beacon of sense and reassurance. He would collect his phone, call his mum . . . and they'd go from there, like the Duck had suggested.

He walked across the courtyard and knocked on the back door. There was no reply. He knocked again, waiting for the measured tread. None came.

He opened the door and went in.

'Hello.'

He stopped, listening. Then walked on into the kitchen. It was empty. An unwashed plate by the sink the only sign of life. The photograph of Amy was now in the centre of the table. There was a faint smell of burning. And something else that had changed, disturbed the normal order of the place. But he couldn't figure out what.

He left the kitchen, went down the short corridor, and paused at the entrance to the hallway. Now he could hear something. A kind of restless shuffling, and what might be the low muttering of a human voice. It was coming from Norman Turner's workroom, the large front room to the right of the hall.

At the door he hesitated, reluctant to intrude, unsure, even a little fearful, of what he might find inside.

He knocked. The sounds stopped. He knocked again and, without waiting for an answer, went in.

There had been a break-in. That was his first thought.

A break-in, not by burglars but by vandals. The machines had been smashed. Splintered wood lay everywhere, broken with such violence that Fin could only imagine a madman with an axe. Nothing remained of either the Taisnerius Device or the overbalanced wheel, not even the workbenches on which they had stood. Strewn among the matchwood were papers tightly packed with figures, some printed, some in Norman Turner's crabbed hand. While in the fireplace smouldered more papers and one or two pieces of wood, as if the madman had thought his axe-wielding was not enough and had begun to set fire to the remains, then lost interest.

Amid the chaos, shuffling back and forth like the dazed survivor of some catastrophe, was Norman Turner, head down, feet scuffing the debris. He glanced up at Fin. His normally guarded eyes were wild, but there was nothing of the victim in his look. Fin stared at him as understanding dawned. Turner had done this himself.

Fin stood there in the doorway, not knowing what to do or say, conscious only of a deep sinking feeling. This was the last thing he needed.

After his brief acknowledgement of Fin, the older man had dropped his gaze back to the ground and continued to shuffle back and forth. He was unshaven and haggard.

'I'm glad you've come, Finlay,' he said, after several long moments. He nudged aside a split timber with his foot. 'There's something I wanted to tell you.'

'But . . . what happened?'

'Yes . . .' he replied, 'what happened? What indeed happened?'

He stopped and sat down on the floor, clearing himself a space among the debris.

'I only came – er . . .' Fin stopped. He wanted to get out of this room, out of the house, find his phone and leave. But Norman Turner sat with his head hanging, shoulders slumped. He looked like a child exhausted by a tantrum. Fin couldn't leave him like this. He picked his way through the debris, cleared himself a space beside the older man and sat down.

For what seemed to Fin like a long time they sat there together in silence. Fin could think of nothing to say, suspected there *was* nothing to say.

Eventually Turner let out a long sigh. 'Perhaps I've been on my own too long, Finlay. No one to question me. We all need that, you know. Someone to question us. Make us stop. Think about what we're doing. You follow me?'

Fin nodded, even though he didn't.

'And you, Finlay – you may not realise it but you've made me ask myself questions . . .' He waved a hand. 'No, not this. I don't mean this. You have no responsibility for this. But . . . you know, Finlay, you're the first person to give me the time of day in more than six years.' He was doing his best to keep his voice neutral, but now Fin could hear the emotion straining underneath. 'Not that I would have allowed anyone to, until you appeared. A recluse, that's what I've been. And it suited me. But a recluse has no dignity. That is something you receive only from others. It is other people who dignify you – or not, as the case may be.' He turned to look at Fin and the wildness had left his eyes. 'And you have dignified me, Finlay. You accepted me as you found me. Asked no questions. Even though I must have appeared . . . strange to you.' A smile flickered at the corners of his mouth. 'You judged me on nothing more than what you saw . . . and perhaps what I told you. And I sense your judgement was not harsh.' He looked away.

'There are no words to express the gratitude I feel for that. And that is why I wanted to help you in return.'

Fin felt he was playing some role he didn't understand.

Norman Turner stared ahead in silence for a long time. Then he continued, 'I saw you, Finlay, with your hopes and fears, and I remembered being your age and thinking that anything was possible. But as one grows older one learns to temper one's views of what is possible. And I asked myself, Where is the dignity in pursuing an impossibility? Where is the dignity in delusion? For I knew. A small part of me still recognised the truth. All along, in my core, I knew the untruth, the impossibility, of my machines. Knew that perpetual motion was a mirage, a fantasy. Seductive enough for all that, as even the great Leonardo found out. And, for my purposes, useful too. A convenient obsession. Something to lose myself in, escape from the reality of life.'

He looked back at Fin now.

'But the greatest irony in all this, Finlay, is that that very reality is a mere five miles away. And I didn't know it when I bought this place. Though something surely must have brought me here so that one day I should see it. I didn't even see it when I went to the Open Day. Because I wasn't open, if you'll pardon the play on words. Quite the contrary. I went with my eyes and ears closed. But you, Finlay . . . had it not been for you, I would never have gone there as I did yesterday. Would never have found myself sitting with one of their senior technicians. Never have heard the passion, the conviction with which he spoke of their device, even in respect of the very small amount he was prepared to disclose . . .' He nodded to himself. 'And the thing is . . . whatever else they may be doing there, and hard as I find it to admit this, their science is good. Very good.'

He gestured once more at the chaos of smashed wood

and papers, then let out a long, deep sigh. He seemed to Fin to be retreating, shrinking away inside.

Fin stood up. 'I'll make us a cup of tea.'

Norman Turner nodded.

Fin reached around his back and put his hand firmly under an elbow.

'Come on. Let's go to the kitchen.'

Slowly the older man rose to his feet. He followed Fin through the house like a sleepwalker, pulled up a kitchen chair and sat down at the table. The model of the overbalanced wheel had gone, Fin noticed. Only Leonardo remained. That was what else had been different.

As Fin waited for the kettle to boil, Turner reached for the photograph of Amy and held it in both hands, looking down at it. 'She gave me a life,' he said, as much to himself as to Fin, 'a life I would never otherwise have had. Something to believe in, to fight for. Because that's what we need, Finlay – things to believe in, things that bring real meaning to our lives . . .'

Fin took the cups to the table and sat down. He would drink his tea, make sure Norman Turner was all right, then leave.

'I . . . er . . . came because I think I might have left my phone in your car yesterday,' he said. 'Is it OK if I have a look?'

But Norman Turner seemed in the grip of some distant thought.

'That freshman,' he said, 'at MIT. He was black, you know.'

Fin looked at him blankly.

'The young man they recruited to Groeneberg's society, the Homelands Society. The one they hunted. He was a black man.'

'What? You mean . . .'

Turner ignored the question. 'Yesterday, when you were talking about the trainees, the trainer – the one who attacked you – '

'Sean.'

'Yes. It reminded me . . . Something missing, not right – when we first spoke about Walter Groeneberg. That's what I wanted to tell you about. So I went back to refresh my memory. Last night. To keep my mind off other things.' He gestured at the front room. 'Not that it did much good.'

Now Fin was sitting upright. 'Do you mean . . . Are you saying . . . that Green Energies could be a racist organisation?'

Norman Turner shrugged. 'Perhaps, perhaps not. But their founder was certainly involved in what could be construed as a racist incident. It's all there. In the archives.' He nodded. 'I thought you should know.'

'But . . . but – it doesn't make sense. I mean, if they are – what would Maia be doing working for a racist organisation? Maia of all people!'

Norman Turner looked at him. 'That may be what you have to find out, Finlay.'

Fin jumped as the room was filled with the shrilling of an alarm. Midday. The older man rose, walked to the counter and turned off the alarm. Then he returned to his chair.

'Don't you . . . ? Aren't you . . . ? I mean, your walk . . .'

He shook his head. A strange, curt movement. Began to sit down, then swayed. Put out a hand to steady himself against the table.

'I think I should lie down for a little while,' he said.

'Are you all right?' Fin began to get to his feet. 'I mean, d'you need a doctor or anything?'

'No, Finlay. I will be fine.' He gave a small smile. 'Thanks in no small part to you.'

He held out his hand.

Fin took it, noticing how grey the older man's face appeared. Despite the strange light that had now returned to his eyes, he looked ten years older.

'You sure you're OK?' asked Fin.

'Yes, thank you. I'm quite fine, Finlay. Now, I believe you should be going. And by all means check the car for your phone as you leave. You'll find it open.'

THIRTY-EIGHT

As he left the courtyard Fin glanced over his shoulder. The farmhouse door was closed. There was no sign of movement in the kitchen. He walked down the track a little way, then stopped and turned on his phone. There was a message from the Duck. *got info abt teeth thng. cll me.* Fin dialled back, but the Duck's voicemail was on. He left a message and walked towards the cliffs.

The car last night . . . Norman Turner's revelation about the black student . . . For a moment he pictured himself as the terrified young man, running for his life through the woods . . . Whatever the Duck had discovered, things were starting to come together, though he still couldn't give them concrete shape in his mind. And right now he longed to be able to stop trying, to hand it all over to someone else. The thought that Maia might somehow be caught up in an organisation of racists made his blood run cold.

Nevertheless, he was sweating as he walked up the alley to Number Thirteen half an hour later. Even before he put his hand to the front door he could hear their voices in the kitchen. He walked in. They were sitting at the kitchen table eating ham sandwiches and drinking tea.

'You're back early,' he said.

'Bloody leg started playing up, didn't it?' Danny's voice had the familiar ring of martyrdom.

Kath raised her eyes in resignation.

'Sorry, Dad,' said Fin.

Danny shrugged and took another bite of sandwich.

'You want one, love?' Kath said.

Fin shook his head. He pulled up a stool and sat down.

'How's Nan?'

'She's all right. She'd forgotten to take her pills again. Silly old trout.' Kath shook her head. 'You OK?'

Fin nodded.

'Did you get my note? That Mr Hunter was here again?'

'Yes, I did.'

'Do you know what he wants? I mean – he seems very persistent, doesn't he . . . ?' She looked at him. 'There's nothing wrong, is there, love?'

Fin took a deep breath.

'Well . . . yes. In a way. Maia's here.'

'Here? Where?' Kath's eyes widened. She put her hand to her heart.

'Oh Christ,' said Danny.

Fin ignored him. 'Seal Island. She's working for the Institute. And I think she could be in some kind of danger.'

'You *what*?' Danny's eyes narrowed. 'You and your—'

'Shut up, Danny,' Kath snapped. 'Just shut up and listen, for once in your life.' She turned to Fin, eyes full of anxiety. 'How d'you mean, danger? Is she all right? Have you seen her?'

Fin reached for his mother's hand. 'Yes, I've seen her, Mum. And she's OK. At the moment anyway. But listen, I need to tell you everything . . .'

As Fin spoke, Kath looked straight at him with an expression of growing horror. Danny stared at his plate, but at the first mention of Norman Turner he bristled.

'That weirdo? You haven't been listening to him, have you? He's—'

'He's what?' said Fin angrily. 'Helpful? Clever? Lonely? You don't know the first thing about him. You've got no righ—'

'Don't you tell me what my—'

'Calm down, everyone,' Kath begged. 'Danny –' she glared at him – 'let Fin finish.'

Danny glowered as Fin continued with the story. When at last he finished there was silence around the table. Kath looked grave. Danny's gaze gave nothing away. But he was the first to speak.

''Sfar as I'm concerned, she's made her bed there and she can bleedin' well lie in it.'

'Daniel Carpenter!' Kath sat forward, her voice sharp with outrage. 'Your daughter, your—'

'She's no daughter of mine.' Danny's face was reddening. 'I told her that when she left, and I've had no reason to change my mind.' He snorted. 'Murder and plots and racist thugs. Sounds like you been readin' too many thrillers, son. Load of old bollocks, if you ask me. Don't want nothin' to do with any of it.' He reached for his stick and began to heave himself up from the table.

'Perhaps that's because you're one yourself.' It was out before Fin could stop himself.

Danny paused halfway to his feet. 'One what?'

Kath was looking at Fin, shaking her head. But suddenly all the fear and worry was boiling up in him like magma ready to break through the earth's fragile crust.

'A racist, Dad. Isn't that right? You wanted white kids really, didn't you? Not little niggers like Maia and me.'

He couldn't stop himself now, even though he knew it wasn't really true. He was sick of his father, sick of his misery, his self-pity, sick of his pretence at mending his ways.

'I bet you didn't come home today because your leg

232

was playing up. You came home because you're scared of people looking at you and saying, "There goes the cripple." Well, if you'd ever done anything half useful in your life, you'd have a bit more self-respect.'

'You . . . you little –' Danny was struggling to his feet again. Kath looked stunned. But Fin ignored them both and went on.

'And you haven't even got the guts to help when Maia's in trouble. You might be a cripple, Dad, but that doesn't mean you have to be a spineless cripple.'

Danny was now upright. He had begun to raise his stick in fury. Fin leaned across the table and grabbed it, wrenching it out of his hand so that Danny, taken completely by surprise, lost his balance and sat down again heavily, his mouth wide open in astonishment and fury.

'So –' Fin was shouting now – 'what're you going to do?' He reached over and poked his father in the chest with the stick.

'Fin –' interjected Kath in horror.

'That's what I'd like to know,' he went on, ignoring her. 'What're you going to do? Because you're going to do something whether you like it or not.' He prodded his father again. Danny let out a bellow of fury, but remained seated. 'I'm not going to let you off that chair till you tell me what. This is my sister. Your daughter, you gutless creep. And I'm not going to let you sit back and do nothing when she could be in real danger.'

He stood there holding the stick, out of words, glaring at his father and breathing hard.

Both his parents were staring at him now in shocked silence.

'OK,' he said, steadying his breathing. 'This is what I'm going to do. I'm going out for half an hour,' he lifted the

233

stick and Danny winced, 'and I'm taking this with me. And when I get back –' he glared at his father – 'you'd better have decided what you're going to do.'

He walked to the door. Turned to look at them.

'See he does it, Mum.'

THIRTY-NINE

A lbert Smith left Sally's cottage and took the path towards the harbour. There was a distant rumble of thunder. He glanced seaward. Out beyond Gannet Rock, great swollen towers of cloud the colour of lead were piling up on the horizon. He could feel the tension in the air. It pressed on his temples.

He had dropped in late in the morning for a cup of coffee. Fragile was not a word he would normally have associated with Sally, but that was how she'd been looking lately. Even, at moments, slightly haunted. But she'd seemed pleased to see him and he'd managed to keep the conversation light, avoiding anything that might lead on to the subjects he knew had been troubling her, the bombings and the dreams. By the time he left she'd seemed more cheerful.

Now, as he crossed the harbour, he saw a familiar figure pacing the quayside below the wall, back and forth. Sally had told him the other day that Kath had finally given Danny the rocket he deserved, threatened to leave unless he pulled his socks up, and to everyone's amazement it appeared to be working. Even so, if he had Danny Carpenter for a father, Albert mused, he'd probably do his fair share of pacing, pondering the meaning of life. His heart went out to the solitary figure.

Fin heard footsteps across the harbour. His spine tingled and he turned around. It was only Albert. The adrenalin was subsiding, his breathing returning to normal, but beneath the anger he still felt wired, on edge.

There was another message on his phone. A text from the Duck. *sthng to tll u. jst lvng. b over in an hr. meet sme plce?* He hadn't heard it come in. Fin dialled and heard the voicemail message again. He must be driving, unable to pick up.

Fin replied, *OK*. Then made his way back to Number Thirteen.

Kath was in the kitchen. There was no sign of Danny. She swung round as Fin came in, tight-lipped but clearly relieved to see him.

'You shouldn't have done that, you know.'

Fin nodded. 'I'm sorry. I just . . . had to let it out. Where is he?'

Kath glanced up at the bedroom. 'Said he thought he was going to have a turn. I put him to bed.' She shook her head. 'You frightened him.'

'I wanted to.'

Kath sighed. 'Well, yes . . . I guess he deserved it.' Tears welled in her eyes. 'How *is* she? How's she looking?'

Fin pulled up a chair. 'Well, she . . . she – looks fine. Just the same, pretty much. Hasn't changed.'

'Really? Just the same?'

She was twisting her wedding ring.

'Yes.'

'And what about us?' A tear made its way down her cheek. 'What did she say about us? About not being in touch?'

'We didn't have much time to talk, Mum. All I know is that she was angry – really angry. With me. For coming. And with Dad, still . . . And she was frightened too, like I said.'

'And she wasn't . . . even – a tiny bit pleased to see you?'

Fin looked out of the small kitchen window. A seagull perched on a neighbouring chimney pot, intensely white against the leaden sky.

'Yes, I think she was at first. But then – it was . . . like something else took over.'

Kath nodded. 'I never knew anyone more stubborn.' She blew her nose. 'Anyway, I've rung the police, like you said.'

'You have?'

'Yes. They said they'll have to interview you. But they won't be able to send anyone out till tomorrow.'

'Why not?'

'Because we're in for a big storm, apparently. And there's a spring tide. They're expecting storm surges later tonight. They've got the entire force out. Going up and down the coast, making sure people in low-lying areas are ready for it. No one to spare, they said.'

'And you told them everything?'

'Yes, everything. Charlotte. Maia. Sean. Hunter's visits. The car. Even the thing about the black student in the States.' She gave him an awkward glance. 'I mean . . . they were very polite and everything. But I think they thought I was some kind of lunatic. If they hadn't had your name already because of Charlotte, they'd probably have told me to stop wasting their time.' She looked at the table. 'Trouble is, love, it's all guesswork, isn't it? We don't even know it was Hunter that was driving the car . . .'

Fin felt the anger rising again. 'Now you're sounding like Dad.'

'No.' She reached across and put her hand on his. 'I'd do anything to have her back here now, home and safe. You

237

know that, love. But I'm just trying to be rational. See it from their point of view.'

'Then we've got to convince them.' The frustration made him want to lash out. He should have known this was how they'd react. He *had* known it. Maia had been right, that was the irony. There wasn't a single shred of hard evidence. He shouldn't have given up so easily. Shouldn't have listened to the Duck's advice. *Hey, man, time to offload . . .* He should have carried on on his own. Found a way to get back on to Seal Island again. Talk to Maia some more, find out more . . .

'Fin . . . ?'

He looked down. He'd bent the handle of a teaspoon back on itself.

'I . . . I just – don't know whether you believe me or not.' He tried to straighten the spoon and it snapped. 'Look, Mum, I *know* something's not right. I know it. *I know it.*' He banged the table, half the teaspoon still clenched in his fist. 'You've got to believe me. You've got to!'

Kath looked at him for a long time. 'I do.'

'Good. Then we've got to sort this out, Mum. With or without the police. We'll find a way. Look, I'm meeting Poacher's friend, the Duck, any minute. He says he's got some information about Sean. Maybe that'll be what we need to convince the police.' He started to get up. 'And if it is, I could go over to Cliffton and turn up at the police station anyway. They'd have to see me, surely. Could you maybe borrow Sally's car?'

'Well . . . ye-es. I'm sure I could. I'll go over and ask her.'

'OK.' He glanced at the kitchen clock. 'I'd better get going. Just need something from upstairs.'

Kath stood up and put her hands on his shoulders,

looked up into his face. 'Be careful, love. And I do believe you, I really do. I'm just . . . worried.' She let her hands drop and forced a smile. 'Anyway, fingers crossed for The Duck, OK?'

'Fingers crossed.'

He went upstairs, leaving his mother standing by the kitchen table.

'Oh Maia, darlin',' she said to the empty room, 'I hope to God you're OK.'

At the top of the stairs Fin heard a grunt from his parents' room. He stopped.

'That you, son?'

'Yes.'

'C'min. Somethin I wanna say to you.'

Fin opened the door and went in. Danny was lying on top of the bed fully clothed. The good leg straight. The injured one half bent. There was a can of lager and an empty half-bottle of vodka on the bedside table. Fin's heart sank.

'I'm sorry, Dad,' he said before Danny could get a word in. Anything to avoid another shouting match. 'I went too far. I was just . . .'

Danny waved him down. 'S'OK. S'OK. Not your fault. I know. I know. Frightened. Worried. Nall that. But police comin now, be OK. Listen though. Things I said bout Maia. Shouldna said em.' He gave a sigh and gazed around the room. 'Course she's my daughter. Had our differences, f'sure. But glad to see her home. Course. Do anythin to get er back, yeah?' He gave Fin a half-focused look and nodded to himself. Then lay back on the pillow and closed his eyes.

'OK, Dad. If you say so.'

Fin closed the door behind him. He walked across the landing into his own room, shaking his head as he went.

FORTY

The Duck looked flustered as he got out of the van. 'Really sorry, man. Flat battery. Couldn't get her started.'

They walked quickly out of the car park and along to the same spot on the beach as before.

'You OK?' the Duck asked, sitting down.

'Well . . .' Fin told him about the car being driven at him. About Danny's reaction to the news that Maia was here. About the police's lukewarm response to Kath's phone call. And finally about his visit to Coldheart Farm and what Norman Turner had told him about the black student. 'So . . . am I OK?' He looked at the Duck and shrugged. 'Who knows? More to the point, is Maia OK?'

The Duck shook his head. 'That's some heavy shit. And it looks like I've got some more here.' He had placed his jacket on the sand beside him. Now he fished in the pocket and pulled out a sheaf of papers. 'Still, maybe this'll get the cops interested.'

He handed Fin an enlarged image of the emblem from Sean's cap badge.

'OK, first things first. Is this the one?'

Fin pulled the cap from his rucksack and compared the badge with the image.

'Looks like it. Same number of teeth. Same shape,' said Fin.

The Duck nodded. 'Except they're not teeth. They're

waves. Seven waves. And the big one at the left-hand end is the seventh.' He paused. 'The Seventh Wave, Fin.'

Fin looked blank.

'My story – the one I told you in the Cathedral cave. The old couple and their seven sons. How weird is that, eh?'

'I . . . I don't get it.'

He pointed to the image. 'This belongs to an outfit that calls itself the Seventh Wave. And that story was about the seventh wave. Pure coincidence, eh? No connection between the two? Maybe not . . .'

'Yeah, OK.' Fin couldn't keep the irritation from his voice. 'But what's all this got to do with Maia?'

'Sorry.' The Duck gave an apologetic look. 'Getting carried away. What's it got to do with Maia? Hopefully not too much.' His voice became more measured. 'Thing is, I've seen this before.' He tapped the paper with his finger. 'Last year I was travelling in eastern Europe. Met up with this crazy Ukrainian biker and we ended up hanging out with a bunch of skinheads. In a graveyard in Kiev.' He looked at Fin. 'One of the scariest evenings of my life. These guys were serious racists, man. Nazis. Like, real hardcore. And some of them were wearing the badge. Here.' He passed over the rest of the papers. 'Have a look.'

Fin took the topmost sheet. Predominantly black and red, with sidebars carrying images of swastikas and skulls, it looked at first glance like the home page of a heavy-metal band. Despite the incongruous-seeming photographs of flaxen-haired, blue-eyed children, the page reeked of violence and destruction. But it was the top banner to which Fin's eye was drawn, and on it, in white gothic script, the words *The Seventh Wave*, followed by the emblem, also in white with a dripping bloody crest to the biggest wave. Beneath, in the centre of a smaller red banner, were the words

Racial Purity. And below that was a sentence in quotation marks, which read: And the Seventh Wave shall come, and it shall be Mighty, and it shall Cover the Face of the Earth and Sweep it Clean of Filth Forever. Then a table of contents listing news, articles, essays, speeches, posters, music, a chat room and links to other sites.

He flicked through the next few pages. In an essay entitled *Origin of the Species,* someone quoted from the Old Testament to argue the inferiority of black, brown and Jewish races. There was a feature on survival and living in the wilderness. A series of stories about white people who had been 'unjustly' convicted of racial assault, maltreating migrant workers, denying the Holocaust – all proof, so the introduction explained, of how the liberal press conspired to undermine the truth of white supremacy. There was a 'Homeland' section, with more photographs of blond Teutonic-looking children and apple-pie moms in gingham aprons, accompanied by an article that asked readers if they would like to see their womenfolk raped, their children's throats slit, by the rising tide of black scum. There were listings of CDs from bands with names like Aryan Avengers, Hammer Death, Seventh Wave Surfers, American Daymare, Crematoria.

'I listened to some of that,' said the Duck quietly. 'Last night. I tell you, man, if you believed in the Devil, you'd say he was there in that music.'

Fin only half heard him. There was a grotesque fascination in this outpouring of racial hatred. Now he was looking at a 'shopping mall' of skinhead and Nazi paraphernalia: jackboots, swastika armbands, knives and knuckledusters, posters of the Führer, of Ku Klux Klansmen with their fiery crosses, of Genghis Khan and Senator Joe McCarthy. There was even a board game called Ethnic Cleansing. And then a page innocuously entitled 'Poets Corner – share your well-written poetry with other Seventh Wave Surfers!' One caught his eye.

> The nigger was looking at my wife
> So I slit him with my knife
> Now the blood is dripping red
> And the nigger lies there dead
>
> Soon my town will all be white
> Blacks and Jews we will fight
> We don't like their dirty ways
> Use our blades to end their days

Beneath, someone had posted, *Wow, that's really cool!*

The fascination had turned to revulsion. Fin shook his head. Pushed the paper away, sickened and enraged by what he had read. How could there be such mindless hatred in the world? What was it in these people's twisted lives that made them feel like that about other human beings they didn't even know? Human beings like him and Maia.

He stood up, breathing hard. 'I – didn't know . . . I mean – I . . . I've never seen . . .'

'Stuff like that?' The Duck looked up at him. 'There's loads of it on the Internet.' He shook his head. 'This old world is still full of hatred, man.'

'And . . . and Sean's part of something like *that*?'

'Seems so.'

'But . . . what if what's going on in the labyrinth has something to do with all this? What if it's not about security, but about some kind of racist training programme . . . ?' Fin paused. 'They were all white, the men there, now I come to think of it. My God . . . this could be even worse than we thought.' He was pacing up and down the sand. 'Does it mean the Institute's into all this too? Do they know where Sean's coming from? Could they be doing some kind of secret racist stuff . . . ? It doesn't make sense – what's this got to do with wind power, or Maia?'

'I don't know. But look, Fin, it's possible. There's shit like this going on right under our noses. All the time. And mostly we never know about it. Religious sects, cults, secret societies, banned political movements, gangs, the tiddlywinks club – who knows, man? There's secrets everywhere. Some dirtier than others.'

'But . . .' Fin stopped pacing, 'if it's true, then Maia could be in really serious danger.' His pulse had started to race. 'We've got to do something. Now.'

The Duck nodded. 'Like go to the police.'

'And say what though?' Fin's voice dropped. 'It still doesn't get us anywhere. Say Sean belongs – which will be hard enough to prove just from a badge on a cap that might be his – that doesn't mean the Institute's definitely involved. See . . . if we could make the link, then I think the police would be interested. As it is, we just don't have anything concrete.' He shook his head. 'I mean, I'll still see them. Tomorrow, if it's too late for Mum to take me over today – and I guess this is one more thing to add to the list. But . . .' He aimed a dispirited kick at the sand.

'So what about your man Turner?'

'What about him?'

'He seems to be the expert on the Institute round here. You sure he's told you everything he knows?'

Fin shrugged. 'I don't know. Maybe not.'

'Worth trying again, surely . . .'

Fin walked down to the water's edge. Growls of thunder echoed across the sullen expanse of ocean before him.

'You know, yesterday I liked the thought of handing all this over to someone else. But . . . I'm not so sure any longer. Right now I'm tempted to forget about the police. Just get back on to Seal Island. See Maia again. Save her myself.'

The Duck stood up. Joined Fin at the water's edge and put a hand on his shoulder.

'Don't do it, man. Not yet.' He came round so he was facing Fin. 'Because if you're really on to something, these people will be dangerous. No question about it. And I mean, like, really dangerous.' The laconic note had left his voice. He was looking at Fin intensely. 'The cops might not be taking you seriously yet, but I am. I've been in some dodgy situations in my day. And believe me, this is starting to look really bad.'

Fin stared over the Duck's shoulder for a long while.

Then he turned for the car park.

'OK. We'll go up to Coldheart Farm.'

FORTY-ONE

Maia switched on her desk lamp and sat back, massaging her neck with her fingers. Seven o'clock in the evening, and the sky was almost dark. There was a loud rumble of thunder. The lights flickered. Her computer screen faltered, went black, then came to life again as the system began to reboot.

'Shit!'

In the labs there was full surge protection and standby power, but they hadn't got round to it here in the administration block. She waited, then reloaded the document she'd been working on. Scrolled down, banged her hand on the desktop.

'Shit! Shit!'

She'd lost the last hour's work. Terry wanted it tomorrow. A report from Ashgabat. They came in in this ridiculous fractured English, like the instructions for Taiwanese battery-operated toys. Which would have been funny had she not been the one who had to tidy them up before management saw them.

She began again where she had last saved the document, trying to ignore the fact that now she would probably be here till ten. Trying to ignore the headache that was building with the approach of the storm, the noise coming from the next-door office, movement, laughter, the low thump of some kind of dance music. Sean. He'd been running the labyrinth programme again today. He was always pumped up afterwards. He'd got his two assistants in there with him – in theory holding a debriefing, in practice getting pissed.

She wished she was seeing Terry tonight. Five minutes in his presence would be enough to take away all the feelings of tension and pressure and irritation . . .

But Terry and Eugene had been tied up for the first half of the afternoon, and now he was busy with other things. Meanwhile, she had a job to finish. She forced herself to concentrate.

We are delight to propose you this up-to-dates . . . Where on earth did these people learn their English?

The door of Sean's office opened and voices spilled loudly into the corridor.

'For Chrissakes, Sean,' she muttered. She pushed her chair back with an angry movement and stood up.

After a while the voices dwindled away.

She continued typing, now careful to save every paragraph or so.

The thunder was drawing closer. Occasional flashes of lightning threw the outlines of the trees outside into stark relief. Maia longed for the storm to break and clear the air, relieve the pressure that was making her feel trapped and claustrophobic.

The back of her neck bristled. There was someone behind her. She spun round in her chair.

Sean. She hadn't heard the door open. Now he was half-way across the room.

'Working late, Maia?' He grinned.

'God, you gave me a fright.' Maia put a hand to her pounding heart. What Fin had told her about Sean had made her feel jumpy around him, she realised. In fact, Fin's visit had made her jumpy about everything.

Sean kept approaching. Hoisted himself without asking on to the corner of her desk and crossed one leg over the other. She could smell alcohol on his breath. He grinned at her.

'Fancy a drink?'

'No, thanks. I'm working. So if you don't—'

'Oh, go on. Just one. Keep me company.'

'No, Sean. I've got to finish this. So please—'

'Not even just a little one . . . ?' He was still grinning. But she could feel his eyes roving across her body, undressing her.

She stood up angrily. 'Look, Sean, I didn't invite you in here. I've got work to do. And you're drunk. So do me a favour and piss off.'

He ignored her. Still sitting on her desk, he leaned forward and leered.

'What colour panties you wearing, Maia?'

'*What?*' Maia took a step back.

'Or maybe you're not wearing any.'

Maia felt the blood rush to her face. 'That's not funny, Sean. Now get off my desk, please. And go.' She began to walk round him. 'Or I'll find someone to come and throw you out.'

Sean said nothing, but his hand shot out and gripped her wrist.

'Let *go* of me.'

Sean tightened his grip.

Maia let out a gasp of pain.

Sean grinned.

'So you don't fancy me, eh? Never wondered what it would be like to be with Seany-baby instead? When you're up there in the sack with *Doctor* Whitelands.'

He filled the word *Doctor* with venom but Maia took no notice. She wriggled and twisted furiously.

'If you don't let go, I'm going to start screaming. You creep.'

Sean continued to grin. 'So I take it that's a no.'

'You're bloody right it is. Because you revolt me, Sean. You always have and you always will. And I suspect you've got a prick the size of a peanut. Which is probably why you attacked my brother. To make yourself feel like a man. Now let—'

Maia yelped as his free hand caught her on the side of the face.

'You black *bitch*!'

Now Sean was no longer grinning.

'*What* did you call me?' Maia's cheek smarted and her eyes watered. But even as he grabbed her other wrist and held her pinioned in front of him, she felt nothing but rage.

'You black bitch,' Sean repeated, spitting out the words. 'Think you're something special because you're working here at the Institute? Because you're fucking the Director? Well, you got another think coming. You're nothing more than window dressing. You think that jumped-up South African jerk-off will protect you when the Project really starts cooking? Hah! Let me tell you, monkey girl, you'll be first in line for the chop. Just like your brother and all the rest of the sambo bastards. Believe me, Doctor Terence won't be looking after you then. You'll be disposable. Just like your little friend Lottie, and she wasn't even black . . .'

'What are you talking about? What Project?' Maia had stopped struggling.

Sean's eyes widened in mock horror. 'Oh dear. Did

Seany-baby say something he shouldn't? Did Doctor lover-boy not tell you why you're really here?'

'What are you *talking* about?'

'I'm talking about a clean planet, Maia. You know: "Renewable energy for a clean planet." Which means clean of all the shite like you. Black shite. Brown shite. Jew shite. And we've already started, you know.' He was crowing now, his face shining with drink and self-importance. '*My* crew. *My* trainees. Operation Gumbo . . . Operation Korma . . .'

'What? I don't know what you mean.'

'The West Indian market.' He gave a vicious smile. 'The Curry Quarter.'

'Oh my God!' It burst from her. 'The bombings! Oh my God . . .' For a moment her body went slack with shock and she thought her knees might buckle as the truth of what he had said hit her. Then she recovered herself and began to struggle again. But he was strong. He held her easily as he continued.

'Yes, Maia. A clean planet. That's what it really means. And whatever the Doctor *thinks* he's grooming you for, he's wrong. Because come the day, there'll be none of you left. Not one, believe me. I'll see to it personally.' He thrust his face into hers. 'So now, you nigger bitch, let's see about those panties . . .'

He let go of her left wrist and lunged for the hem of her skirt. As his head came forward Maia hit him in the nose as hard as she could with the flat of her palm. He reeled back, a startled look on his face. Then grunted and lunged forward again, hooked an arm around her and began dragging her to the ground. She scrabbled at the surface of the desk but there was nothing to hold on to. Her fingers closed on something solid, her paperweight, and she grasped it as she crashed to the floor. She felt a sudden excruciating pain in her scalp as Sean grabbed her hair with one hand, forcing her head back on to the ground, while with the other he lifted her skirt and tried to force his knee between her clenched thighs. He was breathing heavily, a reek of alcohol, and muttering obscenities. Maia waited a moment longer, then scissored open her legs so that he lost his balance. As he fell forward she raised her arm and hit him hard on the side of the head with the paperweight. There was a dull crunch and he collapsed on top of her. She lay still for several seconds, winded and gasping for breath. Then wriggled out from underneath him and stood up. As she did so his body gave a convulsive shudder and something spilled from his mouth on to the carpet. Then he was still.

Only now did Maia notice that the lights had gone out. She stood for a long time in the darkness, trembling from head to foot. More than once the office was lit by lightning, clearly outlining the prostrate body and, by its head, the stain that darkened the carpet.

At length she managed to pull herself together enough to straighten her clothes and mindlessly retrieve the paperweight. She placed it back on her desk. It was the Green Energies office issue, clear glass containing a miniature turbine. She found her bag, left the office and hurried along the darkened corridor, down the stairs and out past the un-manned security desk. Somewhere at the back of the building it sounded as if someone was trying to start a generator. Thankful for the blackout, she ran from the administration block and followed the unlit path through the trees to her cottage. Once inside, she locked the door, then went round making sure all the windows were also locked. Finally she went to the kitchen and poured herself a glass of water. She drank it in one, and as she went through to the sitting room the lights came back on.

She sat down on the settee, took her mobile phone and her tattered address book from her bag, turned on the phone, checked the signal and placed it on the table in front of her. Then sat straight and took long, deep breaths until the trembling stopped.

FORTY-TWO

Fin looked out to sea as the van accelerated up the hill from Easthaven in the dusk. Lightning crackled and danced on the darkening horizon. It seemed as if the rim of the world had sprung alive.

He had phoned Kath from the car park, and she had listened in horror as he told her what the Duck had discovered and what they thought the implications might be. He'd registered the concern in her voice as she asked him if he really needed to go up to Coldheart Farm, but she'd reluctantly agreed that if that was what it took to find the one thing that would convince the police, they should go.

'Just take care, love,' she'd repeated, a tremor in her voice, 'and get back as soon as you can.'

Now the van rattled along the empty road across the headland towards the farm. The journey took only five minutes, ending in the glare of security lights as the sensors detected their arrival in the courtyard.

The engine died and a deep silence settled. They climbed out and the lights went off, leaving them in darkness. The Duck stood for a moment, looking at the house.

'Doesn't look like there's anyone here,' he said.

Fin glanced around. The car was in the stable as usual.

'He'll be at the front.'

He went to the back door and knocked.

After some time, when there was no reply, he opened the door and walked in. The Duck followed.

'Hello . . . It's me, Finlay.'

No answer.

He put on the passage light.

They walked past the darkened kitchen and on down the hallway. Light spilled from the big room to the right, but no sound.

Fin pushed at the door.

It swung open and he stepped inside.

The room had been cleared. Apart from the marks on the panelling where the rack of joiner's tools had been fixed, there was no trace of the workshop or its contents. The piano had been pulled out from the corner. The lid was up, the stool was in place and there was music on the stand. A large oriental rug covered the floor. Arranged around the fireplace were a settee and two armchairs, in one of which, lit by the standard lamp at his shoulder, Norman Turner was fast asleep.

'Norman,' Fin said softly. He began to walk towards him.

But the Duck put a restraining hand on his arm, then shook his head, a strange look on his face. For some time he was silent. Then he said, 'He's dead.'

Fin's heart missed a beat. He took a step closer. Norman Turner's body was still. No rise and fall of the chest. No breath entering or leaving the partly open mouth. No flutter of an eyelid. A grey, waxy look to his complexion. And yet . . . he wore an expression that Fin had never seen on him before. A look of profound peace.

The Duck walked over and knelt beside him. Felt the skin of his cheek. Placed two fingers at the throat and held them there for some moments. Then stood up, nodding to himself.

Fin looked on, feeling oddly detached, as if this was

some hospital scene with which he had no connection. Yet it seemed, equally oddly, to come as no surprise.

The Duck touched him on the arm.

'I'm sorry, man.'

Fin nodded. He had wondered for a moment if the Institute might have had something to do with this. But a second glance at Norman Turner's face was enough to dispel the thought at once. Wherever he was now, it seemed that he had gone there gladly. Could he have committed suicide? Fin thought back to their last moments together in the kitchen, the way he had ignored the alarm clock's summons to walk, the unhealthy pallor, the strange light in his eyes. Fin guessed that he would only have had to skip his pills. Could you commit suicide by *not* doing something? Suicide by omission? And did it matter anyway? It was just a word. For what had happened, it seemed clear to him now, was that Norman Turner had reached some kind of agreement with himself. Something had taken place that had allowed him to stop struggling with the world, to let go at last.

'You all right?'

Fin returned to the moment. Nodded. 'Sorry. Yes. He had a heart condition. I don't think he was quite right this morning. After . . .' he gestured round the room, 'going crazy in here.'

The Duck nodded. 'So . . . what now, eh?'

'I don't know. What do you do when someone dics?'

'You call a doctor. Or the cops. Again . . .'

For a moment Fin entertained the strange thought that Norman Turner was listening to their conversation, hearing every word, perhaps even smiling at their dilemma. 'Let's talk in the kitchen,' he said.

The Duck followed him.

Fin sat down at the kitchen table. He felt dazed. Norman

Turner was dead. It seemed such a momentous thought, considering what a short time they'd known each other . . . He glanced around the sterile room, empty but for Leonardo, still on the wall, and Amy, now in pride of place on the centre shelf of the dresser. Fin looked at her again and wondered what responsibility she held, however unwittingly, for the moment that last breath had slipped like a butterfly from Norman Turner's lips. What responsibility did anyone hold for the way another person's life turned out . . . ?

'Leonardo, eh?' said the Duck, walking over to the picture. 'Did you know there are only two things known about his childhood? One, that a kite flew down and hovered over his crib when he was a baby. It brushed his face with its tail feathers. He always thought it was an omen. The other is that he went up into the mountains – hiking, I guess – and came across a cave. He looked into the mouth and was paralysed with fear at the thought of what might be inside. Yet he was dying of curiosity to find out.'

'What did he do?'

The Duck smiled and shrugged. 'He never said.'

The lights flickered. Seconds later there was a loud clap of thunder. At the same moment Fin's phone rang. Startled, he took it from his pocket. It was a number he didn't recognise.

'Hello?'

'Fin?'

'Yes.'

'Fin . . . it's Maia.'

'Maia . . . *Maia* . . . Maia? Are you OK?'

'No. I'm not.' There was a note of desperation in the voice. 'Something – something's happened. I need to get away from here.'

'What happened, Maia? Tell me.'

'I . . . I think I've killed someone.'

'What? You *serious*? OK . . . OK. You *think* . . . are you sure?'

'No, I'm not sure . . . but – everything's going wrong here, Fin. I've got to get out.' The voice cracked. 'Fin, I'm . . . I'm frightened.'

'OK. OK, I'll help you. It'll be all right. I've got a friend here with me. We'll come. Straight away.'

'Yes, but there's a prob—'

'Maia. *Maia*? You there?'

The connection had failed. Fin fumbled to find the last incoming number and dialled it. Engaged. He disconnected quickly. The Duck was looking at him.

'Maia – she's in some kind of troub—'

The phone rang again.

'Sorry. I thought someone was coming. It's OK now. But, listen – I'm going to have to be quick. I'm in the cottage right now. But I don't think I can stay here. They'll find out soon and come for me. It was Sean. He tried to . . .' She was choking back tears. 'Sean tried to rape me, Fin. But it's not just that. There's something really, really bad happening here. Some kind of racist thing. To do with the bombings on the mainland. Sean said they did it . . .'

'*What?*'

'I know. Fin? Fin . . . ?'

Shocked, it took him a moment to reply.

'Listen, Maia, can you get to the main gate? My friend's got a van. We'll come and pick you up.'

'That's the problem. Tide's coming in – you won't get across. Anyway, there're security cameras all over the place.'

'Are the lights on – where you are?'

257

'On and off. But all the security systems are on backup power. Oh Jesus, Fin, what am I going to do . . . ?' Her voice trailed off.

'OK. Listen. Maia – you still there?'

'Yes.'

'Is there anywhere you can hide? Anywhere on the island?'

'I . . . I don't know. Yes, there must be. I'll . . . I'll think.'

The Duck was nodding. He held out his hand for the phone.

'Maia, listen. It's Fin's friend here. You know the sea caves? . . . You do? Good . . . Yes . . . no, it doesn't matter. I'll tell you how. OK, there's one called the Vestibule. The old smuggler's cave . . . No? Don't worry. The path leads down into it . . . Yes, I can tell you where it is. So what you should do is head over there. Right now. Aim for the standing stone by the cliffs. You know it? . . . Ring us again when you get there and I'll tell you how to get down into the cave. You'll be safe there. I promise.'

He handed the phone back to Fin.

'Maia, you OK with all that? You'll be all right. Just get there. We'll handle it.'

'OK.' Her voice sounded small and far away. She rang off.

Fin looked at the Duck. 'Sean tried to rape her.' His legs felt weak. His voice didn't sound like his own. 'But that's not all. She thinks they're the ones who killed Poacher. The bombings, it's them. So we're right – about everything . . .'

For a moment the Duck stared at him.

Then they turned and ran for the van.

FORTY-THREE

Terence heard the first drops of rain hitting the window behind him. The lights had been off for twenty minutes. Now they were back on again. He turned from his desk to see fat trickles on the glass. It had been a long, tiring day and he'd been planning to go for an evening run in defiance of the approaching storm. The idea of pushing himself against the leaden atmosphere appealed to him, challenging the weather to help relieve him of the tension which it itself had partly created. But now, at last, it seemed that the storm was breaking. It would be folly to run the cliff path in the kind of conditions that were forecast.

He turned back to face the room, clasped his hands behind his head and stretched. It had been a day of two halves, to borrow from the idiot football commentator. The labyrinth programme had gone particularly well. Sean had curbed his more brutal impulses and been rewarded by an exceptional group. They had selected three out of twelve to go on to Schloss Adler for the full training programme. Normally it was one, two at the very most. But today, according to Sean, in addition to their performance in the labyrinth, one had demonstrated unusually good knife skills, while another already had some rudimentary bomb-making knowledge. If even two of them went on to become fully fledged operatives, it would be a triumph for the Institute.

There was another flash of lightning, followed almost

immediately by a deafening crack of thunder, directly over-head, it seemed.

Then there was Eugene. Eugene was still concerned about the Carpenter boy. He had warned him off once di-rectly, with the car, and twice by way of messages left with his parents. Although he had no evidence that the boy was up to anything, Eugene had an instinct for these things, which Terence trusted implicitly. In his twenties Eugene Hunter had spent three years on the Mozambique border with a tracking unit of the South African Army. There he had learned, and done, things he would never forget. And now his instinct, he had told Terence this afternoon, was that the boy was up to something. That he was planning some kind of further trouble connected with Maia. And if that was so, then they might have to consider getting rid of Maia. Or perhaps even both of them. Because once the integrity of any of the staff became compromised, it was just too dangerous to have them around, as had proved to be the case with the unfortunate Charlotte. Not that they had ever planned for her death to take place quite so close to home, but Eugene was an opportunist, another quality for which Terence respected him, and the opportunity had presented itself there on the bridge in the fog. No one, not even Eugene, could have anticipated Maia's brother being beneath the bridge at that moment.

The rain was striking the window behind him with great-er intensity, and now there was the first sound of wind.

So now Eugene had gone to Cliffton. A couple of hours off, he had said. Terence couldn't begin to imagine how Eugene might spend his leisure time, how he could ever get that calculating mind to slow down. Shopping mall, book-store, coffee shop, gallery, even brothel. He couldn't make any of the images fit . . . Anyway, on the way back Eugene planned to stop in at Easthaven for one more attempt to find the boy and, he said, talk some sense into him; though what Eugene meant by 'talking', Terence didn't care to guess. He sighed and stood up. Glanced out of the window again. Well, he might not be able to go for a run, but there were other ways of relieving tension. Would this have to be the last time? Oh Maia, Maia . . . He prayed not.

He tidied his desk, switched out the lights and left his office. Maia might well still be working. He had given her the report from Ashgabat late on in the day. He took the stairs down from the second floor and walked along the corridor. He opened the door to Maia's office. It was dark and empty. He would call her at the cottage. He stepped inside to use the phone, putting the lights on as he did, and took a sharp breath. Sean lay on the floor by the window, a small pool of blood by his head, a livid bruise spreading down from his temple, around his right eye and on to his upper cheek. Terence crossed the room in two strides and knelt beside him. Felt for a pulse. It was almost imperceptible. He stood up and dialled the emergency number. Thank God they kept a medic on the staff. Something like this couldn't possibly be handled by anyone from outside.

'It's Terence here. I'm in room nine, second floor of the administration block. We've got an injury, a head injury. It looks serious. Get over here as quickly as you can and deal with it. I might not be here when you arrive.'

He put the phone down. Looked at the unmoving body and shook his head, then picked up the phone again and dialled Maia's cottage.

There was no reply.

He dialled a final number. 'Eugene, I've just found Sean in Maia's office. Unconscious. He's been hit on the head. Hard, by the look of things. I don't know whether Maia's involved, but she's not here and she's not answering at the cottage. I think you need to get on to the boy now. And keep an eye on the parents too, in case she made a run for it and she shows up there. Call me on my mobile when you get this.'

He put down the receiver. Leaving the lights on and the office door open, he ran from the building and out towards the cottage.

Seal Island

FORTY-FOUR

A wind had got up while they'd been in the farmhouse. Now raindrops exploded against the van as it rattled down the hill. For a moment the sky was lit by jagged tongues of lightning. Fin could almost feel them, like the high-voltage charges of rage that went forking through him. Sean's leering face filled his mind and, with it, a single idea, a single hope. That Maia hadn't killed him, so Fin could finish him off. It was dawning on him with horrifying clarity that this attack wasn't just an assault on Maia, but on Fin too, on black people everywhere.

As darkness settled again he looked for the lights of Easthaven but couldn't see them. Nothing. And on beyond, across the narrows, where normally a scattering of lights winked on the mainland, nothing. There must be a blackout. The only light in the whole world seemed to be the headlamps of the van, their beam struggling to penetrate a few yards into the increasingly turbulent void.

Ten minutes later the van slowed and they began to bump down the track to Salvation Cove. At the shore they stopped and in the moments before the headlamps died, Fin glimpsed the white line of surf beyond the shingle. Then there was darkness again, and added to the sound of the wind the rumble of an angry sea.

Fin and the Duck unclamped the kayak and lifted it off the roof of the van. The Duck retrieved a set of paddles, a wetsuit and a helmet from inside. Fin's eyesight was starting to acclimatise to the darkness. Now the Duck was stripping down to swimming trunks and T-shirt in preparation for putting on the wetsuit. Fin could hear a new sound, the low boom of waves breaking out in the bay.

'Isn't – I mean . . . are you going to be OK? Out there.'

The Duck nodded. 'It's not far. And we're protected by the reef. It'll never get that bad in here.' He pulled the zip of the wetsuit to his throat. 'You want to try Maia?'

Fin took out his phone. Then jumped as it rang.

'Fin, where are you, love?'

'Oh, Mum, hi . . . um . . . still up at Coldheart Farm.'

'I was getting worried. Everything OK?

'Yeah. He's . . . er . . . telling us some interesting stuff. But it's going to take a bit longer.'

'What's all that noise?'

'Just the wind. I'm outside. Went to get something from his car. It's blowing really hard up here now.'

'You in the dark?'

'Yes.'

'Us too. So you really think what he's telling you will help?'

'Yes.'

'Good. But get back as soon as you can – won't you, love?'

'Soon as we can. Bye.'

He rang off. Then glanced guiltily at the Duck. 'Seemed like the best thing to say . . .'

The Duck nodded.

Next Fin dialled Maia, but there was no reply.

'She's probably out of range.' He was starting to have to shout to make himself heard. 'There must be dead spots on the island.'

The Duck was transferring things from the van to the

kayak. A flashlight. A coil of neoprene rope. A spare wet-suit. His own clothes in a waterproof bag.

Fin dialled again. Still no reply.

Between them they manhandled the kayak down the shingle.

For the next fifteen minutes Fin tried repeatedly to call Maia, his anxiety rising like the wind.

'OK,' said the Duck eventually. 'I think I'd better get over there anyway.'

Fin stared into the void for a long moment, wrestling with the thought of the dark water.

'I'll come with you,' he said.

The Duck raised an eyebrow.

'You don't know the island. I do. If . . . if anything's hap-pened to her, two of us will be better than one.'

'OK. But what about getting back?'

'Take her first. Then come back for me. Or I'll wait till the tide's out enough to walk.'

'Sure?'

'Sure. I can't not be there for her.'

'Cool.' The Duck rummaged in the kayak and brought out the spare wetsuit and waterproof bag. Shivering, Fin began to strip off.

Five minutes later they had left the land behind. Fin felt as if he was attached to a tightrope walker on an unsteady rope as they sliced through the waves. Only the precision of the Duck's paddle strokes maintained their balance and prevented them from toppling into the depths. In the darkness, with wind and spray battering his face, waves breaking constantly over the kayak, they could have been a hundred miles from land. All Fin could do was grit his teeth, pray that the Duck could see where he was going and try to imitate his confident paddling. After what seemed like an age, they began to hear the sound of the sea crashing into the caves ahead, a strange echoing roar, followed by a long sucking rush. Then the cliffs started to materialise out of the darkness. A larger wave than the rest caught them broadside on. For an instant Fin thought they were going to go under. He braced himself as the kayak rolled to one side, the water rushed up at him, and then the craft righted itself again.

The Duck turned, gasping and spitting, salt water streaming down his face. He grinned, and shouted something Fin couldn't hear.

They were coming close to the cliffs now, cutting across the waves so as not to be swept headlong against the rocks. The Duck's paddle swooped and dipped, braked and steered as if it was a living thing. Fin watched his companion's back and shoulder muscles flexing and straining as he struggled to keep the fragile craft on course for the dark mouth of a cave.

For a moment he lost control in an eddy and they began to spin, then regained their bearings. With a sudden surge of movement that left Fin's stomach behind, they shot through the cave mouth and into the darkness. The Duck lifted the paddle clear of the water and a few seconds later there was a crunch as the bows bit into shingle. The Duck climbed out. Fin followed. Together they dragged the kayak up the narrow, sloping strip of beach. The Duck retrieved the flashlight and turned it on. This was quite different to the Cathedral, small, low-ceilinged and reverberating with the noise of the sea crashing in through its mouth. The shingle ended in a wall of rock which curved towards a cleft in the right-hand corner. Here Fin could see that rough steps had been cut into the stone. At waist height was a rusty iron ring where once a rope must have been attached to guide people in the darkness. They moved the kayak further up the shingle and laid it lengthwise along the foot of the wall.

'We should change,' said the Duck, retrieving the bags with their clothes in them. 'It'll be too cold to stay in these.' He opened the first bag and passed Fin a small towel.

Five minutes later, the Duck leading with the flashlight, they set off up the steps.

Maia had been drenched within a hundred yards of leaving the cottage. Now, as she crouched behind what remained of the wall of one of the tumbledown dwellings at the ruined village, she was beginning to shiver. The rain was coming down in sheets, and the wind was so strong that she'd had to stoop so as not to be blown backwards. But for the last couple of minutes she'd been stuck here as a powerful searchlight probed the rough ground on either side of the road. The truck that trundled at walking pace towards the main gate was the one they normally used for night work down at the turbine park. It must be the only light on the island now, she thought. Just after she'd left the cottage there'd been a blinding flash of lightning, an almost simultaneous crack of thunder, and the electricity had died. Since then, as far as she could see, nothing had come back on. Perhaps even the backup system had been knocked out, though the night was so wild that she probably wouldn't be able to see anything anyway.

Between the ruined village and the shoulder of Lookout Hill there was an expanse of nearly half a mile of undulating ground with nothing but tussocks of rough grass and patches of bog. The road ran through the middle of it. It was likely that the truck would turn round at the gates and come back again. Meanwhile, she couldn't risk getting

269

caught in the open. So she crouched and shivered as the wind buffeted her from all directions. She pulled her phone from her pocket and began to dial Fin again, then stopped and put it away. Maybe her pursuers had something that could pick up phone signals.

Maia had no doubt that she was in danger. If the presence of this truck, its searchlight sweeping the darkness like some vast, all-seeing eye, was not enough, she had only to think of what had happened to Lottie, poor Lottie, and how it was now all too clear why she had died . . . The terror was unlike anything she had ever experienced before, a kind of cold, crawling sensation, accompanied by a racing heart and a mind that lurched from frantic activity to blind panic and back again. Yet although she'd registered what Sean had said, could link it now to Lottie's own discoveries, she couldn't associate the feelings of terror with Terry or the Institute. The idea that Terry might be out looking for her, perhaps with the intention of killing her as Lottie had been killed, simply wouldn't lodge in her mind; she couldn't accept the thought that the Institute was a training ground for some kind of clandestine racist army, and that somehow she had had a part to play in it all . . . Prey to so many conflicting thoughts and feelings, she was beginning to fear she might disintegrate.

Five minutes later the wall above her head was briefly illuminated again. She ducked down. So it was coming back. Good. She turned into the wall for shelter and faced away from the road and the wind. Then froze. A flashlight was coming up behind her, following the line of the shore, the route she'd taken from the cottage. It was only a wavering pinprick of light in the howling darkness, but it was approaching. So now she was trapped. Desperate for somewhere to hide, and unable to use her own flashlight, she crawled along the foot of the wall, feeling her way in the darkness, reaching up every so often for anything that might shield her from any downward gaze. And was eventually rewarded with the sensation of having entered a cavity of some kind. There was solid stone above her, in front of her, and on both sides of her. It was the deep hearth in what remained of the cottage's gable wall. She squeezed in, turned round and crouched there like a hunted animal, trembling, her heart in her throat.

For some minutes nothing seemed to happen. The beam of the searchlight continued to slide across the stones, the angle changing a little each time as the vehicle moved slowly forward. And then, before she even saw the approaching flashlight again, she sensed the presence of its owner, close by, out in the darkness to her right. She curled down into herself, hardly daring to breathe, praying she was invisible. And now a small pool of light was moving across the ground almost directly in front of her. It stopped, played backwards and forwards, nearly brushing her shoulder, and began to move on. Then her phone rang. She fumbled in her pocket to switch it off. But the beam had stopped moving again.

Seconds later a hand was reaching down and a voice was saying, 'It's OK. It's OK.'

It was Terry.

FORTY-FIVE

Eugene Hunter had known before the movie started that it would annoy him. But a certain nostalgia for the dangerous days of his youth had drawn him to see it, and that feeling had been satisfied. The scenes of pursuit and violent combat in the bush had set his heart racing. But the idea that the kaffirs had some right to the diamonds . . . Who had the expertise, the technology, the organisational skills to work the mines? Not the kaffirs. They were lazy, thieving bastards without a brain between them, whose only right was to a pick and shovel and a twelve-hour shift in the darkness where no self-respecting *blanke* would ever have to see them. No. That was just limp-wristed Hollywood drivel.

He snorted as he came out of the movie theatre, turned on his mobile and listened to Terence's message. He quickened his pace. At the car park he marched straight to the front of the line of startled moviegoers and late-night shoppers waiting their turns at the ticket machine.

'Doctor on call,' he said, holding up his phone as someone began to remonstrate. 'Emergency.' The muttering died away.

Only once he was out of town and heading for the bridge, the lights of Cliffton falling behind, did he realise what a wild night it was. Even with the windscreen wipers going full speed he could scarcely see the road ahead. Caught in the headlights, something glinted through the driving rain. The caravan at the viewpoint, where he sometimes stopped for a pie, now lying on its side with its roof partly ripped off. And, strangest of all, no lights to be seen anywhere. The normal roadside landmarks, the pub, the filling station, the farm shop, all in darkness. Everywhere north of Cliffton, it seemed, was without power. They'd seen the Met Office warning earlier in the day, of course. The chief engineer had flagged it at the morning meeting. Deepening low coinciding with a spring tide, severe gale- to storm-force winds in coastal areas, high risk of localised flooding, possibility of storm surges. The turbines had been shut down at midday, and everyone had carried on working as normal. There were no buildings on Seal Island close enough to the shore to be affected. Though depending on the severity of the storm, the causeway might be submerged for longer than normal, which meant in turn that he might have to stay in Easthaven tonight. The Ship Inn, or one of the village bed and breakfasts. He grunted at the thought.

But now there were more important things on his mind. The Carpenter boy – he had never felt comfortable about him, since that very first moment under the bridge with the girl's body. And it wasn't just that he was part kaffir, and so fundamentally untrustworthy. There was something knowing about him. He looked like a beach bum with those dreadlocks, but he didn't think like one. He was shrewd; Eugene could see that. He figured things out, listened to people and made up his own mind . . .

Then there was the girl, Maia, his sister. Eugene had been keeping an eye on her for a long time now. Partly because she was the Svensson girl's room-mate and so almost certainly privy to some of the muck her friend had been raking. Partly because of Terence's infatuation with her. Eugene had warned him, of course. But vanity was Terence's weakness. A pretty girl telling him he was God, and his judgement went straight to hell.

Then there was that cocksure little bastard Sean, who didn't know when to keep his mouth shut, his fists in his pockets or his fly zipped. A disaster waiting to happen, Eugene had always thought. And now, by the sound of things, it had. Had he not been so good at running the labyrinth programme, they would have slung him out long ago. He sighed. What a bloody mess. Well, at least most of it would be contained on Seal Island. Sean wouldn't be going anywhere, and the girl couldn't on a night like this. Which left only her brother. This time Eugene would wait all night for him to show up, if he had to.

He was on the bridge now. He still thought about the incident whenever he crossed it. The girl looking queasy, asking to stop, getting out and leaning over the parapet. Him waiting for her in the car, staring into the fog, and then the moment when his impatience was eclipsed by a sudden blinding sense of opportunity. Him getting out of the car and walking up behind her. Her turning at the last minute and starting to shout as he tried to grasp her around the waist. Her surprising strength and the kick she'd landed on his shins, which had made him yell. The struggle lasting twenty, maybe thirty, seconds, until he'd finally got a proper purchase on her and tipped her backwards over the rails . . .

Had he done the right thing? He dismissed the question at once. You did what you did in life and accepted the consequences.

A movement caught his eye. A light swaying in the darkness, somewhere out there in the narrows. Eugene was a creature of the land. The idea of being at sea on a night like this made him tighten his grip on the steering wheel. Whoever they were, he hoped for their sakes that they were putting in to Easthaven.

FORTY-SIX

Fin and the Duck stood in the meagre shelter of the standing stone. The flashlight was off, now that they were out in the open and could be seen. Here on the cliff-tops the wind would have torn their clothes from them, were they not already flattened to their bodies by drenching squalls of rain. In the short time since they had landed, the sound of the sea breaking against the cliffs had grown from a rumble to a sustained and furious roar.

Fin shook his head in frustration and put the phone back in his pocket. He crouched down at the foot of the stone, motioned to the Duck to do the same, cupped his hands at the Duck's ear, and shouted, 'She's still not answering. What do we do?'

'Find somewhere more sheltered. Where we can hear ourselves think.'

They stood up and made for the shoulder of Lookout Hill, a vague thickening of the darkness ahead. The wind was at their backs now, pushing them along in violent gusts that threatened to bowl them over.

Five minutes later they crested the grassy shoulder of the hill and at once felt the wind ease. Fin moved closer to the Duck and said, 'So, what—'

But the Duck grabbed his arm and pointed downwards to where two lights were visible. One a floodlight or searchlight of some kind, since it seemed to be moving, though very slowly. The other much smaller, little more than a pinprick, moving jerkily through the darkness beyond.

'We should go and see what's going on,' shouted the Duck.

Fin nodded. There were people down there who had tried to rape his sister. People who, it seemed ever more likely, had murdered her room-mate and were responsible for the death of his best friend. Violent, hate-filled people who wished ill on unknown others simply because of the colour of their skin. Even though the thought terrified him, it fuelled his anger and drove him on.

Invisible in the darkness, they made their way down the slope and out across the flat ground beyond towards the road. The lights were some way off now, the smaller one appearing only intermittently.

'I think we should split up,' shouted the Duck. 'See what we can find out. Keep out of sight. Just watch and listen. No heroics. Meet back here in an hour. OK?'

'I'll take the small one,' Fin volunteered. 'There's a ruined village over there. Bit of shelter at least. Let's meet there.'

The Duck nodded.

'See you in half an hour then. You'd better have this.' He handed Fin the flashlight. 'I won't be needing it, not following that thing.' He squeezed Fin's arm. 'Good luck.'

The Duck set off along the road, leaving Fin to strike out towards the shore.

'It's OK. It's OK.'

Terence's voice was soothing, as if he was talking to a frightened child.

'You're OK now.' He put a hand gently on Maia's arm. She wrenched it away.

'Come on. We'll go back to my place. Get you warmed up. Then you can tell me what happened.'

Maia looked at him, his hair blown by the wind, rain dripping down his cheeks.

'He tried to rape me. That's what happened.'

She saw the concern in his eyes and felt at once like collapsing into his arms. Letting go and weeping like a child until he made everything all right again. But no, she mustn't, couldn't . . .

'And you hit him?'

She nodded.

'Well, he's not dead. But I think you probably fractured his skull.' He gave an ironic smile. 'Sounds like he asked for it. Come on. Let's get you back indoors. It's terrible out here.' He stepped over a pile of stones and began to walk away from the cottages.

Maia followed him in a frenzy of indecision. Perhaps it really would be all right if she just went along with him. Perhaps everything would be back to normal by tomorrow morning. Perhaps Lottie's death really had been suicide and everything that Fin had said, everything that Sean had said, had been lies. For a strange moment, here among the tumbledown cottages in the howling, rain-lashed darkness, Maia found herself back at Schloss Adler, chanting the morning mantra. *I commit to a clean planet. Mind and body. Heart and soul. I commit to a cl—*

'Maia.' Terence was playing the flashlight on her. 'We need to get going.'

The rain stung her cheeks. Should she make a dash for it? Now? In the darkness? But she would never outrun him. Oh God. What was she to do? Fin and his friend would be going crazy waiting. Just go along with him, she told herself. Buy time to think. *I commit to a clean planet. Mind and body. Heart and –*

Drawn along by the beam of the flashlight, she was putting one foot in front of the other like a sleepwalker. Maybe this was what it was like to go mad. Maybe she was losing her grip on reality. Here in the dark on this island, a mere five miles from the family she had pretended for nearly a year didn't exist. This island populated by people she didn't know any longer whether she could trust, one of whom was the man she loved, who stood for so many things she believed in – or thought she believed in . . . But surely he'd make everything all right, wouldn't he . . . ? *I commit to a clean planet. Mind and –*

She stumbled and fell. Felt the cold, wet ground against her cheek. Sensed Terry bend down to help her. Wanted to curl up and lash out at the same time. But did neither. Meekly allowed him to lift her to her feet and steer her forward through the darkness again, one arm around her waist. Her mind starting to shut down now, too exhausted, too shocked and distressed to function properly. An odd feeling, but not unpleasant, almost peaceful in its own way. Like falling gently into some deep place in the earth. Or being inside a house where someone was going around closing the shutters one by one against the storm so everything would be warm and safe inside. And then maybe they'd make love, and afterwards she'd lie in Terry's arms and listen to his voice as he told her how beautiful she was. Now she had begun to cry. There was a salty taste among the raindrops. It was nice to cry here in the dark. Maybe it was the rain that was making her cry, because she was crying quite hard. Her shoulders were shaking too. But it felt good, the release, something washing clean inside her. Though it was hard to walk when she was crying as hard as this. Shaking all over and walking – it wasn't as easy as you'd think to do both at the same time. And of course she had to keep doing both or else Terry would be cross with her. Very cross. And what was that noise? That wailing noise that she could hear even through the sound of the wind. Oh yes . . . oh my God! It was her. She didn't know she could make such a loud sound. And now someone was shaking her, to see if she could make the sound louder still . . .

Fin was fifty yards behind them. Far enough off to be out of range of the flashlight, close enough to catch glimpses of the two moving figures that accompanied it. He had been following them for nearly ten minutes now. They were going very slowly, but even so he reckoned they must be close to the labyrinth.

One of them fell. He froze as the other stopped and bent down. He waited a moment, then took a few paces forward, thankful for the rain and the dark and the crashing of surf on the nearby shore. The figure being helped to its feet looked like Maia. The other was a man, he didn't know who. They moved on, veering to the right as they skirted what Fin imagined must be Hangman's Rock. A short distance later the figures stopped again, more or less by the cutting that ran down to the labyrinth. Something was going on. The Maia figure was shaking her head. Was that a cry he heard above the wind? Now the other figure was stepping closer to grasp her by the shoulders and shake her hard so that her head flopped like a doll's. And then she fell down again. The other figure stood for a moment, then bent down a second time and hauled her to her feet, put his arm around her waist and half supported, half dragged her down the cutting towards the labyrinth.

Fin waited to see whether they would come out again, but they didn't. A sliver of light appeared. Either the electricity had come back on again or the labyrinth had its own power supply. He took out his phone and texted the Duck. *at labrnth. dwn frm old vllge, ft of hngmn's rock. cm now.* Then he dropped to the ground and wormed his way across the sodden grass to the edge of the cutting.

Light spilled from the mouth of the mine that had gaped at Fin with such menace all those years ago. He looked at the sliding metal doors for a long time, confused by what he had seen. By the impression that Maia was not captive, did not seem to be in the company of this man under duress. That what had taken place had not seemed like an altercation, but rather as if the man, whoever he was, was trying to shake sense into her. All of which was so very unlike the Maia he knew. And yet . . . the terror in her voice when she'd phoned had been real. So who was the man? Her friend or her enemy?

Fin got to his feet. Hugging the grassy wall of the cutting, he made his way down to the doors and peered through the gap.

A broad passageway led away from him, the start of the old shaft, its walls and ceilings naked rock. The floor had been concreted over to provide a level surface. Ten yards in, it broadened into a large elliptical chamber. Here, facing the entrance and standing either side of another dark opening in the rock, were two Portakabins, from one of which issued the light.

Fin walked to the edge of the chamber. It was quiet and still after the violence of the storm. Keeping to the shadows, he worked his way around the edge of the chamber and across the mouth of the second exit until he came to the lit Portakabin. Its end window was too high for him to see in. He glanced about for something to stand on. There was junk in the space beneath the cabin. He spotted a plastic crate, gingerly extracted it, climbed on to it and very slowly raised his head to the level of the window. He was looking into what seemed to double as a control room and first-aid post. At the near end was a large console with rows of faders, knobs and buttons. Mounted above it a rack of a dozen small CCTV screens. At the opposite end were a table, a couple of chairs and a shelving unit holding bottles, tubs and rolls of bandage. Slumped in one of the chairs, pale and tear-stained, Maia gazed blankly ahead. Standing beside her was a slim man of medium height and clean good looks. He appeared to Fin to be in his forties, with a lightly tanned complexion and dark hair flecked with grey. He was holding out a glass of water in one hand and two white pills in the other. Fin wondered whether he might be a doctor. Now Maia began to shake her head and motion him away, but the man was insistent. He put down the water glass and took one of Maia's hands, uncurled her fingers and pushed the pills into her palm, then lifted her hand to her mouth. Still she refused. Now the man looked at her with exasperation and began to speak. Fin couldn't hear his words but he could see that the more the man spoke, the more his exasperation was turning to anger. Still shaking her head, Maia seemed to be shrinking back in her chair before his gathering verbal onslaught. Then she began to cry. The man reached out with both hands, as if to shake her again, and a look of pure terror came into her face. She got to her feet and at the same time lashed out. The man winced and shouted something as her fingernails raked his cheek. Then he lunged for her. She fell. He went down after her.

Fin had seen enough. He leaped from the crate, ran to

282

the Portakabin door, wrenched it open and strode across to where the two bodies grappled on the floor. He bent down to grab the man by the collar. The man looked up with a startled expression, which turned to one of angry recognition. Letting go of Maia he rose to his feet with a speed that took Fin by surprise. He roared something in what sounded like a foreign language, then punched Fin hard in the stomach. Fin gasped and staggered backwards, avoiding a second blow. The man made a grab for him, but Fin managed to twist away and make for the door. The man jumped at him and together they rolled down the steps. Fin felt jarring blows to his back, his elbow, the side of his head, and the man was strong. He pinioned one of Fin's arms to the ground and was reaching for the other when Fin drove his knee up as hard as he could. The man grunted in pain and rolled away, releasing his grip.

Fin needed to get the man away from Maia . . . He scrambled up and glanced around. The Duck should be here any minute.

The man was climbing to his feet.

Fin turned and ran headlong into the darkened tunnel.

FORTY-SEVEN

Caught in the headlights, heavy plumes of spray were breaking over the harbour wall as Eugene Hunter rounded the corner by the darkened Ship Inn and drew up on the quayside. He got out of the car and stumbled as the wind caught him. Two fishing boats rocked at their moorings. It was still a couple of hours till high tide, and already water was washing out of the harbour basin, spilling across the road and the pavement.

Eugene turned up his collar and walked towards the alley, the cottages of Easthaven mere shapes in the blackout. He couldn't imagine how anyone would want to live in anything as miserably cramped as one of these lightless hovels. But then the Carpenter woman was half kaffir, and her husband was a cripple and a drunk. It probably suited them.

He strode up the darkened alley and rapped on the door of Number Thirteen. After a moment the woman opened it. Her eyes narrowed.

'I'm sorry, he's not here.'

She began to close the door, but Eugene put his knee against it.

'Who is it?' the husband was calling out.

'Mr Hunter,' she said over her shoulder, still struggling to close the door.

'Tell him he's not—'

Eugene pushed the door hard. The woman staggered

and stepped aside as it swung open. He walked into the small kitchen, slamming the door shut behind him. Candles guttered in the draught. The man sat at the table, radiating hostility and alarm. The woman moved warily round to stand beside him. She was good-looking in her way, with strong features and large eyes, but her skin was that pale coffee colour that he most disliked, evidence of the pollution that was everywhere these days, an insidious, incontinent mingling of the races. And the man – well, he was a wreck. Drinker's complexion, self-pity and bitterness etched in the lines at his eyes and mouth.

'What exactly is it you want with my son?' the woman asked.

'That's between him and me,' said Eugene. He looked around. A living room across the tiny front hallway. Stairs to the upper rooms. He walked to the foot of the stairs and glanced pointedly upwards.

'So where is he then?'

The man bristled. 'None of your bloody business.'

The woman put a hand on his shoulder.

'He's right,' she said. 'It's not. But since it makes no difference, I'll tell you. He's spending the night with friends. On the mainland. And now –' emboldened by her speech she took a step forward – 'if you don't mind . . .'

Eugene thrust up his hand and she stopped at once. It always amused him to see how people responded so reflexively to sudden, firm gestures. 'But . . . I . . . do . . . mind . . . Mrs . . . Carpenter.' Slowing his speech added a note of menace. He reached out with a foot and hooked up a chair. 'All right if I sit down, is it?'

Neither of them replied. They looked at him, trying, and failing, to keep the apprehension from their faces. He sat down and leaned forward with his elbows on the table, gazed at them, then said levelly, 'Your son, Mr and Mrs Carpenter, is in a great deal of trouble, OK? Were this any other organisation, I don't doubt that the police would already have been called.'

An odd look crossed the father's face. He seemed about to say something. But the woman gave him a sidelong glance and he went silent.

'Your son,' Eugene continued, 'has trespassed on Seal Island, OK? It's private property, as you know. His actions were illegal. And furthermore, he has seriously harassed a member of our staff.'

The man's face had turned red. 'Our daughter, you mean,' he burst out, despite his wife's urgent shake of the head. 'And it wasn't harassment – he was worried about her. About what you're up to at that place of yours. Our son is one of the best. He's a smart lad who never harassed anyone, I'll have you know. So you watch what you say about him, *Mister* Hunter.'

Eugene examined a fingernail.

'And while we're at it,' the man went on, 'perhaps you could tell me why we've not seen hide nor hair of our daughter these last twelve months, eh?'

Now Eugene returned his look. 'Family matters are not our concern. Our concern is that she is our employee and she has been harassed by your son. Our concern, *Mister* Carpenter, is that he doesn't do it again.' He began to rap his fingertips on the tabletop. 'And I would like to advise you, as his parents, that if he does, we, the Green Energies Group, that is, may well be . . . what shall I say? . . . moved to discover that you, Mr and Mrs Carpenter, are the instigators of his illegal and antisocial behaviour. So I suggest that you take extra care to make your son's business your own from now on. And I would think particularly hard before making any allegations concerning Green Energies' activities.'

Eugene wasn't expecting the stick. It arced through the air, handle first, and smacked down on the tabletop a couple of inches from his face. So close that he couldn't avoid flinching.

There was a flicker of satisfaction in the man's eye as he roared, 'Are you threatening us, you bugger?'

Eugene composed himself. Then equally swiftly snatched the stick. Stood up. And in a single movement snapped it across his knee.

The man and woman gaped at him.

'Threatening?' he said mildly. 'Oh no. Just giving you a little advice. That's all.'

The woman was the first to recover herself. She marched around Eugene angrily, opened the door and held it for him. Wind rushed in, rattling the kitchen window and blowing out the candles.

'Whatever you call it, Mr Hunter, we don't want it. So now will you please go and leave us in peace?'

He set down the two halves of the stick on the table. Adjusted his glasses. Then walked past the woman and out into the alley.

He stood outside for a moment, glancing up. No glimmer of candlelight from the upstairs rooms. He'd thought she was telling the truth about the boy not being there, though he was less convinced about him being on the mainland. Anyway, Eugene hadn't got where he had in life by believing everything he was told. He walked down the darkened alley towards the crash of the sea against the harbour wall. How much did they really know? More than they were letting on. But the walking-stick trick had impressed them. He could tell. The cripple couldn't have handed him a better prop if he'd tried. You could break almost anything if you knew how to hold it, where to put the pressure. Wood. Bone. Whatever . . .

The wind halted him at the end of the alley. Where *was* the boy though? And what about the girl? He took out his phone and rang Terence. There was no reply. He wasn't unduly worried about her. The weather seemed to be getting worse, if anything. Even if she hadn't been found by now, there was no question of her managing to get off the island. But the boy . . . well, now that it had come to it, he had no choice but to wait. He glanced along at the Ship, at the dim glow of lamplight at its window. Pub gossip was often the best intelligence you could get, worth putting up with clammy sheets and the smell of stale beer for a night. He turned up his collar again and walked out into the wind.

FORTY-EIGHT

The tunnel was not as dark as Fin had first thought. Every so often there was a low voltage bulb enclosed in a small wire cage in the ceiling. He seemed already to have passed half a dozen. And there was noise. Not just his own breathing, loud in his ears, but the echo of two pairs of pounding feet. He was holding his distance from the man, but he didn't know how much longer he'd be able to keep up the pace. His lungs were starting to ache. And the tunnel seemed to be narrowing. Not only narrowing, but shrinking. Soon he would have to lower his head.

He ran on. Aware that the longer he could keep the man in pursuit, the more time the Duck would have to take care of Maia without interruption. He had just begun to stoop when without warning the tunnel opened into a smaller chamber whose floor plunged away into nothing a few feet in front of him. He stopped and glanced around. There was some kind of ancient-looking hoisting gear mounted in the roof of the chamber. It must once have lowered and lifted the miners' cage through the unfathomable blackness of the shaft that dropped away beneath it. To his right there was nothing but solid rock. To his left, two tunnels, one dimly lit with a set of rusty-looking rails running down its centre, the other pitch dark.

Why he chose the unlit tunnel, Fin didn't know, perhaps some primitive instinct of the hunted to seek darkness. With his pursuer gaining, he plunged onwards, and within a few paces all light was gone. The tunnel began at once to incline sharply downwards. Running as fast as he dared with only the scrape of rock on his outstretched fingertips to guide him, with no knowledge of whether the next step would slam him into something solid or pitch him out into thin air, produced in Fin a feeling of terror such as he could never have imagined. Within a short time he was drenched in cold sweat, his heart hammering fit to burst, and always the screaming temptation to reach into his pocket for the flashlight. His pursuer had no light with him, otherwise he would surely have turned it on his quarry. So long as Fin remained in the darkness, therefore, there was always the chance he could duck away from the main tunnel if the opportunity presented itself. But so far his fingers had met nothing but a continuous wall of rough rock. The air was chill and damp, and Fin noticed a metallic taste on his tongue. The tunnel continued to drop, twisting every so often as it led downwards in a descent that seemed to go on forever. And then, suddenly, there was no rock at his fingertips.

He stopped at once, paralysed at the prospect of what might, or might not, be in front of him. His pursuer was now only a few paces behind. Fin groped at his back, and the fingers of his right hand met rock. He stepped out of the mouth of the tunnel just as his pursuer burst through and also stopped.

For a little while the man stood panting in the darkness. Fin guessed he must be within touching distance. Then he spoke. His English was perfect but his vowels were slightly clipped. It came to Fin. This must be the director, Whitelands, a South African.

'I know you're here. And what you should know is that you're trapped. In a minute I'm going to walk back up that tunnel. You can come with me now. Or you can stay here. But be assured, there's no other way out. And I'll be waiting for you. So the sensible thing to do would be to come now. We can talk when we get to the surface.'

Fin held his breath. The man might be bluffing. There might be more than one exit. The old tin mines had ventilation shafts, he knew. The man might mean to have Fin killed the minute he appeared. But more than anything else, the same instinct that had made him choose the darkened tunnel now urged him not to reveal himself.

'I see,' said the voice. 'Well, if you stay, that's your choice. But I should warn you that in that case I will activate the labyrinth programme as soon as I return to the surface. And believe me, knowing that it's coming will be no preparation. You will experience fear and stress beyond your worst imagining. You will be lost down here, terrified and disorientated, with no thread to help you as you try to find your way back – the only way back. Passages will appear and disappear. Shafts will open and close. Shadows will move. You will face choices that might lead you to safety or into the jaws of the beast. You wonder what it is, this modern Minotaur. All I will say is that it will be present at every turn you take. And you will know it when you meet it because *you carry it within you*. So stay if you wish. But if you cannot conquer your fear, you might not come out with your reason intact. Assuming you come out at all, that is . . .'

He turned. Fin listened to his footsteps retreating up the tunnel. When he could hear them no longer he reached into his pocket and brought out the flashlight. The feeling of relief as the darkness receded made his knees weaken. He was in another chamber, a little larger than the last one, with no shaft dropping away into the depths, but with five identical tunnel mouths at more or less equal intervals around its circumference. In the roof of the chamber, fifteen feet or so above his head, there was a light fitting like those he had seen earlier. He played the beam on to it, reassured by the presence of something man-made in this subterranean wilderness. There was not only a light bulb in it, he now noticed, but what looked like a sound speaker and the lens of either a camera or a projector. He played the beam around the walls and spotted something else. Two of the five tunnels had grooves cut into the rock of the floor and walls, a few inches back from the mouth, as if designed for sliding doors. He looked more closely at one and, sure enough, retracted into the rock was the metal edge of what was clearly a door. So some of the tunnels could be opened and closed. Remotely, he presumed, most likely from the console he had seen in the Portakabin.

He glanced at the tunnel down which he had come. He thought of the thousands of tons of rock above his head. His breathing was starting to feel shallow, pressure was building up inside his head. He had to get out of here. He looked at the other tunnels. One seemed to go up, three went down. He chose the one that went up.

He had gone no more than a few yards when the flashlight dimmed, then died. There was no warning, no gradual weakening of the beam. Just light one moment, total darkness the next. He switched it on, then off again. Took out the batteries and warmed them in his palm, and put them back in. Nothing. He walked on. If the tunnel continued to climb it would surely not be long before he reached the surface somehow.

When he fell it was so sudden that he didn't know what was happening. One moment his feet were on the ground, the next he was in the air. He landed on his back and slid for a short distance, then came to rest. He lay still for some time, panting with shock, then sat up and felt himself. Nothing was broken, though there were aches and doubtless bruises.

Where was he? And what on earth was that sound? It was coming from somewhere in the darkness above him, a muffled rumbling and grinding, as if some object of enormous weight was being rolled back and forth. Had Whitelands activated the programme? Had something been unleashed somewhere within this dark web of shafts and passages and tunnels? Was he in a trap? Or had he simply fallen out of the known orbit of the labyrinth into some forgotten corner of the old mine workings where he might never be found – even if anyone was disposed to seek him? Might he simply die here, alone in the darkness?

His heart was beating fast, his breath coming short and shallow. He felt as if he was close to losing control, as if something might snap inside his mind and he would start screaming and then fall into oblivion, or madness.

He forced himself to take long, deep breaths. They calmed him. They also produced an echo which suggested to him that he was in a larger space than any of the other chambers. His heart rate was slowing, the panic retreating to the corners of his mind. He stood up, turned round and explored the rock behind him with outstretched hands. It sloped away, sheer, smooth, without even a fingerhold, for as far as he could reach. He pulled out the flashlight and tried once more. Nothing. Then he remembered his mobile. He reached into his other pocket, took it out and turned it on. Never had he been so pleased to see the small glowing rectangle of screen, the date and time, the lit keypad. In this absolute darkness it was more than light. It was hope. Even though he knew it would never work down here, it was something that made the possibility of a world beyond the imprisoning darkness seem real. And that, for now, was enough to lift his spirits. He held the phone up, surprised at how much the pale glow illuminated his surroundings. If he stretched out his arm, he could see seven or eight feet above him. Enough to know for certain that he would never scale the slope down which he had just tumbled. But what else was around him? To his left was solid rock. He edged to the right and was surprised to find that he could keep going. His foot struck something that wasn't rock. He held the phone at it. A length of rotten blackened timber as thick as his thigh, and another. Discarded pit props, he guessed. This place was much bigger even than the Cathedral cave. Above him there were at least two levels of gallery reaching up into the darkness. In the centre, along with more pit props, was a pile of rusting ironmongery and, lying on its side, a small wooden wagon with corroded metal wheels. The rails on which it had once run now disappeared beneath the rockfall blocking the mouth of a tunnel in the far right-hand corner of the cavern. In the opposite corner, the floor fell away towards a still, dark pool of water. Fin wondered where it had come from, and whether it might conceal a tunnel. But it offered no obvious comfort.

He sat down at the foot of the slope and turned off the phone to conserve the battery while he tried to think. The rumbling continued overhead, and now that his ear was attuned to it he could also hear another, lesser sound. A steady drip of water, an echoing pit-pat throughout the chamber. He had felt it as he worked his way around the walls, landing on his head and back. Then a drop landed on the exposed skin on the back of his hand. Moments later there was a scalding sensation as if it had been a drop of acid. And all at once he remembered a school project, sketches of the mine workings running out beneath the sea. That was what he was hearing, the rumble and grind of boulders on the seabed, agitated by the storm. So perhaps Whitelands hadn't activated the programme after all . . . Meanwhile, the drips – it was all coming back to him – were salt water that made its way through the porous rock, reacting with minerals on the way, to create this stinging liquid that rained from the roof of the chamber.

How ironic it was for someone frightened of the ocean deeps to find himself beneath the very bed of the sea, with not only fathoms of water but thousands of tons of rock bearing down on him. Fin could feel panic and despair crawling in from the corners of his mind. There was no way out of here. He had played right into Whitelands' hands. All the director needed to do now was precisely nothing, leave Fin down here to rot, accidentally lost in the labyrinth, which he should not have been in in the first place. Fin could only pray that the Duck had not been caught and that eventually someone would come to find him. If not . . . How long would he last down here? He had nothing to eat. He might possibly be able to drink the water in the pool as long as it wasn't toxic like the stuff that was coming through the ceiling – and if he wanted to prolong the end, that was. You could survive on water alone for a surprisingly long time, he remembered reading; a couple of weeks, maybe even more. But he would have lost his mind before then.

For a long time he took more deep breaths, trying to calm himself. Then he turned on the phone again for comfort. He would allow himself five minutes of light at a time. It was past midnight, at least three hours since his mother had rung. She would be desperate with worry by now.

In the light from the phone he could see a few square feet

295

of the wall at his side. It was scarred by the miners' tools, the tracings of lives lived out in the bowels of the earth. Men and boys, fathers and sons. Working long hours in the darkness, raggedly clad, undernourished and exhausted. The only light provided by a candle held in a leather band around the man's head. The boy holding a metal spike in place against the rock as the father swung his long-handled hammer at it, again and again, hour after hour, hoping for the soft bite of the spike in a seam of tin, rather than the sting of unyielding rock . . .

Had that scene ever played itself out here, in this chamber? Fin wondered. He stared into the darkness for a long time. At length he shook himself, fumbling in panic for the phone. The screen came back to life. It had lapsed into sleep mode. His mind cleared a little with the return of the light. He stood up. He couldn't sit here and wait for a rescue that might never come, any more than he could sit here waiting to die. In any case, there was Maia, not to mention the memory of Charlotte and Poacher, the dead of the bombings, the unsuspecting people everywhere who were to be the targets of whatever atrocity the Institute might be planning next. For all their sakes he couldn't give up, couldn't let the racists get away with it. Would never, if he got out of here alive, let the racists get away with it again, ever . . .

There were two possible means of escape. He picked his way across the cavern floor towards the tunnel blocked by the rockfall.

FORTY-NINE

Maia was seeing everything as if in a dream, or through a veil. Things were going on all around her but she felt disconnected from them, as if they weren't really anything to do with her or the reality she presently inhabited – which felt, she had to admit, strangely comfortable. Rather as if there was a layer of invisible cotton wool between her and the rest of the world, protecting her from everything that was unpleasant.

She remembered a loud noise and falling down in the wind and rain, then being in the cabin place where Terry wanted her to take some pills which she didn't want to take because they'd make her go to sleep, and she had to stay awake because . . . because . . . well, because something . . . And then Fin had suddenly turned up. God knows where he'd come from. That had been a surprise. But he hadn't stayed very long. He and Terry had had a fight about something and then they'd both run off, leaving her there on her own. She hadn't liked that much. She didn't want to be on her own. And she hadn't been feeling great . . . kind of wishing she'd taken Terry's pills after all so she could just pass out. And then, after a little while, things had started to become very confusing indeed. This funny little wiry guy had appeared. All in black with a black rucksack and a mysterious kind of smile. Who asked her if she was Maia, and if she was all right, and would she like some help. And she'd said, Yes, she bloody well did want some help, because she wasn't really sure where she was, and everyone else had fucked off and left her here. Oh yes, and Sean had tried to rape her.

So anyway, the little guy had said he was a friend of Fin's and he'd come to help, or something like that. Which had seemed good. And they'd been about to leave when he'd suddenly told her to sit down again, and he'd nipped behind the door. Then Terry had come back into the cabin, and the little guy had stepped out from behind the door and touched him, just touched him, on the back of the neck, and Terry had fallen down. Then the little guy had taken some rope out of the rucksack and tied Terry up and they'd left him there. After that she hadn't been quite so sure she wanted to go with the little guy any longer, and she'd started to cry. But he'd talked to her a bit, and smiled a lot, and there was something about him that made her feel safe. Though one thing she didn't understand was why everyone wanted to fight Terry all the time. Or rather, she thought there probably was a reason but she couldn't remember what . . .

So then they'd set off in the dark again. It was a wild and stormy night, but the little guy had shown her the way. They'd seemed to go across the whole island – why, she wasn't quite sure, when they could just have gone in the car and driven out through the gates and over the causeway. But he'd said this was the best way, and that seemed good enough for her. So she'd kept on following him, and eventually they'd climbed down some steps and, well . . . here they were. In a cave. A cave that was so noisy they had to shout at each other. And there was this kayak. She'd been frightened that he was going to go off in it and leave her. But he'd said no, there was something about the tide, and then he'd be able to take her across. So they were just going to wait here for the moment and maybe Fin would join them. She hoped he would. She wanted to see Fin. She didn't want Terry to hurt him. But most of all she wanted those pills she hadn't taken so she could go to sleep and not hear all the roaring and crashing of the sea trying to get into the cave.

FIFTY

Fin sat panting at the top of the pile of fallen rocks with his head in his hands. Stinging droplets rained down on him, and his exposed skin was starting to itch. He felt close to despair.

The wall of the chamber had collapsed from a point well above the mouth of the tunnel, and the resulting rubble had spilled back into the tunnel itself, as well as out into the cavern. There were chinks and cracks, of course. A mouse might have found a way through, but not a full-grown man. And the rock had come away in large slabs, much too heavy for Fin to move by himself.

As he climbed back down again, the words of a song came into his mind, a line describing an old woman as being as 'black as a crow in a coal mine'. For some reason it now struck him as hilarious. Was he as black as a crow in a coal mine? He began to laugh. The laughter rang through the chamber, echoing along the upper galleries, into corners and crevices and around the unseen roof. Then the sound began to frighten him and he stopped laughing.

The grumbling silence returned. He shook himself. He had to keep thinking rationally, and reason told him that he had just eliminated one of the only two possible exits.

Now he turned his attention to the wagon and the pit props. Might he be able to use them to build some kind of platform high enough to scramble up to the level of the first gallery? It was about a dozen feet above the floor of the

chamber, and in the absence of any obvious connection between levels he guessed that each gallery must be accessed
by its own tunnel.

The wagon was almost as heavy as the rocks. After a
struggle Fin managed to haul it upright, then push and drag
it to the foot of the wall, where eventually, using an iron
bar and piles of stone, he succeeded in levering it up on to
its end. Then, on top of it, he assembled a platform of pit
props, flat stones, a couple of old oil cans and other bits
and pieces of scrap metal. When it was ready he clambered
up on to the wagon, then on to the platform. It rocked but
held steady. He reached up and his fingers found purchase
on the lip of the gallery. Pushing with his toes, heaving
till his shoulder muscles screamed, he scrambled over the
edge and stood up. The feeling of satisfaction was intense,
a glimmer of hope in the darkness. He reckoned he was
about halfway along the gallery, although he couldn't see
either end. Counting as he went, he walked to the left and
after twenty paces came up against solid rock where the
gallery ended. He walked back again, scanning the wall in
case he had missed anything. Twenty paces. Then another
thirty paces. To be confronted by another wall of rock. The
gallery was sealed. They must have got to it by ladder from
the floor of the chamber.

He sank to the ground, convinced that he was going to
die.

It was a long time before he could bring himself to think
of the only remaining option. It scared him so much that
he kept pushing it away, back into the darkness. But the
urge for self-preservation would not let him ignore it. He
thought of the American he'd read about whose hand had
become trapped between rocks when he was hiking in
the wilderness. Realising that he had no prospect of ever

being rescued, since no one knew where he was, he had freed himself by sawing through his wrist with a penknife. Where did you find that kind of courage? Fin remembered wondering at the time. Now he knew. When certain death was the alternative, courage hardly even came into it. What had particularly struck him was the man's answer to the question 'How could you endure such pain?' 'It was simple,' he'd replied. 'I knew that with every cut I was another minute closer to freedom.'

Well, Fin didn't have to perform self-amputation. But he did have to investigate a dark pool and then possibly swim underwater into a tunnel of unknown length. Was that freedom or suicide? He had no way of knowing till he tried. But it was surely preferable to sitting here in the darkness and starving to death, or going insane. Drowning ought to be all right, as ways of dying went. Some people who had nearly drowned had afterwards reported the experience as being dreamlike. And at least he would be doing something to try to save himself.

Fin had never known such a feeling of fear as this. His insides were like water and his legs felt as if they would give way at any moment as he stood up and lowered himself back down to the floor of the chamber, then walked over to the pool.

It extended too far into the darkness for him to be able to see where it met the wall of the chamber, even when he held the phone out at arm's length. So he couldn't be sure whether it concealed a tunnel or not. The only way to find out was to get in and swim over. He stripped naked. If there was no tunnel, and this was just a pool contained by the corner of the chamber, then he didn't want to wait for death in wet clothes. He stood and shivered at the edge of the water, then lowered himself in and gasped. It was icy. It was also deep. He couldn't touch the bottom with his feet. And it was salty, though thankfully not stinging like the drips from the roof. It must have found some other route through from the seabed, which might turn out to be to his advantage.

Shuddering with cold, he swam out into the darkness. After a few strokes his fingers met solid rock. He moved one hand down below the waterline, searching by touch for an opening. There was none. He started to paddle sideways, moving along the wall, feeling as he went. And suddenly, there it was, the absence of rock, just water, as far forward as he could thrust his hand. And then, even better, his raised arm came out of the water before it struck the roof of the cavity. Which suggested that if the roof of the tunnel was level, there would be a space above the water all the way through. Not very much, three or four inches, but in that space there would be air he could breathe. And that made this worth risking.

He turned and paddled back to the edge, then got out and pulled on his clothes over his chilled, dripping flesh. If the tunnel did lead him out, he was going to need to be dressed on the other side. The only casualty would have to be the phone. It wouldn't survive the immersion. And if – he hardly dared form the thought – if he had to come back, he would be glad of the light for as long as it lasted. He switched the phone off and placed it on the rock, a conundrum for anyone who might find it in years to come. Then, for the second time, he lowered himself into the water and swam out to the wall in the pitch darkness. He found the tunnel mouth again. The idea of going in head first and not being able to turn round was too much, so he turned on his back and very gingerly, paddling with his hands, led with his feet. As it was, he couldn't fully extend his arms, but there was enough width, even here in the roof of the tunnel, for him to work them at his side like flippers. He needed to keep his head right back in the water, his nose almost scraping the ceiling. After a few strokes he let his head up by mistake. It bumped the rock and he took in a mouthful of salty water. He began to panic and paddled hastily back out again. He trod water, calming his breathing and trying to ignore the bone-numbing chill. Then he set off again. As long as he kept his paddling and breathing slow and steady it was all right. There was enough space between the water and the roof. And plenty of air, he kept telling himself.

He continued like this for an unknown amount of time. It was utterly dark and even the grumble of boulders on the seabed had retreated. The only sound was his breathing and the soft splash of his movements. And then the thing he most feared happened. His feet struck an obstacle. His heart began to thump faster. Struggling to keep his head back, he let his body drift down into the treading-water position and paddled towards the obstacle. Put out his hand. Felt rock in all directions. Felt a scream coming. Forced himself to keep breathing steadily and reached down as far as he could. Just when he felt he could reach no further there was no rock, only water. He hung in the dark treading water for what seemed like an eternity, wrestling with himself. Go back or risk going forward? Freedom might lie ahead, but so might drowning. Might. *Might*. What was certain was that freedom didn't lie behind him. 'With every cut I was that much closer to freedom.' He took the deepest breath he could and dived down through the darkness. Felt the bottom of the obstacle, hauled himself beneath it, kicked forward, rock scraping his back, lungs starting to burst. He kicked again. More scraping, panic building, driving forward with his feet, chest on fire, then suddenly nothing.

No rock. And starting to rise, expecting to feel rock against the top of his head, praying for air space, but no rock. Rising and rising. And then no water, but air – wonderful, life-giving air – filling his burning lungs in great heaving gasps and gulps, as the salt water streamed down his face and he blinked and blinked again. Because here there was not just air but light. Dim, but light all the same. Light and air. Light and air! Were he not still treading water, he would have turned cartwheels.

He wiped his eyes and looked up. The light was a long way above him, perhaps a hundred feet or more. But it didn't matter, he was out of the cavern. And there, a few feet in front of him, were what looked like steps cut into the rock. He paddled to the water's edge, clambered out and, without even stopping to shake himself, began to climb.

FIFTY-ONE

Outside the Ship, Albert stepped into the darkness and the wind caught him. He pulled up the hood of his coat and set off homewards, salt spray stinging his cheeks as he went.

Now that the weather had broken at last, everyone seemed less on edge. The atmosphere in the pub had been a good deal more cheerful this evening, aided, no doubt, by the oil lamps that stood on every available surface, defying the blackout and softening faces with their warm glow. It was as if the storm signified the end of something. Or the beginning of something. Even Shirley Archer seemed on better form, Albert thought. It was still less than a month since her lad had died, but she was a strong woman, Shirley, and tonight the banter at the bar had rippled back and forth as she teased and chided the regulars, her large presence spilling over the counter and out into the furthest corners of the room. Enjoyed by all except the sour-looking newcomer, a small balding man with spectacles, who sat at the end of the bar with a half-pint, refusing to be drawn into the proceedings. Silent though he was, his presence was an intrusion. Albert could tell he was irritating Shirley from the way she stood with her back turned to him.

Albert lifted his face to the wind. It had swung round to the north, which meant that things were going to turn worse before they got better. Meanwhile, he was going to get a good soaking from the spray that soared over the lamp posts.

His eye was drawn into the darkness beyond the harbour. To where a navigation light was swaying back and forth like a firefly, somewhere out in the open water. It had been there for at least a couple of hours. He'd seen it on the way over. They must have their anchor down, he imagined, waiting till they could get into harbour.

Albert gave a shiver.

He wouldn't like to be out there tonight. No matter how good his anchor.

FIFTY-TWO

Ten minutes after emerging from the tunnel, Fin rounded a bend and saw the Portakabin ahead of him.

Shivering with cold and dripping with water though he was, his whole body, from the pit of his stomach to the ends of his fingers and toes, tingled with elation. He had found something down there in the darkness that would change him forever. He had been tested as far as a person could be tested, and he had come through. Nothing would ever frighten him again; nothing would ever be the same again. Whatever Whitelands's version of the Minotaur, Fin had met his own down there in that cold black water. And he had vanquished it.

He forced himself to slow down and approach the space ahead with caution. He could already see that the entrance doors were still ajar, much as they had been however long ago it was . . . Two hours? Three? A lifetime? The lights too were still on. He crept up the last few yards of the passage. There was no sound coming from the Portakabin. Fin retrieved the crate and stepped up to peer through the window. At the far end, in the dispensary area, there was evidence of a struggle. Both chairs lay on their side. Sitting on the floor, his back to the wall and his wrists and ankles bound with what looked like the Duck's blue rope, was Whitelands. Between his teeth he held a pair of office scissors with which he was now trying, with little success, to saw through the rope at his wrists.

Fin wondered for a moment whether he should go in, take the scissors and confront him with Maia, Lottie, the bombings . . . But he decided against it. Not now. What he needed most was to see Maia with his own eyes, to know that she was safe. The answers could come later. And unless someone came along and untied him, Whitelands was going to be there for a long time.

As he stepped down from the crate a different thought struck him. He walked across to the other Portakabin and tried the door. It was open. Inside were boxes and crates, tools and other items of maintenance equipment, and what he had been hoping for, a row of metal lockers. Two were empty. The third had several pairs of black overalls hanging inside it. Fin took one down and held it against himself for size. It would do. He scrambled out of his wet clothes and pulled on the overalls. On the back of the door hung a waterproof jacket. He took this too. Now only his shoes were wet. He could live with that.

He left the Portakabin, slipped through the doors and out of the labyrinth into the night. The wind and rain in his face felt sweeter than anything he could have imagined. He set off towards the sea caves.

The island seemed deserted. Perhaps, once he had found Maia, Whitelands had stood down the rest of the search party. Fin hurried on, casting a glance in the direction of the ruined cottage. If the Duck had Maia with him, he wouldn't be waiting there. He would have gone straight to the shelter of the caves, or maybe even have got her back on to Whale Island by now. Fin struck out towards Lookout Hill.

Twenty minutes later the standing stone materialised from the darkness. He stood for a moment, scanning the ground for the opening, concealed in the seaward side of a grassy bank, where the steps ran down to the Vestibule cave. He noticed that the sea sounded different. Although the storm continued to buffet him as violently as before, the roar and crash of the waves seemed less loud. And then he realised that the wind had changed direction. Now it was bearing down from the north, and the waters around the sea caves were sheltered from the north by the bulk of Whale Island. Fin made his way down the steps, feeling a tightening in his stomach as dense darkness closed in on him once more.

He stepped on to the shingle and gasped as a light came on, full in his face, blinding him. A hand gripped his arm and seconds later let go.

'Wasn't sure who you were for a moment,' said the Duck. He stood back, looking Fin up and down, taking in the strange clothes. 'You got wet?'

Fin nodded.

'But you made it.' He grinned. 'Where've you been?'

'Down a mine,' said Fin. 'Have you . . . ? Is she . . . ?'

The Duck shone the flashlight away from the steps to where Maia was sitting on the shingle with her head in her hands, rocking to and fro as she stared with an unfocused gaze at the mouth of the cave. She had not yet registered Fin's arrival.

'Is she all right?' Fin asked.

The Duck nodded slowly. 'She's somewhere else right now. Best place for her. For the moment anyway.'

'Drugged . . . ?'

'No, no. Not drugged. Just, like . . . out of it. Shock.'

Fin walked across to her and she looked up. There was recognition in her eyes but no emotion.

He crouched down and put his arm around her shoulders. She made no attempt to move away. He stayed there

310

for a long time, not speaking, listening to the noise of the storm, feeling his sister's closeness. She said nothing either, but after a while she let her head drift sideways on to his shoulder.

The Duck had been standing guard at the foot of the steps. Now he walked over to them. Disturbed by the sound of his approach, Maia pulled away from Fin. She sat up straight again, drew up her knees and clasped her arms around them.

'Were you waiting for me?' asked Fin as the Duck sat down on the shingle at his side.

'No. Just waiting till it's safe to go.'

'How long have you been here?'

'Couple of hours.'

Fin nodded. 'Good work with Whitelands.'

The Duck grinned. 'You saw him?'

'Trying to cut himself loose with a pair of blunt scissors in his teeth.'

'Good luck to him.' The Duck looked at Fin. 'And you? You all right, man?'

He knew, Fin thought. Knew that something had happened. And also knew not to ask what.

'Yes,' he replied, 'I am.'

The Duck reached across and put a hand on his shoulder. 'Good. Because we need to get out of here now.'

'I've got to ring home,' said Fin. 'Mum'll be going crazy. You got your phone? Lost mine.' It seemed too complicated to explain what had really happened.

The Duck passed it to him. He dialled but there was no signal.

'We'll be there in under an hour,' the Duck said.

'I'll go up to the top and give it another try once you've gone.'

The Duck nodded, then turned to Maia. 'We're going to go in the kayak now, Maia. OK?' His tone was quite matter-of-fact. 'She can wait in the van while I come back for you,' he added to Fin.

'In the kayak.' Maia repeated his words, still staring at the cave mouth. 'Good.'

Fin glanced anxiously at the mouth of the cave. The sea might have seemed quieter from the top of the cliff but down here there was little evidence of it. The Duck looked unworried as he readied the kayak, then approached Maia with the spare wetsuit, crouched down again and said, 'You're going to get very cold and wet. Better if you wear this.'

Maia turned and looked at it. Then shook her head twice.

Fin began to say something, but the Duck motioned him to silence. They stood up and walked away a little distance.

'We need to keep her calm,' he said. 'The one thing I can't have is her freaking out in the kayak. It's OK, she'll just have to get wet. I've got more clothes in the van.'

The Duck changed into his wetsuit, then turned to Maia again. 'All right, Maia? You just come on now and we'll get into the boat.'

Maia stood up and walked to the kayak. She waited while Fin and the Duck slid it into the water, then took the Duck's hand as he led her to the shallows and helped her ease herself down into the rear compartment.

'I'll come straight back for you,' he said to Fin. 'OK?'

Fin nodded. He watched the Duck paddle away, Maia sitting still and solemn in the stern of the fragile craft, her normally tight, dark curls now limp and bedraggled. His sister. And friend. Once. Would they be friends again? He didn't know . . . In the physical sense she was back again now. But in another more complicated sense he wasn't so sure that she was – not yet anyway.

By the beam of the flashlight he watched the kayak pass through the mouth of the cave and disappear out into the crashing darkness beyond. He sat back against the cold rock, finally letting the enormity of what Maia had uncovered flood through his mind. Wrestling with it all until he was left with a single question. *Why?* Why would anyone want to save the planet with one hand and destroy it with the other? That was where everything ceased making sense . . .

Fin closed his eyes and let the roar of the sea take him over.

FIFTY-THREE

Kath was at the sink when the maroon went up. She heard a bang like a dull thunderclap above the storm. The sky filled with a burst of brilliant pinkish light. It drifted sideways in the wind and began to fade. But briefly though it lasted, there would not be a single person in Easthaven who didn't know what it signified.

In an odd way it was a relief. Even if for the wrong reason, it signalled an end to the waiting, something to plug the agonising vacuum of the past few hours. She had done everything she could. Rung Fin repeatedly, rung the police again, all to no avail. Cliffton police station was currently being manned by a skeleton staff of two. Finally she had got Sally to drive her up to Coldheart Farm. The lights were out, but they'd gone into the house anyway, as far as the kitchen, where they'd called out. There had been no answer, no sign of life. For the next hour they had driven the length and breadth of the island, looking for signs of an accident. They had even been down to the causeway, but there was nothing parked at the end of the road, and the causeway itself was invisible beneath the breakers that crashed through the darkness. Fin and his friend must have gone over to Cliffton for some reason, Kath convinced herself. Though why hadn't he called? And why wasn't he answering?

They had driven back to Easthaven, worried and dispirited. For the next three hours they had sat in the kitchen, waiting for the phone to ring, listening for footsteps in the alley. At first Danny had been full of the encounter with Hunter and how they'd 'seen him off', as he put it. 'That was good, what you said about Fin,' Kath had remarked as she made the first of several cups of tea. ' "One of the best" . . . nice to hear that's how you feel about him.' Danny had blushed and mumbled something inaudible.

The pink light died in the sky.

'That was a—'

'I know.'

Danny was already struggling to stand up. Muttering to himself, 'The bugger broke my stick.'

Kath took the floor brush from its place beside the fridge and passed it to him. It was a little too long to use as a crutch so he grasped it just below the head and heaved himself to his feet.

She fetched their coats and a couple of torches and moments later she, Sally and Danny left the house and made their way down the alley towards the harbour, where a dozen or more flashlights already winked in the darkness.

A large crowd milled on the quayside. Familiar faces strained anxiously into the darkness for glimpses of what was going on beyond the harbour wall, where now the harbourmaster and a dozen other village men in oilskins were setting up a searchlight and preparing to fire a rope out to the stricken vessel. A fishing boat from Cliffton, so the word went, she had developed engine trouble and had been lying off the harbour all evening, waiting till the storm died down so she could put in safely. But her storm anchor had started to drag and she was in danger of being carried on to the rocks a few hundred yards up the shore from Sally's cottage.

Danny glanced around as they reached the crowd, then

peeled off and began walking away, leaning on the brush like some shuffling nocturnal street sweeper.

'Where are you going?' Kath called after him.

'Make meself useful,' he replied gruffly.

She watched him stump away from the crowd and make for the small group of men by the harbour wall. He wouldn't have done that a month ago, thought Kath. She prayed they wouldn't turn him away.

In his sleep Eugene Hunter heard the maroon going off. Instantly he was back in the bush under the magnesium brilliance of a flare, terrorists running for their lives through the shadows. The vision faded. Sleep began to beckon again. Then a commotion started on the quayside beneath his bedroom window. He grunted and sat up, rubbing his eyes and wondering where he was. Easthaven, it came back to him. The evening in the bar had been fruitless. The locals had closed ranks on him under what had seemed like the telepathic direction of the large brassy Archer woman. He had learned nothing of any interest whatsoever, and had made a mental note to ensure that the Ship's contract to run the Open Day bar was not renewed next year. Then he'd gone to bed feeling tired and irritated and, if he was honest, a little anxious. He'd been unable to raise Terence on either his mobile or his private landline, and the main switchboard was on overnight voicemail. Things were going on on Seal Island and he had no control over them. It was unsettling.

Now he got out of bed, drew back the curtains and stood looking out. Practically the whole village was there, it seemed. There must have been a hundred people or more. They had rigged up a searchlight on the harbour wall. Beyond it, a hundred and fifty yards at most, he could see the vessel, a small fishing boat. Pounded by large waves which every so often broke right over her, she was listing towards the shore. A dozen figures clung to the deck, gesticulating to the group of men by the harbour wall. There was what looked like a puff of smoke, and a rope went snaking out through the darkness. It fell short of the vessel and was hauled back in again.

He stood watching for a little longer. All the time more people were drifting down from the further parts of the village to swell the crowd. The rain seemed to have lessened, but the wind was still blowing as strongly as ever, now coming straight down the narrows between Whale Island and the mainland to strike Easthaven with all its force, rattling the windows of the inn, carrying with it the commotion of voices and the stuttering of the portable generator that was powering the searchlight. He shook his head. He would never get back to sleep with this racket going on. He pulled on his clothes and went downstairs and out into the crowd.

FIFTY-FOUR

The darkness at the cave mouth was starting to lessen as the kayak nosed in from the sea. Fin's heart leaped with relief. The Duck paddled up to the shingle. As the craft came to rest he slumped forward, exhausted.

Fin walked to the water's edge.

'Is Maia OK?' he asked.

The Duck grunted and nodded.

'Sorry, man, I'm bushed,' he said without lifting his head. 'She's in the van, safe and warm.'

Fin squatted down by the kayak.

'Thanks,' he said. 'Thanks for all you've done this evening.'

The Duck looked up with a wry grin. 'Thank me when we're back on Whale Island.'

'Do you need a rest?'

'Yeah, I'll take five.'

As the Duck closed his eyes and steadied his breathing, Fin sat on the shingle and watched light seeping into the archway of sky ahead of him. So this was it. This extraordinary night was coming to an end at last. Maia's phone call seemed like a lifetime ago. Tiredness was starting to take hold and he was struggling to piece together the sequence of events in his mind . . .

Eventually the Duck sat up straight.

'OK. Let's get out of here.'

Fin waded into the shallows and helped turn the

kayak around, then climbed aboard to take his place at the rear.

With a weary gesture the Duck raised his paddle. Fin followed suit and they made for the mouth of the cave once more.

FIFTY-FIVE

Caught in the searchlight, out beyond the harbour wall, a solitary figure in an orange survival suit swayed beneath the cable. The crowd held its breath. The man's progress had been smooth at first, but now something had gone wrong. The tackle had jammed. He hung there above the waves. Meanwhile, the vessel seemed to be drifting ever closer to the shore. It appeared to the onlookers as if the cable was the only thing preventing her from being swept on to the rocks.

Eugene mingled with the crowd. There was talk that the coastguard helicopter was on its way. They would need it, he thought. With the man stuck out there on the cable, it seemed unlikely that they would get everyone else off before she ran aground. Eugene scanned the faces around him. Crowds like this made for interesting opportunities. They were magnetic, they drew people in, and they offered a cloak of invisibility. Things could go on unnoticed in crowds. He wondered if the Carpenter boy might show up . . .

Halfway between Seal Island and Whale Island, Fin and the Duck were struggling. The waves were less high than on the way out, but they were close-packed and powerful. Added to which, with the spring tide running, a fierce current raced through the narrow channel. It was doing its best to drag the kayak out to sea.

This was the Duck's fourth crossing that night, and it was clear to Fin that he was fast running out of steam, his paddle strokes faltering. Fin was doing his best to keep going, digging the blade hard into the water with each stroke. But this battle with the waves and the current was starting to sap his energy too. Despite the exertion, he was beginning to shiver. He was almost tempted to put down the paddle and fall asleep, right there in mid-channel. There was a question gnawing at him too, though he was too weary to engage with it. Why, when he had finally got a signal on the Duck's phone, had there been no reply from Number Thirteen? He had no idea what time it was, but dawn was thinning the eastern darkness. They should have been in bed, surely, or waiting for him to call . . .

He forced himself to think of Maia and Poacher, and paddled on.

In his bungalow on the hill, Albert Smith thanked Sally again for ringing and put down the phone. He was always a heavy sleeper, and tonight, despite the storm, had been no exception. He threw on a jumper over his pyjamas, then his overcoat, pulled on his wellingtons and set off as fast as he could for the harbour. From his vantage point above the village he could see a searchlight and a lot of people at the quayside. Then a bend in the road took them out of sight. When they returned to view, another beam had joined the first, though this one was playing over the water from above. A search-and-rescue helicopter hovered there in the dimness of dawn. Beneath it, listing in the waves, was a fishing boat – the one whose light he had seen earlier, he guessed. It seemed to be attached to the shore by a cable from which dangled a tiny figure. He shuddered to think what it must be like swinging helplessly above those furious, hungry waves. He walked on as fast as his legs would carry him. As he approached the Ship Inn his thoughts returned for a moment to the sour-faced stranger who had sat silently at the bar the previous evening. Then he was round the corner and into the crowd . . .

At Salvation Cove Fin and the Duck hauled the kayak out of the water and collapsed on the shingle, chests heaving, unable to move. It felt to Fin as if they'd paddled a hundred miles.

They lay there for a long time, till eventually the Duck groaned and climbed to his feet. Fin reluctantly followed him, and they dragged the kayak up to the van. In the front seat Maia appeared to have fallen asleep. She didn't stir as they heaved the kayak on to the roof and secured it, then changed from wetsuits into dry clothes. The Duck into jeans, Fin into the overalls.

Only as they climbed into the cab did Maia sit up and look around. She was wearing the Duck's spare fleece and jeans. Frayed and oversized, they gave her the appearance of a refugee which, in a way, she was, thought Fin. He squeezed up next to her and took her hand. She didn't resist. Her skin felt cold and damp.

'We're going home now, Maia. Back to Number Thirteen.'

A shadow crossed her face. She frowned as if she was trying to remember something. Then the frown faded. She nodded and closed her eyes.

Ten minutes later, as they turned down the hill towards Easthaven and noticed the activity at the harbour, Fin's first thought was that Kath had already persuaded the police to come, and now they'd arrived to seal off the island. Then he took in the helicopter and the stricken boat.

'A rescue,' said the Duck.

Maia opened her eyes. 'You mean another rescue,' she said quietly.

'Another rescue,' echoed Fin.

Maia looked at the Duck. 'What's your name?' she asked.

The Duck smiled.

'Dave. Dave Leduc. Though everyone calls me the Duck.'

He caught Fin's eye and winked. *So now you know.*

'Oh.' Maia lapsed back into silence.

Fin glanced at his sister and felt a spring uncoiling inside him. Journey's end was in sight. Now they could call the police with confidence. As long as Maia was in a fit condition to make a statement to them, it would soon be over.

They were on the final approach to the harbour. Ahead, where it turned the corner at the Ship, the road was solid with people.

'We'll have to walk the last bit,' Fin said to Maia. 'You OK?'

She nodded.

They parked as close to the corner as they could. Grey was seeping across the sky from the east. Fin glanced towards the narrows, where the sea still bucked and heaved beneath the squalls of spray that streamed like sleet from the crests of the waves.

As they turned the corner a cheer went up from the crowd. A winchman was being lowered from the helicopter to the deck of the stricken vessel. On the harbour wall, meanwhile, hands were reaching up to release the orange-suited figure of a man from the harness that attached him to the cable and lower him to the ground. In the background, standing by the portable generator with what looked like a brush in one hand and a fuel can in the other, was a figure that seemed to be Danny. Fin looked twice to be certain. Then the crowd swallowed them up.

The whole village was there, it appeared, but most people were too gripped by the drama being played out beyond the harbour wall to pay them much attention.

Keeping to the back of the crowd they made their way past the Ship. Fin stepped close to the Duck and said, 'Just seen my dad over there.' He pointed to the harbour wall. 'And I guess Mum will be here somewhere too. Let's get Maia into the house. Then one of us can come back out and find them.'

The Duck nodded.

They walked on a few paces. Then Maia stiffened and stopped.

'What is it?' Fin asked.

She seemed unable to speak. He followed the direction of her gaze to where, a few paces ahead, a short, balding man with wire-framed glasses stood in the crowd.

'Hunter,' he said urgently to the Duck. 'We'll have to go round the back way.'

But at that moment Hunter turned towards them. His eyes widened in surprise, then narrowed. He moved with startling speed. Before Fin had time to react, he had el-bowed his way to Maia's side. With one hand on her wrist and his mouth close to her ear, he whispered something that made her freeze in terror.

He steered her a step closer to Fin and said softly, 'I have a knife against your sister's back, OK. You come with me now. If you do anything to attract attention, I'll stick it in her. Start walking.'

As Fin turned, heart pounding, and began to walk back the way they had come, he realised that the Duck was no longer with them. At the moment Hunter had approached Maia, the Duck had stepped sideways into the crowd and melted out of sight.

'Keep going,' came Hunter's voice behind Fin.

As they drew level with the entrance of the Ship, the door opened and Shirley Archer appeared holding two long tubes of paper cups. Behind her, carrying a catering-sized Thermos, came her husband, Stan. Shirley paused to get a better grip of the cups in the wind. Hunter, Maia and Fin stopped directly in front of her, their way blocked. Shirley looked up.

'Fin!' she exclaimed. 'Not leaving, are you? You're just who I need. There's thirsty lads over there – your dad among them, I see.' She raised an eyebrow. 'So here – give me a hand with these.' She began passing him the cups, then paused. 'Maia! I didn't know you were back.' Fin stood there, feeling Hunter's presence behind him. Maia said nothing but turned her head away. Shirley's look of surprise changed to one of puzzlement, then to a scowl of disapproval as she caught sight of Hunter. Fin could see her trying briefly to work out what was going on.

'Anyway,' she said briskly, 'can you give me a –'

Her eyes widened as the Duck stepped forward from the crowd, his arm flashing out. Hunter grunted and went down on his knees, the knife skittering out of his grasp as he did so. Shirley gasped and stood smartly out of the way. Maia cried out and grabbed at Fin as Hunter shook himself and struggled to get up. People were turning to see what the commotion was. Now the Duck had Hunter by the arm, forcing it behind his back.

'He was trying to kidnap my sister,' yelled Fin from the doorway of the Ship, where he stood with a protective arm around Maia's trembling shoulders. 'And we think he was involved in the bombings on the mainland. Hold him!'

Shirley had recovered herself. She turned towards Fin with a look of astonishment.

Hunter was twisting and turning. He finally wrenched himself out of the Duck's grasp and began to run. Shirley's look hardened. She moved smartly forward and stuck out a foot and Hunter went down again.

'Give us some help here,' she yelled. Before Hunter could get up, a hefty bystander fell on him. Several other men joined in, and within a short while a kicking, struggling, cursing Hunter was immobilised.

'Get off me,' he yelled from beneath his captors. 'This is assault. This is outrageous. Call the police, someone . . .'

'Keep him there,' said the Duck. He drew Shirley aside and spoke to her. Fin stood with Maia's head buried in his shoulder, watching Shirley's face darken with horror and disbelief, then turn pale with rage. Ignoring the spectators, she strode back to where Hunter lay piniomed on the ground and stood for several moments, hands on hips, looking down at him.

Fin wondered whether she might be going to kick him. But something else happened. The rage left her face. Her features crumpled, her shoulders drooped and she began to cry. After a while her husband walked out of the crowd and put an arm around her, and for some time she stood there sobbing quietly, unable to move. A large blonde woman in a black T-shirt, lost in grief.

'Come on, love,' said Stan Archer eventually. 'You need to get indoors.'

She dabbed at her eyes and nodded. 'You tell them all what he's been up to,' she said to the Duck. She turned to Hunter's captors. 'We'll lock him in the cellar till the police come.'

She allowed herself to be walked into the pub.

The men hauled Hunter to his feet. He stood defiantly, his face betraying nothing. He didn't look at Fin or Maia as he was marched inside the Ship after Shirley and the door swung to behind them.

FIFTY-SIX

With the coming of dawn, it seemed that the storm had taken on new life. Terence Whitelands could feel the wind buffeting the 4x4, hear its howl above the noise of the engine, as he reversed the trailer down to the water. He opened the window to look out as he negotiated the last few yards. The rain had strengthened again. It stung like fine gravel against his cheeks. Even here, in the sheltered inlet on the tidal flats, foam-crested waves surged towards the shore. He had never seen the water so high over the causeway. It was almost lapping at the gates.

The one thing for which he was grateful, in all the chaos that otherwise surrounded him, was the fact that Green Energies had decided when they had bought Little Knossos that it was essential, in case of medical or technical emergency, to be able to leave Seal Island at all times, even when the causeway was submerged. To this end, a small boat was kept in a boathouse a little way along the shore from the main gates, while at the opposite end of the causeway, on Whale Island, a vehicle stood permanently in a lock-up.

The trailer's wheels disappeared beneath the waves. Terence stopped and turned off the engine. Asked himself yet again why Eugene was not answering his phone. Eugene always answered his phone, no matter what time of day or night, no matter where he was. His last message had been to say that he had visited the Carpenter parents and was now spending the evening at the Ship, where he might also have to stay the night, to try to get information on the boy's whereabouts. He would deal with the Carpenter girl and the Sean situation in the morning, as soon as he could get back to Seal Island. Meanwhile, Terence was not to worry.

But that had been hours ago, before the shambles at the labyrinth. And now Maia had vanished, spirited away by her brother's accomplice, whoever the hell he was, crafty little sod. Dangerous little sod. The knowledge that the brother himself was trapped in the labyrinth gave Terence momentary satisfaction. But it was eclipsed by the gnawing anxiety that he had lost not only Maia, but also control. That she knew more than he realised, and now she was off the island, about to blow the whole thing wide open. But that was what the induction programme at Schloss Adler was designed to prevent, and it had never failed yet. Yes, but there was always a first time. And how had things got into such a state anyway? Where had he screwed up? In taking Maia into his bed in the first place? No. She was to have been his personal triumph. She, or someone like her, had always been part of the Committee's plan, and Terence had long ago resolved that it would be him who produced the perfect candidate for assimilation, here on Seal Island, just as he had convinced himself that intimacy would be a necessary part of that process. So was it with Sean that he had gone wrong? Sean, whose youthful arrogance and hot temper reminded him so much of his own younger days. Should he have paid more attention to Eugene's reservations about him? Yes, probably. That had been a mistake. He could hear his father's voice, feel the pain of the heavy bible thudding into the side of his head. 'No, no, my boy. That is not right. You did not learn it properly.' His cheeks stinging with shame and guilt at having let his father down again . . .

With dawn spreading across the sky, turning the world around him a dim, troubled grey, he climbed out of the 4x4 and began to slide the boat off the trailer and into the water.

Eugene was the only person who could sort this out now. It had all gone too far. Terence needed to find him as quickly as he could.

FIFTY-SEVEN

The fishing boat was twenty yards from the rocks. Two figures remained on deck, the skipper and first mate, so the word went. The winchman was making his fourth descent from the helicopter, but he would not be able to take them both off at once. Beneath him, the sea was a frothing disc, flattened by the downdraught from the helicopter's rotors. Most of the crowd had surged forward to the harbour wall to watch the final stage of the drama being played out in the gathering light.

The winchman landed on deck and began helping one of the figures into the harness. Now there was only a thin ribbon of water visible between the boat and the rocks. The winchman and the other figure seemed to be having a conversation. Then the winchman gave the haul-up signal to the helicopter and he and the harnessed figure were lifted clear of the deck. A few moments later there was another gasp from the crowd as the remaining figure, bulky in survival suit and inflated life vest, hurled himself into the sea.

Outside the Ship, only a few people remained. Maia had stopped shaking and was silent.

'Come on,' said Fin. 'Let's get you home.'

He put his arm around her shoulders. The Duck fell into step on the other side of her. They began to make their way around the back of the crowd. But they had gone only a few paces when there was a woman's cry. People were standing aside, making way for someone. Kath burst through and stopped in front of them, her eyes wide with expectation.

'Maia!'

She took in her daughter's pale face, ill-fitting clothes and bedraggled appearance.

'Oh my darlin'!'

Tears formed in her eyes. She opened her arms wide.

Maia stood for a moment, looking at her uncertainly. Then from deep in her chest came a sob. She stepped forward and sank into her mother's arms.

Standing there in the dull light of dawn, with the roar of the wind and the sea, Kath held her daughter close and murmured her name over and over again.

Some people turned away. Others looked on, voices dropping to whispers. Sally and Albert had caught up with Kath. Sally's eyes filled with tears, and Albert passed her his handkerchief.

Fin and the Duck also stood by, uncertain what to do now. Fin felt deflated, as if everything he had thought, breathed, dreamed in the last few weeks had had this moment as its conclusion. And now that it was here, he had no part in it. He was just a bystander like everybody else. An empty, exhausted bystander . . .

His thoughts were interrupted by a further cheer from the harbour. 'They've got the final guy, the one in the water,' someone called out. People were turning away to see what was going on. Then there was more movement as Danny came shuffling breathlessly through the crowd, leaning on the brush.

He stopped a couple of paces from Kath and Maia. Kath had her back to him. Maia's face was buried in her mother's shoulder. But she sensed his presence and looked up.

'Hello, Maia.' He gave a hesitant smile.

Maia looked at him without emotion.

Danny's gaze slid away, then back again.

'Are you—'

He was cut short by a sudden gasp of horror from the crowd as every head turned to look out into the narrows. Where now, under a lightening sky, the surface of the sea seemed to be rising, swelling upwards, gathering itself into a black wall of water several metres high.

Fin heard a groan behind him. He glanced round to see Sally Lightfoot slumped on the ground, Albert Smith crouching at her side. But he couldn't keep his eyes from the sea for long. Now there was not a voice to be heard. For several moments people stood transfixed as the dark wall of water reared up and began to advance with gathering speed down the narrows. Then, as one, they turned and fled for the safety of the hill behind the cottages.

Sunk in thought, half mesmerised by the steady sweep of the wipers, Terence Whitelands was on the approach to the bridge before he realised that he'd missed the Easthaven turnoff. He cursed. It was easily done, a matter of habit. His car journeys almost always took him to the mainland, seldom to the village.

He drove on. He couldn't stop and turn on the bridge itself. He would have to wait till the roundabout at the far end.

As daylight seeped into the sky, his anxiety had begun to ease. Between them, he and Eugene would get the situation back in hand without too much trouble. They would have to let Maia go, of course. In the legal sense. But they could surely discredit anything she and her family might come up with. Who would take the word of a dirt-poor, half-black family from Whale Island over the might and reputation of the Green Energies Group? As for the boy's accomplice . . . he looked like a gypsy. The police wouldn't give him the time of day. The Institute might even press charges against him for trespass and assault. That would teach him. And then there was Sean. That was trickier, he had to admit. It would depend on how badly Maia had hurt him. God, he would love to have seen it though, fiery little bitch that she –

Terence never saw or heard the wave. Just a flicker of movement out of the corner of one eye. A slow-motion moment of falling. And then he no longer understood what was happening to him in all the water and darkness . . .

EPILOGUE

Fin stood on the deck of the ferry and looked at the bridge, or what remained of it. Seeing it like this, from the water, brought it home to him that Whale Island truly was an island once more. The sea had reclaimed what rightfully belonged to it.

A freak meteorological event was how it was being described. Not that the event itself was a freak – storm surges were not unknown in these waters – but the scale of it was. The exceptionally low atmospheric pressure that accompanied heavy storms could also create a kind of vacuum into which the surface of the sea could be sucked upwards. This was how storm surges were born, and a wave of three or four feet in height was not uncommon. But coinciding with the spring tide and the confined, shallow corridor of the narrows, this wave had risen to a height several times greater than normal. It had surged down the narrows with enough force to destroy the central pier of the bridge. A fifty-yard section of carriageway on either side had collapsed into the sea, leaving a shattered concrete stump in the centre of the channel, and, either side of it, two ragged tongues of carriageway, facing one another across a hundred yards of empty air. Now, two months later, there were allegations that Green Energies had bribed the local authorities to turn a blind eye to corner cutting and cost savings during construction, and that since the day it had opened the bridge had been a catastrophe waiting to happen.

A public inquiry was to be held and prosecutions seemed likely.

Fin stood at the stern rail watching the houses of East-haven recede, their colours drab under a grey autumn sky. They had been lucky there. The solid breakwater of East-haven's harbour wall had taken the brunt of the wave's force, and by the time it had washed over the road and up to the first cottages, it had only been a couple of feet in depth. Damage had been limited to a few spoilt carpets and ruined household possessions in the houses nearest to the water.

Now, as the ferry pulled away, Fin could still clearly see the Ship Inn. The dark entrance to their own alley, if he squinted. Sally's whitewashed cottage, the last in the village. Then, further on, a lonely sentinel on its headland, Coldheart Farm, now with a For Sale sign at the end of the farm road. While across the water, at the Cliffton crematorium, Norman Turner's ashes remained in storage as the lawyers posted announcements in newspapers up and down the country, requesting that some relative come forward to claim his estate and remains. So far, none had.

Fin glanced at the bridge again. There was something hypnotic about the sight of such a huge structure, seemingly so strong, built with the benefit of centuries of experience, the most modern technologies and materials, torn down in seconds by the forces of nature.

Whitelands's car had been found, but not his body. *Seal Island Institute Director in bridge tragedy*, or variations on that theme, had been the headlines in all the local papers. *Respected South African scientist and sustainable energy expert Dr Terence Whitelands died in tragic circumstances when the Whale Island bridge was brought down by a freak wave* . . . Then the usual platitudes about Green

Energies' leading role in global wind-energy research, and the vital work undertaken by Dr Whitelands during his time as Director of the Seal Island facility.

With the bridge down, the police had finally arrived by helicopter around mid-morning on the day of the storm. Hunter had been taken to Cliffton for questioning. Fin, Kath, Danny, Shirley and the Duck had all given statements, taking their turn to sit with two policemen in the bar at the Ship. Maia had also been persuaded to talk to them, but five minutes into the interview she'd collapsed in tears and Kath had had to take her home.

The next three weeks had passed in an agony of frustration until the police had called again. Fin would never forget the feeling of growing despair as he'd sat in the kitchen at Number Thirteen and listened to the police telling them that Hunter had been released without charge, and that although they had taken what the Carpenters, Mrs Archer and Mr Leduc had said seriously, and an investigation was underway, it was a delicate and difficult matter to pursue, owing to the seriousness of the allegations and the international nature of the corporation in question. There were also some doubts as to whether the available evidence would stand up – lack of proof, and the key witness's inability to provide a full statement. They would keep everyone informed, of course, but this kind of thing could take months. Miss Carpenter was free to bring a civil action for unlawful detention, if she chose, but they would advise against it because it might interfere with their own investigations, it would be costly and, given the reputation of the Green Energies lawyers, they didn't think she would get very far.

Counting down the days till he left for university, Fin woke each morning to a sense of smouldering, powerless fury. Gently he had coaxed from Maia as much as he could about the Institute's covert activities, most of it learned from Sean in the moments before he attacked her, it seemed. The double meaning of a 'clean planet'. The Institute's hand in Lottie's death. And the fact that Maia herself was being prepared for some kind of future role in their plans. Though when he asked about Schloss Adler a strange glazed look came over her, and he didn't pursue the subject.

Meanwhile, life continued as normal on Seal Island. A short item in the local paper reported that despite the tragic loss of their director, work on the Super Turbine would continue and Green Energies would be offering their fullest cooperation to the inquiry into the collapse of the bridge. There had been no more bombings on the mainland. No more busloads of security operatives arriving on the island for training. And nothing more on the story of Sean Rafferty, the Institute employee who had sustained severe head injuries from flying debris during the storm.

But what sort of world was it where Green Energies could be prosecuted for breaches of building laws and health-and-safety regulations, as seemed increasingly likely, when what they ought to be answering were charges of murder and terrorism? What kind of justice was it that weighed Terence Whitelands's life against Lottie's and Poacher's? Whitelands had never been properly called to account, unless the wave could be credited with a will of its own. It was certainly no justice for the many dead of the bombings. No justice for Maia either, who was currently 'taking it a day at a time', which Fin knew was her way of saying she was going through some kind of private hell, so painful at moments that he could hardly bear to see it. Although she was at least receiving professional help, and she was strong. There were days when Fin caught glimpses of what seemed like the old Maia – even if he knew that in reality the old Maia, as much as the old Fin, was illusory, that neither of them would ever be the same again. Which didn't alter the fact that he loved her. He always had and he always would. And part of that loving meant believing in her, trusting that she would find her feet again.

There were times when he wondered whether he'd dreamed it all. He thought of Norman Turner's remark about nothing in the world being all good or all bad, and wondered whether it was possible that Green Energies' technological intentions were as good as their racist ones were bad – but then his thoughts returned to Poacher and Lottie, and the rage flared up again. Rage that a corporation could sponsor such hatred and violence and use its power and wealth to get away with it. Rage that anyone could believe they were entitled to persecute another person, verbally abuse them, physically assault them, attempt to rape them – for any reason at all, let alone what was nothing more than an accident of birth. Rage that there could be such a sickness, such a madness in the world and no obvious antidote for it . . .

And yet . . . there was an antidote, of a kind, surely. Poacher's friendship, the Duck's unquestioning help, Kath's love for Maia and him, Shirley Archer's courage in grief, Norman Turner's devotion to his young niece, Fin's own love for his sister, even Danny's wish to make amends . . . These were the good things in the world, never to be lost sight of, no matter how high the tide of hatred and violence might rise.

As the days passed, Fin began to understand that more even than his darkest moment in the labyrinth, this question of what was right and what was wrong was changing how he looked at life. That perhaps there really were certain things about which, from now on, he had no choice. That when he came across ignorant, vicious prejudice in the future, he would no more be able to cross to the other side of the road than he could now cross what remained of the Whale Island bridge. And because of what had happened down there in the cold, black water of the mine, when he did encounter it he wouldn't be afraid.

Seagulls flocked to the wake of the ferry. Someone was throwing bread over the side as she lumbered towards the old landing stage, a mile up the narrows from the bridge. The jetty had been hastily brought into service again, along with the ferry herself, rescued from a dry dock at Cliffton. Now childhood memories flooded back on the sweetly oily smell of the fuel, the haze of heat around the funnel, the low rhythmic shudder of the engines. Fin recalled the excitement of outings with Kath and Maia to go shopping, to visit his nan, to see the circus and, later, the routine of the daily trip to school in Cliffton – where now he was heading to spend his last night before university with his mother and sister.

In the days immediately following the storm there had been a dreamlike quality to life at Number Thirteen. All four of them were back under one roof again, and yet it was as if none of them quite believed it. Maia withdrew to her room, where she spent most of her time sleeping or listening to music. Much as he longed to be with her, Fin realised that for the moment she was best left alone. The medication she was taking helped keep her mood stable, but when she did appear, mostly for meals, it felt to Fin as if they all trod warily with her, Danny in particular. There was a sense that something was brewing inside her, her own storm.

And then, one night at supper, the storm broke.

Without any warning she turned to Danny and said calmly, 'Do you want to know why I really hate you?'

Danny flinched. 'Why?'

'Because I found out that you'd been having an affair with Linda Steerman – before the accident happened. And that meant all that self-pity, all that "Gus let me down" stuff, was just bullshit. Bull . . . shit . . . Dad. You were living a lie. And it made life hell for the rest of us . . .' She paused. 'You wrecked Gus's marriage. That's why he didn't fall over himself to help you out. And I don't blame him. You wrecked his marriage and he was too decent to tell everyone about it. How you didn't wreck your own too, I've no idea.' She glanced at Kath. 'I think you're either a saint or the biggest idiot on the planet, Mum. And whichever you are, it didn't do Fin and me much good.' She turned back to Danny. 'Anyway, that's why I went. Because if I'd stayed I would have tried to kill you.'

She stared at her father till he looked away. Then she stood up and left the room. Kath watched her go, watched her husband hang his head, his shoulders slump, her look of incredulity giving way to one of fury.

'Danny,' she said, 'you bloody fool.'

She rose from the table and walked out of the front door.

Now Kath and Maia were living together in a rented flat up the hill from the Cliffton waterfront. It was what was best for Maia, Kath said, and it was near the clinic. Kath had a job at the supermarket. Maia did part-time work in a charity shop. Meanwhile Fin had decided it was easier to stay at Number Thirteen for the last few weeks. But tomorrow, at long last, he was catching the train for university.

Tonight they were going out for a farewell meal. He knew Kath would want to hear about Danny. How was he? How did he look? Was he drinking? And Fin would answer that Danny was OK, that he was doing well. Then he'd put his arm around her and give her an admiring kiss and a hug and say, 'You're doing the right thing, Mum.'

And it was true. Danny was OK. He seemed to be managing to stay off the drink. And he was remorseful, almost painfully so. The previous evening, Fin's last on the island, they'd gone to the Ship together. Shirley had made a fuss of Fin, told him if ever he wanted a holiday job he'd got one, then taken him aside and confided that she was talking to a local politician and a couple of journalists she knew to see if there was any way they could dig up some hard evidence of Green Energies' terrorist activities. She was hopeful, she'd said, hopeful she could do something that would really bring the bastards to justice and honour the memory of Peter and all the others. Danny had stood by, an unfamiliar look on his face, which it had taken Fin a moment or two to identify as pride. And then, even though Fin wasn't in the mood, he'd insisted on buying him a pint, something he'd never done before. And as Fin raised his glass, and Danny sipped a tonic water, the same look of pride had returned. Fin had realised that the pint was Danny's way of acknowledging that his son was now a man.

Then Danny had talked. He'd told Fin how terrible he felt about everything that had happened. How his life had been a mess for so long. How, among other things since the accident, he'd found it so hard watching his son growing up able-bodied, taking his fitness for granted, when he knew that he, Danny, could never be active again. And how he'd promised himself for Kath's sake, for all their sakes, that he would get himself together now and be a good husband and dad, if they would give him the chance. And Fin had listened, wondering whether he would ever be able to forgive his father for the way he'd betrayed them all. Finally, Danny had paused and looked at Fin with watery eyes, and Fin knew what was coming.

'Will she have me back, son? D'you think she will?'

'I don't know, Dad. I just don't know,' Fin answered truthfully.

Danny nodded slowly, then said with a crack in his voice, 'I miss her so much.'

The jetty was drawing near now. The ferry had put her engines into reverse to manoeuvre herself alongside, against the current. The Cliffton bus was waiting. Tomorrow evening Fin would be at the opposite end of the country, in another reality, one he so far knew almost nothing about. He thought again of his holiday project. He'd found it impossible to get down to it since everything that had happened. *Life Is a Bowl of Cherries*. He wouldn't say so. Definitely not. But he didn't have to hand in the storyboards till the end of the first week. There was still time. And although he didn't yet know what the story was going to be, he could see the bowl clearly now. He knew what was in it. Some big ones, some small ones. Here and there a bruised one. Some the colour of blood. Some as dark as plums. Some missing their stalks. Several pairs of twins. Some sweet, some tart, some sour. And a couple of rotten ones.

The ferry was tying up, the pedestrian gangway being lowered, but first they had to wait for the vehicles to roll off. A pair of motorbikes rumbled out ahead of the cars. The Duck was never far from Fin's thoughts at the moment. They'd seen each other a few times in recent weeks, though Fin had noticed a subtle distance, as if the intensity of what they had been through together was too much. It sat between them like an unfinished meal. But Fin hoped they'd digest it in time. This was someone he didn't want to lose touch with. Anyway, the Duck had already said he'd come and visit Fin at uni as soon as he could.

Now he remembered the afternoon at the harbour wall, just after Poacher had died. 'You can't feel for everyone, man,' the Duck had said. 'You can't carry all their stuff as well as your own. You need to look after yourself first. Then you can take care of everyone else. If you still want to.'

Yes, Fin thought as he walked down the gangway. Look after himself. That's what he would do for now. Look after himself while he prepared for what he really had to do in the world. Because the time would come when he'd be ready to take them on, the bigots and racists. Deep in his heart he knew it would.

ACKNOWLEDGEMENTS

My thanks to Jess Smith for the story of the seventh wave, Margaret Oscar for keeping me straight on race, Marilyn Denbigh for help with the kayaks, Anelia Varela for the Afrikaans, Annie Blaber for sanctuary at Castle Wearie, Ruth Alltimes and Talya Baker for their expert editorial eyes, and my wife, Sarah, as always, for her insight.

Also by James Jauncey

the witness

From the shelter of the pine trees, through the falling snow, John watched as the men kicked down doors, shattered windows and fired their first shot. Later, among the ruins, he found a boy too terrified to tell John his name.

Now the only witness and the sole survivor are running for their lives, and every choice John makes could mean the difference between life and death . . .

Shortlisted for the Royal Mail Scottish Children's Book Awards 2008 and the Highland Children's Book Awards 2008

JULIA BELL

DIRTY WORK

*In my head I am not here on this dirty mattress. I am up
above the earth, where the air rushes against my face . . .
This is where I go in my head while they pay for my body.*

Money doesn't buy happiness. Hope may be spoilt, but she's
sure that as far as her preoccupied parents are concerned,
she's hope*less*.

Oksana thought the West would offer a better life –
instead, sold into prostitution, hopeless doesn't even begin to
describe the bad dream her life has become.

Oksana and Hope are thrown together in terrifying
circumstances: their only chance of survival lies with each
other. But how do two girls with so little in common find a
way to meet in the middle . . . ?

'**Gritty . . . pitch-perfect . . . provocative**' *Observer*

SUZANNE PHILLIPS

The body of a young man was found in the locker room at Madison High yesterday afternoon.

For some kids, school is a war zone. Walking through the doors is like crossing into enemy territory. Some kids run for cover. Some fight back.

The unflinching and unforgettable story of a boy pushed too far.

LIAN HEARN

The Harsh Cry of the Heron

Lord Otori Takeo and Kaede have ruled for over sixteen years. The Three Countries are at peace, but the violent acts and betrayals of the past will not lie buried. An embittered warrior, a renegade Tribe leader and a boy whose heart is filled with hatred all seek their vengeance.

Against these gathering threats, Takeo draws strength from his love for Kaede, but even this is not beyond the reach of their enemies . . .

The Harsh Cry of the Heron is the dazzling continuation of an epic and unforgettable story that began in *Across the Nightingale Floor*.

A selected list of titles available from
YOUNG PICADOR

The prices shown below are correct at the time of going to press.
However, Macmillan Publishers reserves the right to show new retail
prices on covers, which may differ from those previously advertised.

JAMES JAUNCEY

| The Witness | 978-0-330-44714-0 | £6.99 |

JULIA BELL

| Dirty Work | 978-0-330-44571-9 | £5.99 |

SUZANNE PHILLIPS

| Burn | 978-0-330-43229-9 | £6.99 |

LIAN HEARN

| The Harsh Cry of the Heron | 978-0-330-44961-8 | £6.99 |

All Pan Macmillan titles can be ordered from our website,
www.panmacmillan.com, or from your local bookshop and
are also available by post from:

Bookpost, PO Box 29, Douglas, Isle of Man IM99 1BQ

Credit cards accepted. For details:
Telephone: 01624 677237
Fax: 01624 670923
Email: bookshop@enterprise.net
www.bookpost.co.uk

Free postage and packing in the United Kingdom